The Lost Song

To Bob,
friend + mentor
Steve Effingham

A Novel by

Steve Effingham

ISBN: 1542891310

ISBN 13: 9781542891318

For my wife Tina, for the love and joy she brings to our life's adventure

The Song

The woman found the boys huddled in the darkness a few hundred yards off the River Road just outside the town of Kenner where they'd been hiding since late afternoon from the gangs of vigilantes running the countryside on horseback looking for the fugitive Robert Charles. Word was out among the whites, trumpeted in their newspapers and over the telegraph, that Charles had fled the scene of his savage murder of two police officers in New Orleans and was leading an army of blacks in a servile uprising against the white citizens of Louisiana. The boys had let out that morning, the destination being a lumber camp outside the town where they intended to earn money playing music for the workers. Now, no black person was safe from the mob and every black man was in danger of being taken for Robert Charles himself. When the boys were discovered missing in late afternoon, the woman let out in search of her two nephews and their three friends.

She found them crouched in the brush with their musical instruments, her nephew Chiff arguing in desperate whispers with his brother Stonewall and their friend Jean as the other boys watched silently with tear soaked faces. When they heard her voice in the darkness admonishing them to keep quiet as they could easily be heard down on the River Road, and to follow her through the pitch black night, they formed up like ducklings and quietly obeyed. She led them through darkened fields and finally up a steep rise until they reached what appeared against the night sky to be a thicket of young trees, but was actually the top of a line of old Pines with trunks at the bottom of a crude staircase of stones as the mound

1

of earth they'd climbed dropped at the top like a cliff. At the foot of the stone stairs, they stood in front of the door to a cabin made of thick logs built into earth beneath the mound. The trees before the cabin hung over the front creating a cave-like space of pitch darkness. The boys huddled together, arms wrapped around their instrument cases and each other. The woman rapped on the door of the cabin and a light inside dimmed as the door opened.

"Oh, Mother Luzinda," said a woman behind the door. "Thank the Lord you've come back. You brought some more lost lambs, God bless you, Mother."

The door opened just enough for the group to enter, the light from a kerosene lamp rising slightly as the door closed revealing a single room filled with a dozen or so people huddled along the walls and lying in the center of the clay floor. The boys looked about at the silent faces illuminated in the flickering light as they filed into the room and sat in a line against the wall.

"Mother Luzinda?" whispered Chiff, "they call her *Mother* Luzinda."

The woman stood in the center of the room, hands on her hips, scrutinizing the shadows lining the wall and strewn across the floor.

"That's our auntie," said Chiff.

The woman stepped lightly across the floor, carrying a lit candle, carefully maneuvering among the huddled forms, retrieving an old tin canteen from a sack, the inscription of the U.S. Army embossed on the battered metal, and handed it to a man standing in the shadows.

"Be so kind, sir," she said, "to offer this water round to our brothers and sisters."

The man took the canteen and the candle and moved around the room, bending to the ones on the floor, waiting while each took a drink, then moving to the next figure, everyone shrouded in the dim light, taking only a sip and passing it back. Finally, the man reached where the boys sat and stooped down, handing the canteen to a woman sitting close by. The woman woke a small boy sleeping in her arms, who whimpered softly.

"You have to take some water, Steven," she said.

The woman held the canteen to the boy's mouth then handed it to the man without drinking, waving him off when he offered it back. She wore a man's hat pulled low and when the man holding the candle raised the light and saw her face he sat down next to her, nudging one of the boys, Jean, over to make room.

"How did you find you way here, sister," he said.

"Mother Luzinda brought us in," the woman whispered. "Me and my boy was walking the River Road, trying to make our way to Lutcher and a white man told us they was searching for Robert Charles and they wanted any colored folks they could get and we best get off the road. We did what he told us and sure enough men come by on horseback, a whole bunch of white men, pushing some poor soul ahead, saying he must be part of Robert Charles' gang and they would sure enough hang him unless he say where Robert Charles was hid. Me and my boy got down in the brush and stayed there until Mother Luzinda come along, moving through the brush like an Indian. The Lord must have sent her, cause I don't know where she come from if he didn't. She brought us here, God bless her."

"Good to meet you sister," said the man. "My name is Buddy, Buddy Bolden."

"My name is Louise Castro, and this is my boy Steven."

Jean stared into the candle light as they spoke.

"I been in the middle of this thing from the start" said Bolden. "That's why I had to leave New Orleans, that's where I live, all my life I been there, and my daddy and my grand daddy. I ain't never seen such a thing as this."

Bolden handed the canteen to Jean and motioned to him to pass it down the line of boys. As he shifted his body to face the woman he removed a canvas sack from under his coat and the light from Mother Luzinda's candle hit the bell of a cornet inside the bag like a shooting star catching Jean's eye. Bolden noticed Jean staring and looked at him curiously then turned towards to woman.

"I stayed hid all day long," said Bolden, "watching white men riding back and forth on that road, cussing and hollering. After dark I started moving, wandering, not knowing where I was or which way to go till Mother Luzinda found me and brought me here. The place was full of folks when I got here."

"Mother Luzinda found everyone in this room and took us all to safety," said an old man.

"Praise God, it's true," said Bolden. "Brother Floyd over there told me Mother waved him off a freight train slowing down to pass through Kenner. He seen this little bitty black woman waving for him to jump and he did. Ain't that right, Floyd?"

"Sure is brother," replied a man holding a guitar. He gently stroked the strings as though testing the volume in the small room. His touch was so soft the notes spread out in waves, mixing with the hushed voices and the silence, audible, yet somehow also still.

"Mother sure enough saved ol'Zed Floyd," he said. "How could I know those peckerwoods was stopping trains and pulling all the niggers off? I don't know why I did get off just cause she was waving, but I did."

"How long can we stay here?" came a small voice in the shadows.

"Don't be playing no guitar, brother," said another.

"That's all right," said Mother Luzinda. "No worry for now. We're safe in here, children. Those night riders won't be crawling through all that brush in the dark. Besides, this ol'shack is just about under the ground. No sound comes out long as you keep things low. We're safe until morning."

Floyd let his arm fall slow and easy, touching the strings in a line from top to bottom. He lowered his head, running his fingers like spiders over the shinning neck of the guitar. The notes were stinging and Floyd cringed as he struck the strings like they were live wires or the neck was hot metal. It seemed the guitar was whispering the story of Robert Charles, spitting sparks Floyd strained to contain for fear the fire might burst from the guitar and burn the innocent refugees all around him. Mother Luzinda's eyes blazed as she watched Floyd's fingers dancing over the guitar.

"Yes, this is a solid ol'cabin," she said. "Men took refuge here many times. I know that for a fact. They did it back in 81 when the colored men in these parts gone out on strike. Wouldn't work for no one unless they got a dollar a day cause we couldn't live on no less. The white man tried to arrest all those they figured was the ringleaders. Get arrested and no one sees you again. The colored men wouldn't let'm take those men, so they hid them here and in other places. Most of those men been slaves once and a heap of 'm fought for the Union army, too. And long before those men was in here, slaves found sanctuary in this very cabin, way back in eighteen-eleven. I heard it from my grandmother. They rose up and freed themselves, hundreds strong, marching from plantation to plantation. The white man needed the militia to drive them back. My grandmother told us some hid out and never was found, some made it back into the swamps, some even hid right smack in the middle of New Orleans for the rest of their days and wasn't never found out. My grand-mother seen it herself. "

Floyd raised his head at her words, continuing to play, and she looked at him nodding as she spoke.

"Yes sir, it's true," she said. "My grandmother seen it in her time and I seen it in mine. Colored folks is a nation she say. Seeing all of us in here now, I spect she was right about it. Colored folks is a nation."

Floyd lowered his head, "Yes, Mother," he said.

"We got to be," said Mother Luzinda. "White man don't want us in his nation. Even Uncle Sam don't want us and we saved his nation in the war. Seems to me, we got to be a nation if we are to survive at all."

"I heard that's what Robert Charles say too," came a voice.

"That's my understanding," said Mother Luzinda. "Cept, Robert Charles wants our nation to be in Africa and I just can't see giving up land you spent so much sweat and blood for, so much living and dying on, spent all our days trying to make into something. Seems to me, I got a right to die right here."

"God bless you, Mother," came a voice.

"God bless Robert Charles," came another.

"Oh, dear Lord, yes," said Mother Luzinda. "God, bless Robert Charles. He truly is an angel of the Lord, a warrior, like those slaves that marched these roads carrying nothing but cane knives and axes and those colored men that was striking – they didn't have a thing to protect themselves but their numbers and the work the white man needed them to do. So much of our blood washes this land."

"I believe Robert Charles is just as those men," came a voice.

"Oh yes, it's true," said Mother Luzinda. "Won't let no one turn him into nothing less than what he is. A free black man. No, he'll kill first. Kill and be killed."

"So much killing, Mother," came a voice from the shadows. "What will happen to us?"

"I don't know," said Mother Luzinda. "I fear to God, Robert's ordeal ain't done yet. You heard what the good brother from New Orleans said. So many of us suffering with Robert Charles today. It seems we all got a heap of suffering ahead of us. But I do believe, if they find Robert Charles, they'll be hell to pay. He'll go hard, real hard, take fifty, a hundred with him. And they'll be flames too, they'll try to burn him, alive or dead, they'll try to do it."

"I met Brother Robert once," said a man, his voice coming from the bodies reposed in the darkness of the floor, and the woman next to Bolden said, "Please tell us about him."

"I was on the waterfront in Algiers and he was selling African papers and we started to talking. That's what he did. He sold those papers. We had a nice talk about it. He seemed to be a good man."

"I met him myself," said Bolden. "It was on a Saturday. Recently too. I'd run into an old friend of mine on Poydras Street in New Orleans and Robert came along while we were talking. Robert is a nephew of my friend's wife. Lord knows what's become of them. He was with a woman. She was his sweetheart and I think maybe I was showing off a bit for the lady and he was smiling. Everything was fine. I invited him to come hear my band play sometime and he said he would. I ran into him again two nights later, just like that. I was on my way to work and he was on his way to meet his sweetheart. He had a friend along, a young fellow. They got him in the Parish Prison right now. Robert said after he left his gal that evening he'd come by, but I never did see him again. That was Monday night. I reckon he must have met up with those police a short time after."

"Poor Robert Charles," said someone.

"Oh, you best believe he'll make them pay the price," said Mother Luzinda. "His death will cost the white man dearly. Robert Charles is one expensive nigger. He's a warrior, a black warrior, warrior of the black nation. Their bullets may fall like rain and the devils' flames rise but Robert Charles won't never be anything less than a man."

"They ain't got him yet," came another voice. "He may just get away, may escape somehow. We all gonna make it over, after all."

"Yes, we will all make it over," said Mother Luzinda. "We will all see Robert one day."

Floyd's guitar rang like a sparkling carpet beneath Mother Luzinda's voice, stars shooting as she spoke, waves of oceans undulating with her breath, indistinguishable from the breath of everyone in the room, indistinguishable from the meaning of what Mother Luzinda said, what they all knew to be true. She rocked on her heels, arms folded across her breast, gazing at the pitch black ceiling of the cabin like a vast starless void, a portal to ancestors and loved ones, irreconcilable slaves and union strikers, bad niggers and black warriors, as if she were listening to voices and just repeating the words they spoke. Floyd played gently as though he believed he was carrying Mother Luzinda himself, lifting her closer to the voices speaking to her. He closed his eyes, hunched over the guitar, popping metallic dissonant rhythmic notes, sweet somehow, yet biting, stinging, and a bass line running, continuing even after Mother Luzinda stopped speaking. She held her forehead in her palm for a moment then descended to the floor amidst the huddled bodies.

Floyd played in the silence; his playing was silence itself. His voice rose softly, the sound seeming to emanate from somewhere else in the room, from the floor or the walls, or the mouths of fugitive slaves, generations of fugitives, unknowable utterances called forth by the exhortations of Mother Luzinda and the others and by Floyd's guitar.

"You've heard the story of Robert Charles," he sang. *"And all the things he done. Shot a white man with his pistol, cussed the others when they run."*

The light from the lamp flickered with the movement of Floyd's head swinging as if each would cease if the other ceased, as if everyone in the cabin depended on the light and on Floyd's voice for existence.

"He was setting on a door step," sang Floyd, the diction clipped and articulate. *"Waiting for his gal to show. He checked his forty-four pistol when he heard the police whistle blow."*

Then came a burst of notes and a tangle of rhythm and Zed's finger sliding on a single string in the shrill and foreboding sound of the policeman's whistle.

"He was just setting on a doorstep, a dreaming of his dear, hey you low down nigger, why you sitting here?"

Everyone's heart sank at the words, but they were inevitable, automatic, true. The rush of notes following seemed to say the same thing the words said, except more excruciating, yet they seemed to be transforming into something else, something beautiful.

"The policeman drew his billy, Robert dragged him in the street, the other fired his pistol, knocked Robert off his feet."

"He's all right," came a voice.

"Yes, the police stood a looking, didn't know which way to go, till Robert took his pistol, and fired that forty four."

"He is all right."

"Yes, Robert aimed and fired as he was kneeling down, policeman moaned and hollered when his body hit the ground."

There was a stirring in the room, everyone sitting erect as Floyd tossed clusters of notes at each pause of his voice.

"Early in the morning, they tracked Robert to his room, that's when Robert used his rifle, sent two more to their doom."

"Lord have mercy."

"Well you should have seen them police tremble, you should have seen them run, you should have heard Robert curse those devils, then disappear with his gun."

Only Floyd's hands were visible, floating across the neck of the guitar, illuminated by the lamp, his head a shadowed black form, swaying gently, his voice disembodied. All else was silence in the room as he played, sound embedded within silence, sounding only to those in the cabin, past and present, and maybe future too, maybe future generations, people no longer refugees would hear the silence, feel the sound. The voice trailed off, then it was Floyd speaking, his hands still caressing the guitar.

"That's *The Robert Charles Song*," he said, "first of it, I spect. There's more to be told. We don't know how his story ends yet. I reckon folks will be singing of Robert Charles for some time to come."

He launched off again striking the strings violently, struggling to modulate the impact, fighting the relentless force, riding the anger of Robert Charles' resistance as his spirit danced around the room. The boy, Jean, sat wedged between his friend Stonewall and Bolden, their bodies motionless as if the flesh had fused. The silence in the echoes of Floyd's playing was deep and dark, bottomless. Bolden shifted his weight and Jean saw the cornet glittering in the lamplight, rise slowly to Bolden's mouth and rest there for some time as if he were listening or thinking or perhaps dreaming. Jean felt Bolden's body tense as he breathed into the horn. His fingers eased over the keys but no sound came at first, until finally something emerged, tentative, groping like a baby reaching, sweet like sunlight and blue sky, a melody filling the silences of Zed Floyd's raging. It seemed to Jean as if the sound were coming from inside of himself, then it seemed to be outside, in the room, yet no one moved, no one made a sign. They seemed to be hearing without listening or listening inside themselves.

The sound of Buddy Bolden and Zed Floyd emanated from every corner of the cabin, from every breast in the room, like when Mother Luzinda spoke, it wasn't just her speaking. She was listening and repeating what she heard and when Floyd sang it wasn't just him singing. They were his hands moving on the guitar but the voice was coming from everywhere in the room at once. The sweetness of Bolden's cornet was deeper still, farther back, a prophesying or a trajectory of some sort dancing above Floyd's distorted chords. Something so new it startled, so new it was hardly audible, filling the room like fresh air, pure oxygen, stimulating something so deep no one needed to speak, no one needed to look up, so natural the sound ran along the flesh like sweat dropping, breath inhaled and exhaled, thoughts darting, secret individual thoughts and thoughts everyone in the room shared simultaneously and somehow knew it. Floyd struck bitter sweet percussive jabs below Bolden's melody, the suffering and disappointment of the guitar met the unknowing innocence of the horn like lovers, roses wrought by fire, hate and love merged, transformed into wholeness.

The boy, Jean, felt Bolden's upper arm flex as he pumped the keys and saw the side of his face glimmering with wetness. No one else looked at Bolden or said a word, but seemed to be dozing or peering inwardly into the blackness of the ceiling. Jean looked down the line of his friends huddled against the wall, sleeping, peaceful, heavy, dreamless sleep and his eyes closed slowly without his realizing it.

"the snapshot"

Imagine, the legendary trombonist from New Orleans, Jean "Kid" Auger, at age seventy-nine, playing Dixieland Jazz on the deck of an ersatz riverboat called the Mark Twain on a man-made river at Disneyland. The sun is unrelenting, yet the crowds keep coming. Wave upon wave of pale faces dripping perspiration, endless cameras dangling in a sea of heat rashed necks, countless families dressed in matching shorts and shirts. They seem doped from the heat, yet inexorable in their insistence upon having fun. They move from one attraction to the next as if falling forward. They deluge pop and flavored ice concessions and wait patiently with the stamina of camels in endless lines. The temperature will peak at 96 degrees, yet Kid Auger looks suave and cool, clean as a whistle. The dry heat in Southern California is a pleasure compared to the steamy humidity of his native Louisiana. He is a small framed man, thin and wiry. He wears his gray hair long, oiled and combed straight back. He watches the people from the deck of the Mark Twain as it motors slowly towards the crowded dock, gently blows a piece of tobacco off his tongue and absentmindedly moves the slide of his trombone back and forth.

"You cue the trombone song," he says to Johnny St. Cyr, who winks and nods. St. Cyr holds his banjo around the neck with one hand and wipes the sweat off his forehead with the other hand. He is the leader of the band, the Young Men of Jazz. At seventy-five his carriage is still strong and erect. He's taller than the Kid, with dark brown skin and gray hair brushed back, still handsome, even with the deep lines and puffiness of age. In his youth he was a longshoreman, a card-carrying member of the black Longshoremen's Protective Union Benevolent Association, No. 2. He's always said Jazz is workingman's music, because only workingmen have the stamina to work all day and play all night. He stands on the deck of the Mark Twain, a few feet behind Auger, stroking the banjo with rapid chords, his head tilted forward, smiling as Auger lets out a smeared trombone note and the band launches into *When The Saints Come Marching In.*

A few steps to the right of St. Cyr, Paul Barbarin beats a snare drum. St. Cyr looks at him and winks. Barbarin carries the snare strapped around his neck and balanced at an angle against his stout frame. The horn-rimmed glasses make him look like a college professor despite the straw hat tilted on his head. The man drummed in street parades in New Orleans in the early twenties, over forty years ago. He's the son of Louis Barbarin, renowned among black New Orleanians in the 1890s and still alive back home. These men are more than top of the line musicians or seasoned veterans. They are icons to the music. They were literally on the scene when Jazz music began and are still at it today. No matter that the crowd doesn't know who they are.

And, they're still a stylish lot even after all these years. The red stripped blazers and straw hats can't belie the fact. The Kid is a particularly dapper fellow. Even in the stripped suit of Disney he moves with the same elegance he did as a young man in New Orleans sixty years before. The Kid always looks good. After all, it was the girls who first named Jean Auger, "the Kid." He can still manipulate his trombone too, if not with the vigor of his youth, with a more subtle style.

The throng of tourists squeal at the burst of music from the Mark Twain. They applaud and wave to the band while a man standing on the dock at the top of a paved ramp bordered by a maze of iron handrails shouts into a hand microphone.

"Welcome to Disneyland, ladies and gentlemen. You are listening to the legendary Young Men of Jazz. How about some applause for these hard working boys? They've come all the way from New Orleans to play for you today."

The people clap and click cameras as the boat moves through the dirty water, gently bumping the dock, and the crowd picks up the song, *"Oh when the saints, come marching in, oh when the saints come marching in . . ."*

"Ladies and gentlemen, Mr. Johnny St. Cyr and his Young Men of Jazz, starring the world-famous Kid Auger, will be just one of the attractions at Walt Disney's fifth annual Dixieland Festival at Disneyland during the month of September. I don't want to give too much away, but word has it, none other than Satchmo, Mr. Louis Armstrong will be with us this year."

A ripple of recognition runs through the crowd at the mention of Armstrong's name, then a smattering of applause. Paul Barbarin makes eye contact with St. Cyr, who barely dips his head toward Auger as Barbarin picks up the tempo, starting and stopping, St. Cyr. filling each hesitation with quick strokes and the band bursts into *Auger's Trombone Stomp*. Cornet, clarinet and trombone punch out the melody to rapid-fire snare beats; then a military fan-fare in unison; then all three horns ad-lib around each other. Some people clap in time to the music and most everyone is swaying, strutting like they've seen in photographs of Mardi Gras, waving their index fingers from side to side above their heads and rolling their eyes.

On the Mark Twain, a crew member pushes through a pair of louvered double doors. He moves away from the doorway and Mickey Mouse, Donald Duck, and Goofy strut past onto the deck marching in time to the music. The collective voices on the dock increase in volume at the sight of the three characters. Auger looks them up and down shaking his head.

"I feel for you boys," he says. "I really do."

"Where the fuck is Cinderella?" says Mickey Mouse, "I ain't dying of heat stroke alone."

"She's coming, she's coming for Christ's sake. Give the kid a break," says Donald.

Goofy grumbles, "She's making the same money we are, ain't she?"

Suddenly Cinderella steps into the sun shielding her eyes, a smile pinned to her mouth and waves to the adoring mob.

"I'm here, you lousy bastard," she says, scowling at Mickey. "Now let's see you dance for the people."

The characters prance around the deck of the Mark Twain as the band plays. The excitement on the dock is reaching a dangerous pitch. The sight of the lovely Cinderella is too much. Everyone seems to have forgotten the temperature, swinging their arms about like automatons, waving frantically at Cinderella and calling out to Mickey and Donald and Goofy. When the boat hits the dock, two attendants lower the gang-plank and people flood on board surrounding Cinderella, Mickey, Donald, Goofy and the Young Men of Jazz.

"Move slowly, please folks, watch your step please, don't run kids, hold on to mom or dad's hand until you're safely aboard."

A young woman stands at the turnstile counting bodies as people rush aboard and when the little ship is filled to the limit she moves a metal bar across the narrow entrance stopping anyone else from board-ing. Disappointed tourists wave and click, lifting the little ones above their heads and pointing them towards Mickey and Donald.

St. Cyr glances at Barbarin, a signal to sustain the tempo that Auger takes as a sign to up the energy and plays a phrase so economical and on the beat the notes seem perfect and the other musicians grin and look at Auger with surprise. Mickey and Donald dance around the band hold-ing open parasols in the air. Cinderella sways her hips beneath her stiff sparkling gown, waving her wand, as Goofy grabs the closest woman and tosses her out by the arm, snapping her back and going cheek to cheek as if she were a rag doll. The woman's children laugh and jump up and down, delighted to see their mother thrown about by Goofy. Her husband staggers in a circle around her and Goofy, searching for just the right angle, points his Polaroid and in a flash freezes his wife, Goofy, and a side view of the straw-hatted Kid Auger, slide extended skyward.

Thursday, August 12, 1965

Dr. Valentin Nieting stood within the maze of handrails, pressed among the sweating throng next to the dock as the bar dropped blocking the entrance to the Mark Twain. Dr. Nieting, most recently ex-professor of Anthropology at the Free University of Berlin, vainly tried to block the sun from his eyes with a Disneyland brochure as he peered across a sea of people. The Young Men of Jazz were completely obscured by tourists except for sun flashing off Kid Auger's trombone swinging above their heads. When the crowd parted Kid Auger was there, thrusting his trombone slide at Goofy, shooing him away from Cinderella as the people on the dock applauded and laughed.

Nieting whispered, "What can this mean?"

He ran his fingers through his hair and grasped the back of his neck.

"Things appear to have taken a bad turn for the old man," he said.

Giggles shot up from two children standing next to the professor, reaching no taller than his thighs. They looked at each other and cracked up, tickled as hell by what he'd said, as Cinderella, Mickey, Goofy, Donald, and the Young Men of Jazz swayed in unison on the deck of the Mark Twain. Nieting mumbled to himself, unconcerned about being overheard.

"This is a regrettable development. Those old Negroes were once the real thing, and now they perform with cartoon characters."

Nieting stared as Donald Duck danced with his hands on his hips, dodging the slide of Kid Auger's trombone.

"Somehow, I can't help feeling shame for Auger," he said.

The children at his feet stared up with crooked necks, hanging on his every word. He glanced down then back at Auger.

"Surely, the performance is a ruse, a set up." He chuckled bitterly. "If only they would shove the damned characters aside, clasp hands above their heads and chant 'Malcolm X Lives.' Perhaps the duck will raise the flag of North Vietnam."

Finally, the children could stand the suspense no longer and bellowed like just-hatched birdies begging for food. They thrust their arms above their heads and closed their eyes tightly, squeezing out tears until hands mysteriously emerged from the mass of sweaty bodies and lifted them high enough to witness the spectacle. But, the music had stopped and the performers were exiting down a gangplank and disappearing behind an enclosure of bamboo.

"All the way from Berlin to interview an old man in a striped suit and straw hat? Kid Auger prancing about with Mickey Mouse? Valet to a fairy tale princess?"

The Mark Twain chugged off as Nieting pushed out of the maze of tourists, looking towards the pathway where it appeared his subject might emerge.

Kid Auger was a revolutionary, he thought, *a disturber of the peace. He would never placate middle-class idiocy. His intent must be to mock the audience. How marvelously insolent that would be, taking the ignorant mob for a ride. This was a masquerade then, an astounding farce. Push the spectacle to the extreme and the meaninglessness explodes in your face.*

Nieting rushed from of the turnstiles, high stepping over children, squeezing by a pregnant woman, jogging past restrooms and a concession stand around the corner to a service entrance where he spotted Kid Auger standing alone under an awning, a folded newspaper under his arm and his trombone case leaning against the chain link fence. He appeared agitated as he unfolded the newspaper and repeatedly slapped the front page headline with the back of his hand, moving his lips as though in a heated conversation. There was no doubt who the man was, however. It truly was Kid Auger.

Nieting strode up to Auger and introduced himself and the old man smiled and the two shook hands. However, the professor could not help being nervous standing before his hero, and without pleasantries launched into an impassioned overview of his current project, at least the parts he believed would be efficacious to reveal at that time. He described the assignment for the journal MerzKraft to write an article on Buddy Bolden, the first man of Jazz, and to interview him, Kid Auger, possibly the only man alive who actually worked with Bolden. Perhaps out of intimidation, standing before the great Auger, or because he was not completely forthcoming when he described his intent, he spoke too rapidly, and Auger, appearing confused, leaned wearily against the chain link fence and watched Nieting run his mouth.

"You might want to slow up a bit, son," said Auger. "I can't hardly make out what you saying. Where you say you from, Germany? Oh, they love me in Germany, all over Europe. I was over there several years back. Fine people."

Auger's voice was gruff, but somehow gentle, with a slow guttural Louisiana accent. The sound calmed Nieting and the old man smiled reassuringly.

"Now, my daddy's folks was from Lorraine," said Auger. "Lorraine, France. My daddy, he spoke French, but some of his relatives, they spoke German. No one spoke English, though. Not a word. I didn't learn myself till I was maybe eight or nine. See, my mother was a Creole girl. She spoke Creole, French, Spanish. What magazine you say sent you here?"

"MerzKraft," replied Nieting. "It's a small journal but very well respected."

"MerzKraft?" said Auger. "I don't know that one. What can I do for you?"

"We wish to publish a feature article on Kid Auger," said Nieting.

"I thought you said you was writing about Buddy Bolden," said Auger.

"Yes," said Nieting. "Buddy Bolden as seen through the eyes of Kid Auger. MerzKraft believes you are the most important Jazz man alive.

We want you to tell our readers about your life, about Buddy Bolden and how it was to work with him. We want to give our readers the true Kid Auger. We want the story from a man who lived it, someone who can put it in the correct social context."

"I'm just a little ol'trombone player," said Auger. "I don't know nothing about big ideas like that. I just want to make folks feel good."

"Please, Kid," said Nieting. "May I call you Kid?"

Nieting continued before Auger could answer.

"Allow me to interview you," he said. "I've come all the way from Berlin simply to speak to Kid Auger."

"I don't think I can help you," said Auger, frowning. "No one's interested in old time stuff anymore. It's all that rock and roll nowadays."

"That isn't true of our readership," said Nieting. "I teach at university, in Germany, my hometown, Berlin. I assure you our youth are highly interested in your career. They want to know what the future holds for Kid Auger."

"I'm an old man, now," said Auger. "The future don't hold as much as it did."

"Kid," said Nieting, "You'll be disappointing thousands of young Germans who look to you as a hero. They don't want Beatles, they want real American music. The music of the Negro. The music of New Orleans. They want Jazz."

"Well, since you put it that way," said Auger, "maybe I can give you a little time. Just so long as you ain't one of those troublemakers."

Auger picked up the instrument and stepped into the sunshine just as a golf cart pulled up driven by an attendant.

"Be here tomorrow afternoon," said Auger. "Four o'clock. We can talk some more then. Don't forget Johnny St. Cyr, now, or Paul Barbarin either. They been around a long time, too."

Auger walked past Nieting then turned back and pointed the rolled up newspaper.

"I don't mind talking as long as you ain't an agitator," he said. "Too many youngsters today don't know how to work. All they do is complain.

Anyone who wants to work can work. Some people nowadays think the government owes them a living because things ain't fair. Well, that's bunk. This is the greatest country in the world. Anyone can make good here. I'm proof of that. That's what I'll tell you about tomorrow, too."

Auger hoisted the trombone case into the back of the cart and climbed aboard.

"Yes, Kid," said Nieting. "Thank you. Tomorrow then."

Auger smiled and waved as the driver leaned on the horn and pushed into the tourist-clogged path.

"That crazy old trickster," said Nieting speaking to himself. "Of course he was putting me on. How serious I must have sounded. 'You ain't no agitator are you?' Certainly I am, just as you are. Why couldn't I have said that? And, those pathetic candy cane suits must be part of the joke, too."

Nieting sat at a metal picnic table beneath a drooping pepper tree, fanning himself with a Disneyland brochure. "It's all too much to believe. It's as though the Kid was lying in wait to trick me and I walked straight into it. 'Yes sir, Kid.' I was a perfect fool. No doubt he is having a good laugh right now."

He watched Johnny St. Cyr and Paul Barbarin walk from the bamboo enclosure and climb aboard a waiting golf cart and on an impulse gave a rebel yell like he'd heard a redneck do in New Orleans. A drunken white man had shouted the yell the first time he'd heard it, inexplicably perturbed at his conversing with an elderly Negro musician on a street corner. He hadn't known what it meant at the time, until he was told by his companion. Nieting gave the rebel yell among the tourists of Disneyland, expropriated it for Kid Auger as a tribute to Negro Jazz. St. Cyr and Barbarin didn't seem to hear as the cart pulled off and the people around him laughed as though he were simply expressing the joy of being at Disneyland.

"Brilliant," he shouted. "Nothing short of brilliant."

Nieting was ecstatic as he walked through the gates of the glittering castle-facade into the vast parking lot and waded into the sea of steaming cars, shielding his eyes from the glare of a thousand chrome-reflections.

"The old man hasn't lost it," he said. "Amazing."

Take the oppressor's phony culture and turn it on its head, he thought. *Push it to the extreme, spend it and leave the empty husk. Celebrate the sterility, the emptiness. Auger has taken bourgeois vapidity to its farthest limits and exposed the absurdity of American life.*

The professor spotted the bulky black case of the tape recorder in the back seat of his rented sedan. He winced when he touched the red hot door handle and jerked his hand away, chuckling as he shook the pain from his fingers.

"The only man alive who may possess knowledge of Buddy Bolden's lost song has agreed to an interview."

Nieting let out another rebel yell as he started the car, for himself this time, celebrating what he believed would be the final step towards a great achievement. The interview with Auger could very well reveal what had been allusive thus far in his travels. His mind danced with the sound of Kid Auger's trombone as he drove north on the Harbor Freeway towards Los Angeles. He emitted yet another rebel yell out the car window that dissolved into the ecstatic shrill cry of an aboriginal coming of age ritual he'd once documented in an ethnography, a call that no defender of the white supremacy would have ever deigned to emit, which was just as Nieting intended.

The sedan sailed in the freeway traffic like blood shooting through the brain, an electric current careening above the shingled roof peaks, vast tangles of utilities poles and wires and odd headed palms languish-ing in the glowing mist. The Southern California landscape was surreal, if ever anything was, and somehow the strangeness seemed appropriate to his mission. Kid Auger had been a vivid force in his life. The sound of his trombone coming from the record player had always held more resonance for Nieting than the voice of any real person he knew. Auger existed in another world yet was as real to him as the buildings lining the Zossener Strasse where he grew up.

Below the freeway, to the east, a great fire raged, a large flat building engulfed in flames, spewing black billows, turning afternoon into dusk for a hundred yards before sunlight knifed through illuminating the lanes of the concrete roadbed strewn with debris like a battlefield. The world appeared to be a wasteland. It seemed natural that he would finally meet Auger in the flesh in a place as weird as this. After all, Auger existed nearly exclusively in his mind until now. Wasn't it appropriate that their meeting place mirror what was inside of him?

Yet, Professor Nieting was on the verge of a great discovery and he knew it. He was close enough to what he sought to taste victory and thus thoughts of his benefactors came to mind, of his Uncle Max above all else. It was only six months since his uncle had passed away. Cancer had taken him, not quite one year after the passing of his life's companion, Heinrich Menk. The two had shared their domestic life since the end of the war. Together they'd raised Valentin Nieting. They were his only family. Everyone else had died in the war. Val was eight years old when Max rescued him from the camp for displaced persons and brought him home. It was Max and Heinrich who sent him to university, supported him during his years of study through the doctoral work at the Free University of Berlin where he went on to become a professor of anthropology until his tenue there was abruptly terminated. His firing was precipitated by the signing of a petition, along with 3000 students, demanding the right to free speech on campus. The Rector had banned the use of university property for workshops on the American invasion of South Vietnam and the students would not have it. The expulsion was handed down in February 1965, several days after his uncle died. Uncle Max would have been proud of Val being fired for political actions. To be despised by the establishment was the least one could achieve. Had his uncle been alive, Nieting would have had a difficult time keeping him from joining the ranks of the students.

Uncle Max was responsible for most of the good things in Val's life. He was even the cause of his being in the U.S. working on his current project. It all came about during the final days of Uncle Max's life. He'd shared a hospital room with an American named Randall Marquette who was also in the last stages of his struggle against Cancer. Marquette was from New Orleans and a musician and he and Max became fast friends. He'd spent the last twenty years of his life as a sort of musical vagabond, traveling across Europe, "playing for his supper" as he put it, spreading the word of New Orleans Jazz and having the time of his life. He told Max, "I got no one looking after me when I leave and no one looking for me when I arrive. I'm a happy man."

After years of wandering Marquette Randall found himself playing solo for the final set of his life. The presence of Max and a few others seemed sufficient for the old man. At least he betrayed no regrets spending his final few days regaling his small audience with tales of his life in music and his friendships with the greatest artists his hometown had produced. Kid Auger and Louis Armstrong and Jelly Roll Morton were among his intimates. He seemed to have been everywhere and known everyone of any consequence. Max reveled in the first hand renditions of the eloquent griot's stories, stories they all knew were being told for the last time.

It was inevitable that the pain of the Cancer intensify and the orations of the Poet, as Max dubbed his friend, more and more descend into drug induced ramblings. The day after the news of Malcolm X's murder on February 21, 1965, reached Randall he became possessed by a great anger. He screamed in burning agony at the vermin consuming his insides and raged at "those god damned pecker woods, those dirty motherfuckers the Klan" and how they were the reason he'd left home all those years ago and was now dying alone. He cursed the lynch mobs and Jim Crow, "all that motherfucking American bullshit." He called for death to the murderers of Malcolm X, striking out at the air, reaching for someone or something, flailing his arms until he was deemed a danger to himself and tied to his bed in restraints.

In the final hours of his life, Randall became obsessed with a man named Robert Charles, a freedom fighter he called him, who resisted a lynch mob of thousands of whites in New Orleans in the year 1900 and succeeded in killing a hundred men before he made his escape. He said his uncle told him the story of Robert Charles when he was a boy. He claimed everyone he knew, knew who Robert Charles was and what he did.   Randall lay on his back staring at the ceiling as he spoke, seeing Charles holed up in the second story of a house on Saratoga Street near South Rampart with a Winchester rifle and a barrel of homemade bullets as whites fired from all sides. He appeared in a window for a split second, discharged his rifle, a white body fell and he jumped from view as a hail of gunfire swept the wood framed house like rain. The whites finally set the structure afire to smoke him out, but they couldn't kill Robert Charles as all the newspapers claimed they did.   Another black man was mistaken for Charles and his body mutilated by the mob. Robert Charles escaped those devils, according to Randall, and was never seen again. Randall struggled to give witness. He spoke to Robert Charles like he was in the room. He exhorted his uncle to tell all the children about Robert Charles. He begged his sisters not to weep for Charles' suffering. He was tortured by Cancer, yet fought to tell all he knew. The story came out in shattered fragments, jumbles of words, then succinct images before veering off into indecipherable anguish.   Several times he became lucid and spoke of a song, a lost song he said, a ballad written in tribute to the great Robert Charles composed by none other than Buddy Bolden. When he descended back into the agony and chaos of morphine, he pleaded with Bolden to play the song, to teach him the song, "we need that song now to carry on the struggle, we need Robert Charles, our people need war- riors, we need that song Buddy, please, Buddy teach me. How did we lose that song? How could we let it slip away? Please Buddy, teach me. We need that Robert Charles Song."

Max awoke one morning to find Randall's bed occupied by another man. Two days later, Max departed himself.

When the suggestion arose to write a piece on Buddy Bolden's lost song for the magazine MerzKraft there was no question that Nieting would accept the challenge. The idea came from his uncle's friend, Oscar Worst. He'd been a constant visitor of Uncle Max in his final days and was greatly moved by Randall Marquette's deathbed testimo- ny. He believed that such a song must exist. In fact, he remembered reading of the song and its suppression in the biography of a great New Orleans Jazz man.

Oscar had been publishing MerzKraft intermittently since the mid-1930s. Uncle Max told Val the early numbers, all of which were lost in the war, regularly carried his father's drawings and photos of his sculptures and from time to time even his writings. Oscar Worst was like a relative to Val. He was a colleague of Uncle Max and Nieting's father in the old days before the war and a Jazz buff who survived the Nazis. He even managed to save his record collection from the SS, Allied bombing, and the Russian occupation. Worst was a passionate Jazz fan as far back as the 1920s when Nieting's father first played Auger's Hot Creoles records at a party. Oscar recruited Nieting to search for the song and his uncle would have hardily approved. Who better to conduct the search for the lost song than an out of work anthropologist, a deposed radical and son of the man who first gave him the music of New Orleans? Worst would publish the song in MerzKraft along with an article by the young anthropologist Dr. Valentin Nieting.

As Nieting's rented sedan shot up the freeway towards Los Angeles, he saw Oscar Worst in his mind, the day they agreed to recover Bolden's lost song.

"How will you find the song, Valentin?" Worst had asked. "So much time has passed. Bolden died thirty-four years ago, broken and all but forgotten."

"Men like Bolden are never forgotten," Nieting had replied. "A song is like a memory, it can be repressed but still lingers beneath the surface. A great injustice has been perpetrated by the whites. We can correct this injustice. We can restore The Robert Charles Song to its rightful owners."

"Yes, Valentin. Tell me more,"

"You see," said Nieting, "as Negro Jazz emerged out of New Orleans to the rest of America, to Europe, and to the world, it was expropriated and reconstituted into something it was not meant to be, something that did not benefit its originators."

"What does this mean, Val? Be specific, if you please."

Nieting had hesitated, watching the corners of the editor's lips slowly curl into a grin as the implications of his pronouncement became illuminated in his brain like a string of Christmas lights.

"Ah yes, you are correct, Valentin," Oscar had said. "I understand now. The black man was once a slave. The whites are accustomed to taking his things. The Americans treat the Negroes very badly. Everyone knows this."

"The whites have created a myth of the origins of Negro Jazz," replied Nieting. "They believe they've made Negro culture their own. In the process they have drained the music of its potency. Bolden's lost song is untouched, pristine. It still reflects the power of Negro resistance in the refusal of Robert Charles to submit."

Oscar clapped his hands and nearly squealed. "Yes, yes, you know, just yesterday, I was reading an article in a banal rag, a fan magazine fit only to clean one's ass. The editors concede the origin of the rhythmic elements of Jazz to the Negro but reserve the ownership of melody and harmony to whites, to their European heritage. As if the truth is meaningless. As if art were real estate. It was an old issue Val, from before the war, yet it managed to make me beside myself with rage. The trumpeter LaRocca was quoted as saying Negroes had nothing to do with the creation of Jazz music. He claimed working-class white men invented Jazz. Can you believe it, Valentin?"

"Yes I do, Oscar. For this reason our quest is great. The recovery of the lost song will unleash knowledge gained through struggle and once again be at the service of its originators. We must return *The Robert Charles Song* to the Negroes."

"But how?" asked Worst, leaning forward and blinking. "Time is running short. The people who may know Bolden's song are dead now or will die soon. From what I've read there are only a handful of souls, a few still living in New Orleans, elderly and poor."

Worst held his hands behind his back and paced about the room, head down, finally stopping short and waving his finger at Nieting as he spoke.

"You must go to New Orleans," he said. "We'll find the funds some-how. Nothing must be allowed to get in the way of this project. You must speak to whoever you can find who knew Bolden or may have knowledge of the song. Who will you interview, Valentin? Who is still alive who could make a difference?"

Nieting hesitated again, watching Worst twitch with anticipation.

"Kid Auger," he said.

"Yes, of course, Kid Auger," said the editor. "He was there at the very beginning."

"That is correct, Oscar," said Nieting. "He may be the only man living who actually worked with Bolden and he is alive and well in California."

"You know, I've said many times," replied Worst, slapping his palm with the back of his hand. "Auger is clearly the most important man left of the original New Orleans Negroes. And that includes Louis, even though some might consider that a crazy thing to say."

"I concur, Oscar," said Nieting. "Auger stands at the top with Morton, Oliver, Louis and Bechet. They were the first great Jazz men to bring the music to the outside world."

"Yes, yes, Valentin," said Worst. "Your father would be so proud if he were alive. You know what he would have said, Valentin? 'Make it sensational!'"

Worst was delighted with his statement and skipped across the room to the phonograph, pointed his forefinger at Nieting and cackled with joy.

"*Make me a Pallet*, eh?" he said. "I've been listening to this selection quite a bit lately, as if I knew we would have this conversation. Isn't that a marvelous coincidence, Valentin?"

Nieting was taken aback, was breathless for a moment.

"Quite so," he said. "Miraculous, actually. Splendid."

Worst lowered the arm of the phonograph.

"Bolden's composition played by the great Auger," he said.

He swept his arm towards the record player as Kid Auger burst out, playing a single note for several bars, altering the duration of each breath, twisting the note like a tympani, transforming the quintessential simplicity of a repeated tone into a soul-firing original once-in-lifetime statement. The ensemble followed on his heels improvising collectively amidst the crackling and popping of the old record. Worst clapped in a spasm of delight and he and Nieting sealed the deal with a handshake.

Nieting wiped a few tears from his eyes as he reached the junction of the Harbor and Santa Monica Freeways. "Dear old Oscar," he said softly. "My wonderful co-conspirator."

When Professor Nieting referred to Oscar Worst as his co-conspirator, he was the victim of a rush of euphoria. He knew better than that. It was Uncle Max who was his true co-conspirator. He was his mentor and benefactor and the only father he'd ever known. It all began with Uncle Max. It was he who put everything in motion. It was because of Max that little Val Nieting had heard of Kid Auger in the first place. According to his uncle, Val had listened to Kid Auger in his mother's womb. He'd kicked in time to the syncopated beat inside her belly causing a living room filled with his parents' friends to break into laughter and applause as his father, Emil, ear to his mother's stomach, beat out the rhythm in the air. This was related to Val by his Uncle Max, his father's best friend. Uncle Max had introduced Emil to his sister and blessed her marriage to the young sculptor, half Jewish, Anarchist, Dadaist, and connoisseur of American Jazz. He lived with her long enough to conceive Valentin before he fled. Like everything else in Val's life, it was the war that wrecked his family. Uncle Max was the only one besides Val that survived. He was the reason Auger and his father existed for Val at all. He conjured their presence in stories, wove a legend for the boy, described the bizarre collaboration, passed on reminiscences nearly swallowed by the all-consuming fire of bombs and the horror of concentration camps. He made Emil Nieting and Kid Auger a presence in the boy's life.

Kid Auger was even involved in his father's fleeing. It came about because of an art exhibit held in an old Berlin warehouse. It was the first exhibit in years because of the Nazis repression. It was early 1937, just before Goebbels' exhibit of so-called degenerate art. Uncle Max told the story many times, always with absolute relish as if telling it for the first time.

"They said we were degenerates, Valentin. Hitler vowed to cleanse the fatherland of our kind. They were clamping down all over, for years they'd been confiscating people's work. So many of our most brilliant colleagues had already left Germany. Hausmann was in France, Richter and Grosz were in America, Schwitters was in Norway. We all believed the days of free expression were over, that it was suicide to stage an exhibition, but your father wouldn't accept that. Everyone was underground by then. Nevertheless, your father decided that we must have a showing, regardless of the consequences.

"It was a defiant exhibit, quite radical, I'd say. In the entrance of the warehouse was a sculpture of a human buttox made of paper mache. The surface was smooth and shined like flesh and it was lined with human hair."

Nieting remembered Uncle Max being so tickled when he spoke of the hairy ass that his eyes filled with tears.

"It was made by your father," he would go on. "Bristling with genuine human hair. Oh, who is to say? He may have inserted something else, a bit of fur from the kitty. But, all of us contributed our pubic hair, men and woman. He solicited the pieces at a party after everyone was drunk. He walked around the room taking donations in a cloth napkin. The next day he carefully inserted our gifts into the wet plaster and dried it into a perfectly real hairy human posterior. A burn appeared across both cheeks, a brown blistering Swastika, like the SS had applied to people we knew. The sight of the ass was hilarious at first glance, but on closer examination it became disturbing, macabre, tragic.

"But that was your father," Uncle Max would say. "He always told the truth, even when it was a terrible truth. Oh, how we loved him. He was the heart of our group. And, how he loved Kid Auger. It was Auger, out of the entire ensemble, whether it was his group or Oliver's or Morton's, it was always Auger's trombone that your father heard above all else. I would say, it was the engine of his philosophy, the essence of his moral view. He called it 'the wail of the complete rejection of power.' Isn't that something? That's what your father heard in Kid Auger's music. He said it was surrealistic, a dreamscape, modulated yet free, unashamedly sexual, a driving force. He once described the drummer Baby Dodds as a mountain of syncopation, a solid rock with moving parts, and playful above all else, funny, joyous. These are the attributes that power distains, that threaten the existence of tyrants. Your father said these things.

"The day we heard Kid Auger had retired, had given up music completely, I was astonished. We read that the Americans had simply stopped listening to the music of New Orleans and that the music of Kansas City was suddenly the rage. Armstrong changed his style because of it. This was in the thirties, Valentin. Your father was beside himself with joy and I didn't understand. How can you be happy that the great Auger has thrown away his art?

"'Do you know what Auger is doing now?' your father asked.

"'No, no,' I told him, 'I don't know what the great Auger is doing? Tell me.

'He is running a chicken farm,' he said, 'in California, in a place called Watts. Can you see the chickens parading in a line behind Auger's trombone? Dada *is* chicken shit. And the press thought Tzara was only being difficult.'

"I don't know if your father loved Auger more for playing his music or for giving it up; anyway, I was telling you about the exhibit. On the second day, a group of Nazi Youth showed up at the gallery. They were older boys, sleeves rolled above the elbows, all carrying clubs. They pushed through the entrance and formed up beneath your father's hairy ass.

"We knew they would come," Uncle Max would say sadly. "We knew someone would inform. We only had the courage to be there because of your father."

Uncle Max would brighten. "They hesitated under the hairy ass when they realized the gallery was crowded and they were clearly out manned. For a long moment we all stood silently, every one of us just staring at the Nazis. I don't know if they would have left on their own. We'll never know because your father approached them, carrying a piece of artwork, a collage; words and photos cut and torn from magazines with bits of brown paper, old clothe and foil pasted on a wooden board. There were pictures of Hitler and Goering with grotesque grimaces and lines of generals with the oversized mouths of baboons pasted onto their faces. There were Swastikas flying around like bats, everything distorted, juxtaposed into screaming images shooting in straight lines like sabers. It was glorious, shrill and inflammatory. Quite lovely really, and not your father's. It belonged to Heartfield. Your father held the piece for John for years, kept it hidden from the Nazis after he'd fled. But that didn't stop your father from using it.

"Natty Dominque was playing on the phonograph when the Nazis came in," said Max, "booming throughout the warehouse, *Heebie Jeebies*, I believe it was. I still get the heebie jeebies every time I hear it because I can still see your father walking towards the Nazis, holding the piece at his side like a weapon at rest, very calmly, and facing them like a western cowboy, a gunfighter. Unbeknownst to the Nazis, he was listening to the vocalist scat singing, concentrating on the voice, Johnny St. Cyr I think. And when Mr. St. Cyr called out, 'hey Kid Auger, play that thing, boy,' your father drew back Heartfield's collage and smashed the nearest Nazi across the face on the beat just as Auger punched out the note. Your father always loved the grand gesture.

"With the crack of the board on the Nazi boy's face, everyone inside the gallery charged. We did it without a plan. We rushed at them, wrested the clubs away and beat them into the street. They were outside in the gutter in seconds with all of us after them, on them like wolves. There were no police to be seen. They must have known of the plan to attack the exhibit and thought the Nazis would easily destroy the gallery, so they withdrew from the neighborhood. But, we routed them. Men, women, the artists beat them back. Your father stood in the street swinging the collage above his head, howling like a Red Indian.

"We all quickly left the gallery and went to the home of a friend, a place we thought would be safe, and danced to the music of the great

Auger. Your father sat next to the phonograph hearing nothing but Kid Auger, Kid Auger laughing, Kid Auger goosing the asses of Nazi Youth with the slide of his trombone, Kid Auger propelling the wooden collage into the face of the Nazi boy as he drove the ensemble. Baby Dodds suddenly playing wood blocks as though answering your father's blow. Omer Simeon whistling his clarinet like birdies singing when the boy went down, and Natty trumpeting the charge."

Max would hold his stomach and shake with laughter until the tears ran down his face. So many times, he would embrace his little nephew, take him in his arms, standing behind him as though he were covering him, shielding him from the harshness of the truth.

"That was the last time we saw your father," he would say in a whisper. He always sounded perplexed when he said it, as if failing to grasp the meaning of his own words. "It was only a matter of time before they would come after him" said Max, "so he fled. They were going to murder him or send him to the camps. It was very dangerous. We all had to stay out of sight after the exhibit. We couldn't associate with one another after that. None of us saw your father again. We were told that he fled to Paris. He worked in the underground for a period. A colleague of Emil's from that time told me he once wore a captured SS uniform and infiltrated Nazis headquarters and freed several members of the Resistance. Frenchmen. I believe they were affiliated with the Surrealists. The day before Hitler captured Paris, he moved on to England in the dead of night, across the channel in the small craft of a fisherman. Members of the Resistance arranged the transport because it would have been too dangerous to hide him in France after the Nazis occupied Paris. In London he was active in counter-intelligence, as I understand it. We were told he died there, murdered by agents of the SS. He succeeded in killing his assassins before he died. Friends told us of it, but we were never able to bring his body home. He was so young, Valentin, just twenty-eight years old. He could have had a brilliant career if he'd lived. But we mustn't think of the sadness. Valentin, if only you could have seen the looks on the faces of the Nazis as we charged and the perfect timing of your father's blow. Just as if he was part of Auger's band. They are bound together, Valentin. Emil and Kid Auger are truly brothers."

As Nieting traveled west towards Santa Monica, the image of uncle dissolved like mist into the sunshine. To the north, the sky was bright and deep blue, no longer the toxic dreamscape, the eerie image of another planet. Los Angeles looked like a Mediterranean city, the buildings white like bones scattered across the basin, splashing part way up the hills at the base of the mountains.

Nieting believed at that moment that everything would be revealed. Buddy Bolden's song would be plucked from the collective unconscious and returned to its rightful owners. It was he, Professor Valentin Nieting, who possessed the power to reclaim, illuminate and transmit the knowledge essential to the creation of a new world. The solidity, the affirmative weight of all he'd learned during his sojourn to America came back as he drove the freeway west towards the ocean. Everything he'd learned in New Orleans the week previous to arriving in Los Angeles had enhanced what he already understood about the power of culture and the inevitability of revolution. The song would be a functioning model of his thesis. He hungered to tell someone, to confide how he'd been confused at first by Auger's performance.

He'd been given the address of a poet by a friend, a colleague at the Free University, a professor named Hans Gartenbauer. The poet's name was Arnold Snellman and in Professor Nieting's estimation he was a great poet. He was a contemporary, just a few years older than Nieting, highly esteemed among radical literati of Berlin. He'd come to America several years earlier on a fellowship as writer-in residence at a West Coast university and was currently living in a small converted garage near the beach in Venice, California. He would most certainly be amenable to entertaining an educated countryman, according to Nieting's colleague. If he were in need, Gartenbauer had told him, the poet would no doubt put him up, that is, if the professor didn't mind rather rustic accommodations. Snellman was a mystic his friend said, and paid little attention to bodily comforts. The prospect of speaking to a like-minded German was a relief to Nieting.

He desired to discuss Kid Auger, to explain the marvelous, perplexing experience of witnessing his performance at Disneyland.

Nieting rebel-yelled, waving his left arm out the window like a bronco busting cowboy as the car descended the loping south bound entrance to the San Diego Freeway. After some time, he exited at Venice Blvd. and wheeled westward, fingering the map laying in the passenger seat as he organized his thoughts for the poet. After several wrong turns and retracing his path, he arrived miraculously at Rose Avenue in Venice, the street where Snellman's garage apartment was supposed to be. He took a right at Rose and drove several blocks, finally making a quick U-turn when he spotted the address given to him by Hans Gartenbauer. The first impression was promising. The house was a neat Craftsmen-style cottage with a front porch, the overhang supported by tapering columns, pyramids cut short at the apex and behind that, Morris-style strained glass hanging in the leaded glass picture window and more stained glass in the small window in the door. Nieting parked on Rose and in moments was making his way through a sandy alley to a tiny yard crowded with cactus and palm plants and a sandy patch of lawn littered with piles of dog feces. Beyond the lawn was Snellman's garage or rather the back of the garage, the car entrance apparently on the opposite side facing an alley.

The sight Nieting encountered as he approached the back entrance was disturbing, like the aftermath of terrible violence. The back door had been torn from the hinges. A piece of white tape with the name F. Zarathustra written in pen was glued above a broken doorbell dangling from electric wires. When he peered inside he noticed that the doors on the other side were also gone. He walked around to the alley entrance, carefully stepping over broken glass from a side window. Inside, the space was filled with debris, the corpse of a cat, dried and petrified, hung on the wall next to a bronze crucifix with the face of Nietzsche pasted over the face of Christ. Open flat on the floor was a hard bound copy of Spengler's *Decline of the West*, mildewed and bloated from dampness, the pages pasted into collages with cutouts from magazines. Twisted mounds of clothing lay about like sculptural renditions of tornados, piles of wet newspapers, apparent drafts of poems, garbage in varying stages of decomposition, old sneakers, ancient flip flops, torn up books, half consumed food cartons, and broken furniture lay about in a chaos. A terrible stench permeated the place. After several moments of silently pondering the fate of the poet, a man appeared out of nowhere, startling Nieting. He announced that he was the owner of the property and with that introduction began to spew angry questions.

"Are you a friend of his? You're a foreigner, aren't you? Do you speak English? Can you pay what he owes? The police know your friend. They know him real well. He better not come around here without the money he owes me. It'll go easier on him if I don't press charges. Look at the mess he made. Do you know how much this will cost to clean up? Plenty, I promise you that. Are you related to this guy? You're not a junky are you? I have dogs inside, German Shepherds. They're pretty fucking mean. Can you contact his family? They're liable for his debts, you know. He was a real nice guy until he started messing with that shit. Now, he's a wreck, damaged goods, won't last much longer. It's a shame. This was a nice little unit before he got his hands on it. Fucked up, he's one fucked up son of a bitch. He said he was a poet. Junkies always say they're poets. How can a junky be a poet when junkies don't give a shit about anything but the needle. He might have been a poet once, back in Germany, but not anymore. Look at this place. Imagine living like an animal and still thinking you're better than everyone else. That's a fucking junky for you. Poet my ass. That god damned needle does it every time. I've seen it too often. I don't have any sympathy either. He did it to himself. They all do. Sick. They're all sick. That's the reason I hate junkies. I never would have let him set foot on my property if I'd known. How much money do you have? Someone has to pay for this and it ain't gonna be me."

It took some time before Nieting succeeded in convincing the man that his affiliation with Snellman had never been consummated. At that, the landlord shifted gears, rubbing his forehead and apologizing. He informed Nieting that he might find Snellman at the beach, where the junkies regularly assembled to panhandle and get high and offered directions which Nieting gladly accepted. "Tell your friend, as bad as I want my money, I'd rather set my dogs on him. If I ever lay eyes on him I'll let them kill him. Tell him that, will you?"

The question of Snellman was perplexing. He was a great poet after all, and a decent man according to Gartenbauer, at least before his apparent fall into heroin addiction. Perhaps Nieting could locate the unfortunate fellow, offer to relay some message home or contact someone who might be of help, Hans perhaps, someone who might rescue Snellman from the terror of his Venice, California nightmare. Nieting skipped over the piles of dog shit and made his way through the sandy alley. Within fifteen minutes he'd parked near the beach. The blue horizon of the ocean was visible down the block as he locked his car.

Venice was a sleepy town on the perimeter of the sprawling city, an odd corner of poverty, incongruous beneath towering palms. For a little over a year, the City of Los Angeles had been engaged in the first phase of urban renewal on and around the beach front. Nieting felt an eerie nostalgia, seeing streets with gaps like missing teeth where buildings had been demolished and piles of debris left behind. The images of the bombed out Berlin of his youth against the incongruous sound of pounding surf and the smell of the ocean unnerved him, as if all of Europe was blown to bits and the Mediterranean Sea had become the coast of Germany.

A lone drum sounded in the distance. Nieting imagined the drum beats darting into the air, slowing into a high arch, then accelerating as they dropped, splashing into the Pacific. At the end of the street was Ocean Front Walk, a paved walkway, twenty feet across, separating the white sand from lines of rundown storefronts and beat up apartment buildings. As he scanned the beach for the poet, he spotted a Negro sitting under a green pagoda at the sand's edge clutching a conga drum between his thighs. Nieting headed towards him. The weather had changed in a matter of minutes without his realizing it. The sky was thick with low clouds and the ocean obscured by fog except for white water tumbling onto the shore, rumbling as it hit and hissing as the foam fled back into the gray mist. The overcast sky seemed to bring a strange clarity, a closed-in stillness, a vividness enveloped within a curtain of gray. The few souls on Ocean Front Walk appeared to be moving in slow motion to the pulse of the man in the pagoda caressing the drum, as if he was eliciting everyone's heart beat, as if the drum were the force behind all their lives.

On the water's edge, three desperate souls, ragged and emaciated, stumbled across the wet sand, jostling each other like tragic keystone cops, their figures etched starkly against the mist as they hurried towards some pathetic business. "There are your drug addicts," said Nieting. "Perhaps they are off to meet the poet Snellman. Perhaps he is one of them." He started onto the sand in pursuit and halted after a few paces as the three made tracks down the beach, their figures growing smaller in the distance. They finally darted back towards Ocean Front Walk, gesticulating wildly, debating some incomprehensible point or plan, knocking into each other, pulling one another's clothing, each scratching at their skin and tearing at their hair, before the trio slipped of out sight between two abandoned brick buildings. Ocean Front Walk shot like an arrow directly north from the spot the three ant-like creatures disappeared into the decaying structures of the city. Nieting's gaze rose a few inches from that spot to the mountains touching the blue sky like a Mediterranean kiss, then followed its extension westward as it thrust with primeval tenderness into the soft flesh of the ocean and disappeared into its undulating fluid, each body vivid, flexed, distinct until the instant of fusion.

The mist at Venice Beach had cleared. Miraculously, everything opened up and the sand glowed in the sunlight. Nieting's eyes ran along the horizon of the Pacific, on the line of blue against blue behind the path the three junkies had passed, perhaps the ghost of the German poet among them.

A gong sounded, vibrating in a sustained flow that hung in the air, a strange internal background that Nieting didn't notice until a bearded young man standing in the doorway of an old storefront on Ocean Front Walk, wearing nothing but briefs, banged the gong a second time. Nieting turned at the sound of voices as a set of double doors opened and a crowd of people moved out onto Ocean Front Walk. They came from a one-story building of tan stucco with a Star of David above the doors and smaller ones in-set in arches of stucco on either side. The man hit the gong again and the conga in the pagoda answered with delicate finger tips. The man holding the gong grinned and nodded exaggeratedly so the man in the pagoda could see his approval, then disappeared inside. The people exiting the temple were elderly. They didn't respond to the weird sounds, didn't seem to notice, as if such strangeness was an everyday occurrence. They filed out of the building, sitting on benches and milling about in front of the synagogue.

Nieting gapped at the old people. It was as if the past had suddenly appeared before him, as if he had summoned them with his brooding over poor Snellman, as if they'd lined up at his behest, as if his mind had emptied itself of them and he stood before himself or rather some lost part of himself. *Listen to them, chattering in their Yiddish*, he thought. *Some among them might have known father. They might have been his friend. They might have been our neighbors.*

For all the wonder of the appearance of the old Jews at just that moment, the only thing Professor Nieting, the researcher, the social theoretician, renegade anthropologist, knew to do was stare, to look as closely and as deeply as he could, to consume the images as some strange food for his mind. The only emotion he trusted enough to set free was his amazement. Why were they all sitting there? Had they truly assembled because of him? They seemed to be waiting for something. His eyes jumped to the numbers tattooed on the arm of an old woman. He towered over the old people; not one of them would have come up past his chest. They sat in a row on the benches, pointed at the ocean and at Nieting who faced them, his eyes riveted on their arms. He'd been noticed the moment he walked among them and now, staring with his mouth hanging open, nervous titters tinkled from the benches, old elbows attached to numbered forearms poked surreptitiously at their neighbor's sides. An old man with his hands apocket asked the line of ladies on the bench, "What are you girls looking at?" and one replied, "That nut right over there, look, right in front of your face. How can you miss him?" Her neighbor whispered loudly, "My god, whatz he doing? Whyz he got his mouth stuck open like that?" and another replied, "Looks like he's doing caca in his pants."

A few giggles squeezed from the bench and gasps of amazement at the wide eyed nut. Finally, a woman laughed and it spread like a ripple in water until they were all laughing, everyone laughing except Nieting. The laughing kept up, getting worse until they were all howling and reeling on the benches. Nieting looked back in wonder, oblivious to the joke. He didn't know why they were laughing, had no idea it was the sight of him, incongruous absurd gapping man. The old people laughed like a street mob. Nieting turned and looked towards the ocean for the source of the joke and the laughter grew louder. When he looked back quickly to see what caused the increase in intensity they laughed harder still. Old women raised their arms in laughter, slapped their thighs, jabbed each other with their elbows, tried to smother screams in their hands, wiping their wet eyes with balled up tissues.

The man in the pagoda rushed a steady pattern of drum beats like water spraying or tall grass swaying or a peacock's tail spreading in a soft breeze as an old man stepped up to Nieting's side, standing barely up to his elbow and squeezed his arm. He wore a tattered tweed jacket that was once quite sporty, a bit wild even, but was dingy, torn at the shoulders and frayed at the sleeves and too tight across the back. He had a hat on, a sweat stained Panama that hid his eyes until he looked up at Nieting. His face was deeply lined and unshaven, scared with age, and his eyes sparkled. He grinned a wise-guy grin, jaunty, playful, he was a real card the old man, a jokester. His eyes twinkled as he gripped Nieting's arm, almost affectionately, "job well done kid, you slayed'm my boy," and Nieting's body grew stiff. It was his father. It was Emil Nieting in the flesh. But, he was an old man, not the dapper artist, spiritual chum of Kid Auger he knew from the old photograph kept by Uncle Max. Yet, there was no doubt who the man was. No question besides the fact that his father was dead twenty five years.

The old man lowered his head and the face disappeared beneath the hat. He was mugging to the crowd on the benches, trying to keep the laughter going even as they calmed finally, dabbing tears from their eyes and sighing with relief, gratitude for the break in hilarity. The conga came up and Nieting looked away, towards the man in the pagoda, seventy-five yards off, then back at the old people. The man in the tweed jacket disappeared for a moment until Nieting saw him standing against the temple chatting with several old men, the tweed coat slung over his shoulder like a young rake, not an old man, or an old Jew, or a survivor of the camps. The numbers on his arm were visible and clear twenty yards off. He turned his head away from the others and looked at Nieting, as if he knew Nieting was looking for him, and winked. He winked and grinned and rocked on his heels, then bent into the group and out of sight. *Father?* Nieting wasn't thinking. It was the face. He'd only seen it in a photograph, yet he was quite sure it was his father's face. In a moment, he found himself at the side of the synagogue, his hands on the old men, moving them aside, searching for the tweed jacket and Panama hat that hid his father's eyes. The others drew back, disturbed, alarmed at the pushy young man and that intense stare again, only this time the incongruity wasn't funny.

"Vatch out dere," said one of the old men.

"Get avay from us," said another.

"I'm so sorry," said Nieting. "I thought I saw someone I know, knew once, someone I should have known."

"Vhat?"

"Shhhh. . . don't say no more. He's mishuga."

"No, I'm alright now. Forgive me. I'm a stranger here."

This is what they look like, he thought. *I haven't seen one up close for all these years. Is California a graveyard? The netherworld? They look like ghosts, but they're not ghosts. They're old Jews splashed like shards of glass to the ends of the earth.*

Nieting left the old men looking after him and shaking their heads and started towards the man with the drum. He reeled slightly at first, regaining his stride as voices from behind spoke.

"I figured he was a drunk."

"Shhh, don't say nothing till he's gone."

Nieting edged up to the pagoda where the black man worked the drum, finally dropping on the bench like a weary traveler. He smiled and nodded and the man nodded back without smiling. He was a young man in his early twenties with thick horn rimmed glasses and a sparse beard that thickened at the chin into a kind of natural goatee.

"This place is quite weird, isn't it?" said Nieting. "To use an over worn phrase, it's rather surrealistic. Do those old Jews always congregate there?"

"They got a community center for the old people," said the man. "That's a synagogue. That all right with you?"

"Yes, of course. They startled me, that's all. They're from another time and place. I didn't expect to see them here."

"I figured you were a tourist," said the man, chuckling, "the way you crept up here with that simple-minded grin on your face. Like you were lost or something. Yeah, Venice can be funny all right. It ain't just you."

Nieting scanned the hunched figures of the old people sitting on the benches and standing around temple door. The tweed jacket and Panama hat were nowhere to be seen.

"It seems like the past keeps catching up with me," said Nieting. "Even far away from home, even in America."

"That's the way it is," said the man. "You can't escape your history. It's around you all the time. Stays with you whether you want it or not. You only think it's catching up, but it never went anywhere to begin with."

He spread his fingers wide and flicked the tips on the drumhead like rain drops.

"It's a good thing, too," he said. "Helps a man understand why things are like they are. If you ever do really lose the past, you're as good as dead. The only way you can survive is to know the past."

"That's quite right," said Nieting. "I'm afraid people have forgotten that in my country. In some ways nothing has changed."

The man turned away, towards the ocean and continued hitting the drum as though the conversation with Nieting had come to an end.

"You know, in Germany the authorities do not allow young people to congregate in the streets, in public places to make music," said Nieting. "You will be arrested. It has happened many times. Young people are detained for dancing to American Rock and Roll music or simply playing the guitar in public. To those old Jews it would be all too familiar, I'm afraid. People have chosen to forget these things. Nowadays however, more and more, the youth sees through all of this. Yet, when they question these things they are attacked. The authorities use sticks and dogs. The police break up peaceful demonstrations. I realize that Germany isn't the only place where this occurs, yet that is no consolation at all. We aren't the only ones to suffer this, nor the worst victims. For instance, we were particularly appalled at what they did to Malcolm X."

The drumming ceased like a heartbeat stopping as the young man jerked his head and cringed. His eyes hardened.

"Don't you talk about Malcom," he said. "Presumptuous motherfucker. Get the fuck away from me."

"I merely mentioned the murder of Malcolm X," said Nieting. "Why are you angry? Surely you've heard he was killed."

"Are you FBI or fucking LAPD?" said the man. "I got nothing to say to you."

"I could never be a member of the police," said Nieting. "I lived under the Gestapo. I'm not even an American. My name is Dr. Valentin Nieting. I am a professor at the Free University of Berlin, or I was. I've come to the States to research an article on Buddy Bolden, the legendary Negro musician."

Nieting hesitated. He would not tell the man the true nature of his work. His job was to ask questions, not volunteer information to strangers, even Negro strangers. Besides, there was always the possibility the man might be a government agent himself.

"Do you know of Kid Auger?" asked Nieting.

"I heard the name," replied the man coldly.

"Tomorrow I will interview the Kid," said Nieting. "I met with him yesterday and he was quite supportive of my project."

The man answered in the form of a four beat figure tapped on the drum head, each beat of the skin suspended amidst another unheard beat, perhaps in the man's mind. He played it over and over, the deep sound resonating as a physical sensation, a vibration in the center of Nieting's chest. Nieting listened for a few moments then said smiling, "You remind me of some kind of wondrous municipal worker, like your drum is the only thing keeping all of this life moving. I'm afraid if you stopped drumming, we would all disappear."

The man worked the congas calmly, yet somehow managed to evoke the illusion of several drummers playing. His torso was relaxed yet his hands flitted so quickly over the drum he appeared not to be touching the surface, as if signaling some complex incantation above the stretched skin. He remained silent for several moments as he worked his hands, then spoke finally.

"Who'd you say you're gonna interview?"

"Kid Auger," replied Nieting. "The famous Negro musician. He's a Jazz trombonist. Perhaps the greatest that ever lived. I met him this morning at Disneyland."

The man threw back his head and laughed.

"Disneyland? There ain't no Negroes at Disneyland."

"It was Disneyland, I'm sure," said Nieting. "I was a bit surprised about that myself. He wasn't at all like I'd expected him to be."

"No? What'd you expect the Negro to be like?"

"I expected so many things, a thousand things. But, not Disneyland. I didn't truly know what Disneyland was until I was there. It was quite shocking, overwhelming actually. Until I realized his act was a put on."

"What do you mean, put on?" said the man.

"There were nothing but tourists there," said Nieting. "Whites, nothing but whites. They were ignorant and no one knew who Kid Auger was. When they announced Louis' name over the loud speaker, only a few responded, as if they'd never heard of him. Everyone in Germany knows Louis Armstrong. He is known all over Europe. I thought all the Americans revered him. Yet, they appeared quite removed. It is true, the people enjoyed the music. They seemed quite content, like cattle really, like contented cows. The situation was strange. Like a weird dream where nothing has any value, where everything has been drained of its meaning. Yet there were the Young Men of Jazz. They were a band of old Negroes and they called them the young men. I was fooled completely at first. I'm a bit ashamed to admit it now. Auger has always meant so much to me. I was completely taken in by the joke."

"You think there was a joke, huh?" said the man. "Sounds like more of the same to me. Business as usual. Status quo. What's the point?"

"It was a put on, don't you see?" said Nieting. "Auger wasn't what he appeared to be at all. He was like a mirror really, reflecting back onto the audience their own emptiness, the vacancy of their existence. He was mocking them. Later when I spoke to him, he made statements about America being the greatest nation in the world and I fell for it. I mean, I thought he was being sincere. I was speechless. My heart sank. I felt like I wanted to grab him and beg him not to say those things. When he left I realized it was all a put on, a critique of sorts, or a protest."

"That don't make sense," said the man. "If no one knew what he was doing, there was no protest, right? If the people you want to effect with your protest ain't aware that there was a protest, there ain't no god damned protest. Whitey went home sky high and never knew a thing. Your man didn't confront them with any kind of reality. Ain't that right?"

"That's not the point," said Nieting. "Auger has no obligation to educate ignorant reactionaries. You should have seen it. They were like robots. I felt as if there was no flesh and blood present besides myself and those Negroes."

"What is the point?" said the man. "He did it specially for you, right?"

"Certainly not. He had no idea I was there. He didn't know me at the time. Or perhaps he did do it for my benefit. No one knows."

The man laughed.

"Right. They were all there because of you. Old Walt build the damned park for you, too. All those whites were probably actors. Probably some Negroes in white face in there too. You must be a pretty important man."

"No, of course not," said Nieting. "Auger's intention was clear. He simply hoped that someone, a few at most, might understand. He was trying to speak to those few, not to that mass of cretins. It seemed like a farce to me. I don't know what else to make of it."

"What you say is not logical, my friend," said the young man.

He looked blankly at Nieting, hitting the drum, moving his fingers around the circular top, shading the tone and phrasing the beats almost like words, as if to show Nieting he spoke a language Nieting did not understand.

"No" said Nieting. "I'm certain it was a joke."

"Don't sound like a joke to me," said the man. "Let me tell you something. The system is slick. See, if a black man makes a name for himself, if he starts *saying* something, first thing they'll do is try to buy him off. I seen some good folks change their tune just like that, because the white man let a few crumbs drop off his table. Anyone who does like that, needs the scraps so bad he's willing to sacrifice his people, ain't shit anyway"

"Yes, of course," said Nieting. "It's called 'selling out.'"

"Right," said the man chuckling. "Selling out."

"But that's not Auger, I assure you. His music was always an act of disruption, a rejection of authority. Bolden must have been the same way. I'm positive of it. America is the sell-out, not Kid Auger. There are things that have been stolen that must be returned. I believe it is vital to view the culture of the American Negro within the proper context, that is, white supremacy."

The man slid his hand across the drum head with a hissing sound, then a pop, hiss, pop, hiss, pop.

"You got that right," he said. "What you say your name is?"

"Nieting. Professor Valentin Nieting."

"I'm Rene Lawson. I like your outlook, professor. You took me by surprise earlier. You got to be careful being so forward like that. Someone else might have been real offended. Malcolm's name shouldn't be spoken so casual, not by no fucking white boy. It's too important to folks. It ain't safe to be throwing it around if you don't know who you're talking too."

"I'm learning that to be true," said Nieting. "Rene, I thank you for your patience. I really wish to help, not exacerbate things."

"You gonna put this is a book or something?" said Rene. "And you think that old Uncle Tom is gonna be the missing link between you and Buddy Bolden. There's plenty elders besides Mr. Disneyland."

"There is no one like Kid Auger," said Nieting. "I've already interviewed most of the old timers in New Orleans and was unable to find what I need. I expect Kid Auger to add the final piece to the puzzle. There is information that only he possesses. He was there at the beginning, you know. I am confident he will add some insight to what I've seen in New Orleans. I witnessed an absolute confirmation of the true nature of peoples' culture in New Orleans. I saw Negroes using the music the way they must have in Bolden's time. I witnessed a Negro funeral. I was invited by a friend, a Negro friend. He is a wonderful man. He'd worked with Bolden and all of the early Negro Jazz men. He taught me many things. He insisted that I experience the Negro funeral. It was an amazing spectacle. The people paraded all over the city, even through the white business district."

Rene listened intently, nodding his head slightly at first, then rapidly as Nieting said more. He took a joint from a small leather handbag and lit up.

"You should have seen how the whites looked at the Negroes as they passed," said Nieting. "Yet the Negroes didn't seem to notice or care. They weren't an oppressed minority any longer, at least they weren't for that moment. They were transformed by the music. It was more than a symbol of resistance, believe me. It was almost an act of rebellion or at least portended the possibility of it."

"That's god damned true," said Rene, "and the white man knows it. He's scared shitless. He got black people in concentration camps. It's a systematic type thing. See, the music is dangerous. It's one of the ways we organize ourselves, teach ourselves. It's an African thing. Music ain't shit if it don't lead the people to revolution. It ain't shit if it don't change your life."

"Yes I know this," replied Nieting. "My father was assassinated by the Nazis. He believed in revolution as well. His mother was a Jew, but they killed him as much for being an artist."

"No shit," said Rene, squinting through the smoke and drawing on the joint. "They're killing people here, too. For being black, brown, red. They go after the artists for sure, always after the truth tellers."

Rene offered the joint to Nieting, who took it without hesitation. He toked the joint and handed it back to Rene.

"Yes, I know," he said. "Even in Germany we know this. We were quite shocked when they killed Malcolm X. If you'll forgive my saying so."

"Malcolm and a shit load of others," replied Rene. "They kill black people every day. They've lynched us, shot us, poisoned us, locked us up, forced us into exile. We've had four hundred years of it. But that's all changing now. Black people understand what's been going on. That's the difference. We won't take the same shit no more. Times are changing fast and the white man can't keep up. He knows his time is short."

"Do you think the whites will give up their power?" asked Nieting.

"Give up power?" said Rene. "Shit, they won't give up nothing. No one gives up power. It's human nature to seek power, not to give it up. But that's old news. What's new is the black man ain't in the asking mood no more. We'll take what we need if we have too. There's more niggers in the world than whites."

"But, you are a minority," said Nieting.

"Black, brown, red and yellow people, what you been calling Negroes, are a majority in the world. There's too many of us for you to take us militarily."

Nieting felt a rush of shame and lowered his head.

"I'm interested in the part the music will play in this change," he said.

"Oh, the music's all over it," said Rene.

"Can you tell me what you mean?" asked Nieting. "Perhaps offer the name of an artist. This would be helpful in my research."

Rene relit the joint, his eyes suddenly becoming wide and earnest.

"You ever hear of the Black African Diaspora Ensemble?" he said. "We call it, the BAD ensemble for short."

Nieting nodded his head apologetically and shrugged his shoulders.

"Then you ain't as hip as you think you are," said Rene. "Talk about African family, man, those folks got it going on. Morris Triplett is the founder of the group. You could say he's the leader. He's a master musician, teacher, composer, band leader. He does it all, man. I work with BAD, that's my home base. I stay up here in Venice, but I go down there and play, where the elders are. I don't usually mention this kind of thing to no strange white people, but I guess you're all right."

Nieting nearly swooned, high with the weed and the scent of the sea and the sound of the drums. He clasped his hands around his knees and rocked back and forth.

"That sounds beautiful, man," he said.

Rene drew deeply on the joint and handed it to Nieting.

"What kind of black music you say you writing about?" he said.

"Early Jazz," replied Nieting. "The beginnings of it, in New Orleans."

"Dixieland?" said Rene, raising his eyebrows. "BAD don't play no Dixieland. Only the real thing. We play Great Black Music. Strictly for the community. None of that *Concerts By the Sea* bullshit, either. See, it ain't that that's not our music too. It's all black music. We got old timers who know New Orleans music. We got our elders right there with us. Even Dixieland is black music. It's more the spirit I'm talking about. We play everything, all kinds of music. Our people been all over the world and all music made by Africans is connected, no matter where we are. There are common threads. Things we all do and all understand cause we come from the same blood, the same folks, even though we might live in different places or speak different languages, see?"

"Yes, they're called Africanisms," said Nieting. "I am familiar with the concept."

Rene drew back. "The real Africanisms can't even be seen by the white man," he said. "His eyes and ears don't pick it up. He's not equipped to perceive that kind of thing. It's the spirit and the meaning and the reason for playing that separates us from the white man. He can't copy that. He can't put his finger on it."

"I'd like to hear these men perform," said Nieting. "The Black African Diaspora Ensemble and Mr. Triplett."

"You can't hear'm outside of South Central Los Angeles," said Rene. "Watts is one of the places to go, if you're as serious as you say you are."

"Where is this place?" said Nieting.

"I said, in Watts man," replied Rene, "the heart of the ghetto. Not too many of your kind go down there nowadays without a gun and a badge."

"Watts?" said Nieting, handing Rene what was left of the joint. "Kid Auger lives in Watts. Perhaps he knows this group you're speaking of. He may know your Morris Triplett. I'd like to go to Watts and speak to him."

"Go down to South Park most any Saturday and you'll find them," said Rene. "You need a car to get down there, though. Ain't no bus lines going directly to the ghetto."

Rene sucked on the remainder of the joint, finally giving up and tossing away the tiny end. He placed his hand on his chin, mused for a long moment then smoothly patted the drum head. Each touch resonated in the hollow beneath the head like blood pumping.

"Not that you're the kind who would worry about this," he said, tilting his head as though considering an idea or perhaps simply listening to his hands dancing on the skin of the drum, "but if anyone gives you any trouble down there, if anyone asks you what you're doing down there, just tell them you're European, you ain't white."

Nieting struggled to keep from grinning.

I'm not white. Not what's really meant by white. Not what the American Negroes mean by it.

"Thank you," said Nieting. "That's very decent of you. I'll remember that. But, I believe you're wrong about Kid Auger. I've studied his work for years. Ever since I was a child, in fact. I realize my rationale may have sounded contradictory, yet the beauty of his music is that it is absolutely irreconcilable with authority. It turns white supremacy on its head. I used to marvel at the thought of how those southern crackers must have hated Auger and hated his music. How they couldn't help imagining their frail white daughters mounting a giant Negro every time the music was played within their hearing. They must have shit themselves, don't you think?"

Rene screamed with laughter, rolling backwards and kicking his feet into the air.

"Whatever you say, brother."

A young white man wearing leather sandals, white chinos, a tee shirt and dark sunglasses shouted "hey Rene" as he walked briskly past the pagoda.

"John," said Rene, "What's up, brother?"

"Black and white over on Rose, coming this way. They'll take your drum if they catch you playing. Remember they got us banned for the time being."

"Thank you, brother Haag," said Rene. "I was just splitting anyway."

"You ain't got to go. Just zip your drum up in that bag. Those bastards can't keep us from being here."

Rene slipped his conga into a cloth sack and hoisted it onto his shoulder. "No, I'm gone John, wait up, I'm coming. I don't want to lay my eyes on LAPD today. So long there, brother Nieting. Good luck with your Negro. If you do go down to Watts, don't talk so damned much. Don't be afraid to listen either."

Nieting rose and called after the men.

"Thank you so much, Rene. I can't tell you how much help you've been. Good luck to you, man."

Rene pointed his forefinger at Nieting and trotted off until he caught up with his friend and the two fell in together.

"I'm surprised to see you down here," said John

"What do you mean?" said Rene

"You know what's going on, doncha?"

"I just got in from Tucson," said Rene. I ain't even been home yet. I don't know nothing. What's up?"

"You ain't heard?"

"No, I ain't heard."

The two men disappeared behind a building into a side street. Nieting laid back on the bench beneath the pagoda. He thought of the horde of mindless tourists at Disneyland with the deep disgust of an initiate, the member of an inner circle, practically as a black man would.

According to Rene, this Morris Triplett lives and plays among the Negroes, just as Bolden did. The true music is still among the Negroes. Perhaps he knows something of Bolden's lost song . . . and as Rene suggested, a European of good will, someone who understands the music and understands the struggle, would be welcomed by the Negroes of Watts.

Nieting glanced to the corner where Rene and his friend had turned onto the side street and did a double take. The old man with jacket slung over his shoulder and the Panama hat tilted slightly upward on his brow was lingering there with his hands thrust in his trouser pockets. Emil peered at his son like he could see inside his head, grinning that grin, speaking with his eyes, dada gibberish, his face clearly discernable even at the distance of a half a block, numbers on his forearm glowing against yellow flesh.

"It can't be father," said Nieting. "That's just an old Jew."

The old man pointed his body up the side street like a dancer on a stage and when he locked eyes with Nieting he pushed his hat forward further still, winked, and disappeared behind the building. Nieting sensed that the man would be gone when he reached the corner and he was gone.

◆ ◆ ◆

Two black figures rimmed in flaming orange stood between Nieting and the sunset filling his rear view mirror as he sped away from the corner of

Imperial Highway and Sepulveda Blvd. One of the two, a teenaged boy, thrust his middle finger up like a flaming dagger, gesturing to Nieting, who pressed the gas causing his car to burn rubber and spew exhaust fumes in the couples' faces.

"God damned white chauvinists," said Nieting. "Thieves, expropriators, punks."

He'd met the couple a mere hour before. They'd hailed him on the street in Venice as he approached his parked car. They were teenagers, a white boy and girl, and had asked Nieting if he were going anywhere near El Segundo. When they discovered his destination was a motel on Imperial Highway, the girl explained that there was a faster, far easier route than the freeway if he would let them show him. Nieting acquiesced and the boy immediately piled into the back seat, holding a guitar case across his lap as the girl hopped into the passenger side next to Nieting. Everyone was all smiles when they started out and it stayed that way for most of the ride, even as Nieting's mind swirled with thoughts of Auger and all the things Rene had said about him and about Morris Triplett, and of the fate of poor Snellman, and the vision of the old Jews and the man who looked like his father, and stranger yet, acted like he knew Nieting. It all came back in indecipherable waves of images, an overwhelming barrage of impressions. Yet, he was determined to act graciously, to be attentive and appropriately inquisitive towards the two young people in his car. He was a teacher, after all. It was his job to draw young people out, to encourage and inspire them.

"So, you must be musicians," he said, and the young man in the backseat piped up, "I am. I play the Blues. I'm a Bluesman. She sings. She's a Blues singer. We do a Jimmy Reed thing. We do other things, too, or we used to, ya know, folk stuff, even some cowboy songs, but we stopped all that. Now, its Blues straight out. Personally, it's all I can do. The only thing with enough guts for me."

"I don't know Jimmy Reed," said Nieting.

"You don't know Jimmy Reed?" laughed the boy. "Man, what a square."

The boy was cock-sure of himself and worse, he made no reference that Nieting could discern to where the Blues originated. He glanced at the boy in the rearview mirror and wondered. The boy gazed out the window, so full of himself he seemed to toss his hair back like a pony and Nieting became piqued.

"Blues is Negro music," he said. "Why would you attempt to perform a music you'll never be able to master?"

"What's that supposed to mean?" said the girl.

"Simply, that I've never understood why white people would venture into an art so far afield from their own experiences. Particularly, when so many Negroes perform the actual form themselves, the real thing, so to speak."

"That's fucked up, man," said the boy. "I don't know where you get that shit. There's plenty white people playing Blues, the younger generation is keeping it alive, man, bringing it out to more and more folks. We learned from B.B., Muddy, and Wolf, but we got plenty to say ourselves. It ain't about that anyway. It's about the music, man. Fuck it, I hate that shit."

"Calm down, Stevie," said the girl.

"No, no, I don't give a fuck. That talk is fucked up."

"You really don't believe what you're saying," the girl said to Nieting.

"Of course, I do," he replied. "Whites can't play the music because they don't know what it means. Their reasons for playing are different from the Negro's reason. Besides, Blues music is a part of a revolutionary oeuvre. I was told that by a Negro friend. Someone who knows."

"What the fuck is an OHV-WHA?" said the boy. "We speak English, here, man."

"All we want to do is play music," said the girl. "Music is universal. It has nothing to do with colored people any more than anyone else."

"Music may be universal," said Nieting. "Just the same, Negro music reflects Negro life. In a country like yours, the gap between the lives of Negroes and the lives of whites is vast, too vast to be bridged from a position of privilege. The white man has no understanding of what the music is. He can be no more than a pale imitator. I have no doubt that you've reduced yourselves to offering a tepid approximation of the authentic form."

The girl gasped and turned quickly towards her companion, her mouth swinging wide. "I think that's a prejudiced thing to say," she said.

"That's bogus, man," said the boy. "It's bullshit. It's about soul, man, about feeling. It's all about the music. It ain't got nothing to do with skin color, man. What kind of bullshit is that? Anyone can get the Blues. It's about fucking human beings, man, it's about people, not color."

"You know, your position isn't unique," said Nieting. "In Europe, Gypsies are the object of a similar kind of imitation. People want their music, but they don't want Gypsies. You see, when art is not based on life experiences, it is necessarily paltry by comparison to the real thing."

"You're a foreigner," said the girl. "We don't see things that way in America. We're more free here. We play whatever music we like. Younger people love to hear us play Blues."

"Younger white people, you mean," said Nieting. "Correct? Descendents of slave owers, the very people responsible for the suffering of the Negro."

The boy banged his fists into the back of the front seat, jolting Nieting as he shouted, "Fuck this, pull over, let us out."

They'd finally come to Imperial Highway and the girl said, "There's your street," and motioned eastward. Then Nieting was alone in the car, the two figures inside his mirror, rimmed by the glow of the setting sun, growing smaller as he drove off.

"What an impossible little prick," growled Nieting. "My god, Rene wouldn't have considered them for a moment. He wouldn't have spoken to them at all."

The setting sun in Nieting's mirror appeared to accelerate as it dropped below the western horizon, leaving the sky to the east dark and the streets suddenly illuminated by streetlights. He felt fatigued, as if someone had pulled the window shade on the world and reminded him that he was bone tired. Yet an agitated energy ran through him. The events of the day crowded into his mind, a spiraling mass of impressions, impossible to grasp all at once. He began to panic, then felt the urge to weep and didn't understand why. An irresistible sense of loneliness, a physical sensation, filled his body. The bright red neon sign of the motel appeared, blinking IMPERIAL MOTER LODGE above the electrified thoroughfare. His body buzzed like the sign as he clutched his head in a wave of exhaustion.

He wheeled into the lot and parked beneath the second story balcony where his room was and dragged himself up the stairs. As he placed the key in the lock, the door to the next room opened and a man and a woman exited. The man was inebriated and the woman clearly a prostitute. They passed behind Nieting without a word. He could smell them as they walked by. Inside his room he was hit by a wall of heat and the stench of cigarettes and human sweat. He sprawled on the bed, his limbs like dead weights, whispering "a good night's sleep, Nieting, just a good night's rest and you'll be fine." He dozed for a moment, then twitched and roused, thinking, *I should put on the television. The world could be in flames for all I know. I haven't heard the news or seen a newspaper for days. No, Nieting, sleep now, just sleep.*

The door slammed next door, rattling the window panes in Nieting's room, then the shriek of woman's laughter followed by a man's voice. Nieting's eyes popped open.

"That fucking whore is back," he said. "And she's got another customer."

The voices boomed through the walls, then a loud bang as the whore and the john hit the bed, the headboard slapping the wall directly opposite Nieting's bed on the other side. His eyes opened wider. Sirens in the distance, dozens of sirens crawling over the landscape like every cop in L.A. must be rushing somewhere, and that slapping, steady now, causing his bed to vibrate with each thrust of some stranger's hips, a muffled gurgling, guttural and obscene and she gasping. Nieting curled into a ball on the bed and clutched his guts. He struggled to breath. The room was an oven and the dirty air devoid of oxygen, yet it didn't occur to him to do anything except press the sweaty pillows over his ears like a sick child.

"Pathetic whore," he said. "God damned degradation. Why must human beings wallow in filth? Why must they choose to descend to the lowest depths? Like that poor wretch Snellman, the weakling, the coward, the fool." Nieting sat upright, clutching the pillows against his gut and growled at the wall. "Surely, if anyone has an excuse to destroy himself, to end this ordeal, it is I."

He fell back and squeezed two pillows over his ears, ignoring that they reeked with the stink of countless bodies. *What did I say?* he thought. He felt like a child who accidentally told the truth when he'd intended to lie. He'd caught himself, realized he'd blurted out an assessment of his life that he was not prepared to consider. Sirens pierced the pillows like pin pricks shot with electricity, running up and down every nerve in his body, and the bed pounding next door, the incessant slapping, jolting the bed, and someone droning a low gurgling moan, a he or a she, Nieting had no clue, grotesque breathing. He felt about to vomit and curled into the fetal position. *What excuse would I possess to destroy myself?* Nieting was frightened. He would have run from the room, bolted to nowhere if he had any strength at all. Only his stomach, which threatened to rise up into his throat, and his mind, flooded with images, still filling, all of it rushing in flickering flashes, so rapid he couldn't keep his eyes closed, only his stomach and his mind were alive, the rest of his body dead, heavy, a trap to keep him from fleeing.

Yet, he must have dozed, even as his mind spun uncontrollably, because he found himself in the flat where he and his mother lived for a time towards the end of the war, in the darkness of the parlor, in the cold sparseness, huddled on a tattered carpet, a key rattling in the door and a man there, letting himself in, seeing little Val crouched in the shadows, patted his head, saying "hello little Jew." He removed his coat, a huge grey coat with great square shoulders and insignias and a red band on his arm and the Swastika like the one burned onto his father's sculpture of the hairy ass, only more uniform, immaculate black in a circle of pure white in a field of deep red. He placed the coat on the back of a chair and entered the room where Val's mother was. He heard them speaking through the wall and wondered why she would speak to the man and not speak to him. Then, he heard the sirens; they sounded when the planes came and the bombs and Val huddled deeper into the rug. The sirens moaned as his mother moaned in her room and the man grunted like the roar of airplanes and the bed rattled as the bombs fell nearby. His mother did not cease her moaning no matter how close the explosions came and the man did not cease his grunting, as if they already knew what was going to happen or didn't care. Val cowered, tormented by the siren of his mother's whimpering and the bombs of her bedstead punching the wall.

He awoke at the Imperial Motor Lodge to the whore in the next room moaning against the distant sirens, dozens of sirens, there must have been a war going on in the outreaches of Los Angeles. Nieting rushed into the bathroom and spewed vomit into the bath tub. He rinsed his mouth in the bathroom sink, doused his face with cold water and staggered back to bed. *Mother* he thought. *I haven't thought of her for so many years. I have considered suicide, haven't I? Many times. How can a little boy have thoughts of suicide?*

Nieting wept softly. He remembered the Nazi in the dream very well now. He'd been a family friend before the war, in his parents' circle, too long ago for the boy to actually know him from that time, but he'd heard the man and his mother conversing, speaking of the old days. They spoke freely in front of him, as though he couldn't understand what they were saying. Val was a Jew, a quarter Jewish, which was enough to allow the man to blackmail his mother, make demands, force her to do the things he told her to do in exchange for his silence. She took the man into her bed, took his friends into her room anytime they showed up at her door. Val understood she had no choice. It was because he was a Jew. The Nazis took her because she was harboring a Jew and the Russians took her because she was harboring a German. After the war, it was the Americans who paid to enter her room. She took men into her bed in exchange for money to buy food for her son. When she died, he was sure she was fleeing him, that she couldn't bear to sacrifice her soul any longer. It was too much for any human being to endure, to much to give to keep anyone alive, even a son.

The woman in the next room shrieked and Nieting cowered. His hands shook and his stomach tightened. He tasted vomit. *Yes, I did wish to kill myself.* Sirens wept outside the motel room and voices argued behind the wall. The door slammed, rattling the window panes. There was quiet for a time, a quarter hour or more, until foot steps outside returned and the door slammed and voices boomed drunkenly and then the bed pounded again, slapping the wall next to Nieting's head. He heard music coming from somewhere in the distance and strained to hear beyond the racket in the next room and the terrible whining of the sirens. He recognized the sound of Auger's trombone and was amazed.

"Who would be playing that music here?" he said. "Can I be imagining this? No. It's there. Kid Auger."

The volume increased, as if the sound were coming closer. It was sweet and lyrical, sentimental even, the pulse driving, yet carefree, reckless perhaps.

"I could never forget that sound," whispered Nieting. "I've played that record a thousand times."

He saw the little boy at the old phonograph, beneath the huge horn, lifting the arm and carefully placing the needle down and Auger emerging, making the sound of his mother's moaning disappear, hilarious, surreal, delicious colors, fiery red, neon yellow, green and purple like a peacock, flowing from the horn of the phonograph, washing over little Val, causing his mother's voice to cease, her suffering to go away.

But, there was no phonograph when I was with mother. I'm sure there wasn't. We barely possessed enough clothing to go outdoors. The Nazis took everything. I'd never heard of Kid Auger then, not until Uncle Max saved my life and told me the story of the hairy ass.

Nieting trembled as the woman next door gasped with every thrust in unison with the headboard slapping the wall. He tried to clear his mind, to picture himself, to see the child, poor pathetic little boy, placing the recording on the circular bed, slowly allowing the needle to alight onto the disk as his mother cried out in an incomprehensible combination of grief and pleasure until Kid Auger covered her voice as if placing a cloak over her flesh. *We had no music then. I knew nothing of Kid Auger then. Emil. Yes, Emil was there. I was with him. I was with my father.*

He saw his father perched on the arm of Uncle Max's old easy chair, leg folded over his knee, those perfectly pressed tweed trousers up high over his ankles. His clothing was eccentric, funny even to the boy, yet immaculate as he watched his little son listening to Kid Auger. He watched over little Val, told him to play the record one more time so the sound of his mother's moaning would cease to torment him. The sirens never stopped and the head board tapped a steady rhythm as Nieting lay on his back, arms stretched out and streams of tears flowing from his eyes.

I was at home at Uncle Max's flat, he thought. *Mother was dead by then, yet, I still heard her voice. Yes, I heard her for some time after she was gone. How long? Month or years? I heard her with those men and played Kid Auger to drown out her cries. Father was there. He came to see me many times. He stayed with me. I've met him many times. He and Kid Auger saved my life. I'd vowed to kill myself. I needed to silence her voice, but father was there and he wouldn't allow me to do it. He told me it was fine to play the music over and over, all day long. If I didn't I would have heard mother's cries. Father and I spoke. We never used words. We didn't want anyone to overhear us. Kid Auger silenced the terrible noise. How her voice reverberated inside of me until Kid Auger washed it away in rivers of sound.*

Nieting covered his sweat soaked face in his hands. Nothing could be denied. It was too late. He had remembered. The sirens sounded closer now, a fire truck wailing and clanging on Imperial Highway. Nieting sat upright and shrieked with the sirens, beating his breast with closed fists, cursing his mother, the whore, and his father the phantom and cursing himself, bellowing, "murderers, murderers, killers, rapists," choking on tears and spit and sweat, pulling his hair, tearing at his clothes, digging his finger nails into his flesh. Suddenly, a voice from next door and a fist pounding on the wall, "Shut the fuck up, you fucking freak." It was a woman's voice, slurring, shrill and angry, and a man's voice, "fucking douche bag." Nieting began to laugh and in a moment was overcome with laughter. He lay back down and screamed laughter as the wall exploded with fists and threats and the sirens answered, so close by Nieting believed they were inside his head, the whore must be in there, everything was so near Nieting was sure he'd taken the entire world inside of his brain. He clutched his guts and opened his mouth wide and all the sounds, the sirens, the whore's filthy threats, the wall beating, the bed slapping, his mother's moaning, even the planes and bombs poured from his mouth, from the depth of his soul, from his bowels, streaming out like vomit, shooting from his mouth, everything spewing from Professor Valentin Nieting's body.

◆ ◆ ◆

Kid Auger stretched his legs in the back seat of the limousine, cradling a newspaper in his lap as he leaned wearily against the trombone case propped up beside him on the leather upholstery. He rubbed his face with his palms and sank down with a long sigh. He couldn't shake the feeling of fatigue. He'd been dogged of late by an unrelenting weakness, so bad he'd decided to quit taking his own car to work. He'd simply lost the desire to drive, let alone fight the traffic to Disneyland. When the fatigue came on he was helpless. It invaded his entire body, leaving him depressed and utterly spent. The music was the only thing that could lift him, make him feel alive again, but the exhaustion seemed to come on stronger once he stopped playing.

His only comfort was the thought that his wife, Suzette, was out for the day with their teenaged daughter Celine and wouldn't be home when he arrived. Just that morning he'd avoided explaining to her why he'd suddenly decided to avail himself of the Disneyland limousine after always resisting her suggestions to do so. He dreaded the idea that his young wife, Suzette being in her mid-fifties, see him in such a state. It would only serve to worry her. He closed his eyes tightly, grateful for not having to mask his weariness. He dozed until the front page headline he'd been reading when the German boy approached him appeared in his mind like a billboard.

WATTS VIOLENCE

His insides tightened as he reached for the paper and held it up.

1000 RIOT IN LA
POLICE AND MOTORISTS ATTACKED
Routine arrest of 3
Sparks Watts Violence
8 Blocks sealed off

He'd overheard something on the TV news the night before as he was readying for bed, but was too tired to take it in, hoping that somehow he'd misunderstood what was being said. It had slipped his mind after that until he saw the headline the next day. He tossed the paper onto the floor of the limo and clutched his forehead between his thumb and forefinger trying to massage away the knife-like pain.

Only last week, during a break in a performance at Disneyland, Barbarin remarked on what a powder keg South Central LA had become. He predicted an explosion if somebody didn't do something to avert it. It was because of the police, he said, always pushing folks around and doing worse things. He insisted that there were regular back-room beatings of black men at the Firestone police station. He claimed everyone in the community knew about it. "They might pick a man up for anything," he said. "Just walking down the street. They take him back there and give it to him good. Men have died in that station. The cops just say the nigger was resisting. They beat folks' asses every day of the week. And besides that, there are too damned many poor people with nothing to do but think about how poor they are. They can't live nowhere else besides south Los

Angeles, because they don't have no money and the white man won't let them live nowhere else. You ever take a look at a map of L.A.? I have. Black folks live in this skinny little line starting downtown and running south. That's it. Can't go east or west, just fill up that little corridor, pack it tight with poor black folks."

When Auger had remarked that they should just move somewhere else if it was so damned crowded, just as he had, Barbarin replied, "They ain't allowed. The whites made it legal to deny us a home with that Proposition 14 bullshit. They voted on it. You know that as well as I do. And the schools all gone to hell, so you can't get no decent education so you can't get no job, which they won't hire you for anyway because you're black. That's why we got so many of our young black men just hanging out in the streets. It makes a man sick. There ain't no jobs for black people nowadays. Nothing."

Auger got hot when Barbarin said it and snapped back, "Anyone who wants to work can work," and Barbarin came back in his usual salty manner. "Niggers always work, and look what it gets them."

Barbarin had a way of getting into Auger's face, even across a bandstand. Both men were piqued and the argument would have escalated if St. Cyr hadn't called the tune to start the set. When the set was over, the subject didn't come up, but now the headline was right there. Barbarin was correct, if not about the reasons, at least about the result. Yet, it was Suzette that worried Auger the most. She must not have been listening to the television the night before either, because she hadn't commented. He was sure she would be frightened by what was happening in Watts. He would have to convince her that they were in no danger, that their lives and home were safe from those militant blacks, the criminals, thugs, the haters of white people. It seemed bad news was all over the newspapers and television. There was always something involving black people to upset Suzette; constant out cries over church bombings in the south, black students and white students brawling at a local high school, protests at city hall when Mayor Yorty blocked the release of federal funds for poverty programs, incessant demands for voting rights, desegregation, integration, as if this wasn't America after all. It was all too much and Suzette was simply too sensitive to the reports. Television news was the most upsetting. The sounds and images of black people talking fast and sharp-edged, angry, demanding, threatening, saying things Suzette could not fathom, not only scared her, but enraged her as well. "Why do they hate us so? Why don't they try working for what they want instead of demanding it on a silver platter?"

She even voiced satisfaction over the murder of Malcolm X the previous February, as if his death enhanced her and her family's personal security. Auger dreaded the conversation they would have, what he would have to say to quiet his wife's fears. He didn't blame her, he mostly agreed with her. *Why do people have to make trouble? Why can't they just live and let live?* He agreed with her, but the discussion would be unsettling nonetheless, frightening perhaps, and Suzette would take for granted that they were together every step of the way. His hands trembled as he gazed out of the tinted window of the limo, musing over how far he'd come since the days of his youth in Louisiana. The past was worlds away, galaxies, solar systems. *We had our problems back then*, he thought. *I can't say we didn't. Things was always hard on colored folks. But, I could pretty much go where I wanted, move on both sides.* The headline from the jumbled newspaper was visible on the carpet of the limo. **1000 RIOT**. Auger shuttered. *It wasn't that long ago that I lived in Watts myself. On and off for nearly twenty-five years.* He opened the electric window in the limousine a crack and the air flooded in, blowing his hair as the car sped down the freeway. He raised the window and smoothed his hair. *Suzette has no idea the places I been. That little girl was a long way from Watts and a million miles from Pine Grove Plantation. I had to come a long way to find her.*

Auger picked up the newspaper and read . . . "sporadic rioting continued early today as crowds of rock-throwing demonstrators broke through police lines while turning the area around 116th Street and Avalon Blvd. into a scene of near chaos."

He brushed the newspaper aside and lowered the window again, allowing the warm breeze to flow gently across his face as the limousine maneuvered the winding circular streets of his Brentwood neighborhood. When the limo pulled up to his house, Auger realized he was shivering and his face running with sweat.

"You had that AC jacked up too high," he said, as the driver held the door of the limousine and Auger, motioning to the trombone case he was too weak to carry, dragged his exhausted body out and onto the path leading to his front door.

◆ ◆ ◆

Dream: *Before first light, a newspaper blows down Rampart Street in New Orleans, soaked slick in the drizzling rain, whipping like a magic carpet, snaking through the air and slapping against the white-washed wall of the French Opera House. He rushes through the darkness squinting to see the news.*

LOS ANGELES TIMES
THURSDAY, AUGUST 12, 1965

NEGRO WILL BE BARBEQUED FOR MURDER

Below the headlines, blocks of words obscured, shadowed - a voice reading the words, his voice, but the words are not intelligible. Urgent need to read the words. The headlines rise, carried upward by hundreds of colored balloons. The words are clear against the sky and the world can see the words. The words will incite the world to violence, call the world to fulfill the meaning of the words. No place to hide. The words are everywhere. Any nigger will do. Laughter. Any nigger will do. Laughter. Any nigger will do.

Auger awoke in a puddle of sweat like blood and cried out, bolting upright in bed and staring into the blackness. A thin line of bright light framed the closed drapes of the patio door. He was at home in his bed, napping since he returned from work. It was still afternoon and he'd only been sleeping a short time. He swung his legs over the side of the bed and held his head in his hands then staggered to the bathroom sink, doused himself with cold water and looked into the mirror.

"What'll I do?" he whispered. "I just can't get no rest. It don't make sense. I can't work like this. What'll I tell Suzette? I can't face the fellas in this condition. I don't want Johnny or Paul to see me. I just can't do it."

Sunlight flooded the room when he opened the drapes on the sliding door to the patio and stepped up to the glass, shielding his eyes against the fiery yellow disk shimmering in the blue water of the swimming pool. The Eucalyptus trees that marked the edge of his property stood dead still in the summer heat.

Auger showered and dressed. Suzette and Celine might be home anytime. In the living room, he sat in a large red leather recliner facing the front door waiting for his wife and daughter. When his hands began to shake, he tried to calm himself, yet the panic rippled through his body in waves. He drew full breaths, exhaling slowly, staring out the window above the front door at the head of a towering palm tree motionless against the blue sky. He tried to dispel his worried thoughts by thinking of Suzette and Celine, just last week dancing cheek to cheek in this very room to an old Hot Creoles record. He'd laughed until tears ran down his face, and now the thought calmed him and his eyes grew heavy. Then, the fear came on again, a sensation filling his body like water filling a glass. He jerked towards the television, reaching to turn it on and stopped short. He knew what the screen would show – Special Bulletin – Watts, Watts, Watts. *Niggers just don't want to work if you ask me. They got to tear everything down and make it hard on everyone.*

Shoes scrapping outside on the front walk. Auger jumped upright in the chair as a bundle of mail shot through the slot in the door, sliding and scattering across the polished floor.

"I can't take it. I'm too old. It'll kill me. Ain't no way I can go to work tomorrow. I hate to leave Johnny short but I got too. And that god damned interview."

Auger scowled like a madman and looked about the room.

"That Kraut wants to know about Buddy Bolden. I don't have the stomach to talk to no white writer. I don't give a damn if he's European. Europe don't make no good damned difference to me. He's white and they ain't nothing but grave robbers looking for treasure. They don't want the colored man nowhere but in his place, but they want every last thing the nigger's got. Every last thing. What we got inside and what we got outside. They want what we do, what we remember, what we make, but they don't want us. They think what colored folks have is free pickings for any white man. Why's he want Buddy so bad? Why can't he let him rest in peace? They don't want us when we're alive. They want us when we're dead. They love us when we're dead. The deader the better."

Auger saw movement out of the corner of his eye and quickly turned his head, but there nothing except the dark eye of the television. He glared at the TV, rubbing his face with his palm, sighing, then gesturing earnestly at the screen.

"Ain't too many men alive even know what Buddy sounded like. He never made no records. He was gone by the time we was doing all that stuff. He sure enough died hard, too. Alone. Hardly no one knew his name when he passed on. And now, all these years later, the white man wants him again. Buddy Bolden helped set this this damned thing going, he started it, and they want more still. They don't even know what he sounded like and there's no way they ever will. I got something they can't have."

Auger stared out the window above the door, past the palm tree into an ocean of blue light.

"There was a time I didn't know nothing but to follow Buddy. I might have lost my mind back then, too, if it hadn't been for him. Everything was in that music."

It arose out of nowhere, slowly, quietly, like a whisper, so soft a heart-beat could drown it out. When the air conditioner clicked on, Auger had to concentrate to hear, and when the air conditioner shut off, it was there, clear and still rising. He fell into perfect stillness, smiling as the sound grew deeper. Teardrops oozed from his eyes as he listened, foot crossed over his knee and suspended in air, swinging gently as Buddy Bolden played his cornet. Bolden playing. Caressing the air with notes, rising and falling, bending tones for agonized, unending seconds, then sprint-ing, quick-fingered, stopping at the edge of a great black abyss, sway-ing over the edge, slapping his thighs and blowing again, rising up this time, flying aloft. Buddy Bolden's cornet rang in Jean Auger's head as he walked the River Road along the Mississippi River, so clear he was sure he heard it with his ears instead of in his mind and stopped to listen for the direction of the sound. When he cocked his ears the sound vanished. He took off walking and Bolden was there again, punching out notes to a tune Jean heard him play just two weeks before, Fourth of July, 1900, from the open door of a boxcar on a train stopped in La Pointe, Louisiana, near Pine Grove Plantation where fourteen year old Jean Auger lived. He knew the instant he heard Bolden that first time that his life had changed. He would never see or hear the same way again. He danced on the River Road, strutting, tapping his thigh to the music.

The old man was at home in Brentwood perched on his red leather recliner as Bolden disappeared into the agitated cacophony of screech-ing crows in the palm tree outside of his house.

"For Christ's sake, man, get hold of yourself."

He rubbed his knobby knuckles into his eyes.

"Wake up, boy. C'mon back. That was a day dream. It was god damned real, but it was a dream."

Two crows circled the head of the palm outside the window above the door, striking each other with black beaks, battling to run the other away from the perch on the top of the tree. Auger rose from the chair shaking and shuffled across the carpeted floor to a wall of photos beneath which was a record player and a wire rack of long playing records. Dozens of photographs with signatures scrawled, nearly every musical association of his professional career was pictured on the wall. Louis Armstrong, Clarence Williams, Sidney Bechet, Jelly Roll Morton, King Oliver. A publicity photo, circa 1923, of the Hot Creoles, Johnny St. Cyr, young, handsome, smiling. Barbarin and Auger, arms slung over each other's shoulders, standing next to a U.S. Army transport plane in an airfield in Berlin, 1946. Auger's life was pictured on the wall of his living room and only Buddy Bolden was missing. Auger had never seen a photo of Buddy Bolden. He looked at the pictures and mused.

"Buddy sure missed the pay off." he said. "But he had plenty of fun, plenty women, and all the whiskey. He just left us too young to get any benefit from what he started. That's a real shame."

The men and women in the photos looked at Auger with shinning eyes, Bill Bojangles Robinson suspended in air in a dance leap, Jimmie Noone with horn thrust out in the heat of performance, Luis Russell and Auger with drinks in hand in a fancy Harlem nightspot, a portrait of Duke Ellington, handsome like a movie star.

"We did have some fun," said Auger, speaking to the photographs.

"Buddy missed it all though, didn't he? He missed so much, but he was a happy go lucky sort of fellow. He wouldn't have held anything against the rest of us who gained from what he did. He would have been the first one to say he didn't do it alone, that he didn't start things by himself, unless he was drunk, then he'd claim he created just about everything, including Adam and Eve."

Auger slipped a record album from the wire rack and scrutinized the vintage photograph on the cover. *Kid Auger's Hot Creoles*. Natty Dominique holding his cornet as if offering it to the viewer, Johnny St. Cyr, Omer Simeon, Zutty Singleton looking towards Kid Auger holding his forefinger aloft as though instructing the band. They were all young, bursting with health and promise, impeccably tied down in black suits, everyone's hair slicked just right, postures relaxed, sophisticated even. Auger flipped the album over and perused the back. It was the long playing type, a 33 1/3 reissue of the 1925 session that had first made him famous. The number one song on the second side was *Make Me a Pallet*. Buddy's tune. Auger caressed the picture of the Hot Creoles and spoke gently to the album.

"The day we recorded that song we toasted Buddy and dedicated the performance to him. Everyone lifted their bottles and cups and drank to Buddy Bolden. The cut came off smooth as silk, hot like fire and everyone said they felt like Buddy was in the room. But, when the record come out, Buddy wasn't listed as the composer of the song, even though everyone knew it was his piece. The label read, *Make Me a Pallet (words and music by the Lott Brothers)*. Those Lott boys were known for that kind of thing. It seemed they was always being sued or suing someone over royalties or contracts. It was a dirty business. There was nothing I could do besides watch my own back. Where ever Buddy is, I bet he's getting a laugh out of those Lott boys, too. A right bitter laugh maybe, but he wouldn't have let it get him down. He wasn't that type of man. Buddy knew what was what. He wasn't nobody's fool. What else could he do but laugh?"

Auger placed the record on the turntable, pushed the button, the needle alighted and the Hot Creoles flew into *Make Me a Pallet*. The cornet, trombone and clarinet swelled into crisp punches on the beat until the cornet took the lead, playing Bolden's melody as the other horns danced above and below.

"I showed that lead line to Natty Dominique. That's Buddy's line note for note. Natty played it pretty good, but you know, not as good as ol'Stonewall way back when we was kids at Pine Grove. I taught Wall the notes, too. He never played it smooth as Natty. Natty was a professional musician and Stonewall was a field hand, all his life just a field hand. But there was something closer in his phrasing to Buddy's. I showed Wall the notes, but he was there the day Bolden played it too, so he knew how it should go. Natty put his own flavor to it, and that was alright with me. Wall was happy sounding as close to Buddy as he could because he was playing just to make himself feel good and he loved how Buddy did it."

The cornet on the recording sang perfectly modulated, clear and bell-like, swinging Bolden's notes with such beautiful airy élan that Auger knew the day they laid it down he had a hit.

"I had no way of knowing Natty's reading of that melody would live forever with that record, would be more famous than Buddy Bolden himself."

Auger straightened up, arching his back and patting his hands lightly, following Natty's cornet trampolining off the rhythm. Then he heard Buddy's raspy non-notes shadowing Natty's refined tone, playing the melody just a shade behind Natty, twisting his own line like it was taffy, changing, distorting, and finally blowing in unison with Natty, stride for stride, breath for breath, until Natty stopped altogether like he lost his nerve, and it was just Bolden. Auger heard it. Buddy playing the song the way he played the first time Auger heard him. That was the day he was set free.

It was on the Fourth of July in the year 1900 and the old man could see it clear as day, he and Chiff and Stonewall Matthews coming to the station with Uncle Andre to load a shipment of goods arriving from New Orleans. The engine gushed steam when Andre pulled the wagon around the station house into the yard. Chiff called out, pointing at a black man dressed in a pin-stripped suit and wearing a brown derby, pacing back and forth next to the train car and shouting into the gathering crowd.

"Come on over and join the True Friends' Society's excursion to Baton Rouge," said the man. "Only seventy-five cents round trip. That's right, it's cut rate cause we rented the entire car just to accommodate the True Friends and their guests. Seventy-five cents will get you the time of your life at our very select picnic spot, set aside exclusively for use by colored folks, safe and peaceable, guaranteed. The very finest refreshments will be available, brothers and sisters, prepared by our own Mrs. Annie Ellen Highbend and the True Friends Ladies Auxiliary.

"And if that ain't enough, none other than brother Charles Galloway and his famous band from New Orleans, Uptown, will supply the musical inspiration. Believe me, you will not be able to resist these gentleman. There's only a few tickets left, so step on up. If you'd like a little taste of what's in store for the True Friends this afternoon, look yonder. It's none other than Brother Galloway and his boys."

The man swept his hand towards a box car with an open door and a man perched on the edge, guitar in his lap, dangling his legs over the side. He held the guitar up and stroked a fanfare, nodding at three musicians standing next to him on the platform, a man with a cornet and another with a clarinet and a boy in short pants with a snare drum strapped around his neck, and shouted, "take it fellas."

The cornet let the cue pass, hesitating, watching the crowd as he slowly raised his horn. All eyes were on him as he waited, grinning as the tension built and the crowd stirred. He began playing an old church song, dirge-like and mournful, playing the melody slowly as the drummer played a roll on the snare. The roll was smooth and incessant, like paper being torn, fading and intensifying with every breath the cornet took.

The guitar player yelled "Play it, Mr. Bolden," and a woman in the crowd gasped. "Buddy Bolden, it's Buddy Bolden," and another woman responded, "I told you it was him. Play it Mr. Bolden."

Bolden was a stocky, muscular man in work shoes and overalls with the straps hanging down over a bright red undershirt. He blew with deep quivering vibrato, punching out splayed notes and holding them. When he decided he'd reached the end of the song, he held the final note as the hissing snare seemed to rise into the air and fade away with the vanishing cry of the cornet into dead silence.

Bolden shouted "make me a pallet," jolting the crowd, stomping his foot three times and kicking up a cloud of dust as the band pushed into an up tempo number. Bolden blew so powerfully, it sounded like the horn might explode, so loud they could probably hear it three miles away over on Pine Grove Plantation. Bolden's neck bulged, his cornet shot short raspy bursts like cannon fire, the guitarist banged chords like a drummer, the drummer cracked the rim of his snare with his sticks like a piston, the clarinet spit shrill notes like a frantic bird darting and the people swayed and clapped as a man rushed into the train shouting, "I won't miss Galloway's band this time."

The three men on the ground fell into a semi-circle around the guitar player, all facing each other, pouring their music into a common invisible vessel, hoofing it on the platform, signaling with eye movements, dance steps, instruments swinging, amazing themselves as they strained and sweated. Jean had never seen such a thing. Galloways' band had the courage to jump off a cliff all together and there they were flying, spinning in the air, churning, spiraling. Bolden was in the middle, in the eye of the storm, blowing the melody as the others fell in line around him like birds in formation and Bolden ran a string of notes out of nowhere or from heaven, except they were so dark and beautiful, Jean felt his body lift up, raise off the ground. He was shouting when the train whistle screamed and the musicians halted abruptly in a great rush of steam and noise. People swarmed the musicians, slapping their backs, grabbing their hands as the musicians staggered, dizzy with the music, drunk with it.

The train began to roll and the men scurried into the baggage car, handing their instruments to the guitar player and hoisting themselves up. Jean sprang from the crowd and ran to the side of the car shouting at Bolden. "Mister, hey Mister Bolden, Buddy, hey Buddy. What was the name of that tune?" Bolden looked down and wiped his face with a red handkerchief.

"My tune," he said, and disappeared into the moving train.

Old Auger shuddered in the shadows of his living room and whispered to his friends in the photos.

"Damn, you ain't supposed to see yourself so vivid-like" he said. He spoke into the face of Louis Armstrong. "Why, I can see that child, the child I was, like it wasn't me, like it was a movie." Armstrong was smiling. "There we was at La Pointe station," said Auger, "and the boys was doing all the work loading those crates from New Orleans. I don't know where uncle was, but Chiff and Stonewall was cussing me real hard for just standing there like a dummy while they was straining at those heavy wood boxes. But, I couldn't do no better. I was knocked silly by what

I'd heard. I made my plan right then and there. I could hear Chiff and Stonewall calling me names, mutha-this and such, but they was in the distance somehow and my mind was clicking, clear like Buddy thinks – you know how he thinks cause he shows you his mind when he plays, like it broke open and you get to peek inside. I knew for sure, right then, the time had come to run away from Pine Grove."

Auger whispered to Armstrong, "I don't believe I ever told you this, Louis. It happened before you was born. I decided I would join up with Buddy Bolden, join his band. There was no question in my mind that he wouldn't have me."

"Fuck you. I'm Maury Wills."

A voice outside Auger's front door, then the sound of feet running in the flower bed beneath the window and another voice, farther away.

"No, I'm Maury Wills. You know damned well, I'm always Maury Wills."

Auger hit the button on the record player ejecting the LP and moved to the window. He pulled the curtain aside and saw three boys in the cul de sac outside of his house, neighborhood children, playing baseball.

A boy holding a bat, laughed and shouted, "Maury Wills is a nigger."

"He is not. He's a shortstop."

All the boys laughed as the boy with the bat hoisted the ball up and smacked a grounder. "He's a nigger shortstop," he said.

"He is not," shouted a boy, fielding the grounder and tossing it to another, apparently the first baseman, who yelled, "Yes he is," as he stretched to catch the ball.

"I don't care, I'm still Maury Wills."

"That means you're a jiggaboo, then," shouted the batter and the boys laughed.

"Fuck you, I'm a white Maury Wills."

"You can't be. There's only one Maury Wills and he's a jigaboo."

"All right, I'm Sandy Koufax," shouted the fielder, motioning to the first baseman to move behind the batter and become the catcher so he could become the pitcher. Instead, the first baseman moved to the right, to the short stop position.

"Good, now I'm Maury Wills."

The pitcher yelled, "Motherfucker," and the boys collapsed in the street laughing.

Auger let the curtain drop and rushed to the front door, thrusting his head out and shouting, "You boys want me to tell your folks what kind of dirty talking you do? Now, get on away from here. I said get the hell away from my house."

The boys snapped to attention, two of them appearing frightened at Auger's threat, the third, the batter, grinning sheepishly as they walked briskly down the street. Finally, the boys ran, stopping at a safe distance and shouting something Auger figured must be curses. He was sure he heard the word nigger as he slammed the door and went back to his chair.

"God damned nonsense. Things just don't change, do they? It's the same bull shit now as it's always been."

Auger brooded in his red leather recliner, speaking to the photos of his friends across the room.

"I seen that boy with the bat before. Fat little bastard lives a few doors down. His father is a real estate salesman. Every time I pass him on the sidewalk he tries to get me to sell my house or buy another one. Told me once my investment was safe because all the neighbors signed those restrictive covenants and can't no niggers ever buy around here. He said nigger right to my face, right in front of my baby girl, grinning like he was daring me to say something. I told him I didn't have any restrictive nothing on my house and walked on. It was bullshit, the same old bullshit and it don't end. Ever since I was a youngster there's always someone trying their damnedest to keep me back."

◆ ◆ ◆

Late afternoon light from the window above the front door and sun behind the drapes illuminated the living room. The rest of the house was dim and quiet like dusk. The old man was exhausted. He heard a noise some-where in the house, something fallen or knocked over; perhaps there was no noise, perhaps it was in his mind. Yet, he was sure someone had entered his home. They hadn't come through the front door, unless Suzette and Celine came in when he was dozing. But, those two couldn't be quiet enough to get past him, even if they tried. They'd giggle for sure or drop something or try to give him a peck on the cheek and wake him up. He'd know if they were home. It was someone else. Someone must have gotten in a back window.

Auger's arms and legs felt too heavy to lift. It was the fatigue coming on again. It hit him suddenly and with no warning. There was a thief in the house and he could do nothing. His arms shook as he raised himself off the seat and peeked over the back of the chair. He saw movement back there, a shadow moving about, someone watching him. He called his wife's name, and when no answer came he growled contemptuously, addressing whoever it was lurking in the recesses of his home.

"I ain't killed a man in sometime, motherfucker, but if I have too I will."

Absolute silence, suspicious silence. Someone was there.

"You boys best climb back out that window unless you want your asses whupped real good. No, I'll have you motherfuckers arrested. I know what you look like and I know where you live."

The windows in the back of the house were locked tight, he'd checked it himself when he'd gotten home. No one had come through the front door, either. There was no way in except through his mind.

"You listening back there? You got no business to be in here listening. You don't know me. You don't know what I been through. It don't matter to me what you think one way or the other. You got to be strong to survive, especially when you're a child thrown out on your own with no parents to look out for you."

Auger's body came alive with rage and he pounded the armrests of the chair and shouted at whatever it was lurking in his house. Outside, two crows tumbled through the air near the top of the palm tree, perfectly framed in the window above the door, clutching each other, striking with flailing claws, finally unclenching into a spiraling dance and striking with screeching black beaks. Auger shouted over his shoulder into the house.

"I hear you moving around back there."

The spasm of anger welled inside of Auger, exploding and releasing, leaving him so spent he thought death had finally come. *So be it. I'm ready. Peace. I just want peace. Rest. I want to sleep.* The house was still. Even the sound of his breathing was inaudible. He was beginning to grow calm when he realized the quiet was deepening, descending, spreading out into a black void, a vacuum so complete the absence of sound began to transform into a howling emptiness, suffocating, endless. *This must be death. It ain't so bad. I'll miss my girls though. No, I don't want to leave my girls.* Someone was standing over Auger. His eyes were closed yet he saw something moving in the light through his lids. He felt breath close to his face. *Am I coming to in the hospital? Maybe I died and I'm waking up in the hereafter.* A voice came from far off, a man's voice, clear and resonant.

"All of this anger isn't like you, Jean."

"What's that?"

Auger jumped in the chair, twisting around and propping himself up on his knees and peering into the darkness. The voice came from the hallway to the bedroom.

"Everyone knows Jean Auger is a happy man. People smile at the mention of your name."

"Who's there? Show yourself if you're man enough. C'mon out, motherfucker."

A figure stepped into the living room, a tall shadow preceded by the red glow of a cigarette. The last sunlight shooting through a gap in the drapes caught a face behind the swirling smoke. Auger trembled, straining to see the man's outline then locked on his eyes, white suns, vacant and opaque. The man's accent was Creole. He was surely from south Louisiana. His voice was deep and lilting with a gravelly musicality that was familiar to Auger.

"Calm down, Jean. I'm not your enemy."

The man casually perused the photographs on the wall as he flicked ashes in an ashtray next to the record player. He moved elegantly with feminine ease and when he turned back towards Auger a streak of light caught his face. His complexion was dark and soaked with sweat.

"Who the hell are you?" said Auger. "You're in my mind, ain't that right? I may be crazy but I'm not stupid. This is my home. My house. It's my legal right to kill you if I believe you may do me harm."

"Kill me?" said the man, calmly blowing smoke and chuckling softly. "I've never done you any harm, Jean."

"You ain't starting today neither, I promise you."

The man smiled, shaking his head and drawing on the cigarette.

"You don't recognize me, do you Jean?"

Auger strained to focus in the dim light.

"I don't know who are are,"

The stranger exhaled luxuriantly.

"But you do, Jean. You certainly must have heard of me, and actually we are far closer than that. Does the name Phillipe Deslonde bring anything back?"

"I said I ain't heard of you motherfucker."

The man's face disappeared into the shadows as smoke drifted in a shaft of light. His voice came out of the darkness.

"You do know me Jean. You know me as well as you know yourself. You were there, Jean. You were there."

"I ain't been nowhere, man. Where do you think I been?"

Deslonde snuffed out what was left of the cigarette in the ashtray.

"Running, Jean, running, one is always running, running from the white man. Doesn't it seem so Jean? Why, you're still running from the white man. Isn't that right, Jean?"

Auger growled. "You ever hear the name Kid Auger, boy? That's a name known round the world. If I *am* a runaway, I sure as hell made something out of myself, didn't I? Who the hell knows your name? Tell me that. Who the hell are you?"

Deslonde grinned sadly and Auger became enraged.

"Why are you so god damned delighted?" he said.

"Because you asked me who I am," responded the man. "As I told you, my name is Deslonde. You remember July of 1900, Jean?"

Auger jerked to attention and listened with his face screwed up and his arms folded across his chest like an angry school teacher.

"How the fuck do I know," said Auger. "I mean, I suppose I do. I was alive at the time."

"You'd just arrived in the city," said Deslonde. "Isn't that right?"

"Yes, that's just about right."

"That was a very bad season for our people. Do you remember, Jean?"

"I don't know what you mean."

"That was the season the whites killed our people by the score. They were angry because Robert Charles stood up to the police. The police tried to humiliate the wrong nigger and Robert Charles killed a multitude. You must remember. Do you remember hearing of Robert Charles, Jean?"

"I don't know of no Robert Charles."

"But you must. He was killed the year you ran away from home, the very week you arrived in New Orleans. It would be impossible for you not to know of him."

"I don't know no Robert Charles, I told you."

"You must. It's not possible that you wouldn't."

"You calling me a liar, motherfucker?"

"No, Jean," said Deslonde. "I don't blame you for forgetting. I wish I could forget but it's impossible for me. The memory is the only substance I possess. You must have lived through those terrible times or I wouldn't be here. You must have called me here to make you remember."

"You can't make me do nothing. You sure can't make me remember things I never knew in the first place."

"Robert Charles was my friend," said Deslonde. "I still remember the headline in one of the white newspapers. *July 25, 1900. NEGRO KILLS BLUECOATS. Cursing his victims, fires into their lifeless forms. Negro is Wounded and Takes to the Swamps.* I hadn't seen Robert for weeks. He used to sell the emigration journal, *The Voice of Missions* on the street and would make his rounds delivering the paper to subscribers. Robert was a proponent of African emigration. He believed it was his duty to let his people know they did not have to live and die like dogs, that they could escape from America and live like men and women. I always received *The Voice of Missions* from Robert. I read it because I loved the writing of the great Bishop Turner. 'To the white man the American flag must be a beautiful thing to behold. The American flag is his flag. It represents him. But to the Negro, it is nothing but a miserable dirty rag.'"

Auger shook his fist towards Deslonde's face and shouted.

"Now wait a god damned minute. I don't allow no one to talk that communist shit in here. I only been putting up with you cause I took pity on you. That American flag you hate so bad whupped hell out of Hitler and the Japs. Don't be saying nothing against that flag or I'll take your ass down hard. Do you hear me?"

Deslonde grinned.

"Sorry Jean," he said. "I was merely paraphrasing Bishop Turner. How I exulted in his words. He never failed to write something that would make my heart sing. My god, how the whites hated him. I can't imagine how he had the courage to do what he did. Or how he managed to stay alive. I can't tell you the admiration I felt for Robert Charles.

"You can't imagine the shock, Jean, the sorrow, when I read the head-lines that morning. The drawing of Robert on the front page of the white newspaper looked like a madman. Eyes bulging. They said he was a cocaine fiend and a morphine addict. They said he was violent with his friends, that he beat his fiancée. When they found bundles of emigration literature in his room, stacks of *The Voice of Missions* they said it was proof he was insane, proof that he was a hater of the white race."

"Hate, hate, hate," said Auger. "That's all you niggers know. And there's just no damned reason for it."

"Robert had every right to hate white people, but he didn't," replied Deslonde. "He loved his people and to the whites that's the same as hating them, the same as plotting to cut every white throat in Louisiana. I would have gladly done that if it were in my power, but that wasn't how Robert felt. He was a rational man. He was passionate but he didn't waste his soul hating."

"Don't give me that bullshit," Auger spit back. "Niggers just hate to work, if you ask me. They blame the white man cause they can't make it. That's where all the hate comes from."

The pop and hiss of a match igniting startled Auger into silence as the fire moved through the darkness like a shooting star to the cigarette between Deslonde's teeth.

"I hadn't seen Robert for weeks the morning I saw the terrible headlines," continued Deslonde. "He and a friend, a young man named Lenard Pierce, had gone to visit Robert's fiancé. When he discovered that she hadn't yet arrived home the two deigned to rest upon the front steps of the home of a white man. As you would expect, before long they were confronted by several policeman, white men, who did not hesitate to treat them in the manner prescribed for a nigger. Robert was a quiet man but a man of great passion and of great principle and when he failed to play the role of terrorized darkey, the white men bore down. No one knows what transpired between them. We know nothing except that guns were drawn and fire exchanged. Robert wounded an officer and was wounded himself. Young Pierce was arrested but Robert escaped into the darkness leaving a trail of blood for blocks. Several hours later he returned to his room, perhaps to retrieve supplies or personal items for what surely was going to be a long exile. Before Robert could leave his home, a contingent of officers arrived. Robert shot two of the policemen dead, one being a captain, very popular among the whites, and held the rest at bay, cowering in an adjoining apartment. So terrorized were the police that they remained in the darkened room for hours after Robert escaped, emerging finally at daylight with the arrival of dozens of fellow offices and a growing crowd of spectators. Can you imagine how the death of those policemen enflamed the minds of the whites?"

"Enflamed the mind of whites?" shouted Auger. "It's enflaming my god damned mind right now. Whoever the fuck you are, where ever you come from, you got to go there now. You got to leave my home."

"I asked you a question, brother," said Deslonde.

"I don't want to think about it," said Auger. "I don't believe it ever happened like you're saying. I never heard any of these things mentioned before. If it did happen, I blame that nigger Robert Charles. It wasn't legal to carry no gun in New Orleans. I don't want to imagine what the whites would do."

"You'll know in short order," said Deslonde. "I promise you'll know full well. Robert Charles fled for his life. He disappeared into the community, hidden by his friends, and the whites couldn't find him. Of course that merely raised the pitch of the white man's fear. They lived so close to insanity as it was. If you think of how we existed day in and day out you have to admit there was a significant element of the unreal and any group of people who would enforce such murderous cruelty, such blood thirsty oppression must be a hair's breadth from complete derangement, chaos, frenzy. Robert's presence among them drove the whites to the limit. He was imagined to be everywhere, in the city, in the countryside, he and an army of Negroes whose intent was to murder every white man and rape every white woman. Their newspapers spewed the hysteria like vomit. They called for race war, for our extermination, and in less than an instant a mass of whites rose up."

"I told you stop what you're doing," shouted Auger. "I ain't gonna listen no more. I ain't interested."

"Oh you'll listen, Jean. I'm here at your bidding and you'll listen until my story is finished."

Deslonde carefully crushed his cigarette in the ashtray and lit another as Auger frantically tapped the heel of his palm against his forehead, struggling to awaken and realizing at the same time that he was not asleep.

"Have mercy on me please," he said in a choked whisper. "I'm an old man. I can't take this kind of talk. Leave me alone, for god's sake."

Deslonde listened impassively until Auger stopped speaking.

"For three days the whites chased us down where ever they could find us," he said. "They beat us, Jean, they murdered us, they entered our homes and shot us in our beds. They assembled at night by the thousands and hunted us, pulled us from our wagons, dragged us from streetcars, pursued us down streets and alleys, through yards; anyone with black skin. They held men beneath the light of street lamps to discern the color of their skin if their race was unclear, to discern if he or she was to be a victim or allowed to join their ranks. They shot us, clubbed us, kicked us, they burned our flesh."

"I don't remember nothing you're saying," said Auger. "Not a god damned bit of it. Don't you think I would remember something so terrible? You sure are a troubled spirit, but I ain't got nothing to do with it. I ain't got nothing against you. You got to believe that. You shouldn't take what you read in the papers to heart. Most newspapers just exaggerate anyway. Just to sell more papers. You're a smart man. You should know how it works. Things ain't always what you think they are. Particularly for someone like you, so sensitive. You should have learned from all the suffering you done that there ain't no fairness in the world, no justice at all. Colored folks got to do the best they can. We got to keep an eye out for some advantage and grab hold of it when it comes. Take what talents you got and figure how to use them to get over. Dwelling on the worst don't do you no good. Besides, you ain't really nothing like that nigger Robert Charles. You didn't carry no gun. You didn't kill no police. You might have thought you wanted too, but you ain't that kind. You ain't got nothing in common with a man like you was describing, now do you?

Auger waited a long moment for Deslonde to answer, but he did not.

"I ain't got no more patience for you, anyway," said Auger. "I've listened to you talking long enough. I'm gonna open the curtains and let the room fill up with sunlight and you'll go away, back to the darkness, back to where ever you come from."

"I was in the 25s club in the District that night," said Deslonde. "Do you remember the 25's on Franklin and Customhouse?

"Yes," whispered Auger. "I remember the 25's."

"It was the worst night of violence," said Deslonde. "Wednesday, July 24, 1900. The white newspapers said there were 5,000 white men in the streets searching for black people. I'm here to tell you there were far more than that. Most of our people stayed in their homes with the doors locked, shudders drawn and lights darkened. Only a few dared to venture out. There was only a handful of us at the 25s that night. The place was nearly empty. It was early, around 10 o'clock I believe, but still the crowd was less than usual even for that time of night. Buddy Bolden was there and a few other musicians. Henry Peyton was there. You may have known Mr. Peyton. He could be ornery, would roar like a lion, but was really a very sweet man. There was a Creole boy there, a clarinetist, Pinot was his name. I remember he was sullen that night, brooding because Mr. Peyton insisted that he play string bass and not clarinet. Frank Lewis was Peyton's usual clarinet man. He was supposed to be working somewhere else, but showed up anyway, so the boy was shifted to the bass.

"There were two working girls. I don't remember their names. They often stopped in at that time of evening, before their night's work began in earnest. They always returned just before daylight when the music was at its hottest pitch. They loved Bolden with a passion and would often argue over who would hold his horn during the breaks. They were very kind to me. I liked those young women very much. There were one or two customers, as well, regulars perhaps. I don't remember for sure. The place felt very odd being so empty. It made everything strangely festive, like we were the last people in the world gathered together for the final party. There were so few of us, everyone seemed to be sharing a single conversation. I remember being so hungry to hear Buddy play, as though his music would straighten everything out, would supply the answers, some understanding of all the horror going on outside. No one brought any of that up. It was like it wasn't happening or was a thousand miles away, but we all knew it was close by. We could hear the gun shot. Yet, somehow the scene was intoxicating. I know that sounds foolish. We were all drinking. I was half drunk myself yet I felt a strange closeness to everyone. It was as though in that single moment in time, we were enveloped in a separate world and the outside ceased to have any meaning. I heard footsteps on the banquette outside and a woman thrust her head through the swinging doors and shouted that the whites were coming and they were killing all the niggers. We all sat silently after the woman spoke. She stood at the door waiting for some reaction, but we just sat there, as if we were deciding what to do, almost as though we could choose what was real and what wasn't.

"Peyton was sitting on a chair warming up on his accordion. He didn't stop noodling with the instrument the whole time we were sitting in silence. Finally, he said something like, nothing like that ever happened in New Orleans yet and it ain't gonna happen now. At his words the conversation began again, picked up right where we were when the woman interrupted us. When I looked at the door she was gone. We went right on drinking, talking and laughing. I thought to myself, what does Mr. Peyton mean, never happened before? It's been happening for two days. The thought made me laugh, the irony of it. You see, I was with these men, these musicians. I was with Buddy Bolden and he was a hero to me. I thought to myself, nothing can happen to us. Buddy will just play and the whites will drop their guns, extinguish their torches, and admit, they'd have to admit, this nigger knows the truth, if I follow him I'll be free, with my white skin and doomed soul, I'll be cleansed, my mind unshackled, my heart redeemed, and we can all live like men. I wasn't that drunk, but it all seemed so plain to me that I laughed and laughed. Everyone was laughing, and Buddy raised his horn and blew.

"That night at the 25's as the city writhed in agony we few clung to one another in complete fellowship, like angels, I believe, deluded angels, doomed angels. Bolden was standing at the bar before three shots of whisky. I swear it, he had three lined up, bought for him by the girls, and as he played his horn we were transported, Jean, it was truly joyous. I think that's the reason we didn't hear the whites coming. There was a strange sound, like a roaring in the distance, like thunder far off. Somehow, it made me feel closer to what we were doing, more safe perhaps, like the sound of rain against window panes makes one feel cozy and warm in bed. The girls were on either side, pressed tightly against me. I felt an electric current running between us and their hearts beating as Buddy played. I could hear the girls sighing with awe, amazed, clutching me tighter and tighter. How we all loved each other, Jean. Not a word was spoken between us, but we loved each other.

"Then Buddy stopped playing and I felt someone pulling me and calling my name, shouting as if through some barrier. Their words were muffled and distant, like I was waking from a dream but was still half asleep. There was an explosion then, Jean, so deafening and abrupt my vision disappeared and I saw nothing but white light. The noise was sudden and loud, shrill like demons howling; it was the voices of men, vile, vicious voices and pistol shots and glass smashing and wood crashing. They were flooding into the 25s. The swinging doors flew from the hinges. I saw the string bass smashed like a child's toy and at that moment, I think I became fully conscious for the first time. I saw Buddy rush into the back room where the card games are run, slamming the door behind him. There were guns firing, the terrible cracking of pistol shot. I was alone in the 25s with them, my friends were all gone, caught in the rear of the place. I was in the eye of the storm standing at the bar as the whites swirled about in a chaos of smoke. Somehow I was unnoticed all that time, until I made for the door and was spotted in the flash of gun fire. A man shouted, "There he goes, get the nigger.""

"I pushed through the crowd and out the door. I vaulted a wagon, Jean. My leg must have broken when I landed. I'm sure it did, but I ran anyway. I turned into an alley and saw black faces huddled. There were young ones among them so I retraced my steps and bolted from the alley into the heart of the mob, surprising them and somehow managing to dash by into the streets of the District. They were on me, Jean, they were never out of sight. Every time I looked back their numbers had increased. People kept joining the chase. It was terribly amusing sport for them, a carnival of devils by the sound of it, shrieking and laughing.

"I'd run several blocks. I think I may have been on Conti Street when one of their bullets finally hit the mark and knocked me off my feet. My leg was burning and I heard them cheering joyously. I got up and began running towards Back 'o Town, but turned over to Customhouse Street. The street was unlit so I ran close to the buildings hoping to lose the mob in that long dark block. Just as I hit the side of the street all the electric streetlights illuminated, crackling and buzzing, exposing me to the mob.

"When they saw me, the most unearthly moan rose up, all at once, one devilish spirit crying for joy. They surged down Customhouse, two hundred strong by now. They might not have caught me Jean, even with my leg broken and bleeding. The distance between us was increasing, but when I reached Villere Street, there were men waiting. I looked over my shoulder and saw a white man wielding a club, gaining on me because I hesitated at the men in front. He was a large man and never would have caught me if I hadn't slowed. The blow came and I fell to the street. It was only a second before I was up, but they were all over me by then. There was another blow and I fell backwards into a deep rut in the street that was filled with water. A puddle Jean, I was lying in a puddle and in moments the water was thick red. They fired on me, Jean. They kicked me and slashed my flesh with blades.

"I suppose I lost consciousness, but somehow I knew what they were doing. I saw everything. They tore at my flesh like dogs until they grew fatigued. I could hear them walking away, bragging about the part they'd played. 'I took him down first.' 'Hell you did, it was John knocked the side of his head, and that sent him down.'

"I lay in the puddle when one of them looked back and thought he saw me moving. They all returned and after another round they began to argue as to whether I was alive or dead. The conversation regarding the state of my existence became quite passionate. They poked me with sticks seeking signs of life. As ignorant as they were, they were quite thorough. Finally one of them decided to check my breathing. I was pulled from the water and tossed on my back. They lit matches and one of them had a candle and they looked into my face and still couldn't figure it out. The men with the matches thrust them into my eyes. They finally tired of the game and tossed me into the puddle, pushing me beneath the red water as a man shoved past them, cursing, saying he'd settle the question. He put a shotgun barrel against my chest.

"I don't want to know," shouted Auger. "I don't want to know. Help me Jesus. Please have mercy on this old sinner. Please Lord."

Auger flailed his arms about, trying to run but his feet were rooted to the floor. He could feel the carpet lift as he tried to raise up. Deslonde simply waited, smoking his cigarette in the shadows.

"I may have been dead by then, Jean, because I was standing among them. I was able to survey the crowd. There were a dozen men standing over my body still hungry for the kill, exhorting each other to break off and continue searching for fresh victims. Scores of men were slowly drifting off or standing in the street conversing when someone shouted that the police were near. All the lights in the District were dark then, yet the streets were illuminated by torches, hundreds of torches, from Villere all the way down Customhouse to Franklin. It was a beautiful sight I think, the light reflecting off the houses, shimmering in the bloody puddle were I lay."

Auger saw the thickened water undulating, cresting in tiny red waves as an electric trolley rumbled down Customhouse, forced to stop by the crowds of men, some of whom searched each car for black people then waved the motorman past. He saw the lump of black flesh three quarters submerged in a sea of red, motionless, glistening in the torchlight. The movement of the water set Auger's head spinning and he fell into the street, landing on his back on the rug of his living room. He looked up at Deslonde smoking beside the wall of photos, flicking ashes into the ashtray next to the phonograph.

"Now *you* mustn't be so sensitive, Jean."

Spittle shot from Auger's mouth as he struggled to answer, but no words came, then finally a choked whisper.

"Remember what? I don't remember those things. I swear it."

The muscles in Auger's chest and neck tightened as he lay flat on the rug. He felt his face contorting and his tongue becoming thick and numb. *A fucking stroke?* He couldn't move his neck or head but he could see Deslonde out of the corner of his right eye drawing deeply, finishing his smoke. Auger's eyes shot to the left, landing on the television set, darkened, obscured in shadows except for the last daylight streaking across the top. There was a photograph of Celine on the television in a gold colored metal frame, taken on her birthday three years before, sweet sixteen. The camera caught her laughing, head thrown back and her mouth open, her blue eyes wide and clear and her auburn hair lifting off her shoulders as she twisted towards the lens, towards him, Auger. He'd made her laugh. He could always make her laugh, with just a look if he wanted too. She held the heart shaped locket he'd given her for her birthday between her thumb and forefinger, lifting it for the camera when something he said set her off into a fit of hysterics. Auger fixed on the photograph.

I ain't ready to leave my baby girl yet. I ain't gonna die this way. This ain't no stroke. This is all in my mind.

Auger rolled onto his stomach and lifted himself to his feet. He thought for a moment he might have been asleep all along, except that he felt Deslonde's presence, still there, silently watching.

"I think you done your best," said Auger. "There ain't no more for you to do . . ."

He turned and gasped at the sight of Philippe Deslonde. The room was aglow as if from torchlight. The walls danced with the reflection of fire. Deslonde stood before him, naked save for tattered remnants of bloody clothes. His thighs showed deep gashes and white bone, his groin was a bloody void, his chest an open cavity like a gutted animal, and what was left of his torso was dotted with holes and slashes from bullets and knives. Sections of his face and head were gaping spaces of red flesh and hair and his eyes were viscous white globes, opaque and unseeing. He held his arms aloft as if welcoming Auger's embrace.

Auger covered his eyes and moaned, "Sweet Jesus."

He jerked his head towards the top of the television. Celine was fresh and alive, the blueness of her eyes shined like a sunlit lake. He shielded his gaze when he turned back to Deslonde, but Deslonde was gone. The house was still. There was no one there. Auger was alone. The living room curtains were dimly lit by the last of the day's light.

Auger fled to the bedroom, pressing his palms into his ears with all his strength and cowered next to the bed. The front door slammed, shaking the sliding glass door in the bedroom and Auger snapped to attention. At the sound of his daughter's voice he instantly took himself in hand.

"Daddy, are you home?"

"Yes sweety, Daddy's in the bedroom."

He affected a leisurely gate and moved to the glass door and opened the drapes.

"Daddy, come quick. You can see smoke in the sky outside. You have to look, daddy. It's awful. It looks like the world is on fire."

Suzette's footsteps patted the thick carpet as she moved through the house towards the bedroom.

"Calm down, Celine," she said. "Jean?"

Auger greeted her at the door with a kiss on the cheek.

"Hi love," said Suzette. "It's true. Looks like world war three from up on Mulholland. The coloreds have gone crazy. They say they'll burn the city to the ground. It's terrible, Jean, terrible."

Auger took his wife in his arms and held her close, kissing her temple and speaking gently into her ear.

"Now don't let your imagination get the best of you, darling. You're talking about a few troublemakers and we got the best police force in the country looking out for things."

"Do you think so, sweetie?"

"I know it. Just this morning I was talking with a police officer down at the park. He was off duty, down there taking his family to Disneyland. He had his wife, granny, little bitty babies. They was having the time of their lives. He said the department got it all under control. They know who they got to corral and it won't take too long. If it was real trouble they wouldn't be giving the man the day off, would they?"

Suzette's face looked strained, the way she looked when she was keeping something inside. Auger tightened his arms around her and rocked gently.

"The man was an L.A. County Sheriff," he said.

"Is that right? Well, the police do know what they're doing. Still, it's frightening. How far do those people think they can go before they get taught a lesson?"

"I don't know, darling. I really don't know."

"I think it's the Communists," said Suzette. "I think they've infiltrated the coloreds from top to bottom. They're so easy to influence, you know. Like children, dangerous, hateful children."

Suzette changed her clothes as Auger stared out the patio window, catching sight of several buzzards sweeping the tops of the Eucalyptus trees in his yard. He jumped when Suzette began speaking again. Her words were like shards of splintered glass.

"The police need to shoot to kill, if you ask me," she said. "The coloreds have got to get the point, period. Before it's too late. Anyone even suspected of starting a fire should be shot on the spot."

At least I'm in the right place, he thought. *At least this is real.*

The sound of Suzette's voice was piercing, but Auger wasn't listening to what she was saying. Instead, he took deep breaths and thought of how much he loved her, determined to stay where he was. He wasn't going back again. He'd vowed it as a child and he vowed it now. He was free. He was never going back.

Nieting in New Orleans

Late July, 1965

What happened at Disneyland was the last thing Nieting expected, particularly after what he'd seen in New Orleans. When he arrived on the West Coast, after spending the previous week in Louisiana, he was triumphant. Although he'd found only a single testimony of value regarding the lost song, he believed it to be of immense importance. He believed he'd deepened his understanding of his subject in New Orleans. He believed he'd discovered what Negro music was all about. He witnessed the music the way it had been in Buddy Bolden's day, the way Kid Auger must have seen it played. At first, he'd been disappointed with what he found there. He interviewed a score of elderly musicians and not one yielded any information about Bolden's song. It was easy enough to get an interview, most of the old musicians were eager to talk, but it proved nearly impossible to discuss the things Nieting needed to advance his research. To a man, the musicians demurred at any discussion of race relations, acting as though Nieting himself could not be trusted. When he mentioned the name Robert Charles, his informants became even less forthcoming, a few turning hostile, questioning his intentions and cutting the interview short. Only a single old-timer even admitted to knowing of Robert Charles. "I just know he killed a lot of white people, that's all." Finally, Nieting decided not to mention his search for *The Robert Charles Song* at all until he could stablish proper rapport with his potential informants, a task that was proving nearly impossible.

In the first two days in the city, conditions rapidly became untenable. He felt swallowed up in the crowds of white tourists filling the French Quarter Jazz venues; everything was a novelty to them. The crowds were so thick at Preservation Hall, he had a difficult time making contact with the musicians. His fortunes seemed to change when he met an old man by the name of Pinot, a clarinet player, collecting donations at the door of a Jazz club. The initial discussion with Pinot went the way of all the others. Not long into the interview, Nieting mentioned Robert Charles, just as he'd resolved not to do. Pinot hesitated for a moment, then continued as if he did not hear the question. Instead he told Nieting about the music happening at Disneyland out in California.

"Yes sir," he said, "If you want the real thing, outside of New Orleans, it's on the West coast. Barbarin's out there. Johnny St. Cyr been there a while. Sweet Emma's going out. Mr. Walt Disney is putting on a festival, Dixieland at Disneyland. I heard Louis is gonna be there next month. I just wish I could go, but no more travel for me, too old."

"Is that the Disneyland of Mickey Mouse and Donald Duck?"

The old man nodded.

"No kidding?" said Nieting. "Will Kid Auger be there? I've heard he lives in California. I'm on my way there to find him."

"Oh, he lives in California for years now," said Pinot. "But don't you leave New Orleans without seeing one of our brass bands. I don't tell everyone about this kind of thing. It's a community event, you know, personal. It's a funeral. Wouldn't want too many tourists getting in the way, good intentioned as they might be. But you're different. You're a scholar, a European scholar. I know they love our music over there, so I'll tell you where to show up tomorrow if you want to see the real thing. You ever hear of the Olympia Band?"

Nieting's eyes misted with gratitude for the old man's generosity.

"I've never heard of them," he said. "You know, when I was a small boy, I always wished I was a Negro."

Pinot smiled.

"Lucky you was a thousand miles away then," he said.

The next morning Nieting set out early, hours before the time Pinot said the Olympia Brass Band was supposed to assemble. The streets were wet from the previous night's rain and the air was damp and hot. Black clouds sailed across the sky and the sun shot streaks of light through the breaks as they fled. Nieting was so overjoyed, so expectant of marvelous things, he skipped out the door of the YMCA at Lee Circle and danced down St. Charles Street. He purchased the *Official Jazz Map of New Orleans* in the gift shop of a fancy hotel on Poydras Street, cheerfully blurting out his uptown destination to the cashier.

"Don't go back there," the cashier had replied. He was a middle-aged white man in a white shirt with the hotel logo monogrammed on the front pocket.

"You European people just won't learn," he said. "I expect you want to see Buddy Bolden's place. That's the most popular one."

The man winked and spoke in a confidential tone.

"Japanese is the worst. They go traipsing back into that neighborhood all smiles, totting cameras, pocket books, and such. Then they get hit on the head or a gun stuck in their side and all their money took."

The man's eyes darted around the shop, empty except for a black man cleaning the glass door.

"That's one of the worst nigger areas there is," he said. "If you're smart, you'll just stay away."

The black man was well within earshot, yet made no sign of having heard the white man's remark. Nieting listened to the white man with some amazement and a bit of satisfaction. He was encountering his first case of overt white American racism and couldn't help smiling. He dismissed the man's advice, but stopped back at his room and left his camera. *No use inviting trouble*, he thought.

The *Official Jazz Map of New Orleans* listed the addresses of dozens of old-time Jazz men in an index with the name and location designated by a corresponding number on the map. Nieting marked the places were Buddy Bolden and Kid Auger lived more than a half century earlier. He caught a streetcar at Lee Circle and rode up St. Charles Street, following the route on the map with his finger. At Clio Street he rang the bell and the trolley rolled to a stop. He jumped onto the lawn next to the track and headed up Clio into the uptown district holding the unruly map unfolded before him.

The houses on Clio were old and the streets covered with a canopy of ancient trees. There wasn't a soul around. It was like walking in a magnificent museum. The houses were almost entirely circa 1900. Bolden and Auger had walked these very streets. Clio Street was bursting with vegetation spilling from overgrown yards. "They saw this very sight, stepped on this very ground." He sauntered slowly, taking in everything. His insides, his heart, his blood, his flesh were racing when a voice called out. "You're going the wrong way."

Nieting turned full circle. There was no one who might have spoken. He'd heard a woman's voice, yet as he looked about, the streets were deserted except for an elderly black woman rocking on a porch swing who didn't appear to be looking at him. She was slumped forward as if frozen, as the swing moved back and forth almost inperceptibley. Nieting looked over his shoulder, suddenly grasping that the voice was issuing a warning. He'd been cautioned several times about going into the uptown neighborhood, each time by a white, the last time no more than an hour previously when he purchased the Jazz map in the hotel gift shop. He proceeded on Clio Street, picking up his stride, unsure if the old woman was the voice that called out or if the voice was speaking to him at all. At the corner of Clio and Rampart, he stopped to reconnoiter, laying the oversized map flat on the sidewalk and crouching, tracing the route to Bolden's house with his forefinger.

He walked to Liberty Street and turned left, going another eight or nine blocks, passing Jackson Street, where Auger once lived, then two blocks to First Street where he made a right. He walked on First to the next cross street, which was Howard, and on the corner of First and Howard he found 2309, Buddy Bolden's house. It was a small shotgun-style duplex cottage built right up on the sidewalk with no set back other than three steps leading to the front door. There were two entrances facing the street, one for each apartment, and one window for each, with a single chimney in the center of the roof that appeared to service both sides of the residence. Nieting felt a shiver as he read the Jazz map.

"The Boldens lived in the right apartment from 1887 to 1905," he said. "Those were the years of his greatest fame."

Nieting stood directly across the street and stared at the house for half an hour until a woman came to the door, stepping onto the front steps and frowning, holding her fists clenched on her hips. She appeared to be looking at Nieting, who turned his head, pretending to watch something at the end of the block. He moved off quickly, crossing the street at the corner and walking down Howard around the back side of Bolden's house. He peered into the yard filled with overgrown bushes and a small garden where a man sat, crouched on a wooden crate, leaning his elbows on his thighs, examining a brass horn, a cornet, holding it up and pumping the keys. He was a young man, wearing only a pair of denim overalls with the shoulder straps hanging down and a black bowler hat. He put the horn to his lips and blew. Not only did Nieting understand instantly who the man was, he didn't question the impossibility of it or what the fact that he could see the man portended. Buddy Bolden had been dead for decades. Nieting knew he shouldn't be seeing him alive in broad daylight. Nevertheless, he raised his hand and waved to Bolden. Bolden lowered the horn and looked over the broken down fence, motioning towards the house and shrugging his shoulders as if to say, "sorry for the woman's unfriendliness. I know who you are. I appreciate what you're trying to do." Then Bolden smiled and raised the horn and blew a sound so odd to Nieting's ears the effect was otherworldly, like it should only be heard by spirits, and Negro spirits at that. When Bolden stopped playing, he rested his elbows on his thighs and grinned, playfully shooing Nieting away, "you got great things to do boy, go on now. You have my sanction for sure, but you got to leave old Buddy, so go along now."

Nieting continued down Howard Street, looking back at the wooden crate where Bolden sat. It didn't dawn on him to ask Bolden about the lost song. He simply smiled and waved and Bolden smiled, nodding his head until he was out of view. Within minutes, Nieting was on Jackson Street, turning left without even looking at the map, certain that was the way to Auger's home. He picked the house out from half a block off, the only one on the street that appeared to be uninhabited. There were no numbers on the front, so Nieting counted out the address by the other houses. 2919 Jackson Street. It was Kid Auger's house. Nieting approached thoughtfully, stopping to observe from different angles, allowing his imagination to adjust so he could see things Auger might have seen, the angle of the roof from a certain point, the texture of the walkway to the door. He held his hands together as he stepped off the sidewalk onto the path leading to the yard. The door and windows of the house were boarded up and the small front yard was overgrown with weeds and wild flowers. A short picket fence lay flat on the ground, grass growing up between the boards and nails protruding from the rotting wood.

It began to drizzle as Nieting walked around the side of the house through knee-high grass and into a small yard thick with unkempt bushes. There was a large pile of debris in the center of the small property, broken-up furniture, an old baby carriage, worn-out shoes, faded clothing, sacks of moldy belongings. It was nearly sixty years since Auger lived in the house, yet Nieting felt a strange excitement as though the remnants left behind belonged to Auger's family. The backdoor and windows were nailed tightly shut, except for an old screen door Nieting grabbed to enter the house, but the door broke loose from the rusty hinges and bounced past him onto the ground. He jumped off the wooden steps to avoid the flying door and staggered backwards into the yard until the wet branches of a bush sprinkled his neck with drops of water. He huddled under the branches as the rain picked up, imagining Auger there, coming and going over the years, wondering who might have been with him.

He imagined a gaggle of little Negro boys rushing out the back door, chasing the one carrying a trombone, fleeing a stout black woman shouting after them in French and the boys giggling and disappearing around the side of the house to who knows where, to the place where Negroes gather to make music; they were off to create Jazz, invent it and change the world. The rundown little structure with its' boarded windows and perforated roof was alive with an electricity that made Nieting want to shout. He closed his eyes and danced in a circle beneath the branches, shaking rain drops from the leaves onto his shoulders and down his back. He could feel the presence of spirits. He could sense the closeness of the past, feel it peeking through the shrubs, waiting to burst forth to reveal itself to him. He had the feeling of being watched and realized there was a man standing on the opposite side of the yard. Professor Nieting found himself standing face to face with his father, Emil, who rocked on his heels beneath a canopy of wet branches.

Nieting's knees buckled and he staggered. He pinched his cheeks to make sure he was awake and cried out in pain. At that moment his mind was perfectly clear, his cheeks stinging, the image before him vivid and, in fact, his father. He looked like the only picture of Emil he'd ever seen, the one Uncle Max kept in a frame with a photo of Kid Auger of the same scale, clipped from a magazine and pasted next to him so the two looked like old buddies. His father grinned like a trickster. His hair was brushed back, sticking straight up at all angles. The sleeves of his tweed jacket were too short, his pants legs too high, the suit too tight. It was clear from the look on his face that he preferred the odd fit. His spats glistened with beaded drops of rain. Nieting stared.

Emil glanced to his left. Kid Auger was there, holding a trombone, shielded from the rain by a drooping wall of hedges. Auger was a full grown man, his father's age, late twenties, impeccably tied down, hair slicked back smooth, every crease in his clothes razor sharp. Nieting could smell his cologne across the yard. Auger smiled sweetly, bending forward to look around the branches, making eye contact with Nieting's father. Emil looked at his son and spoke.

"Do you truly understand the meaning of the music?" he asked. "Why, it's a mallet to pummel generals and priests, a hammer to silence politicians and bureaucrats, a wrecking ball to tear down courthouses and jails."

Auger let out a blast like a lion's roar, then cut the breath short into the sharp jab of a fist. Emil held his face in his hands and laughed, delighted by the collective spontaneity. Auger moved the slide in and out, searching, then played a single sustained note, the tone like velvet, flowing gently, illuminating, and so palpable Nieting saw rain drops splashing off the sound. His father's eyes swelled with tears as he gestured towards Auger.

"There it is," he said. "The breath *is* a river."

The single note finally vanished into the misty drizzle and the two men bowed to each other and turned towards Nieting. They each smiled mischievously, offering their hands to Nieting, which he took from twenty feet away as a gust of rainy wind swept the yard and a cat shot from the bushes, between Nieting's legs and across the yard. Nieting vaulted into the air, bounded over the mangled screen door and came to rest in the corner of the yard next to a pile of broken up furniture. He held his face to the sky and let the drops of cool rain wash the tears as he sobbed. When he turned to where Emil and Kid Auger had been there was nothing there but green hedges waving in the rainy wind. Nieting nearly shouted for them to return, but remained silent. He ambled around the house to Jackson Street and stood several moments in the rain, hands a-pocket, gazing at the old cottage.

"Am I not on the right path?" he said. "Did not my fathers unlock every door?"

As he walked away from Auger's house he absentmindedly slapped the branch of a bush hanging over the sidewalk from a neighbor's yard. He saw the leaves laden with translucent drops, flawless symmetrical domes perched on the green flesh, appearing viscous until his hand caused an explosion of spray. They were universes of perfect order and solidity until Nieting casually obliterated the illusion with his fingers and palm. It was at that moment that he first sensed the great challenge he must face, without even knowing he'd done so. He discerned his mind splitting, a chasm broadening between two irreconcilable selves, one existing in a rational world and the other in some other realm, or perhaps it was a joining of the two into a single inseparable world, a melding of what was real and what was not, an indifferentiation or perhaps a chaos. It came in the form of a speck of memory, a feeling rather than an image, that he'd met his father before in just such a manner, that he knew his father in just this way, that they'd spoken many times. This knowledge was a light glistening on the point of a needle and was lost in the smallest component of a second to the absolute certainty that his father and Auger were leading him, that he had their sanction, that they approved of his direction. At that moment, he sought no more than this, no more truth.

He wandered on Jackson Street in the drizzling rain and turned for no reason onto Liberty Street. The way he reached the corner of Saratoga and Erato without the map was magic. Not until he saw the street signs did he remember that the old Negro musician, Pinot, had told him to be right there at 11 a.m. if he wanted to see the real thing. It was just after eleven and people dressed in black were lingering next to a vacant lot across the street from a two-story wood framed building, a late 19th century structure badly in need of a paint job. The building had seen better days, yet there was still evidence of former glory in its decaying form; in the center of the front was a large ornate dormer with carved woodwork over an arched stone entrance with pillars on either end of a broad staircase leading to two heavy wooden doors. There were eight large windows across the front, shut tight with wooden shudders and one large window in the center over the doorway. An old sign above the door read *TRUE FRIENDS HALL.* Musicians in dark blue uniforms milled about, chatting. Two black limousines were parked at the muddy roadside next to the vacant lot. The crowd of black-clad mourners grew quickly as people arrived from all directions and congregated in silence at the roadside. Neighbors peeked out front doors and from front yards, some coming outside and standing at the edges of the crowd.

An elderly man dressed in a black suit leaned against the limo, smoking, holding a long flag pole with a cross at the top and a banner of silk fringed with gold tassels that read, *True Friends Society – Organized January 14, 1883 – Incorporated March 31, 1885.* The musicians were mostly old men, with a few youngsters among them with Afro's protruding under blue band hats and the word Olympia in gold thread on the front. Nieting noticed old Pinot standing among the musicians and Pinot spotted him and nodded. The grand marshal, a broad chested, gray haired man, somber and serious, in a black suit with a gold sash across his breast, conversed with the limo driver, a young man wearing sunglasses, goatee and a large Afro. A black hearse rounded the corner onto Saratoga followed by two limousines and stopped in the street next to the lot. As if on cue, the doors to the True Friends' Hall opened and a mass of mourners exited. An elderly woman wearing sunglasses beneath a black veil and a man holding an open umbrella over her and another woman shepherding children entered the first limousine as scores of people crowded out onto the street. Finally, a cloth draped coffin supported by six pall bearers floated out into the rain and down the stairs to the waiting hearse where it was deftly slipped into the back. The musicians moved into the road and the hearse pulled up behind and the limos backed up, angling to follow. The grand marshal, in the street now, faced the musicians. He raised his hand slowly over his head and held it there, then dropped it quickly, clutching his side as the band played a dissonant multitude of notes, quivering vibratos, ragged, yet somehow a perfect distillation of grief. He turned and stepped, palm spread across his chest, eyes sadly searching the ground, dropping his head forward on each beat of the bass drum.

The procession inched down Saratoga in the rain followed by a growing throng of mourners, silent except for the sound of hundreds of feet shuffling. A luxurious flood of funeral music enveloped Nieting, sounds of mourning, the sorrow of death transformed into notes that dissipated into air like spent sobs. The rain picked up as the people moved slowly forward, the hearse creeping in front, the band squeezing out agonized dirges, sweet sad hymns, solemn drum beats the grand marshal stepped to as the procession winded through the city streets, finally halting at the wrought iron gates of the cemetery. The hearse and its entourage of limos whizzed past the crowd towards the gravesite, visible through the rainy mist, where a priest and several others waited beneath an awning. Meanwhile, the members of the Olympia Brass Band spread out in all directions, some disappearing into a nearby tavern, others into a house, and a few jumping into a car at the roadside, while the followers milled in the warm drizzle or huddled beneath the shelter of several willow trees.

Men and women dressed in black walked with open umbrellas through the cemetery gate as Nieting stood against a large tree trunk.

After half an hour, the mourners at the grave dispersed, loading into cars as the call rippled through the crowd at the gate, picked up by little boys who charged to the doors of the tavern and the residence calling for the musicians to get back quickly. A grinning trumpet player trotted out of the tavern with a white napkin still tucked in his collar, slurping a glass of beer before handing it off and skipping across the street. The crowd stirred and all eyes were on the line of cars as the hearse pulled behind the Olympia Brass Band in formation just inside the gate and the rest of the entourage came in behind it. The grand marshal raised his hand then quickly clutched his side, pumping the air as the band blew, marching out the cemetery gate as the crowd filled the road behind the procession. They'd traveled no more than a block when the cars made a hard right and sped away from the marchers. Nieting watched the last limo disappear around the corner, then jerked back at the sound of the band blowing. The mood was different now. The horns exploded into a rowdy, blaring melody and the drummers pounded a beat that made the grand marshal thrust out his chest and strut fast for several yards before pulling himself down into a steady dancing walk. The action of restraining himself appeared like some kind of joyous agony and the crowd cheered and everyone danced behind and alongside the band. It seemed as if the number of marchers was constantly increasing, expanding in bodies and in sheer joyfulness. There were children everywhere, dancing, moving in lines, kicking, shaking their arms, laughing, clapping their hands and others following on bicycles, shooting ahead of the parade and circling back, pointing and talking excitedly. He saw women in house dresses with scarves over curler-clad heads standing on the roadside, arms folded, watching, nodding to the rhythms and smiling.

The band wove through the streets, finally moving into a narrow cobble-stoned lane as the people flooded sidewalk to sidewalk. The river of humanity flowed past a beautiful young woman in a sleeveless hot pants suit and a black beret slanted in perfect balance on a ball shaped

Afro, dancing on a car top above the crowd. Nieting laughed at the sight of passing heads turning in unison towards the woman, like she was a queen and the car a reviewing stand as she shook her bottom and twisted her hands as if swimming under water. Then the street opened up, as more people joined the parade and the tune shifted to something Nieting didn't recognize except that it made him want to laugh and cry and he felt his flesh tingling at the drum beats and the sight of the enraptured crowd. He felt himself rising off the pavement. A man dressed in a white beret, white sneakers, white shirt with wide lapels, white belt and white sharply creased pants, slid down a grass parking strip, taking long strides, thrusting one arm all the way forward and the other all the way back, moving his feet as though he were ice skating, so singular and concentrated on gliding, he appeared to be in the wrong picture or dropped from another planet. Another man shot past the man in white, carrying a cup of beer, arms spread in welcome, splashing beer as he hurried in pursuit of the music. He charged past a heavy set woman wearing high heels, her body bursting out of a short, tight, knit dress as she swung an oversized hand bag by the strap. Nieting marveled at the sea umbrellas open and held aloft, jerking in infinite rhythmic variation. He saw men in undershirts and women in robes who'd run from the house at the sound of the music, dancing unabashedly down the street. It was pandemonium, a collective affirmation, an ultimate coming together, pure love.

The parade reached a main thoroughfare, a broad street with two lanes of traffic moving in opposite directions and fronted by large brick buildings, old structures that must have been there in Bolden's day. Nieting pretended his eyes were Auger's as he scanned the rooftops. Children ran through the ranks of the band. A policeman on the curbside stood with his hands on his hips, club jutting out from behind his back, watching blankly. White people stood watching, some grinning, some clapping, a few moving out into the flow, and some huddled in groups glaring at the horde of black dancers. As the army of revelers poured into the street in what appeared to be a business district, everything stopped, everything except the music and the dancing. Business stopped, pedestrians stopped, traffic halted in the intersection as the crowd pranced and skipped through.

Nieting raised a fist over his head and pumped to the bass drum, shouting at the white bystanders through the din, "This is the sound of revolution. You're time is short. Can't you hear it?" He walked with his fist clenched, punching the air to the beat until the procession passed through the business district into a residential area and white faces became fewer. The celebration careened joyously back into the uptown neighborhood, finally reaching the vacant lot on Saratoga Street where it all began. Nieting left the ranks of the marchers and moved to the sidewalk, watching as the band dispersed wearily and the crowd melted away into the day to day life of the city. He drifted off, strolling dreamily in the warm drizzle for over an hour, contemplating the miraculous scene he'd witnessed. He crisscrossed through the uptown neighborhood, walking in the rain down the center of deserted streets. By late afternoon the rain stopped. The sun in the western sky, forcing its way out of the clouds, reflected on the wet pavement and the white-washed house fronts on the east side of the street where Nieting found himself alone.

He pranced down Dryades Street bowing his legs like he'd seen some of the dancers do, when suddenly the empty street began to fill with people, every one coming out because the rain was done, pouring out of the houses into the sunshine, children playing on front steps and running all around, vaulting puddles of rain water, skipping rope, adults calling to one another from doorways. The streets were alive as Nieting hurried past like a ghost, unsettled by the sudden appearance of so many black people. He rushed towards Clio, making eye contact with another person only once, a small child behind a screen door who seemed to scowl and say something Nieting couldn't understand. An older child ushered the angry tot away from the door as Nieting fled past. He quickened his pace, moving towards Clio, as three young men, shirtless and muscular, fell in behind him. They seemed to be keeping pace with him, increasing their speed as he increased his, moving within ten feet and holding steady as he tried to affect a casual gate and yet walk faster still.

At Clio, he cut sharply towards St. Charles, as four more young black men, broad shouldered, two of them shirtless, wheeled around the corner in front of him, moving towards him four abreast while the men behind kept pace. Nieting recognized the section of street as his eyes landed on the old woman who might have called to him earlier that day still sitting on the porch. "You're going the wrong way," someone had shouted, and now the old woman seemed to glance at him, moving her head slightly in his direction then turning away. Nieting bolted between the approaching men, dropping the Jazz map in a puddle of water, pumping his legs for all he was worth and not looking back until he reached St. Charles Street.

Just as he reached St. Charles, the trolley pulled up, overflowing with tourists. Nieting shouted and frantically flagged the trolley as it slowed for the stop and bounded aboard in a great leap. He dropped the coins in the fare box and pushed into the crowd of whites, bending to look out the window back up Clio as the trolley pulled out. The thoroughfare lined with ancient trees where Bolden and Auger had once walked was deserted again.

Before Nieting left New Orleans for Los Angeles in pursuit of Kid Auger, he spoke to the old Negro clarinet player, Pinot, one last time. On the morning of the day he was scheduled to fly out, as he packed his bags in his room at the Y, a boy appeared in the doorway. It was unclear how long he'd been silently waiting for Nieting to notice his presence, but when he did, the boy stepped forward shyly and handed Nieting a tiny slip of paper. As soon as Nieting took the paper the boy disappeared into the hallway. Nieting followed in time to see the boy hit the banister to the stairs and slide down, feet first, bounding onto the first floor, darting past the front desk and out the door into the sunshine. The note, scrawled in pencil in shaky handwriting on a piece of torn newspaper read, "I got something to tell you about Bolden and that song. Come to the True Friends' Hall at Saratoga and Clio, right away," signed Wilson Pinot.

Nieting caught the Uptown streetcar and exited at Clio, hurrying past the same streets Bolden and Auger had walked, past the empty porch where the old woman had been, to Saratoga Street. A block past

Saratoga he found True Friends' Hall. The old building seemed to eye
Nieting suspiciously as he approached. Its' weathered face appeared se-
vere and unperturbed with its memories of Buddy Bolden and the lives of
countless Negroes, their suffering and their striving, their resistance and
the knowledge they possessed by virtue of it, knowledge Nieting coveted.

He walked up the wooden steps and through the double doors and
halted in the dimly lit foyer. To the left was a darkened auditorium with old
wooden shutters on the windows closed tight. The wood floor sagged
and there was a stage at the far end with an old rostrum and folding chairs
stacked against the walls. To the right was a small room with the door
ajar, an office with a large wooden desk and chair and metal file cabinet
in the corner and an old couch where half dozen children sat watching
cartoons on a TV perched on a portable stand in the middle of the floor.
The children faced Nieting but none raised their eyes from the television.
Straight ahead on the left was a dark hallway leading to the recesses of
the building and to the right a staircase to the second floor. Finally, a man
emerged from the office, having obviously heard the big doors slam. He
appeared startled to see Nieting and addressed him with undisguised
suspicion. Nieting explained the purpose of his visit with equal reserve.

"Mr. Pinot is pretty sick," said the man. "He ain't supposed to get too
excited. If he sent for you, I guess it's alright if you go up. He's up those
stairs, last room on the right. Don't stay too long. He can't take it."

Nieting ascended the creaky stairs as the man watched. At the top
was another dark hallway lined with doors, all closed except one at the
far end, apparently Pinot's room. The starkness, the barren necessity,
the poverty of the surroundings touched Nieting. Pinot had been well
dressed on the first two occasions they'd seen each other. The second
time he'd worn a black suit and tie and a white shirt. Nieting had had no
reason at the time to consider what the man's circumstances might be.
Yet, as he approached the room it was clear that the man who had summoned him to the True Friends' Hall was poor.

Nieting stuck his head around the open door. The room was bright
with sunlight from a window propped open with an old shoe, yet the air was

stale and smelled of sweat. The wall paper on one side of the room had come loose, appearing as though a dirty bed sheet had been tacked onto the wall. Pinot lay on a cot next to a night stand covered with prescription bottles. He opened his eyes just as Nieting looked in, and nodded, motioning for Nieting to come close. The old man looked like Uncle Max in his last days. The memory of the loneliness of death swept over Nieting and his face sunk into a look of despair and his eyes filled with tears.

"Don't be upset, young fella," said Pinot. "I'm just an old man ready for his reward."

He motioned to Nieting to pull a nearby chair to the bedside.

"Take these," he said, handing Nieting several sheets of loose toilet paper. The simple generosity amidst the stark poverty was more than Nieting could bear. He cried as the old man watched him scan the room.

"You ever been poor?' asked Pinot.

Nieting nodded as he blew his nose in the wad of toilet paper.

"Then, none of this shocks you too much," said Pinot.

"I think it shocks me because I was poor," replied Nieting.

"Hard times over there in Berlin after the war, was there?"

"There were so many suffering," said Nieting. "I was far luckier than most."

"Ain't that the way," said Pinot. "I knew you had a lot of sense in you when we first met. I said to myself, this young fella has a head on his shoulders. I never would have sent you to our brother's sendoff otherwise."

"I thank you for that," said Nieting, taking the man's hand in his. "It was truly the most important experience of my life."

"Okay, okay," said Pinot, taking back his hand. "It wasn't all that much. I'll be going that same route soon myself."

"Literally and figuratively," said Nieting chuckling through the tears.

"Don't be joking at a man's death bed, now," said Pinot. "That's bad luck."

Before Nieting could respond, Pinot went on. "Don't be talking so much either. You got to know when to keep your mouth shut, particularly if you interviewing folks. Nothing more annoying than an interviewer that talks too much. That's one thing that always gets my goat. Ain't shit I can tell you if you rather hear yourself going on."

Pinot looked sternly at Nieting, who bowed his head and sat quietly until the old man spoke.

"I ain't got long to live. I know that. But, I ain't complaining. I lived a good life . . . well, I ain't always *been* good, but I had a good time for sure. I had my fun, in other words. I knew the great ones. Jack Carey, Buddy Petit, Keppard, Tony Jackson. I knew Bolden. I didn't mention it to you before because all you writers want to know things and most times just take what we give and go away with it. I know men that told their stories and never did get nothing out of it, never even seen it in print. Some white man just took it away to some other world or some-place colored folks is barred from and it never does do us any good. Our children don't get to see it, don't get to learn nothing from it or get what they got coming. It's like we still giving everything we got with no consideration paid."

Pinot was clearly very ill. His face had been full when Nieting had first seen him, robust and animated, yet now his flesh hung on his skull and his eyes appeared sunken into black rings. Yet he managed to sit up, labori-ously propping himself up on his hands.

"I told you about the funeral the other day cause I thought you seemed alright," he said. "But I wasn't ready to give nothing up bout Buddy yet. I hold my memories close to myself, like I said. I ain't long for this world. I lived too long anyway. My family is all gone. Who would have thought I'd be the last one to go. Believe me, that ain't no good luck. I wish to god it'd been me went last year instead of my poor wife. Even my kids is all gone. If you outlive your children, you know you lived too long. You can see I'm a poor man. None of that matters now. It don't matter when you lie down for the last time. Oh, I got no regrets, don't get me wrong. I could have gone away with all those boys when I had the chance and made all kinds of money. I could be living in Hollywood today if I'd fol-lowed the rest."

Pinot hauled his legs over the side of the bed like dead wood and faced Nieting, groaning as he squeezed his thigh.

"But that wasn't me," he said. "I stayed at the source. I kept it real. Every last one that left ended up changing, Jelly, Joe Oliver, I think it killed both of them, Auger, Louis, all those great musicianers changed. Now, a man can't help but change, but too much money and you forget why you're doing what you're doing. We got our folks down here. It was them give us the music in the first place. You don't up and join another world just like it was another social club. I know Louis always came back and he was always real generous, helping folks out with money, helping the musicianers. Hell, he laid bread on me more than once, when I needed it. And he was always saying how he's a New Orleans boy, real proud, always giving proper respect to the folks that gave him a leg up. He's the only one I know did like that and I'm here to say it still ain't enough. I love Louis. But, you got to stay with your folks. Even if you end up like this."

Pinot motioned around the room.

"Don't get me wrong," he said. "I'm grateful as hell. Thank heaven for the brothers of the True Friends Society. They'll give me a proper funeral, too. I ain't even got a home to die in. I don't mind it, though. I chose it to be this way. No one made me stay close to my people. You do it for the children, the music got to benefit them. It got to be a part of their lives if it's gonna go on. You got to hire them to play the music, you can't exclude them from the benefit of the gift they gave. Once the white man gets wise to what they been doing, he picks it up and next thing you know he gets all the jobs. He controls it all and makes all the money. We end up getting cut out again."

Pinot reached to the night stand and rummaged through the collection of old bottles, finally finding what he was looking for, a pint bottle of whiskey with barely a swallow left. He drained the bottle holding it over his open mouth to catch the last few drops.

"I ain't supposed to do this, but you won't tell nobody. Like I was saying, you take a guy like Barney Bigard when he was with Duke. I'm talking bout the 1930's now. He's a New Orleans boy. I used to give him lessons when he was a kid. He's a a Creole boy, still going strong today. He's with Louis now. Been with him a while. Well, this is the early 30s, and he was doing real good with Duke. They was going places, but the only way that band could make it was to travel, travel all the time, all year for years on end. There wasn't nothing for the colored musicianer in the studio where the big money was. Colored was barred from those jobs, even up in New York City. It was our music they was playing, but the white man took over cause he owned it all, the radio, the movie studios, the big venues. We couldn't get those jobs no way. I heard one time, Fletcher Henderson had his band up to Princeton College, big time white school up north, to play a dance and they wouldn't let colored play where white kids was. They put all these plants, great big pots across the stage to hide the band. Just like they wasn't really there. They couldn't have no black men playing near no white kids so they cover up so they could have their dance and not break Jim Crow. That's right, it was up north and it was Jim Crow just the same as down here."

Pinot held the empty whiskey bottle to his mouth and shook a drop onto his tongue.

"Long about ten years later, Dizzy and them had to go and invent something brand new, all that rebop mess. I never did go for it, but I know why they had to do it, come up with something the white man didn't know about. We got to change our music constantly, always come up with something new. As soon as we put it out the white man picks it up and takes all the work. So our kids lose interest and got to make up something brand new again until the white man gets hip and the whole thing goes on again, round and round. There ain't no group of people in the world created more beauty than our black youth. They're like some invisible power, like in a movie about outer space, and no one gives a damn about them, no one knows they're alive unless they sending them to jail or off to some war. Yet every couple of years they got to invent some new style, just so they got something they can do that nobody else can do. That's the way it's always been. That's what Bolden did too. Him and Galloway and the others, they dressed different, they talked different, and sure enough played music different. Black people is always changing just to stay alive, just to stay at square one."

"What you are saying is truly amazing," said Nieting, "and in a way quite wonderful."

"Nah, it ain't wonderful," said Pinot. "The problem is, youth lacks experience. They think they're the first and only ones to ever do anything, so they're easy for the white man to con, to take advantage. That's how our music always ends up in some barroom, always turns into good-time music, when it was always more than that. I ain't saying there's anything wrong with clowning, with dancing and drinking in some roadhouse. I done it plenty. I probably would have lived another twenty years if I hadn't done it so much. But, we let the white man turn us out. He made whores out of us, selling ourselves like we done. If you don't think selling our music to the white man is like turning a trick, you don't know a god damned thing about what music is supposed to do."

"I believe I understand you," said Nieting. "Music is a means of survival."

The old man continued as if he hadn't heard what Nieting said.

"Now days, people don't care about nothing but good time music," he said. "But at one time our music was about much more than that. It was about all of life, everything, the good and the bad, happiness and tough times. The way things is in New Orleans today, we play mostly for white folks and most of what the music has to say gets lost. White folks don't know it cause it ain't about them in the first place. That's the reason I never left New Orleans for very long. You know down here we never made much money. Even when I was a kid, in the early days all the musicians took a day job. They couldn't make enough to feed their family just playing music. There was exceptions. Take a man like Papa Tio. He worked every night and did parades in the day time and had more students than he could handle. He was an exception in this way. He had some of his family in there working as cigar makers, had a little factory right in the back of their house. His brother Lorenzo and his nephew Lorenzo Jr. was real fine musicians, too. That family did alright, but they was still just working people. Not rich. You had to love making music, you had to love the life. See up north, those New Orleans boys got right into that ol' rat race."

"Rat race?" said Nieting.

"Yeah, you know, chasing after the almighty dollar. Well, you go at the music too hard that a way and the music changes. Everything that ain't feel-good gets cut out. Folks don't need to know what's going on in the same way no more. Used to be you could go to a dance and Buddy Bolden would play that horn and it was like he could see right inside of you and tell just what it was bothering you. He knew black folks, felt what they felt. It was more like church than some kind of simple pleasure. Now I got nothing against pleasure mind you. That's what music is for. I'm still talking about pleasure, see, but deep pleasure, pleasure that comes from being aware of everything that matters, knowing what you been through and where you going. The music gives this to you. I know, no man can really be aware of everything. Hell, we all miss most of what's going on anyways. But in the old days when the music was right, you felt like you could know everything. It was a holy feeling. You know, some folks considered our music profane. The church going folks didn't appreciate it very much. But, we'd get this joyous feeling nonetheless. It was a feeling that made you understand there was more parts of yourself than you could know, parts of yourself so deep, like you was anchored and nothing in the world, not the white man, nothing, could do you out of it, take you out of that deep water, that reservoir. Yes, you are right. I believe it allowed my people to survive."

"What terrible irony," said Nieting.

"Eh?" said Pinot. "What do you mean?"

"It is ironic that something so significant in terms of collective survival could be trivialized in such a way."

"Ironic, is it?" said Pinot. "Sounds right. We was sure enough up against an iron fist. You know when I was a boy, I'd just started to playing with grown men. Times was tough. I was just a boy but I went out with those big men, Bolden, Galloway, Dusen, because my family needed the money. My daddy had his own meat stall in the French Market, his own business, my people always had some kind of business going and times was real lean. My folks didn't ask where I went at night and I didn't tell. Nobody wanted their boy to be working in the District, but we needed the money. I was fifteen years old and I guess they figured I needed to be a man because no one told me what to do and my mama was sure happy to get that money. Course, I would have played for free, truth be told, with Buddy and them, but the money helped us out for sure. Those were some troubled days. The worst of it was the time the white people was all up in arms and looking for Robert Charles because he killed a couple of police. I know you wanted to hear about this first time we talked, but I don't give that up to no strangers, period. It's different now, seeing I don't have much time left."

"I understand, Pinot," said Nieting.

"They was killing black folks all over the city, uptown, downtown, and even way out in the country. Most folks hold up in their houses and even some of those was killed. Whites come right in with guns blazing. Well, to this day I wish I'd stayed at home. I wish I made my daddy stay home too. They killed him, shot him off his wagon when he was going to work. He stopped by the slaughter house and was hauling his goods to the market when they came and shot him, long about three in the morning. They left him to die on the corner of Dumane and Burgundy. Took all the meat, too. Left him to bleed to death."

The old man's eyes hardened as if he could see his dead father's face. He paused and Nieting remained silent until Pinot shook himself from his reverie.

"I near got killed myself," he said. "They was shooting everything in sight, just killing folks out right for being colored. They say Robert Charles killed those police and they was gonna make all the colored people pay. They say they was gonna kill every last one of us and they would have if we didn't start to fighting back. None of the papers ever wrote that up. Our people got a hold of guns and started to shooting back and things calmed down real quick. Just like the Deacons of Justice and Defense do today.

Same thing. Caused the whites to bring in the National Guard. Papers said New Orleans bond rate was dropping in New York City on account of all the murdering. Didn't no one want to do business in such a place. Things wasn't stable. But that ain't really why they called in the troops. Even bad business was a small thing compared to black men with guns shooting back. Yes, sir. Nothing the white man fears more than that.

"That song you was asking about, yeah, we had a song about Robert Charles, but it's forgotten now. I don't know where it came from and it didn't last very long. Folks used to say it was Buddy's tune, but I never knew for sure. I heard it one time on the street and watched the police nearly kill the poor soul that sung it. He said 'don't beat me, I'm only repeating what I heard' and they said 'repeating is enough to get you whupped and 90 days on top of it.' See, that's exactly what I'm getting at. That song, the version I heard, was speaking to black folks. That man had no business singing it where the white man could hear it. Naturally, the white man didn't like it at all. Oh, he understood it alright, but he sure didn't like it. Robert Charles was a great man. A lot of colored people saw it that way. White man kills our people whenever he gets a notion and don't nothing happen. Still going on today. Robert Charles, he said, I'll go, you can kill me, but I'm taking a heap of you all with me. That's what he done. Killed 30 or 35 whites before they took him. Folks had a song celebrating Robert Charles' life. Some never did believe they killed him the day they burned the house he was hold up in.

"That song been eating at me lately. I had a dream the other night and I could hear it but when I woke it was gone. Here I am, bout to say good-bye to this world and I'm fine with that. I lived a real good life. Why, I been around the world with this music. I had it all, so I ain't sorry to go. I just started to thinking about how my daddy died and I wished I'd gone a bit further to change things for folks. I remembered what Robert Charles did way back when – those Deacons got the same attitude as Robert Charles had, today. Well, I wasn't never no gun totter. Still ain't. I just wished I could remember that song. I only heard it once and it stuck with me for the longest time. The words went away first and all I could remember was Buddy's melody, but I never did actually play the song. I don't know why. It was a dangerous song to mess with, I knew that. I'd seen what happens when you play with it, but I don't think that's what stopped me. Maybe it was all too painful or too personal and the last thing I wanted was for the white man to get a hold of it or some New Orleans boy to bring it up north and next thing you know Paul Whiteman be playing it with strings and Irene and Vernon Castle be gliding over the parkay floor to Robert's song and Robert would be done in again. Only this time we'd loose him for good.

"I been trying to remember it now, before I die. We need that song now, we need men like Robert Charles and we need our music. I been laying here racking my brain, trying to bring it back, but it's gone and I can't get a hold of it, you see? Our music keeps us alive. It makes us happy, makes us forget our troubles, but sometimes it makes us remember where we been, what we gone through, how strong we are to survive like we done and sing about it, and what deep souls my people have and the old heads we are to be making music so simple but complicated too. Hell, just look at popular music you got in this country today and you'll see it mostly all comes from us. But, I ain't worried about what's already been took from us, I'm thinking of this song we lost, we let get away. Nothing I can do now. My time ain't long and like I say, its okay with me . . . I'm tired. I done more in my life than most men could do in ten lives. I'm alright. I'm satisfied.

"The one thing I want to tell you is this, don't let nobody fool you and tell you that the music ain't nothing but a good time, forgetting your worries, hell that ain't real pleasure. Real pleasure is deep like your soul, real pleasure is understanding your suffering and making it into something else, something new, something beautiful like our music. You give it to your people and they at least have the pleasure of seeing themselves through their own eyes. Forgetting ain't no pleasure at all, seeing yourself with your own eyes, that's pleasure, that's joyous living.

"You say you looking for *The Robert Charles Song* and you want to give it to the colored people, well then take what I say to heart. Most folks, black and white don't want to talk about such things. Talking about things the way they really are makes folks uncomfortable. Scares the hell out of'm. That's why no one ever mentions Robert Charles no more. That's why we let his song get away.

"I know you Europeans put a lot of stock in your music. Beethoven is considered a pretty big man over there. That's good. Maybe you can see things more clear then, not being from the states, maybe you ain't caught up in all this nonsense about a man's color. Maybe if you find the song you'll be able to tell the truth about it. It don't make no difference to me now. Dust to dust, ashes to ashes. I just wanted to tell you these few things. That's why I called you here. I got no idea if you understand what I'm talking about. A lot of people are coming by to see me lately. They all know, no one goes on forever. I'm just trying to say what I got to say before I go. You're gonna do whatever you do, write whatever you write. I just hope your European readers are smarter than the white folks over here. I hope you remember what the song means and you tell it like it is. Man, they shoot us, lynch us, arrest men for no reason but their color, make them slaves, sell them just like slaves and work them till they die. This is an everyday affair and I ain't talking about back before the War Between the States. It goes on today. I mean the police do it, the judges too, today. It's always been like this. It ain't never changed. We was hemmed in every which way back in Bolden's day too, but there was a spirit coming up, and it was coming right through the music. Buddy knew he didn't make it up, it wasn't him, he was a vessel is all, speaking for all of us. His power was greater than anyone else because the power of all black people was coming right through him. They couldn't kill us all even though that's what they wanted, even though they tried mighty hard. A man like Robert Charles and a man like Buddy, why they was the heart and soul of my people. That's why I been racking my brain trying to remember Buddy's melody, trying to remember *The Robert Charles Song*. Those two men go together. If they'd ever met, my god, who knows what would have come of it."

Pinot closed his eyes. His cheeks were sunken and his mouth agape and he lay still for a long time. It appeared as if the old man had died. Nieting sat quietly, wondering if he should call the man down stairs or simply remain silent out of respect. Finally, Pinot took in a protracted breath and let out a long gurgling snore. He licked his dry lips and moaned as Nieting bent forward and saw his chest rising and falling ever so slightly. After several moments, Nieting tip toed from the room and down the dark hallway. At the bottom of the stairs, the children on the couch in the office elbowed and tickled each other laughing with raucous child joy at something a cartoon character had said or done. He left without addressing the man in the office and on the street he wept.

Little Jean Goes in Search of Buddy Bolden

The old man thought he was safe in his bed in Brentwood with his wife, yet images of his past continued to flood into his mind. He could feel the warmth of Suzette's shoulder and smell her sweet scent as he watched himself in his mind at the La Point Station catching the Yazoo & Mississippi Valley train, then saw the train coasting through the streets of New Orleans and coming to the final stop at the Illinois Central Station at Poydras and Franklin Streets. It was the year 1900, just as Deslonde had said. Jean was thirteen years old. It wasn't that the things he was witnessing were unpleasant. Some of the memories might have been sweet if only he could turn it off, stop the torrent. He was tormented by the thought that Deslonde was behind it all and Deslonde did not exist anywhere but in his mind.

He witnessed himself leaving the train station and entering into the flow of the city, craning his neck in every direction as he shoved through crowded sidewalks, overjoyed to have escaped Pine Grove Planation, to be so close to a new life, so close to Buddy Bolden. Poydras Street was a marvel, lined with buildings of three and four stories with tangles of electric lines crisscrossing overhead and rows of electric street lights. The street vibrated under his feet as an electric streetcar overflowing with riders rumbled through the intersection, young men dangling off the back, clinging to straps with one hand as they smoked and gabbed. A police van sped full bore out of nowhere on Rampart and the traffic in the intersection parted miraculously as the van shot through, bell clanging, causing the horses on Poydras to rear up as the drivers cursed and strained to hold the reins. It was all music to Jean Auger. It was freedom.

The boy conjured the sound of a trombone in his head and in an instant heard it weaving in and out of the street noise, making rhythmic patterns beneath the clatter of the city. He stood on the corner, head tilted back, dust swirling as the trombone pumped and churned. A bass drum joined in, propelling the trombone and Jean tapped a counter rhythm with his foot. He stood among the passersby, his insides shaking like a machine, until the joy of the music made him stagger with laughter. When he regained himself the trombone in his head had stopped, but the drumming only faded then came on stronger. Someone nearby was hitting a bass drum. A snare drum joined in, sizzling a bright military beat that bounced off the buildings causing Jean to turn full circle.

A block away at the intersection of Dryades at Perdido, a group of black men, perhaps a hundred strong, marched down the center of the street beneath an American flag. They slowed in the intersection, moving jauntily in place to the beat of the snare as they closed ranks. Jean rushed towards them among a gang of kids and when they reached the corner everyone scurried into the ranks of the marchers. Jean skipped past the man hauling the American flag and another carrying a banner of blue silk with gold fringe and gold lettering strung from the top of a tall cross shaped pole, *Colored Longshoremen's Protective Union Benevolent Association No. 2 – New Orleans, LA.*

Jean zig zagged through the procession of longshoremen and into the ranks of the brass band marching behind. The musicians wore military hats with the word ONWARD on the front and jackets with rows of brass buttons and plush epaulets. The leader of the band stood to the side holding a cornet. He was a short, light-skinned man with wavy hair sticking out from under his hat.

A boy shouted, "Manuel Perez is the greatest cornet in the world."

"Hell he is," shouted someone else. "King Bolden is the greatest."

"No, it's Perez," came another voice.

Perez walked backwards, facing the band, holding his cornet in his left hand and motioning with his right. He signaled to the Grand Marshall, a tall thin black man wearing a white military uniform with gold stripes on the pants, gold buttons on his coat and gold epaulets on his shoulders. He blew two piercing whistle blasts and the drummers took off as the rest of the band readied their instruments, watching Perez for the cue which he gave with a downward movement of his horn. Everyone blew simultaneously into a blaring military march and stepped in unison. The crowd gasped at the band's precision as scores of children marched mock military struts, following as they moved down Perdido.

The band halted about half a block from Poydras, near the train station, playing *A Long Way To Tipperary* to a slashing up-tempo beat amidst hundreds of people dancing and shouting, until all at once, the music stopped. Perez removed his cap and ran his fingers through his hair, then yelled in Spanish to the bass drummer who began pounding out a staggered beat. Perez calmly placed his hat back on, raised his horn, and in a great, animated gesture, blew.

The band was off on a dime, in unison, Perez swinging his horn as he played, the drummer playing faster and the musicians clicking into the increased tempo. They seemed to rip the music out of the air as the drummers each played a different tempo. Jean danced in a crowd of children, head down, arms up, stepping to every beat, then suddenly stopped and cocked his ears, standing limply amidst the gang of kids. Someone shouted, "Who's playing *Didn't He Ramble*?" and a woman yelled, "look yonder," and pointed past the throng of people filling the street side waiting for the Onward to pass. Everyone turned in a wave, exploding into cheers as the raucous, bittersweet strains of *Didn't He Ramble* rang clear and loud and another brass band, followed by scores of dancing children, swung onto Franklin Street.

"It's the Excelsior," someone shouted. "It's Professor Baquet's band."

The Excelsior moved in loose formation, collars open, jackets off, hats pushed back, blowing like mad for the chaotic rabble of dancers. Professor Baquet walked at the side of the ranks of the Excelsior, carrying a little conductors stick, shaking his head derisively at the band free styling for the dancers. When he noticed the Onward on the street, his head jerked like a lion suddenly aware of an interloper. He signaled the Grand

Marshall whose whistle blast snapped the drummers into a martial beat. The crack of the drums echoed in the street, causing the wild jamming to cease and the Excelsior to ready its horns.

The maze of buildings on Franklin reverberated with booming drums. You could hear Baquet barking at the Excelsior as the musicians tightened ranks and marched directly towards the Onward. The Onward stood its ground, punching out hot ensemble passages as the longshoremen moved out of the line of fire. The bell of Perez's horn, tilted slightly higher than the rest, signaled with subtle swaying movements causing the unit to change sonic directions, slashing into the din of street noise.

Up the street, Professor Baquet nodded to the snare drummer who set off in a rhythm slightly slower than the Onward drummers. The bass drummer jumped in, clenching his jaw as he whipped the drum, followed by the thundering massive brass ensemble. Baquet raised his conductor's stick, slashed the air, and the Excelsior was off marching, each step calibrated to the beat until they came to a sharp stop a few yards from the Onward.

The two bands worked face to face, wailing separate songs, as hundreds of supporters cheered and danced, some dancing to one band, some dancing to the other, some dancing to both, everyone stomping, spinning, dipping, and jumping on the concrete bed of Franklin Street. The two bands played and played, neither missing a beat or a note or loosing focus in the face of the other band's blasting. And almost simultaneously, Perez and Baquet signaled their respective Grand Marshall and each blew the whistle and the bands moved forward into each other's ranks.

The shrill screech of the whistles was lost in the chaos, yet somehow each group responded to the command to march in place within the ranks of the other, playing with impenetrable concentration, chorus after chorus, each unit thrusting blocks of sound at the enemy, brilliantly colored geometric shapes juxtaposed in the air, layer after layer reverberating. The mass of humanity encircling the Onward and the Excelsior became motionless, all the dancers, down to the smallest child, were frozen as the sound became visible, a rainbow of smashed glass spraying from the brass bells and the drums vibrating the breast of every living thing on Franklin.

Then Baquet and Perez must have motioned to their Grand Marshalls and the Grand Marshalls must have blown the signal, because each band suddenly moved off with crisp metallic strides causing gasps and cries from the crowd. The people seemed to exhale collectively as the bands broke away and advanced in opposite directions. After several moments of stunned silence, the crowd awoke, amazed, rising into wild cheering and applause.

Jean's body was released when the bands uncoupled and the space between them opened, exposing the people on the other side of Franklin moving again, countless arms waving, hands gesticulating, torsos twisting and stepping. His eyes fell on two men, stationary on the sidewalk in the center of the animated crowd, motionless amidst the giddy bliss of the people. One of them was dressed in denim overalls soiled with grease and a denim railroad hat. He was short and stocky with a large bushy mustache. The other man was younger and taller and wore white overalls spattered with paint. He carried a bucket in one hand and a canvas tool bag slung over his shoulder. Jean's eyes darted between the two faces as all around people chattered about the meeting of the Onward Brass Band and the Excelsior Brass Band.

"You don't see that too often," someone shouted

"The Onward blinked first."

"No, it sure enough was a draw."

"Like hell, the Excelsior couldn't stand the heat."

Jean's eyes were riveted on the two men conversing across the street as the crowd melted into work-a-day New Orleans. The traffic pushed in from both directions, closing like a curtain as Jean's gaze stopped finally on the face of the younger man. Buddy Bolden. Just like that, Bolden, directly across the street, and just like that, he disappeared behind a wall of horses, wagons, and streetcars. The boy flew into the traffic and when he emerged on the other side, Bolden was there talking to his friend and two others, a man and a woman. He rushed towards Bolden and stopped short, suddenly hesitant, hidden by passersby as Bolden and his friends conversed.

"Buddy, this is Robert Charles," said the man with the mustache. "We was all together back in Mississippi, in Copiah. He's Martha's kin. And this pretty gal is Virginia, Robert's lady friend. Robert, Virginia, this is my old friend Buddy, Buddy Bolden."

"I know Buddy Bolden," said the man. "I've seen Mr. Bolden play his cornet many times. Good to meet you, Mr. Bolden."

"Glad to meet you, Robert." said Bolden. "Call me Buddy."

Bolden smiled, focusing his gaze on the woman.

"Virginia?" he said. "That's a beautiful name. My folks were from Virginia, way back before the war. I never have been there myself, but I understand it is a beautiful location."

"Well, I've heard you play your music, too, Mr. Bolden," said the women.

"Call me Buddy, please," replied Bolden.

"Buddy," repeated the woman. "I've heard you play your cornet, too. Once, on a Sunday afternoon in Morris Park, me and my friend Ernestine happened by, and another time I saw you and some others ride by our house playing on the back of a wagon, advertising something, a dance I think. But, the best time was when I chaperoned a dance for the girls at the Blue Ribbon Social Club, and you and your friends played the music. It was at the Longshoremen's Hall on Jackson Street. You all were very genteel, very respectable."

The woman laughed shyly as Bolden took her hand and lowered his face closer to hers.

"Why, I am truly honored, miss," said Bolden. "You are quite a respectable lady yourself. Where'd you hear me play, Robert? I'll wager it wasn't the Blue Ribbon dance."

"I'd better not say," replied the man, grinning.

Jean stood in the gutter, oblivious to the traffic moving behind him until a voice shouted "Get out of the street you damned fool," and

Bolden glanced towards him then snapped his fingers and pointed at Robert Charles.

"I thought I seen you before, Robert," said Bolden, "It was at Lala's on the waterfront. That's it. You was selling those African newspapers. Going back to Africa and such. You sell a bunch of'm too, don't you? That's what Frankie Dusen says."

"I know Frank real well," said Robert Charles. "We been knowing each other since I come to New Orleans. That's about four years now."

"Dusen said he's been getting his papers from you for a long time," said Bolden. "I didn't know the brother could read till I saw him going over that paper."

"That's Robert for you," said Bolden's friend Silas. "He's trying to take all the colored folks to Africa. I tell him he ought to be making a little money to live on but he don't hear nothing I say."

Robert Charles listened silently to his friends words, smiling patiently then sighing as if he'd heard them many times before.

"I sure enough can understand a man wanting to leave this place," said Bolden.

"Oh, I understand it all right," said the friend. "Who wouldn't? I had it all my life and I still get it from time to time. Just to get out, leave here for anyplace there ain't no white man. This ain't no way to live, the way things are. But, I worked too damned hard to leave what little I got to the white man. I gave too much as it is. This place is as much mine as his, the way I see it; even more mine if you think about it. Our folks did all the work building it. All the white man done was ride on our backs. They'll bury me here. I'd just as soon send the white man back to Europe. Besides, you see in the papers all the time. The white man's swarming all over Africa like the damned boll weevil. You go over there you'll be dealing with the same man. At least here we got our folks and we know the territory."

Bolden looked at Robert Charles expectantly.

"Well, brother? You're the man to answer ol' Silas, ain't you? What do you say?"

"Oh, he don't never try to convince folks who don't already see it like he does," said Silas. "That's one thing I'll give him. He goes straight to them agrees with him. Maybe they never even heard nothing about going to Africa before they see Robert, but they'll go for the idea when they do. Robert can pick'm out of a crowd."

Robert Charles smiled and winked at Bolden.

"That ain't so," he said. "I don't know what folks are thinking. It's just there's enough of our people who see things the same that I don't need to convince no one. I just find the folks who want to go and help them out."

"Ain't nothing wrong with helping folks," said Bolden. "Ain't that right Miss Virginia?"

"Oh no, nothing wrong with helping folks," said the woman. "That's the Lord's work."

"Will you go to Africa with Brother Robert when the day comes?" said Bolden.

"We don't want to open that can of worms," said Silas, turning sideways and motioning with his eyes for Bolden to cease. Then Silas continued speaking as if to change the subject.

"You know they're trying to bar us from the street cars again? The city couldn't do it last time cause the railroad companies said it would be too much trouble figuring out who was colored and who was white. Now they're trying to pass a law in the state saying we got to ride in a separate car with a star on the side of it."

"I heard something about it," said Bolden, "I don't ride the cars myself."

"That ain't the point, Buddy," said Silas. "It's one thing after the next. They're trying to put us back in slavery one law at a time."

"I don't know, Silas," said Bolden.

"Don't know?" said Robert Charles smiling. "They already stole our right to the vote, and it ain't just in Louisiana. They done it in Mississippi. They're doing it in all the rebel states. Legal disfranchisement, they call it. They went and rewrote their constitution so they could say it was all legal."

The woman placed her hands on Robert's forearms and tugged playfully.

"Now you men," she said. "We just met Buddy and already you all talking about serious things, right out in public where anyone can hear you."

"I don't much care who hears me," said Robert Charles.

"Hey Robert," said Bolden, hoisting his canvas tool bag onto his shoulder. "You know the Big 25s club? Me and my boys gonna be working over there for the next few nights. C'mon down if you get the chance."

A streetcar bell hit rapid-fire strikes as the irritated motorman cursed at the jam of wagons in the middle of Franklin, forcing them to the side. Suddenly Jean was surrounded by wagons, spooked horses and angry drivers. He cowered and scrambled, shielding his head as a horse reared back. He ran down Franklin next to the trolley, finally dashing through an opening to the sidewalk. When he looked back to where Bolden had stood, he was gone. Only Buddy's friends were there. Bolden had vanished.

The boy wandered the streets, tired and hungry, wondering what his next move would be. How would he ever find Buddy Bolden a second time? He had a backup plan that could buy him time if the need arose. He had a sister in the city. Her name was Celine. He could go to her house and stay the night, rest and make his final break the next day. The plan was risky. If Celine found out he'd run away she would surely tell his uncle and force Jean to return to Pine Grove. He halted in front of an alley between two brick buildings, unsure of which direction to go, when he heard men talking and someone tuning a guitar. After several moments, he walked back between the buildings.

The men were at the end of the alley amidst stacks of crates and empty barrels. They looked like a couple of farm hands with worn, dusty overalls, soiled shirts, and beat-up shoes. The older of the two appeared to be in his thirties. He sat on a box, bent over a guitar, examining the strings, wiping them gently with a handkerchief. He was a small framed man, almost petit, yet solid and wiry. His skin was copper colored and his light brown hair was parted to the side and combed over into a mass of curls. His eyes were black and his face long and angular. The other man appeared to be a teenager. He was tall and lanky with a black mustache that hadn't yet had its first shave.

"Pull up a box, Larry," said the older man. "And I'll show you what you been bother'n me to show you."

"You made me wait while you drunk up what money we made in that saloon," replied the young man. "Who ever heard of salooning first thing in the morning? You drunk, Zed Floyd. You drunk and we broke."

"I can't teach you how to get along if things is too easy," said Floyd.

"How you reckon things is easy?" replied Larry.

"We ain't in Texas," said Floyd, "we in the city, New Orleans, and New Orleans ain't Texas, no way."

"You drunk, Zed Floyd," replied Larry.

"You ain't seen me drunk," said Floyd.

The older man leaned over his guitar, swaying slightly, and began to play. Jean listened silently, unnoticed as the man sang. At first his voice was more of a moan than a song and the intensity of it startled Jean. Then the moan became words, nasal and shrill, grotesque over the strange harp like ringing of the guitar.

Have you heard the story, how they do in Brazos Bottom? sang Floyd.

"What the hell you doing, old man!" said Larry.

Floyd answered with a verse.

Have you heard tell, way they do in Brazos Bottom?

He hesitated and strummed a mess of disparate chords, then slid back into the beat.

I heard tell, if a nigger sass a white man,
There'll be hell to pay, dear Lord, there'll be hell to pay

"Lower your voice, don't sing that shit!" said Larry.

They shoot'm and they hang'm,
Sure as that morning sun,
They cut'm and they burn'm,
In Brazos, that's how it's done . . .

If the nigger got some kin,

They best pack up and run . . . that's what your mamma said," said Floyd. "That's why she let you come on the road with me."

Larry stood with his head down, holding a guitar by the neck. The man's words frightened Jean and he nervously checked the entrance to the alley.

If folks don't move fast, they do the deal again," sang the man.

If you don't get out quick, they'll do it all again,

Don't you know, in Brazos, Texas,

They kill children, right along with the men.

"You shouldn't do like that, Zed," said the young man. "Why you talk like that?"

"Ain't no other way to tell the story," said Floyd.

"You ain't got to tell no story," said Larry.

Zed Floyd squinted into the bright light at the end of the alley where Jean stood against the building.

"Can't nobody hear, Larry," said Floyd, "cept this fine young New Orleans boy here and he ain't a white man, he don't care . . . you ain't white are you boy? You ain't afraid to hear what this old black songster got to say, are you?"

Jean moved past the younger man and stood before Floyd.

"I play trombone myself," he said.

"Ya don't say," said Floyd.

"Yes sir, got my own outfit out in the country, over to LaPointe out in St. John's Parish. We call ourselves the Pine Grove Orchestra."

"Orchestra? You don't say. That sounds mighty nice."

"Yes sir," said Jean. "I'm in the city on business. I'm looking for Buddy Bolden."

"Buddy who?" said Floyd.

"Bolden, Buddy Bolden," replied Jean. "He plays cornet, and Frankie Dusen, he's a trombone man iike I am. Only older."

Floyd laughed and slapped the front of his guitar.

"Where's your horn at?" he asked.

"I left it back home when I run away," said Jean. "Couldn't haul it on the road cause everyone would know I was leaving. Besides, it was old and busted up. I'm buying me a brand new horn."

"Brand new horn?" said Floyd. "You must be doing pretty good."

"We do alright," replied Jean.

"That's real fine," said Floyd. "Now, my young fellow musicianer, you want to hear a real Mississippi songster pick and sing? Course you do. I been all over every state in the south cept Arkansas and Tennessee and I ain't never seen a worse hellhole than Texas."

The man clenched his teeth and spit and pulled a bottle from his overall pocket and drank, placing the bottle carefully on a crate next to where he sat. He grinned at Jean and winked but his eyes seemed to look through Jean and the boy could see that the man was drunk.

"Why, we are fresh from Brazos, Texas, and the meanest foulest killings you ever seen. June 4, 1900 is a day I'll pray to forget, an entire family this time, the Cabannis family, poor black folks, killed to the last of'm, man, woman, and child, just like the song say. Damnit Larry, stop jumping all around. Can't nobody hear, peoples too far off."

"Hell they are, Zed" pleaded Larry, "why you making fun like that? It's the liquor making you say those things. It ain't nothing but mean, Zed. We trying to escape it and you bringing it right along with us."

"Only one way to leave it behind," said Floyd, "You got to let the music fix this living hell into joy, even if it's bitter and tough, even if it burn like they burned them poor folks."

Floyd picked up the bottle, drained it, and lofted it against the brick wall. Jean giggled at the explosion of glass. He watched as Zed closed his eyes tightly, as if resisting physical pain, bent over his instrument and played.

Baby girl's name was Cute, that's what her father say,
White man told her father, Lord's gonna take your child away,
They put a rope around her neck for all the town to see,
You shoulda heard her papa cry, see his child swing that tree.

"Oh my, good god," cried Larry. "Zed, if you don't quit I'm walking off right now, I swear it."

"Walk off?" said Floyd. "After you begged me to show you how to play guitar, teach you the ways of the road? Anyway, where you gonna walk off too? Back to Texas?"

Floyd swung around towards Jean.

"Hey, my little trombone man, I apologize for my inhospitable companion here. His name is Larry Abrams, and me, I'm none other than Zed Floyd, Mississippi songster."

Jean extended his hand and Zed grasped it and the two shook heartily.

"Very glad to meet you," said Jean, "you sure do play fine guitar and you sing real nice too."

"C'mon Larry," said Floyd, "move your hands on that guitar, show this young fella what I taught you."

"No Zed, we got to keep moving."

Larry bent forward, thrusting his head between Jean's eyes and Zed's hands on the guitar.

"Hey you, boy, we got to go. We got to keep moving. We can't spend no time here. Go on away from here and leave us be."

Jean jerked his head back to the guitar, as though what Floyd said was true and the music would silence Larry's fears, the music would be all that mattered if he would only play.

"Hey boy, you gonna bring the white man down on us," said Larry, his voice choked. "It ain't safe nowhere."

He leaned towards Jean, screwing his face up and speaking in a whisper.

"See, Zed ain't lying bout what happened back in Texas."

Larry leaned over and twisted his neck towards Jean, pushing his face up close. His eyes were round with terror and his face glistened with sweat.

"Boy!" said Floyd, "Shut your god damned mouth and pick up your guitar. Let the song make your mind right. That's the way it works, ain't that right trombone man? Now Larry, pick up your god damned guitar."

"I don't think so, Zed," said Larry, quietly, "look like to me we got nothing we can do but keep moving."

"Keep moving," said Floyd, "that's right, keep moving. It's about time we introduced our musical wares to the good folks of New Orleans. C'mon Larry, put that guitar strap around your neck and quit dragging it. Let's go make some money. I may want to eat later on and I sure as hell will want a drink."

Floyd staggered as he rose, guitar strung around his neck and at the ready and walked to the end of the alley and out into the blinding brightness of Rampart Street with Jean on his heels and Larry walking several paces behind. Out in the full daylight, Floyd suddenly appeared sober as he strode confidently down the side of the street. He wove his way through a traffic jam of wagons and buggies, moving blithely past the nervous horses and irate drivers, pausing as a streetcar rolled by with bells clanging, then crossed, followed by the two boys.

Jean nearly lost sight of Floyd to avoid getting run down by a wagon. When he looked after the two, he saw Larry hustling down Rampart and hurried after him. He spotted Floyd finally come to a stop in front of a store. Bagnetto's Grocery and Saloon appeared to be closed for business. Floyd stepped onto the sidewalk beneath the awning and surveyed the street, looking about for a place to set up. He moved just off an alley between Bagnetto's and the Shanghai Chinese restaurant.

"You sure we be alright here?" said Larry. "Looks like a general goods store or something . . . I don't know Zed, what if they think we stealin?"

"Let's play some music," said Floyd, "If we playing, we ain't stealin. There's money to be made here. I'm tired of walking. Only so far and so long I can run."

Floyd grabbed a crate and positioned it with his back against the building and a full view of the street in both directions. He bent over his instrument and began turning the keys and plucking the strings. Jean hoisted himself onto a barrel in front of Bagnetto's, dangling his legs and grinning in anticipation as Larry rooted about among the stacks of crates just inside the alley for one sturdy enough to sit on.

"Hey you there. You darkies there, stop what you're doing."

Zed Floyd's head dropped between his shoulders, but in an instant he was up, grabbing Larry by the arm. A white man was scurrying across Rampart Street, dodging traffic as he rushed at the two musicians.

"You boys are obstructing traffic and causing a nuisance," he shouted. "I ought to drag you both to the precinct and teach you what we do to vagrants in New Orleans."

The man wore a long waxed mustache, the two points curving upward parallel to the side of his face. The hair on his head was sparse and what there was of it was oiled and combed straight back. He bounded forward waving a police badge.

"We sorry boss," said Floyd, "we jess po'niggahs, din't mean no harm."

The policeman stopped several feet away, admonishing Floyd and Abrams as they quickly backed down the street. He stepped onto the sidewalk in front of the saloon shouting, swinging his arms, drawing back his foot as if to kick, but the two men had moved off and were already disappearing into the bustle of Rampart. The policeman chuckled and stepped under the awning, wiping his balding pate with a handkerchief, finally noticing Jean sitting on the barrel watching him.

"Why do you associate with blacks?" he said in French and Jean replied in French, "I was here when they came along."

Then the policeman spoke in English.

"Does your mother know you sit on the street with vagrant niggers? You people say you ain't niggers, but you can't help acting like them, can you? Stupid little mulatto, a bit of French don't make you white. Move on before I kick some sense into you."

Jean hopped off the barrel and as he hit the wooden walk his trousers jingled with a few coins. The policeman eyed the boy's pockets.

"What do you have there?" he said. "I believe I've stumbled onto a burglary, haven't I? You had those blacks make a commotion while you robbed the shop. Stay still, I say. Don't move. Empty those pockets and place the money on the barrel. Do as I say or I'll shoot you dead."

Jean hesitated and the cop cursed him, "damn you, I'll see for my-self." As he reached out to thrust his hand inside Jean's pocket, a stout, dark haired man appeared on the sidewalk and proceeded to unlock the door to the grocery as he glared angrily at the policeman.

"Hey Trenchard, you here to suck my blood?" he said.

The policeman yanked his hand away from Jean's pocket.

"Ah, Bagnetto," he said.

"No, Trenchard," said the man. "I told you already I will not pay. I pay the precinct, I pay your god-damned superiors, those thieves, not you Trenchard. I pay them to protect me from scum like you."

"Watch what you say, Dago," shouted Trenchard. "Whatcha what you say or I killa you. I've been checking on you. You make damned good money here, enough that you can spare a bit more to stay on my good side."

The man smirked and stood facing the cop.

"I ask about you, too, Officer Trenchard," he said. "You was kicked off the force for stealing money from shopkeepers. Ain't that right? And now you come back and you don't learn nothing. What if I tell your Captain Day what you do?"

Trenchard looked at Bagnetto and scratched his head as Jean took off across Rampart, running furiously in the direction of Canal Street.

"Lucky for you, Dago," shouted Trenchard, "This is official duty. That boy was attempting to rob your store, you ungrateful Sicilian nigger. I'll be back Bagnetto."

"To hell with you, Trenchard," shouted Bagnetto. "They'll throw you off the force for good this time."

Jean fled, hugging close to the buildings and running with all his might. The cop was a madman. He wanted Jean's money and God knows what else. He might even kill Jean. There was no doubt about it. The boy ran for blocks, not letting up until miraculously he came upon Canal Street. The great thoroughfare appeared suddenly, opening up all at once. He must have lost the cop, the way he shielded himself from view, moving through the traffic, using the crowd as cover, all the while staring wide eyed at the city. There were four lanes of trolley tracks running down Canal Street and on either side of the tracks were wide streets paved with huge granite blocks, and hundreds of wagons, buggies, and carts moving in a heavy stream in both directions. There were towering poles of electric lines strung as far as Jean could see, feeding the streetcars and street lights and all the lights in the countless buildings lining the street like canyon walls. Towards the great river, the Mississippi, a huge electrical tower straddled Canal Street with arches big enough for four streetcars to pass beneath. There were ornate buildings of brick and stone and concrete, four, five, six stories high, and commercial signs plastered everywhere, and people, more people than Jean had ever seen at one time, lingering, rushing, strolling, hurrying about, standing in bunches at intersections and crowding sidewalks. He headed down Canal, jumping from sidewalk to street to sidewalk, jostling past people, twisting his neck to see the top of the massive department store, Maison Blanche. The building was six stories high, taking up the entire block, each story with a façade of white columns and archways, all leading to a massive cupola topped by a huge American flag.

Jean was swallowed by a crowd of pedestrians crossing Burgundy Street and by chance looked back to the far side of Canal to the cop who had chased him. Trenchard turned in a circle, blocking the sun from his eyes with his hand and squinting into the endless procession of people. Jean huddled close to the buildings, trying to disappear into the crowd, hurrying towards the huge sign for *Werlein's Music Store* mounted two stories high, a half a block away. Trenchard kept pace on the opposite side of the street, finally stepping into the gutter and charging through the traffic as though he'd spotted Jean. Jean flew past Werlein's and kept running for three blocks to the corner of Franklin Street and Canal. At the intersection, two streetcars passed in opposite directions and Trenchard disappeared from sight. Jean ran behind one of the streetcars as it turned onto Franklin, running beside the car for half a block before ducking behind a wagon parked on the side of the street.

The buildings on Franklin Street were different from great multi-storied commercial edifices of Canal. Instead, there were rows mansions and one and two story buildings with awnings over the banquette and wrought iron-balconies fronting shuttered doors on the upper floors and the swinging doors of saloons on the lower level. Two deliverymen, unloading barrels of beer from the wagon, stopped to rest after lowering a full keg onto the ground, just as Jean appeared.

"Look a dere, Pat," said one of the men, "dey're getting younger everyday, ain't dey? This one should be in short pants, not roaming the red light district."

"You've no place here, son," said the other. "There's nothing here but whorehouses, saloons, and gambling dens, and just a boy, my god John, he's just a child. Son, when you turned off Canal you entered the district."

"As if he didn't know, Pat," said the first man, wiping his face with a dirty rag. "And look at'm panting like a race horse and hiding behind our wagon. It's the law he's running from, Pat, no doubt about that."

"Don't be so hard on the boy, John. Remember, Mr. Anderson started as a lad running love letters and dope to whores and today he's the biggest pimp in the district and an alderman to boot."

"Watch your tongue, Pat, or you'll have more trouble than you want."

"The lad could be another Tom Anderson for all we know. I reckon we should call'm mister or sir."

"Like hell, go along there boy or I'll call the law on you, get on there."

Jean bolted, looking over his shoulder as he ran and saw no sign of the mad cop Trenchard. He slowed at Franklin and Customhouse and stood amidst the trolley tracks in the center of the intersection. There were saloons all around. He read the names of the establishments, The 28s, The Pig Ankle, Shoto's Cabaret, and Big 25s, the place Bolden told the man Robert Charles that his band would be playing the next few nights.

The sound of a piano drifted over the street, odd dreamy notes, released and left to float like bits of ice suspended in air, alone, singular, not strung together by rhythm but by the lingering ringing of the tones melting softly into space. Then there were wild chords, loud, strange notes, sad and weird. Jean couldn't immediately tell where the music was coming from. The front doors of several saloons were wide open and music crawled over the street like smoke. He turned in a circle, trying to discern the source of the bizarre sound as the pianist struck the keys with tremendous force, powerful chords, deep and dark, yet with absolute delicacy and restraint. Perfect clusters of crystal notes ascended and descended irresistibly outward. Jean darted diagonally across the intersection to the entrance of Shoto's Cabaret and crouched under the swinging doors.

In the center of a large room was a piano between two large wooden beams and the pianist seated on the bench next to his neatly folded jacket, his collar open and his sleeves rolled up. He was a black man with a hairline nearly at the top of his head, bulging eyes and a delicate frame. He appeared dainty at the keyboards, yet struck the keys with amazing force.

A bald, heavy-set white man with a snow white mustache sat at a table just to the right of the piano with two white women, one blonde and the other brunette. The women were dressed in fancy gowns and sported shiny jewelry although they appeared exhausted as if they hadn't slept the night before. Their hair, held on the top of their heads by pins and combs had come loose in spots and both were barefooted, their shoes hanging on the back of the chairs. The man had also apparently been well dressed at some point. Now his clothing was in disarray; his white shirt sweat stained and open to his stomach and his tie hanging untied around his neck. His eyes were closed and his head swung in a circular movement as the women watched, circling their heads in anticipation, until finally the man fell forward, landing on his face on the tabletop with a thud.

"Thank gawd he's finally out!" said the blonde.

The brunette gestured to the pianist.

"We never would have left Lulu's parlor, if he wasn't passing out those hundreds, eh Tony."

The blonde dragged herself to her feet.

"What time did we leave the house?" she asked.

"I dunno," said the brunette, "Hey Tony, it's been light for hours, let's get outa here"

"Yeah, let's get the hell outa heah," said the blonde, "thank gawd we can finally get some shut eye."

The drunk man snorted terribly, making a strange whinnying sound before gurgling in a long sputtering exhale. The two put on their shoes and buttoned up as the blonde winked and raised her index finger to her lips and flashed her eyes towards the door. The pianist, disregarding the sign to keep quiet, swept his hands along the keyboard in a wild cadenza, shooting out clusters of notes, a great classical barrage cascading into raucous barrelhouse and zany ragtime, then bunches of notes falling like rain showers, finally crashing into huge pounding blocks of sound, protracted thunder, the pianist's head nearly touching the backs of his hands as he came down again and again, finally thrusting himself back onto the bench, his hands flying upward as though they would have kept going if they hadn't been attached to his arms, as he rose, pushing the bench away with the back of his legs.

"My gawd, Tony," said the blonde, "even after the night we had, you make the hair on my arms stand up."

The pianist smiled demurely and wearily wiped his brow with a silk handkerchief. He squinted and shielded his eyes as he looked out into the bright sunlight streaming in from the street. Jean's head was wedged between the swinging doors like a gaping mask or a stuffed head and the pianist burst into giggles. The two women looked at the pianist, following his eyes to the door and erupted into laughter. The pianist held his hand over his mouth as he laughed. Jean took their mirth as an invitation to enter, but before he could start forward he was thrust into the saloon by a blow from behind and crashed onto the dirty saw-dusted floor. He looked back into the light at the black shadow of Trenchard, fists clenched, the ends of his handlebar mustache quivering. He stood over Jean, reared his leg and kicked him in the thigh with full force.

"God-damned thug," yelled Trenchard, "first I catch you in the act of committing a burglary with two nigger accomplices, then you flee the scene of a crime with your pockets full of stolen money, and now I got you laying out in a saloon with whores."

Trenchard drew back and kicked Jean again with the tip of his boot and Jean cried out and clutched his side.

"You'll do time in the workhouse, I swear it," said Trenchard. "Magistrate Baker shows no mercy to your kind. You'll be lucky to live through what's in store for you. Get up and empty those pockets."

A voice came from behind the bar.

"Hey Trenchard, you old grafter. I ain't seen you since you was tossed off the force in 96 for putting the squeeze on shopkeepers."

Trenchard brought his cocked leg to rest, straddling Jean, looking at the bartender behind the bar casually drying shot glasses with a towel.

"I beg your pardon, sir," said Trenchard, stepping towards the bar, "I was reinstated last year. I am a patrolman in good standing now. Who might I have the pleasure of speaking with?"

Jean rolled beneath the swinging doors and out onto the sidewalk and was up and gone in a flash like a crazed animal, sprinting with all his strength down the center of the street next to the trolley tracks, through intersections, turning after two blocks onto Conti Street, not lessoning his pace for five blocks, finally reaching a run-down, deserted section of Robertson Street. He stumbled in a pothole in the cobblestone and fell forward, skidding on his belly for several yards and coming to a stop against the front steps of a dilapidated old wooden building. He crawled onto the broken down steps of the ramshackle structure, curled into a ball as small as he could, and sobbed.

He lay in the sun for an hour, gradually uncurling, lying limply on the wooden box steps, lulled by the heat, exhausted by the release of sorrow. His knees were stiff and caked with blood and his right thigh and ribs throbbed. He lay on his back dozing, prostrate under the sun. The feeling of intense warmth on his breast was a comfort, a soporific against the abject terror inflicted by Trenchard. The din of the city was a distant, muffled drone, hypnotizing as Jean lay still, momentarily forgetting the man's incongruous hatred until he heard a voice.

"What the hell ya do'in this neighborhood, kid? Doncha know where ya are? Dese are the lowest of the low live in dem shacks, poor nigger whores, dope fiends. Twenty-five cent cribs dey call'm. You'll get killed on a lark. Dere ain't nothing here but death and disease. Go on over to Conti. The cribs dere are a dollar a throw, but you'll be better off."

A man stood clinging to a streetlight and weaving drunkenly, staring as Jean climbed to his feet. He took a bottle from his pocket and drank a long hard swallow.

"A nice Irish boy like you shouldn't be whore'n anyways," he said. "Why, you should be wearing short pants, fa Christ's sake." Jean listened impassively, then limped slowly off as the man continued to talk. "But den agin, I had me first piece when I was still in short pants . . ."

Jean limped over broken cobblestones, passing a vast cemetery behind a wrought iron fence, a city of white washed tombs and burial vaults, a sea of crucifixes, statues, and Doric columns shimmering in the sun. At the corner of Rampart Street and St. Louis, he crossed into the French Quarter, Vieu Carre, the old city, silent and bleached white under relentless sun. You could hear Canal Street buzzing in the distance. He wandered aimlessly for what seemed like hours. He couldn't have found his sister's house if he'd wanted too. He reminded himself over and over that he was too old to cry. That he must find Buddy or all was lost. Finally he arrived back at Canal Street, the far end near the river and the great electrical tower he'd seen from blocks away when he fled for his life from the mad cop.

As Jean sprinted across Canal, he spotted a large congregation of black people moving slowly behind a brass band onto St. Charles Street. The band's instruments gleamed in the sun. It was like a scene from a dime novel about soldiers in Indian Territory, lost until a troop of cavalry suddenly appears on the horizon charging to the rescue, only these were black cavalry with Indians in their ranks and the hostiles were whites. Jean's heart sang at the sight as he rushed after them. It was a funeral procession. He ran to the front where the band walked in loose formation, instruments at the rest. He shouted, "Who are they?" and a black man yelled back, "It's the Pickwick Brass Band. Can't you see ol'Deuce Manetta up there, plain as day?"

Tears flooded his face as he hooted and hopped about, shouting and cheering and waving his arms. The Pickwick Brass Band was an oasis. Jean was rescued. The mourners were dressed so fine. What joy, proclaiming to the world the dignity, the strength, the accomplishments of the beloved deceased. The musicians were all black men, skilled, learned, refined. They made martial music that armies might follow. He trailed along, swinging his arms, holding his head up, bouncing next to the band as though they were working at full tilt, but they were strangely quiet as the parade moved on St. Charles and halted at Poydras in the middle of the intersection. The musicians weren't playing, not even the drummers. It was the sight of them that enthralled Jean. After several minutes, bunches of pedestrians began growing impatient at the large crowd standing stationary in a busy street and some cursed and shouted at the mourners. A white man standing close to Jean climbed the base of a streetlight above the heads of the crowd and shook his fist, shouting "move, niggers." Jean fled into the ranks of the brass band. The musicians were formed into a circle, each man scanning the crowd as Jean huddled among them and the mob of pedestrians grew louder and more hostile.

"Look yonder," said the bass drummer, pointing his mallet into the mob. "There they are. Look at those sons of bitches with them sticks."

"Where?" said the tuba player.

"Yonder," repeated the drummer, pointing his mallet to the rear of the crowd at a handful of men shadowing the parade, clutching wooden bats at their sides.

Jean looked back toward the procession of mourners at four police officers in the middle of the street speaking with three black men in suits and the grand marshal of the brass band.

"You see those low down Mick bastards up there," said a heavy set black man, sweat pouring off his face and soaking his neatly buttoned white shirt. "You can see the clubs plain as day. We are peaceful marchers, sending our brother to rest. They keep swinging them clubs close like they been doing and they'll be more than one funeral."

"Now, first off, my name is Flynn," said one of the officers, "and I don't need no darky telling me how to do my job. Dem men ain't bodder'in no one far as I can see. And I don't like you threaten'n me nedder."

Jean watched the men arguing as some of the people flooding the side of the street screamed at the people in the funeral parade until a streetcar lumbered onto St. Charles causing hordes of onlookers to move off the tracks and into the ranks of the marchers. There was pushing and shouting and finally the police officer hit the heavy set black man with a club. At the crack of the stick against the man's skull there was a collective gasp and shouts of disapproval from the mourners and cheers from the crowd of whites as the man fell heavily onto the pavement of St. Charles Street. Jean ran from the ranks of the Pickwick Brass Band, pushing through a rush of white pedestrians shoving forward for a better look at the action. He hurried to the side of the road, moving quickly away beneath the tall cypress trees lining St. Charles. The thud of the policeman's stick on the man's head sounded over and over in his mind as he walked, fast and furiously. He became frightened at the sight of a white man coming towards him on the sidewalk and crossed to the other side of St. Charles and passed back over after the man had gone by. He turned into the uptown neighborhood on First Street, consumed with the sound of the policeman's stick on the man's head. He wept and moaned like the little boy he was, unconcerned by the passersby staring. He'd seen the men arguing. The heavy set black man wore a dark suit and a white shirt. He must have been a preacher or someone respectable. You have to work hard to have nice clothes. You have to be steady and faithful to have so many friends, to pay respects to a dead friend, to hire a brass band to lead hundreds of mourners. The dead man must have been somebody too, to have such a grand funeral and the heavy set black man must be somebody to be the friend of such a great man and still his skull was cracked by a club and the man fell like a stone on the street.

Jean walked aimlessly down the unpaved roadbed of First Street, carefully stepping over deep ruts carved into the dried earth by generations of horse drawn wagons. His mind was blank, numbed by the terror of the great city, his face tear stained and his knees caked with blood. The street was nearly deserted and peaceful compared to the chaos of Canal Street, until a sound arose faintly in the distance as though carried by a breeze. It was barely perceptible until a pattern emerged, growing more distinct and steady. At first it was like the pistons of some great machine far off in the city, churning incessantly, then the space between each machine thrust opened into lilting echoes like an army marching. It grew louder as Jean walked on, causing chills to run down his back. Voices could be discerned, of many people, swelling like deep water rushing to the surface and hands clapping in unison. Everything seems to come from a small wood-framed church directly in Jean's path a few blocks away. On the roadside, standing perpendicular to the building was a sign, *First Street Baptist Church.*

"It ain't Sunday," said Jean. "It must be choir practice. God damn, what a sound."

He reached the church and nestled onto a patch of soft grass under the shade of a large hedge on the opposite side of the street. He sat on crossed legs and rocked back and forth as inside the church a woman preached and shouted, clapping over a chorus of singers. She slapped her hands together rapidly and sang, slowly and deliberately. *Jesus is real to me.* On the next chorus the congregation joined, singing, *Jesus is real to me.* The voices of women predominated as the sound of a piano, snare drum and all the feet in the church beat a steady rhythm, easy and calm, yet containing so much tension Jean twitched beneath the hedge in excruciating anticipation.

He is real to me, sang the collective voices and the woman replied, *So many people doubt him,*

I can't live without him,
That is why, I love him so, and the congregation sang,
Jesus is real to me, and the woman sang,
In the morning, and the congregation came back thundering,
Jesus is real to me.

The piano rang onto First Street as a million hands clapped and a hundred million souls joyously shouted *Power,* and the woman shouted above it all as the power pulled Jean off the ground and made him dance on the grass at the side of the road. A buggy hauled by a scrawny mule rolled by and the white man driving looked at Jean and smiled, bobbing his head to the music and shaking the reigns, trying to stir the old animal to move faster. Jean held his arms out like wings, turning in a circle, and when the church came around again the front doors burst open and there was Buddy Bolden. Jean dropped to his knees, his arms stretched out as if beholding a miracle as Bolden descended the wooden steps of the church with a woman on either arm, one gray haired and buxom and the other young and pretty, riding out the double doors on the crest of the huge ocean of sound.

"Holy Jesus, its Buddy," shouted Jean, "there he is, its Buddy Bolden."

Bolden flew down the street, stepping and twisting, propelled by the music, the two women hanging onto his arms for all they were worth.

Jean jumped to his feet and charged down the grassy roadside, but Bolden and the two women seemed to be floating on air, speeding away, as Jean yelled after them.

"Buddy Bolden, Buddy, hey Buddy stop, please stop."

The thunderous shouts of the congregation drowned out Jean's voice as Bolden turned the corner. He looked back and saw Jean following, beseeching him to stop, but showed no sign of recognition and turned away. Jean ran after him, pumping his arms, his feet barely touching the ground, yet when he reached the corner, Buddy and the two women were gone. The street was deserted except for the back of a buggy moving off and away in a cloud of dust. It looked like the buggy was flying off to heaven, leaving Jean behind in hell.

"I let him get away," he whispered. "I might be dead before I find him again, mean as this town is. What will happen?"

Then the boy remembered what Bolden had said to the man, Robert Charles. Jean snapped his fingers.

"Big 25s," he said.

Friday, August 13, 1965

Nieting didn't sleep until after dawn on Friday morning and what sleep he did get was riddled with dreams of his mother. The visions of her vanished when he awoke in the early afternoon, yet her presence clung to his consciousness like the stink of whiskey clings to the flesh of a drunkard. The eruption of insanity the previous night had not brought catharsis, only a deepening of confusion, an opening of a vast abyss of lacerations. He'd awakened with his senses impaired, with a hangover of sorts, the image of his mother lingering behind a wall in his mind, undeniably present, nearly audible, as though left alone behind a closed door. Yet, there was no time for such thoughts. The task of his life was to recover Buddy Bolden's lost song, to free Robert Charles from the racist prison of obscurity. There was much work to be done. He was to meet Kid Auger at Disneyland in less than two hours.

When he stepped onto the balcony outside the door to his room into the sun, four women were cleaning the next unit where the whore had been with her johns. The women looked at Nieting with disgust, shaking their heads and chattering in Spanish. One of them held her nose to the side, gripping a bloody sheet at arm's length as she stuffed it into a plastic bag. Nieting noticed the bed and the center of the mattress stained red and fled down the stairway to his car. The eastern sky where the San Gabriel Mountains had been was shrouded in a thick gray curtain and the air smelled of smoke. He rolled up the windows, started the car and pulled into the east bound lane of Imperial Highway. He clicked on the car radio.

A voice came on singing, gravelly yet good natured. *Well hello Dolly . . . .*

"God damn it, Louis," said Nieting. "Why do you perform this type of material? Vomit. Absolute vomit."

Nieting slapped the radio off. His heart sank.

"Louis Armstrong," he said. "What a loss. He is precisely the opposite of Kid Auger. Auger goes to an extreme that turns the mind inside out, threatens to obliterate one's everyday perceptions, exposes the bourgeoisie weltanschauung as a sputtering ghost ship. Armstrong has chosen another path, diametrically opposed to revolutionary consciousness. He is a reactionary, a pandering, obsequious Uncle Tom. What a terrible loss."

"Valentin, stop assaulting Louis, will you?"

It was a man's voice interrupting right on the heels of his rant. The words were muffled, buried within the rattling stream of freeway noise, nearly unintelligible yet somehow piercing. Nieting punched at the radio dial and Armstrong came back. *It's so nice to have you back where you be . . .* He hit it again and Armstrong shut up like he'd been slapped in the face. The voice returned, stern and annoyed.

"What a loss? You never had Armstrong to loose, did you?"

Nieting jumped and the car swerved as he locked eyes with a man in his rear view mirror. He was sprawled back there, legs crossed, head tilted forward, watching Nieting and grinning. It was his father, Emil. Nieting arms jerked and he nearly lost control of the car as horns screamed past and disappeared into the haze. A pick-up truck driven by a young woman passed Nieting on the right. He saw her with a quick side glance thrusting her middle finger up and mouthing *asshole.* Nieting turned fully around and looked Emil in the face.

"Father," he shouted, spinning back towards the road, clutching the wheel, struggling to control of the car.

"Father!"

"Maintain yourself, Valentin," said Emil "Be calm, but, please do tell me, what do you expect from Mr. Armstrong? Can't you allow him the privilege of making a few pennies before he dies? You'd feel better, I suppose, if he left this world pure and impoverished so you could revere him without complications."

"Father," shouted Nieting. "Father."

"Straighten up, Valentin," said Emil. "Get hold of yourself and answer the question. Why do you insist that Mr. Armstrong suffer poverty?"

"That isn't so, father," said Nieting. "I want him to tell the truth. I want the truth. I demand it. I reject the selling of lies. I despise the subversion of genuine human feelings and desires."

Emil dusted the sleeves of his coat and smoothed the lapels. "That's all well and good, Valentin," he said. "You know, it isn't your intentions that I find questionable. The prominence of desperation in your thought trivializes your conclusions. I'm not speaking of passion, I'm referring to disintegration. You are an overloaded electric wire, Valentin. I can almost hear you crackling. I do smell smoke, anyway, your search for this damned song is polluted with a morbid subjectivity. One wonders what it is you're really after."

Nieting was stunned, flabbergasted, amazed, speechless. How could anyone, let alone his dead father, say such things? Question his methodology and even his integrity? The blatant inaccuracy and extreme bad faith were incomprehensible, far more unreal than the fact that his dead father was sitting behind him in a car on the freeway in Los Angeles, so close that he could smell his breath.

A line of military trucks painted in camouflage in the north bound lane of the freeway caught Nieting's eye. They were American soldiers like he'd seen many times in Berlin since he was a boy and the sight was frightening. Not that he feared they would do him harm, rather that they would show up again in his life at all, particularly with the past bursting out of the back seat of his rented car. He thought he might faint until his father spoke.

"What can that old con man Auger give to you?" he said. "You'd be better off interviewing the mouse or the duck. At least the one in that poor gown might give you some pleasure, if only you knew what to do. Besides, what do you want with this song, anyway? It isn't yours, Valentin. Leave these things to the Negroes. They have no need of your assistance."

Emil laughed, his eyes framed in the mirror, cold and dusky blue, the brow flat and expressionless.

"I blame Max for these excesses," he said, his manner off-handed and clearly disgusted. "Don't get me wrong, I never had a problem with homosexuals. I respect all types and always have. Berlin was marvelously free when we were young. It is people who don't love at all that I disapprove of. Yet, Max is oversensitive nonetheless, damaged from suffering, I believe. He wasn't the best influence, Valentin, not for a young boy."

The traffic moved fast and heavy as Nieting bolted from lane to lane across the entire width of the freeway, pushing through, taking his eyes off of Emil only at the split second before darting to the right or left. Emil opened the window and let the wind rush over his stiff hair as Nieting examined him in the rear view mirror. He looked like the only image of his father he'd ever seen, from that single picture of Uncle Max's; the suit with the sleeves too short, shoulders too tight, hair jutting in different directions like porcupine quills, the same grin that may have been good natured or may have been mocking, there was no telling for sure. Nieting's hands shook as he gripped the steering wheel. His blood was boiling.

"You must cease lying, father," said Nieting. "Kid Auger means everything to you. You used to say, 'why waste time painting a picture or writing a thousand words when truth can be distilled in a single sound.' He was your greatest teacher, your inspiration, your alter ego. You used to say it yourself. Uncle Max told me this many times. He told me everything. He told me of the exhibit and the battle with the Nazis and how Auger helped defeat them and how the very sound of his trombone was nearer to your gods than any utterance you'd ever heard."

"Battling Nazis?" said Emil. "I never said such a thing. Near to my gods? What gods? You sound like Max. You're far too serious, just like your mother."

"We weren't over serious, father," moaned Nieting, "We were struggling to stay alive."

"That is true," said Emil, "Still, Max might have done a better job instead of turning a blind eye to your true condition. Did he really believe those fairy tales would save you? He should have helped you remember the truth. You might not have survived, but you wouldn't have ended up in this hopeless situation. A grown man talking to the father he never knew, who died twenty years earlier in Auschwitz, just like they were having tea in a tea shop. Why, you're crazy Valentin. Don't you think so?"

Nieting moaned, "You were an artist. You celebrated rebellion. Does that mean nothing? Why contemptuous now of a different temperament, a free spirit, someone who sees things others cannot see?"

"You are speaking about art," replied Emil. "I've learned a thing or two about that. It's merely form, empty form. You fill it up for your own use and when the air runs out it drops to the ground. There's nothing to keep someone else from retrieving the carcass and using it for their own purposes. Any Hitler or Jesus Christ can do it."

"No father," said Nieting. "What you're saying is not true. I am speaking about your piece, the human posterior with the Swastika and pubic hairs, and how you confronted the Nazis beneath the sculpture, a work that you conceived and constructed, and how you drove them into the street to the music of Kid Auger."

"I never made such a piece," said Emil. "I was picked up after our first discussion of having an exhibit. We weren't able to organize it, let alone open the doors. There were spies everywhere. It was a terrible idea. I must have been drunk. I paid for it with my life. I died in Auschwitz. You wouldn't know, but here's the proof of it."

Emil lifted his right forearm towards the rearview mirror as Nieting turned around. The arm, suddenly naked, came within inches of his nose, the numbers visible, dull blue against yellow flesh, tall as a billboard and Nieting's eyes riveted there. He could feel the car careening forward, was vaguely troubled because he could not see the road, had even lost the steering wheel. How he managed to drive from that point, no one will ever know. He certainly had no idea or memory of it. He saw nothing but himself and Emil conversing, close-ups of their faces and no more.

"You were the old Jew at the beach, then?" he said.

"Well yes, I was," said Emil. "Although, I never was truly an old Jew. I was play acting for you. I died a young Jew, remember. Strangely, I never thought of myself strictly as a Jew until the camps. The Nazis made me understand I was a Jew. That was me at the beach, however. Just trying to be entertaining. You've heard from your uncle that I was a real live wire. His portrait of me is somewhat in character. Collecting pubic hair at a party sounds like something I might do. I wish I had. Good for Max. At least his lies are clever. There was no battle of the hairy ass, I assure you. Nothing remotely like that ever happened. We'd only talked about an exhibit. I don't think anyone would have actively supported the idea. There weren't many of us left by then. We should have gone when we had the chance. It was far too late for that then."

There was a long silence when Emil stopped speaking, a shattering quiet amidst a cacophony of white noise, a million explosions swirling in a sucking sound past the closed windows of the car until he shifted in the seat, re-crossed his legs, sighed, and began again.

"Don't be angry, Valentin," he said. "None of it matters any longer. You're so unhappy. You must do something about it. I could keep you company, just like the old days. The only difference would be that you're a man now. You have the right to choose your own way out. I wouldn't try to stop you this time. Death is not so bad once you get there. It can be terrorizing when you know nothing about it. Better men than you have done it. You'll be able to see the truth of things. It behooves you to at least know the truth. Death frees one, Valentin. Why lie if you're going to die anyway? Lies are only of use to the living."

Nieting looked into the mirror determined to meet Emil's eyes, but he was gone.

◆ ◆ ◆

A strange calm descended upon Nieting after his father left. By the time he reached the exit sign for Disneyland, the haze had lifted and the sky was cloudless and blue. In spite of everything, he felt hopeful, as if he'd just awakened to the brightness of a new day. It seemed clear to the professor that the violence of the previous night and not sleeping in the wake of it and even the impossible pace he'd maintained pursuing *the Robert Charles song* had contributed to his current mental condition, had caused him to see and hear things that could only exist in his mind. He dismissed the idea that his father had actually appeared. It would be grossly impractical to take the word of an apparition, particularly if it contended that a significant portion of his most cherished beliefs were no more than falsehoods. Not to mention its insistence that suicide was the only imperative. Instead, Nieting clung to the conviction that he'd simply conjured the appearance, the result of extreme overwork. He'd pushed himself too hard. The problem was no more serious than this. It was true, he'd allowed his methodology to become permeated with a desperate subjectivity, but that was because the task he'd chosen was so harrowing; entering the collective unconscious of a strange people was bound to tax even the sturdiest of intellects.

Nieting parked in the Disneyland lot, strapped the camera around his neck, grabbed the recorder case by the handle and made his way through the ocean of automobiles to the gates of the park. As he maneuvered through the parked cars he conceived of a new work, delineating the structure in his head and becoming more excited with each stride forward.

Everything happens for a reason, he thought. *Providing the individual possesses the capacity, the rational mind can arrest destructive trends and reign in irrational emotions that impede one's development. The work emerging from this struggle shall be titled* Music and the Negro Revolution – Reclaiming *The Robert Charles Song. It will be a handbook of cultural reclamation and the revolutionary rebirth of colonized peoples.*

Nieting held his face up to the sun and reveled in the warmth and brightness. He skipped between two tour buses parked along a long curb and onto the sidewalk.

1000 RIOT IN LA

Banner headline of a newspaper in a vending machine. He would have run past it if the word RIOT in the banner headline hadn't caught his eye.

He thought instantly of his students at the Free University. They must be carrying on the fight he'd left last June. There was no doubt that they were. He dropped a coin in the machine and grabbed the paper.

"WATTS MELEE" "1000 RIOT IN LA" "WATTS MELEE" "8 BLOCKS SEALED OFF" "WATTS MELEE" "POLICE AND MOTORISTS ATTACKED" "WATTS".

"My god," shouted Nieting, "It's Watts. *1000 people rioted in the Watts district Wednesday night . . . attacked police and motorists with rocks, bricks, and bottles . . .* they've done it . . . *sporadic rioting continued early today* shit, the Negroes have risen. My god, this paper is dated Thursday the twelfth. This has been going on since Wednesday then. How could I not have known?"

A man stepped onto the sidewalk pushing a dolly loaded with bundles of newspapers from a delivery truck double parked on the other side of the tour buses. He greeted Nieting jauntily, stepping up to the vending machine, unlocking and emptying the coin box, removing the unsold newspapers and replacing them with the day's papers. "You just bought yesterday's news," he said, handing Nieting the Friday edition. He let the lid drop, nodded and moved off. Nieting held the paper up.

EXTRA – NEW RIOTING – TROOPS ALERTED

Nieting stood in the middle of the sidewalk fumbling through the unruly pages as passengers from tour buses swarmed past. He rushed into the park, his mind in flames like Watts and halted near the dock where the Mark Twain was, at the same metal table he'd sat on the day before. Crowds of tourists moved around him in absolute oblivion, dumb, uncaring, privileged, not knowing that their make-believe world was hanging by a thread. Mickey Mouse squealed, raising his four-fingered hands above his head, swarmed by children, as cameras clicked in clusters like volleys of gunshot. All about him, the Disneyland scene transpired in lugubrious monotony, passionless joy, absurd like an Auger performance, only unintentional.

Two young men in green Alpine hats sprouting a tiny feather, wearing shorts with red suspenders, knee socks, white shirts and little bow ties were suddenly framed in Nieting's view, directly before the white ersatz peaks of a 150-foot high mountain, the Matterhorn, glistening with bogus snow beneath the desert sun. A waterfall spouting from the side of the Matterhorn spewed small boats of screaming children along a roller coaster waterway into an Alpine lake below. The two young men stood hands apocket, rocking on their heels as Nieting walked between them, greeting him in unison in loud cheerful voices, "velcome to Disneyland." Nieting did a double take and glared, resisting the impulse to thrust his middle finger up into the men's grinning faces.

"Vould you and the kids like to try the Matterhorn ride?" said one of them.

"It is vunderful," said the other.

"Ya, vunderful," repeated the first.

A troop of small girls wearing little tan skirted uniforms and brown berets pushed past, shouting and giggling. As Nieting looked after them he saw the sign.

YOUNG MEN OF JAZZ in Concert – Today – 6 pm

Behind the sign announcing the concert was a fence covered by a wall of ivy and behind that apparently was an outdoor theater. It was four o'clock and Nieting was right on time for the interview with Kid Auger. He folded the newspaper, placed it under his arm, grasped the tape recorder and followed the gravel path to the sunken amphitheater. Inside, he perused the rows of seats descending towards a circular stage. Kid Auger was nowhere to be seen. Nieting walked among the empty seats until he heard a man's voice coming from somewhere back stage. Finally, Johnny St. Cyr, dressed in street clothes, walked onto the stage, surveying the space and nodded cordially at Nieting.

"Has Kid Auger arrived?" asked Nieting. "We have an appointment for an interview at four o'clock."

"Not today you don't," replied St. Cyr. "He's been here and gone. Said he wasn't feeling right and couldn't make it this evening. That's what I get for hiring old men. I'm surprised he didn't call you."

"He doesn't have my number," said Nieting. "I never gave it to him. That is terribly disappointing. May I speak with you, Mr. St. Cyr? I intended to request an interview today of yourself and Mr. Barbarin. Mr. Auger said he'd put a good word in for me."

"C'mon back," said St. Cyr and Nieting scurried down the aisle and followed backstage to an air-conditioned kitchen area with several other rooms adjacent. Nieting set up his recorder on a folding chair and sat with St. Cyr next to a circular table until Paul Barbarin joined them a few moments later. St. Cyr leaned back in the chair, balancing himself on the balls of his feet. He grinned and winked at Barbarin.

"This here is the fella Jean said was coming down to interview him today," he said. "He figures, since Jean ain't here, me and you'll do."

"That right?" said Barbarin, lithely grabbing a chair from against the wall, unfolding and straddling the seat, resting his wrists loosely on the top.

"Well, not really," said Nieting sheepishly. "It was my intention to seek your permission today. I do appreciate your time."

"What can we do for you?" said Barbarin.

"I am an Anthropologist by trade, currently on an assignment for a journal called MerzKraft, to seek out a lost composition by Buddy Bolden. I'd like to get back to that shortly, however, first I would like to know your thoughts about the uprising in Watts?"

Nieting clicked on the tape recorder.

"I don't comment on worlds events," said St. Cyr.

"You can turn that thing off, right now," said Barbarin. "We don't talk for no machine." He pointed his forefinger at St. Cyr. "Remember what happened to Louis when he talked too much?"

"I sure do," replied St. Cyr. "He didn't do nothing but say that those kids back there in Little Rock should be let into high school. That son of a bitch Faubus called the troops in to bar those children. Louis said it wasn't right. Newspapers were all over him for that. Folks said he was a damned Communist. Pops a Communist? He had everyone coming after him. They forgot his job was making music. Making people feel good."

"I congratulated Louis, publicly, in print at the time," said Nieting. "I wrote it in my university newspaper."

"Hell, that don't make no difference at all." said Barbarin, "We don't know you well enough to talk personal, anyway."

"That's true," said St. Cyr. "Who knows what your intentions are? We could wake up tomorrow and find you twisted every word we said."

"Happens to celebrities all the time," said Barbarin. "Particularly Negro celebrities."

"We're musicians," said St. Cyr. "It's our job to make folks happy. All folks. Color ain't important."

A young man in a powder blue blazer approached Nieting and seeing the reels of tape spinning and the microphone set up between the men, announced in a loud theatrical voice, "Mrs. Auger requests that I relay a message to you, sir. She says Mr. Auger is sorry that he was unable to make his appointment today and that you may call him if you'd like and make another appointment."

The powder blue blazer handed Nieting a folded note, turned on his heels and marched off.

"See that," said St Cyr. "I didn't figure Jean would just let you go like that without saying something. That ain't the way Jean works."

"He must really be under the weather," said Barbarin, "if Suzette is calling for him."

"You know how Suzette is," said St. Cyr. "It wouldn't surprise me if she started playing the trombone for him, too."

Nieting cut in abruptly, causing both men to come to attention.

"I have no desire to put words into your mouth or distort your views," he said.

Barbarin leaned past Nieting and clicked the recorder off.

"That's what you say," he said. "How do we know that? We don't know you from Adam."

"You say it's your job to make folks feel happy," replied Nieting. "Don't you feel an obligation to the mass of Negroes living under an oppressive system?"

"What system?" said St. Cyr.

"I know what he means," said Barbarin. "He means we're a couple of niggers and we should stay down there in Watts with the rest of the niggers."

"I don't mean that at all," said Nieting. "It seems to me that there is a purpose to the music. It comes from the people and shouldn't be taken away from them when they need it most."

Barbarin screwed his face up close and glared at Nieting.

"We give music," he said. "We don't take music away from anybody." The volume of his voice rose as he went on. "This is our music. Where the hell do you get off telling me I'm stealing my music from my people?"

"You are the only Negroes here," said Nieting. "I haven't seen any Negroes in the audience. You play exclusively for whites. I'd say you have taken the music away from the Negro community."

"Niggers shouldn't make a living, you mean?" said Barbarin. "You want us all on welfare, begging handouts. If all the niggers ain't poor, strung out, and in the ghetto, you think things ain't right."

"That isn't so," replied Nieting.

"Hell it ain't," said Barbarin.

"Kid Auger would certainly grasp what I am saying," said Nieting. "He is an artist who has always understood the relationship between the peoples' music and revolutionary change."

"What?" shouted Barbarin. "Did you hear that, John? Jean is a revolutionary man. I heard everything now. Everything."

"You don't know what you're talking about, son," said St. Cyr.

"He might have been around during the Revolutionary War, but that's as close as he gets to any revolution," said Barbarin.

"Alright then," said Nieting. "If you insist, I'll give you an example of what I mean. Morris Triplett is on the front line in Watts, right now, as we speak."

"Morris who?" said Barbarin.

"Morris Triplett and the musicians of BANG, right now, as we speak, are in Watts. Yes, in Watts, where they should be, if you please."

Barbarin raised up off his seat.

"Musicians of BANG?" he said. "I've known Morris for years. What the hell is this foreign cracker talking about?"

"I don't know," said St. Cyr. "Listen son, you're not from around these parts. You best not speak to a black man and tell him what he ought and ought not to be doing. You might find yourself arguing with some pretty touchy Negroes. You could get hurt."

"I'm not telling you to do anything," said Nieting. "I am simply relating basic principles of culture. These phenomena are universal. They are the same for everyone."

"Principles my ass," said Barbarin.

"We don't know nothing about your principles," said St. Cyr. "What we do know is you're coming around and telling Mr. Barbarin and myself that we shouldn't be in here, shouldn't be working at Disneyland. You're doing that, and you don't know nothing about who we are, nothing about our music and nothing about our people. This is a very common thing among you whites. Yes, the writers are the worst. You stand right up in our face and tell us who we are. You don't want no part of us telling you who you are. You don't want to hear that. You call that militant. But you can look us in the eye and tell us who we are and expect us to fall in line."

"I have many Negro friends, Mr. St. Cyr, I assure you," said Nieting. "I've been told many times that I am not a white man. I think what is meant by that is, that as a European, I don't think as an American white does. My perspective is in solidarity with the Negro. I'm sorry if stating that simple fact in this manner appears abrupt or vulgar, however, I've not often been confronted by a Negro with this level of hostility and misunderstanding."

"Is that right?" said Barbarin. "We sorry boss. We jest po'niggers. We don't mean nothing."

St. Cyr walked around the table to Barbarin.

"Cool down, Paul," he said. "Can't you see, this one ain't your regular oddball."

St. Cyr mouthed the words, "he's crazy," signaling to Barbarin to back off, raising his eyebrows and brushing his index finger in a circular motion past his temple, saying silently, "crazy," in full view of Nieting as if he were too far gone to comprehend.

"Oh hell, he ain't crazy, he's a motherfucking white supremacist, that's all," said Barbarin. "You got five seconds to get your racist ass out of here before I start tearing it up."

St. Cyr squeezed Barbarin's arm, gently pulling him into the chair. He looked at Nieting for a long moment, then said, "Do you know what it means when a white man looks at a black man and thinks he knows him because he's black?"

"I don't pretend to know you," said Nieting.

"Well then, you heard the man," said St. Cyr, gesturing towards Barbarin. "I wouldn't test him if I was you."

"Very well," said Nieting. "Perhaps the time has come to take sides, whether one wishes to or not. Clearly, we've each chosen our side. Have you ever heard the phrase Uncle Tom?"

"Uncle Tom?" said Barbarin. "You two bit motherfucker, I'll body slam you."

Nieting hastily grabbed the equipment and made for the door as Barbarin shouted behind him, "Sieg Heil," thrusting his arm up in the Nazis salute.

Nieting looked at the two men and scowled.

"Really?" he said, and Barbarin repeated "Sieg Heil," extending his arm towards Nieting as if attempting to strike him.

"Calm down, Paul," said St. Cyr. "He's not worth getting sick over."

Nieting rammed past the door beneath an exit sign as Barbarin shouted, "Seig Heil, Sieg Heil." He pushed through another door of heavy metal, knocking it open violently, causing the equipment strapped to his torso to jerk about like it was trying to escape. He burst outside into a wall of heat and blinding sunlight, but kept moving, nearly knocking over a baby stroller tangled between his legs, cursing "black bastards" and fleeing as the father of the frightened baby pursued him for ten paces, then halted. "What type of a man talks that way at Disneyland," the man shouted. "Are you crazy? You coulda hurt my kid. You are crazy, you're some kind of a nut."

Nieting stopped on the path and looked at the man, clenching his fists, then lunged towards him. He wanted to thrash him, beat his sweaty red face until it bled, but he resisted. "Those niggers would love to see me arrested," he whispered. "That would prove to them that I'm just what they claim I am. I am not. They are just as I described them. Uncle Toms."

A crowd gathered around the father and the baby in the stroller. Barbarin was among them with several men in powder blue blazers. St. Cyr. joined them and pointed through the crowd at Nieting. Nieting ducked around a corner and slipped into the ticket line at the foot of the Matterhorn, looking over his shoulder for pursuers as several powder blue blazers spread out into the crowd. He hustled along a stretch of paved walkway, lugging his gear, finding himself suddenly on a dirt street in an old western town. There were women in old time dresses and bonnets, holding open parasols, conversing on the wooden walkway in front of a building with a sign, First National Bank mounted on the front. Beyond the women, the incongruous mob of tourists milled, necks extended and craning every which way like spooked ostriches. The Western scene was macabre to Nieting, bringing to mind vigilantes, lynchings and impoverished Indians. He walked down the center of the street, glaring contemptuously from side to side.

Two men in broad white western hats and pistols holstered to their hips sauntered across the street in front of Nieting; one wearing a metal star on his chest nodded as he passed, then tipped his hat to the women in front of the bank. The women waved little lace handkerchiefs and in the next instant one of them screamed for no apparent reason. The two men in the street rushed forward just as a series of loud explosions sounded at the door to the bank and three men emerged, carrying leather bags, firing pistols and shoving the women to the ground as they fled. A cowboy dressed in black raced past Nieting, fanning a six shooter at the sheriff who tumbled over a hitching post and splashed into a horse trough, clutching the spot in his chest where the bullet must have struck. The crowd of tourists jumped up and down and cheered, some signaling frantically to Nieting to move out of harm's way.

Dust swirled around Nieting's head as two riders sped past on horseback, fleeing the scene, the leather bags flapping against the flanks of the horses. One of the riders yanked the reigns and the huge horse twisted to a halt, rearing up as the rider hoisted the man in black up, dug his heels into the horse's side and took off galloping around the corner. For a moment the crowd appeared to be stunned by the violence, children looking at parents, parents looking at each other, then everyone looking at Nieting standing in the street. There was enough dirt on his face to remove with his hands and throw to the ground. His mouth was filled with grit and his hair encased in a brittle bonnet. The children began first, pointing at the lone figure in the street, so brown with dust he looked like Rochester in a Jack Benny movie. The laughter started with the kids and in seconds moved through the crowd like an electric current until everyone was looking and pointing and laughing, then flash bulbs began to explode like the mob was shooting at Nieting, a firing squad in Bermuda shorts.

It was a shocking sight. They were a curious bunch, fantastic really. Truly automatons with electric lights behind their eyes, or surgically altered cattle, or part of an incredible farce. They were remote, untouchable, impenetrable. Somehow, Nieting had become the object of their attention, as if he were a rodeo clown, something devised by Walt Disney, a defrocked German college professor about to lose his mind. For an instant, Nieting thought they wanted him to lose his mind, like they were part of the conspiracy. He shouted at the crowd and everyone became hushed.

"Thank you for your concern, ladies and gentlemen," he said.

They watched with intense concentration, waiting silently for Nieting to speak, their mouths poised, ready for hysterical laughter, their eyes beseeching Nieting to extend the ecstasy a bit longer. They looked as though they were formed up for a family portrait, huddled together in front of the saloon behind the hitching post, wearing looks of agonized expectation. There were a few shushes to quiet some giggling children, then they were all dead silent. Nieting chuckled. He had them in precisely the same manner that Kid Auger would have had them. He knew their thoughts and more importantly, he knew what they would do next. For the moment they were his, and he waited, surveying the group from one end to the other. Professor Nieting, however, was not Kid Auger. He was a scholar, a truth teller. He spoke directly, not theatrically, not symbolically.

"So, this is how a racist mob appears," he shouted. "I understand the game now. Those men on horseback were bank robbers and all of you are the lynch mob. It's your job to hunt down Negroes and murder them, torture them perhaps. Then, if the spirit moves you, apply a little fire to their flesh. Just as your grandparents did. I understand why you are all so mirthful. This sector of the park is where you pretend to be your grandparents. But, there are no Negroes here for you to kill. Oh, forgive me. I am wrong about that. If you take the path that lies in that direction, to the theatre, inside of that, backstage, you'll find two old Negroes. You can take them if you'd like. They may put up a fight, but there are too many of you for them to resist. Why don't you go on and do as your ancestors did? Your countrymen in the South still do it today, do they not? Your people bomb churches and murder in the dead of night. Why aren't you laughing? I've told you where the Negroes are. You mustn't be choosey. There are too few Negroes at Disneyland for you to be choosey."

Nieting watched the faces in the crowd, bright with anticipation, appear to drop, one by one, into a disinterested blankness. Only the children continued to giggle, becoming more animated as it became clear that there was to be no big gag, no punch line to whatever it was the strange man was saying. There was no response from the grown-ups, as if a switch had clicked, a sensor used to detect diversion, that becomes activated when one strolls through the gates of the Magic Kingdom and filters out any proximity to troubling sentiments, blatant discontent or inappropriate seriousness. The people simply drifted off. There were no words of reproach or even comprehension. No complaints or differing opinions. Nieting simply felt himself disappearing and shouted as the people dispersed. "If you'd like a more interesting challenge, the Negroes of Watts would be glad to accommodate your wishes. They may even come here to do so, whether you like it or not."

In a few moments the street had cleared. The bank robbers sauntered down the center of the dirt road, back towards the bank, chatting as they led the two horses. As they reached Nieting, the man in black remarked, "You might want to stick around. In thirty minutes or so, you're gonna be able to see a real Western gunfight. How about that? You won't want to miss it."

◆ ◆ ◆

In the parking lot of the Imperial Highway Motor Inn, Nieting carefully lifted himself out of the car avoiding the burning metal surfaces as he mopped the sweat from his face with a rag. He fished in his pockets for change as he walked to a pay phone across the lot. His hands shook as he dialed Auger's number. A woman answered, introducing herself as Mr. Auger's wife, Suzette. She said Jean would be pleased to see him the next day. He could come to their home in Brentwood. Jean wouldn't be working at Disneyland and it would be far more comfortable at their place. She suggested he come "in the afternoon, after lunch, say around two o'clock." Nieting barely spoke to the woman, he simply agreed and she gave him the address. He dragged his gear from the car and up the stairs to the balcony leading to his room. At the top of the staircase, he glanced at the door of the room where the whore had been the previous night. The number nine hung sideways against the cracking paint. The peep hole in the door stared knowingly like the eye of a nemesis. Nieting ignored the contempt he felt from behind the door. He winced at image of his mother's face in his mind. Her face was twisted and painted as the whore's had been. Nieting gestured towards the door.

"There is nothing to fear in there," he said. "Your mother does not reside in room number nine. An unfortunate woman is inside. She is a lost child, as destitute as yourself. Flesh, she is made of flesh and blood. Speak to her. Tell her there is nothing for either of you to fear."

He approached the door and knocked lightly. After several seconds of silence, he knocked again, slightly harder. There was a rustling inside and footsteps approaching and when the door opened, a middle aged man stood before Nieting in his underwear, rubbing his eyes as if he'd just awakened. Nieting looked past him, scanning the empty room. The man sighed and said, "whoever you're looking for, she ain't here. You might want to check with the police if you're interested in her whereabouts. They probably wouldn't mind talking to you, either. They probably would have by now if every last one of'm wasn't over in south central L.A."

Nieting shuttered at the mention of the police. He had no idea where south central L.A. was except that it seemed close by, the way the man gestured eastward. The man frowned and looked Nieting up and down.

"Allow me to explain, please," said Nieting. "I do not wish to do business with the woman. I was here last evening, in the next room, trying to rest as I see you are. I do apologize. I merely wished to speak to her briefly."

"You a preacher, then?" said the man.

"Certainly not," replied Nieting. "I simply want no misunderstanding between us."

The man smiled sympathetically and nodded.

"I understand there was quite a fracas here last night. Get involved in something you shouldn't?"

Nieting shook his head wearily.

"No," he said. "I'm afraid I was an unwilling bystander. I heard them shouting through the walls."

"You mean you didn't know what was going on?"

"Of course, I knew. I am a grown man. I heard them fucking. It seemed like a new man every half hour. I was exhausted. I only wished to rest."

"You got no worry on that score tonight," replied the man. "I can promise you that. That one last night is long gone, though. I mean, really gone. She met up with the wrong stud and he sliced her up something fierce. She won't be sucking no more cock, that's for sure. The Mexican maids came in this morning and cleaned up the crime scene. It was one hell of a fiasco. Did someone a big favor. The detectives were fuming. Good thing she was just a whore."

"That's quite terrible," said Nieting.

"You can rest easy tonight, though," said the man. "I sure don't want no trouble. I ain't that type. I ain't paid for pussey in five years. I'm just here to get some shut eye before I hit the road again."

"Yes, of course," said Nieting. "I wouldn't have thought otherwise. I had no idea how bad things were over there. It is quite shocking . . . although, I am not surprised."

"Sure thing, buddy," said the man. He looked at Nieting with half lidded eyes and closed the door.

"Fucking ironic," said Nieting. "Another whore dead. She may be in hell at this very moment, chatting with my own mother." Nieting recoiled at the cruelty of his words. "God damn you, Nieting," he said. "Have you no compassion, no decency? " He gripped his forehead tightly and growled, "Insanity is enough to drive one mad."

It may have been the timing of the statement that caused Nieting to laugh. It hit like the sound of a stick cracking. He watched himself laugh and thought how crazy that was and laughed harder. As he walked to his room, the door to number nine opened a chains length and the man peeked out and Nieting fell into boomeranging guffaws. *He can see I'm fucking nuts. It's down-right obvious.* The thought tickled him to no end and he let out a string of machine gun giggles, finally shouting over his shoulder, "At least I'm the one laughing." The door slammed shut and

Nieting cracked up more, covering his mouth and doubling over. "It is all too much. Dr. Valentin Nieting is nuts."

Everything became clear at that moment. At the crack of the stick the veil had lifted. Nieting was mad. The knowledge spread over him as a physical sensation, as if his entire body were waking up to the outside world.

"Valentin, you are not well at all," he said waving his index finger. "And what is more, you are insane." He broke into a grin. "Crazy as a gnat. Irrevocably deranged by the suffering of your childhood. How touching. You are damaged goods. You've been told so. Told by a dead man you never met who happens to be your father. Before long, no doubt, you shall become a monstrosity, a shocking entertainment. You are ill. I am a fucking madman. This is a fact one must accept."

Embracing the idea that he was indeed mad after all was a liberating act for Professor Nieting. Insanity wasn't as upsetting as one might think, at least once one accepted the reality of it. There was a rather glorious freedom in owning up to the condition. One was in command, so to speak, or at the ready, rather than at the mercy of spooks and goblins coming and going at their pleasure. Perhaps he could reconcile with Emil now that he wasn't at such a disadvantage; clinging to sanity depletes the greater part of one's creative will. No matter. Emil was of no importance. He was merely an acute symptom of Nieting's malady. The work was the only thing of significance. The song, if only he could recover the song. He'd reached the place of inner certitude that such task demanded. *Music and the Negro Revolution* would be his great work and the centerpiece would be *The Robert Charles Song*. If this were all he accomplished in his life, it would be a monumental fulfillment.

"A single great work," he said, and yet another light came on. The notion of a man's life defined by a single great work flitted like a phosphorescent ping pong ball in the vast surging ocean of images and sensations that overwhelmed him. It may have been tragic, this sense of life reduced to a single gesture, but it was stirring also, because it must be a great gesture to justify an entire lifetime. Perhaps, only a madman could transform the chaos into a vision of perfect symmetry.

Once again, everything was clear. He bought Mexican food from a truck and ate, sitting cross legged on his bed, wolfing the food with voracious lust, in perfect sync with his thoughts on Kid Auger and how one might induce him to reveal what he surely must know. Indeed, there were questions about Auger. His character had been impugned everywhere his name had arisen. Was not this proof of his artistic validity and of the veracity of Nieting's convictions?

"I'll propose to the Kid that we venture to Watts together and offer our services to the Revolution. I'll offer to deliver him to Mr. Triplett's camp. This is the ultimate gesture and the next vital link in my search for the song. We should leave directly from his home. Kid Auger will understand this. Every means at our disposal shall be utilized to assist the Negroes."

Nieting smelled smoke as he huddled on the broken down bed sure the stink of fire came from him, that he'd always carried it, that he reeked of destruction all his life and was only just now able to perceive it. The thought was insane.

"There is no suffering in madness if one accepts being mad," he whispered. "One can come full circle and madness will become true transvaluation."

He leapt from the bed and clicked on the television. Watts was all over, on every channel, bulletins one after the next, breaking news, footage of buildings in flames, firemen dodging projectiles, mobs of Negroes taunting the TV cameras, politicians pleading for calm, whites in gun shops arming themselves against the anarchy of Negro rage. The reports in the media were sensational, biased, designed to enflame the whites. All information was in the hands of the authorities. The real story would have to be gleaned later from the Negroes themselves. There was nothing he could do except wait. Waiting, however, was no easy task.

"Can one in good conscience remain idle when the Negroes are so close by struggling to remake the world?"

This was a rhetorical question. It was Nieting's conviction that he needed a guide, a liaison between himself and Morris Triplett and his community of musicians and that that would be Kid Auger. These men would validate his project and lead him to the lost song. He must wait out of necessity, as a tactical imperative, regardless of the agony of watching the Revolution unfold through the lenses of White Supremacy's cameras. He jumped onto the bed and the head board rammed the wall.

"God damn it, I must go to Watts now," he shouted.

A door in room number 9 slammed and the window panes in Nieting's room vibrated. He shouted at the wall as if explaining his frustration.

"The tide in these struggles can turn at any moment. I must go while the momentum remains in favor of the people, before the authorities bring in soldiers and tanks as they most certainly will."

He lie spread eagle on the bed, staring at the ceiling, sweat pouring off his body to the sound of sirens in the distance and on the television the voice of a TV newsman, breathless, crouched behind a police car with sniper's bullets whizzing past his ears, then, "the American Tobacco Company proud makers of Pall Mall." Nieting chuckled.

"Are you sure you want a light?" he said. The irony was delicious. The Revolution was at hand. What would be the most effective course of action? How best assist the masses of Negroes battling in the streets of Los Angeles? First, he must explain the nature of his work to Triplett and Auger. They must understand the importance of recovering the song. In the process, he would provide them with a language, a system of thought, a means to express the song's meaning in all its ramifications and reveal the philosophical dimensions to the struggle. He imagined himself and Auger being driven through the back streets of Watts. The sound of weapons discharging seems to be coming from the next block. They are taken to a nondescript little cottage and into a dimly lit back room where they are introduced by the driver to Triplett and his lieutenants, a percussionist and a bassist, sitting around a table. Triplett signals and a woman holding a baby leaves the room. The men rise and embrace Auger and then Nieting. They all sit down. No one speaks. They are waiting for Nieting to address them.

"Mr. Triplett, I believe the Kid is with me on this. I think we all agree that the entire world is engaged in the act of revolution. The western powers have lost their grip all over the globe. Colonized peoples are claiming their freedom. It isn't just happening in Los Angeles. There is no question that time is short for capitalism."

"Ah ha," says Triplett, leaning closer, unconsciously stroking his snow white beard.

Nieting looks around the darkened room. There are Negroes standing in the shadows, a gun barrel glistening in the candle light. A man at the window lifts the curtain back slightly at the sound of a car passing on the street. He nods when the car has passed. The room is silent, the hunger for knowledge is palpable. The atmosphere is electric. Nieting goes on.

"It was clear to me even as a small boy upon hearing the music of Kid Auger, that only indigenous cultures can lift us out of bourgeois notions of truth, far beyond internationalism into the realm of mind as a vast collective repository of human knowledge and potentialities available to everyone. Only indigenous peoples have the capacity to create social systems free enough to effect the transformation of humanity."

The truth of Nieting's statement is so concise and direct that the Negroes laugh with delight. A great tension is released. Of course, these men understand the nature of struggle. Nieting is present among them to deepen this understanding.

He goes on, "Once this is understood, the prominence of Asia, of the America's before the European invasion, and of Africa, naturally offer themselves as distinct possibilities, sources of technology and forgotten knowledge. Thus, the peoples of those regions have become leaders in the struggle to reclaim the world. This takes us full circle, takes us home to Watts, if you will."

There is a long silence at the table, during which time Nieting realized he was laying on a bed, a rather foul smelling bed, and forced himself back to the table where Triplett and Auger exhale deeply, releasing the tension of being rapt by Nieting's speech. Triplett offers Nieting a complicated Negro handshake which Nieting does not understand. Triplett laughs and hugs Nieting and Auger throws his arms around both men, a great prolonged embrace. "To the Revolution," says Triplett and the others respond, "To the Revolution."

"My Living Doll, staring Bob Cummings, is brought to you by . . . "

Nieting was on the bed, the room dark except for the flickering eye of the television. White people living on the edge of oblivion and not even knowing it. He flipped the dial and a man appeared, speaking with a deadpan expression.

"Reports are turning up of Negroes wearing red arm bands spotted leaving the scene of many fires, the latest as far north as the Santa Monica Freeway. Fears of an organized invasion of the downtown area have been expressed by city officials who declined to be identified."

The Chief of the Los Angeles Police Department squinted into the television camera like John Winthrop eying the naked breasts of a Pequot woman. Not with lust, with contempt.

"The civil disobedience preached by so-called Negro leaders and Communists is a revolutionary tool that has been used to bring about the overthrow of existing governments. These so called Negro leaders, can't lead at all, except that they've led us into this trouble."

Chief Parker was smug, with a skinny neck and glasses perched on a bird-like nose. He looked like a plucked chicken in an oversized suit, eliciting chuckles from reporters with quips about Negroes and Communists, scowling as he spoke, giving no quarter, conceding nothing, cock sure.

"I don't know anything about what has happened in Mississippi. I do know Negro hoodlums have been held up by Liberals and Communists for too long as people who are deprived individuals, that they had been maligned and abused by society."

The voice ran through Nieting's body like a virus penetrating his sinew, pin pricks piercing the core of his bones. He lay on his back on the bed watching the evening news behind the rapid rise and fall of his hyperventilating chest and twitching feet.

"How can I remain idle when this filthy brown shirt is attacking the Revolution," he said. "He should be liquidated as quickly as possible. The mass of Negroes would take heart at such an occurrence."

The professor rose from the bed. He could wait no longer. He had to get out of the dingy motel room or come apart at the seams. Rene. He needed to confer with Rene.

It was dark when Nieting drove to Venice Beach, taking the route the two teenagers had shown him. He was there in twenty minutes, parked and pacing near the pagoda where he'd first met Rene. He wandered up and down Ocean Front Walk, agitated, rushing up to passersby, asking if they knew a Negro named Rene Lawson then moving off at the confused stares and annoyed rebukes. The fog dropped quickly shrouding the street lights along the beachfront. He walked towards a lighted doorway on a side street where he saw a few people coming and going. Perhaps it was a bar or restaurant, a place of business, a safe haven. Perhaps Rene was there. The painted sign outside read *Venice West Cafe*. Nieting entered as a pretty young woman was leaving. She called over her shoulder into the room, "good night, John," smiled at Nieting and held the door as he slide around her.

Inside the cafe was a counter behind which was a large coffee urn and shelves filled with stacks of cups and plates and an old cash register in front of a large mirror. Chairs and small tables were scattered about the space, a few paintings hung towards the front and posters were plastered all over announcing poetry events, musical concerts, parties past and future. To the left was a tiny bandstand with an upright piano where two young men sat, conversing, each with a guitar across his lap. Behind the counter a man, apparently named John, was busily tinkering with the coffee urn. He spied Nieting in the mirror and turned, greeting him with a noncommittal nod. Nieting ordered coffee, leaning forward against the counter and speaking in confidential tones. When the man placed the steaming coffee down, Nieting said, "Hello John, I was hoping you could assist me. I am looking for a Negro named Rene Lawson."

John looked at Nieting with no expression and resumed working on the coffee urn.

"I recognize you," said Nieting. "You spoke to Rene yesterday on the beach. I distinctly remember your name. Can you please tell me how to contact him? This is a matter of urgent business."

"You got *my* name right," said John, turning his head slightly. "I still don't know anybody by that other name."

"I saw you with him, man," replied Nieting. "We were together yesterday on the beach when you walked by. I was the guy with Rene. You both walked off together."

"That doesn't mean shit to me," said John. He stopped working, turned towards Nieting and stared coldly into his eyes, then went back to his job. "I don't know you and I don't know any Rene."

God damn it, man," said Nieting. "This is not a game. There are forces at work at this very instant, greater than you can imagine."

John faced Nieting, casually wiping a small chrome valve with a rag.

"Is that right?" he said.

"Forget that I asked," said Nieting. "I don't require your assistance after all. Forgive me for intruding. You needn't tell me anything."

He absentmindedly picked a stapled booklet of mimeographed sheets off the counter and flipped through the pages.

"Stuart Z. Perkoff," he said. "I assume he is one of your local poets."

The man held the valve to a lamplight, carefully examining the surface and answered without looking at Nieting. "Yep," he said.

"Have you heard of the poet, Arnold Snellman?" said Nieting.

John looked at Nieting with raised eye brows. "The Filthy Zarathustra?" he said. "Sure, he's right over there, in the back. You should buy him a cup so I don't have to toss him out."

He pointed to the far corner of the room where a lone man sat, hunched over a lighted candle conversing steadily, motionless except for moving lips, his mouth curled as if the words were clever or ironic. He wore dirty cutoff jeans and a tattered t-shirt and sneakers held together with duct tape.   His hair and beard were long and matted, blonde no doubt, yet appearing white in the flickering candle light. He was short and skinny and the hair on his head made him look like a starving lion. He began to swing his face over the candle, grinning and mouthing something as if he were singing.

"Zarathustra?" said Nieting.

"That's your boy right there," said John, placing another cup of coffee on the counter. Nieting paid for the drinks and silently carried the hot cups to the small table in the back of the Venice West Cafe where the great poet sat counting out a march beat in the air with an imaginary conductor's stick. When Nieting handed him the cup, he took it without hesitation. For an instant, the professor was overwhelmed at the pathetic wretch staring up with the clear eyes of the child. The creases of his face were filled with dirt, black lines panted on alabaster, yet the eyes were pristine blue. Nieting introduced himself in German, taking a nearby chair and sitting opposite Snellman. He realized his forwardness was rude, however, Snellman was ill, desperately ill. He took the seat with a paternal air of familiarity and looked directly into Snellman's eyes.

"I don't speak German any longer," Snellman announced. "I've forgotten how to speak German."

"The man over there referred to you as Zarathustra," said Nieting.

"Of course," said Snellman, grinning proudly. "They call me the Filthy Zarathustra. If Nietzsche's Zarathustra had survived what I have survived, wouldn't he be filthy also? Do not answer. We are strangers. My close friends call me simply F.Z. or just Z. I am no longer Snellman. He is dead long ago."

"My name is Dr. Valentin Nieting. I've come from Berlin.   Hans Gartenbauer asked me to extend his greetings to you upon my trip to Los Angeles."

"Dr. Freud?" said Snellman.

"I'm afraid not," said Nieting. "I am a Professor of Anthropology."

"Anthropology?" said Snellman. He laughed with his eyes closed, rubbing his knuckles as if Nieting had told a joke.

"I've wondered if my old colleagues might send someone to inquire after my whereabouts," said Snellman. "Like Marlow after Kurtz, you know? It's been so long since I've corresponded. Sending an anthropologist makes more sense that sending a shrink, don't you think?"

Snellman grabbed his hairy mouth in his hands and shivered in a spasm of laughter.

"I should say, past professor," said Nieting. "I was dismissed from the Free University for inciting my students to illegal and unpatriotic actions."

Snellman shook his head, waving a crooked forefinger at Nieting.

"Very good," he said. "Well done. Who did you say sent you?"

"Hans, Hans Gartenbauer, your friend. He is doing well, in case you are wondering. He is quite engaged these days. He too was fired from his post at the Free University. We were both fired for our political activities."

"Brilliant," said Snellman. "Hans was always a good boy. He was my student once, long ago. I had high hopes for him and he has never disappointed. I did not encourage his political activities, yet to be so distasteful to the authorities as to be run out of the university is something one can admire."

"Much has changed in five years," said Nieting, "Not with the administration surely, yet certainly among the students. Han's and my sentiments are quite widespread these days. We were hardly leaders. We simply supported the students publically. We encouraged them and conducted workshops in political theory. We joined them, actually. They've been prohibited from holding political meetings on campus. Apparently, the real world has no place in university. Discussion of the American invasion of Vietnam is banned. The students are tired of former Nazis making policy and holding positions of power in what is supposed to be a democratic institution. Some of the students have evolved to quite radical positions. They are greatly inspired by the students of Berkeley, you know. You must have witnessed the beginnings of that struggle when you were there. These are exciting times. Events are moving rapidly. We believe Revolution is finally manifesting on a world-wide scale."

Snellman blinked his eyes. "Why, I didn't see a thing in Berkeley," he said. "I saw no struggle. Revolution manifesting? I hope things turn out better this time, although I can't see how they will. My hands were as full then as they are now with the only revolution I can possibly effect."

Snellman tapped his chest.

"Yes, of course," said Nieting. "How is that revolution coming along? How are you, Snellman? What shall I tell Hans?"

"You can see me," said Snellman. "Tell him what you like, or better, tell him you never found Arnold Snellman. That's true, you know. I am no longer the man Hans knew. What's more, I have no intention of knowing ex-professor Hans Gartenbauer, hence forth. Tell him that. Tell him the Filthy Zarathustra says go to hell."

Snellman shrank down, shaking his head sorrowfully. He stared into the burning candle.

"Do tell him to continue sending the funds," he said. "The funds are essential to my survival. I have no family, you know. I'm sure I would be dead within a week without Hans. My death will be grizzly."

Snellman grinned with black teeth.

"I love the word, grizzly," he said. "It sounds like what it is. Grizzly. It may be a colloquial expression, I'm not sure. Perhaps it means gristle, gristly. My kitty died recently, you know. He disappeared for the longest time. I found him in a tunnel, a drainage pipe it was, a huge thing. He was in there dried, petrified. I took him home with me. His death was grizzly and in an amazingly short time he became gristly. You don't happen to have an English dictionary, do you? America is a cruel place to be an artist. Grizzly. I must exist, regardless. Life is grizzly, yet I must resist becoming gristly. Hans must not desert me."

"Hans sends you funds?" said Nieting. "Then, he is aware of your condition? He never mentioned it to me. I am not here to save you, Snellman."

Snellman cackled. "Then what on earth do you want, Herr Professor? Are you CIA?" He gulped the hot coffee. "You smell like CIA, you know? You did come here for me. You are in search of the poet Snellman. Well, he is deceased. You didn't realize you'd come in search of a dead man, did you?"

Snellman's head jerked and he sat upright. From the look of surprise on his face, it appeared that the idea hadn't occurred to him until he heard himself utter the words. The CIA knew of his death and had nevertheless sent agents in search of him. Nieting chuckled and Snellman jumped to attention.

"Do you consider me entertaining, Herr Professor," said Snellman.

"Certainly not," said Nieting, "nor am I affiliated with any institution, particularly of a military or authoritarian nature. However, seeking you out was part of my plan from the outset. It wasn't simply for Hans' sake. I came here to make your acquaintance, to tell you things I believed would please you. I am grateful for your poems. I wish you to understand how your work is still embraced in Berlin, even after the silence of a year."

Nieting touched the Filthy Zarathustra's shiny red hand and spoke gently.

"To this day, your poetry is performed in Berlin, recited by our mutual friend, Professor Hans Gartenbauer, among others. Twice, I've attended his readings of your correspondence from America. I wondered what he and Eduard did with the money they collected. Knowing Hans, I assumed they bought themselves drinks afterward, but now I realize the funds were destined to come to you. And, that is how it should be, Zarathustra. The gift you have given is greater than a few Deutschmarks. You are a beacon still, particularly to the students."

Snellman appeared to be moved by the thought that the students believed he had given them a gift.

"That's very strange," he said. "Public readings, you say?"

Snellman mused, scratching with two fingers deeply into his tangled beard.

"You must do me a service, Herr Professor," he said. "When you return to Berlin, please discourage any such activities."

Snellman's eyes grew large, shimmering blue in the dancing candle light.

"At the beginning of one's career," he said, "one desires to be understood by one's contemporaries, perhaps even by some abstract notion of posterity. However, one realizes quickly that this is not possible. Either the work is misread and taken for something it is not or it is ignored, a blank stare, you know?"

Snellman affected the look of a catatonic then grinned exposing his black mouth.

"Ultimately, one learns to eschew being understood at all," he said. "One gains comfort in other areas. One writes *not* to be heard, out of spite, if you will, or with the hope of contributing to the unseen spiritual disintegration of mankind, hastening of the apocalypse. When a poet reaches this stage, the greatest fear is of being comprehended at all, acceptance being a signification of failure, of not having traveled far enough away. What could be more distasteful than to be used for purposes against which you initially struggled, to be accepted by a world you sought to destroy?"

Snellman glanced around, resting his eyes on a young woman sitting alone at a table in the center of the room writing in a notebook by candle light. He called out, "Hello Dee," and the woman looked up. "Hello Z," she said and continued writing. Snellman twisted the end of his beard between his thumb and forefinger and winked at Nieting.

"In the old days," he said, "there was always pussy to mitigate the doubts, to calm the confusion, something or someone beautiful to cling to, a reality one could sink one's teeth into, eh? Such compensation is no longer available to the Filthy Zarathustra. Now, I find my comfort elsewhere."

Snellman waved his hand above his head dismissively and sighed.

"All in the past now," he said. "Exited with Snellman."

His eye lids began to flutter and slowly close and his head sink towards the table top like it was being let down by a pully. Then, he jerked up fast, raising his arm as if to make a grand pronouncement, pointing his forefinger to the ceiling, but his torso kept going back, his eyes shut tight and his mouth gaping in a dead sleep. His head hit the wall with

an echoing thud as the chair slipped and he slid to the floor in a prolonged crash. He bounced up like a rubber ball, eyes alert again, and
assumed his seat like nothing had happened. John shouted from behind
the counter.

"God damn it, Z, you can't be nodding off in here. I've told you a
dozen times."

One of the men on the bandstand laughed and said, "That's why they
call him Z."

Nieting motioned to John, waving the flat of his palm.

"It's all right, man," he said. "He simply fell. Nothing more. He's with
me. It's cool, I assure you."

John tossed a towel aside, vaulted the counter and rushed to
Snellman's table. Snellman lowered his head contritely as John shouted
at Nieting.

"I don't give a mother fuck who he's with. I can't have him nodding
off, period. I'm taking a chance letting him in here at all. You know the
scene, Z. Finish your coffee and take off. That's it."

"Please, there is no need," said Nieting and John cut him short.

"Shut the fuck up. You don't know shit about it."

Nieting remained quiet.

"Finish up Z, and take off. Got it?"

John strode back to the counter and Snellman, digging his forefinger
somewhere around his ear, glanced after him, switching his coffee cup
with Nieting's cup with his free hand when Nieting looked away. The
move was pathetic, yet Nieting pretended not to see.

"Herr Professor," said Snellman, "may I ask your age?"

There was a silence as Snellman drained the cup.

"Please, you must not answer," he said. "Forgive the question. I
know more than I would like as it is. There are occurrences in this life
that are incomprehensible, yet real, undeniable, yet impossible to relate.
We are marked by such experiences. There are times when this mark is
discernable to others of the same type. I don't know whether the change
is in appearance strictly, or perhaps a spiritual essence of some sort, an

odor that another of the same type recognizes as dogs recognize each other's scent. Or perhaps we become family members of sorts. The kind of family one wishes never to encounter. Of course, I understand we have never met, or have we Herr Professor? It does not matter"

Nieting averted his eyes as if Snellman's black finger tips might reach inside his breast searching for the softest spiritual flesh and run his hands over the festering scars. The poet knew things about Nieting he no longer knew about himself. There was no point in Nieting asking how he knew. Perhaps the contents of his inner being were leaking, breaking through the skin, memories oozing like blood trickling and the poet could see Nieting for what he was. If anyone could fathom the depth of the perversion of Nieting's life it was the poet. Nieting trembled; he wished to be exposed, wished to be identified by the wretched madman as a lost child, as a comrade. He wished Snellman to see through him and yet he could not bear the thought. Snellman wiped his sweaty face with his naked forearm, exasperated, as if he wanted no part of Nieting's problems.

"None of that business has any import now," he said. "I have the means these days to transcend the filth of this reality. Names, even silly fucking nick names, are merely external significations. I am justified in my ways. I have long felt an affinity for the Hindu belief that life is a dream or rather an illusion. There are myriad paths to attaining Nirvana."

"We agree, then," said Nieting. "Nothing remains beyond the work."

"The work?" said Snellman.

"Yes," said Nieting. "You are a poet, Snellman, pardon me, Filthy Zarathustra."

"We are close enough friends now for you to simply call me Z," said Snellman. "I feel you and I know each other well now, as if for an entire life time. We must help one another. We have become close in a very short time."

"Very well then, Z," said Nieting. "What are you composing of late? You have many friends who will insist upon knowing of your progress."

"Progress?" said Snellman. "The idea is a pathetic irrelevance. I am disappointed that you would use such a word. Certainly, I no longer compose. Not in the traditional sense, not in a manner that would yield anything a philistine or a professor would call poetry. I travel light these days.

"You see, I ran out of paper a while ago. Isn't that strange? Paper costs nothing in this country, yet I couldn't afford a piece of paper. I wrote on the edges of newspapers for some time. Carrying all those scraps was terribly burdensome. I'd lose them constantly. I had to ask myself of what use they were. I was forced to discover a new medium, a technique that I find I much prefer. The need for materials is no longer a concern. I compose in my mind, the poem exists only during the act of composition. I always forget the words, the sounds, the music instantly when I cease writing. That is an essential component of the process. It affords an immediacy that is quite stimulating and promotes spontaneity far more profoundly than transcription. Of course, the option of sharing the work with the public is out of the question. This, however, is a positive evolution."

Snellman looked towards the counter, nodded at John and pretended to drink from the empty cup. He spoke rapidly, yet quietly, barely moving his lips, like there must be a sinister eavesdropper within earshot.

"That is," he whispered, "unless one were to employ the technique of electronically monitoring brain waves. They possess the capacity to capture the content of one's thoughts, you know. The Central Intelligence Agency has perfected the technology. This will open the way to actual mind control on a mass scale. I doubt if they would consent to assisting in the publication of a poet's work. I wouldn't know where to inquire, at any rate. I don't consider this an option, realistically speaking."

Snellman peered suspiciously over his shoulder at the wall touching the back of his chair.

"Besides," he said, "It would be madness to expose my whereabouts to the state. They are well aware of the corrosive nature of my writing. They would very much like to acquire my definitive location. They would murder my corpse. This is why I can no longer communicate with Hans beyond a simple bank transfer. I must remain unseen. This is the reason for the hair, Nieting."

Snellman pointed to his head as if Nieting had missed the obvious tactical component of his appearance.

"It's a small price to pay for anonymity," said Snellman. "I consider the inconvenience to be insignificant, if an inconvenience at all, in fact, not concerning oneself with grooming is a great advantage. I am doing quite well this way. Yes, and I prefer the solitude of internal self-publication. I have nothing to say to the public any longer, particularly to Germans. Germany has ceased to exist for me. This journey is singularly my own. There is no need to explain anything. To expect comprehension is absurd. It will not be forth coming."

Snellman hesitated, picking at his beard and staring into the candle.

"I do have need of patrons, it is true," he said. "Hans and a few others have sustained me, afforded me the freedom to pursue my projects."

"How do you keep your money?" said Nieting.

"Why, I have a bank account, of course," replied Snellman. "I receive only a small monthly pittance, by the way, and I have certain medical expenses beyond which, well, you see how I must live."

"Yes, I see," said Nieting. "You asked why I am here, Z. Will you allow me to tell you?"

"Of course," said Snellman, thrusting the empty coffee mug into the air towards John in a mock toast. John shook his head incredulously as Snellman took an exaggerated quaff, then leaned close to Nieting.

"Go on, please," he whispered. "We are friends, close friends. We must help one another. We must confide."

"Yes, of course," said Nieting. "I am currently pursuing the most significant project my career, a defining accomplishment, perhaps the single great contribution of my life."

"Why single, are you ill?" asked Snellman.

"No, I am not ill," said Nieting, "I meant compared to everything else, this work will dwarf everything I've done before. Besides, one never really knows when this life will be ended, unexpectedly, prematurely."

"Ah, professor, don't be so gloomy?" said Snellman.

"Please Z, I am not gloomy. Do not interrupt. I allowed you to speak. Please extend the same courtesy to me."

"Of course, Herr Professor, please go on. We are all we have in America, you and I. We must be kind. We must be patient."

"As I stated," said Nieting. "I am in search of an important oral document that could very well have an immediate impact on crucial events transpiring today, here in Los Angeles and across the US and the world. I've discovered through an informant, an American living in Berlin until his recent death this past March that a song exists describing Negro resistance to a pogrom in New Orleans in the year 1900. According to the informant, the song was composed in honor of a freedom fighter by the name of Robert Charles whose resistance to the white supremacists sparked the pogrom among the whites. The subject of the tribute, Robert Charles, is said to have single-handedly resisted thousands of armed whites, killing many, until his eventual escape. The song however, was suppressed by the authorities and lost among the Negros. I have reason to believe I may be able to recover the song and return it to the Negroes. As you can understand, in these days of renewed struggle, possession of the lost song would be quite advantageous."

"Quite advantageous to whom?" said Snellman, bobbing his head and chucking. "I was being disingenuous, forgive me."

"My original assignment was to write a companion article for a small journal," said Nieting. "You may remember MerzKraft. The presentation of the song was to be accompanied by a contextual piece on the significance of Buddy Bolden, the first great artist of Negro Jazz, as a cultural resistance fighter. According to my informant, it was he who composed the song. My intent is to write of him from the perspective of his own community's interests, from the Negro perspective. Uncovering a song memorializing Negro resistance written by Bolden would put the American white supremacist power structure into context, demystify its workings, thus return to the Negro not only the song and the knowledge of who composed the song, but the power, the revolutionary power of his own culture."

"That is quite a project," said Snellman. "Of course, I agree with you in principle."

"There is more, Z," said Nieting. "My research in New Orleans expanded the scope of the work beyond anything I could have imagined. I witnessed a collective action of the people, an irresistible insistence upon self-expression in the form of a Negro funeral parade. There was something biologic about the process, like a seed cracking open, germinating. I was able to observe the active culture of resistance that is finally manifesting across the globe today. *The Robert Charles Song* will dramatically illustrate this ongoing principle.

"There are several significant flaws in your approach, Professor," said Snellman.

"Not yet, Z," replied Nieting. "There is more still. What I witnessed in New Orleans represented only the rudiments of culture, astoundingly sophisticated as it was. The power of collective action transformed the streets of the city into a zone of Negro power. Discovery of Bolden's lost song will bring us to an even higher level of meaning."

Nieting was breathless. He noticed Snellman's eye lids quivering and slapped his hands resting on the table.

"The great Negro musician, Kid Auger, was a colleague of Bolden at the time of the pogrom. I came to Los Angeles with the hope that he knew something that might lead me to the song. Upon further consideration I am absolutely certain that he possesses knowledge of song. *The Robert Charles Song* was suppressed because it contains revolutionary sentiments far too radical for the time, yet perfectly relevant, in fact, desperately needed today. I've also discovered that there is a man in Los Angeles who may be of assistance. He has taken the complete canon of African derived musics and created a revolutionary organization called BANG."

"What is the man's name?" asked Snellman.

"Triplett," said Nieting.

"Morris Triplett?"

"Yes, I believe that's it."

Snellman waved his forefinger like a teacher correcting a student.

"His organization is known as BAD, Herr Professor," he said. "Black African Diaspora Ensemble, not BANG."

"Are you sure?"

"Quite sure."

"Are you aware of the rebellion of the Negroes of Watts?" said Nieting.

"Anyone who can hobble past a newsstand knows," said Snellman.

"Do you understand the importance of this fact?" said Nieting. "Triplett lives in Watts, you know."

"Yes, I know," said Snellman. "I've witnessed several performances of various configurations of BAD over the years."

"What do you mean?" snapped Nieting.

"Simply, that I've attended performances of Mr. Triplett and his groups. What else could I possibly mean?"

"Where did you do this?"

"Why, in Watts, in the park, and once or twice Mr. Triplett performed in Venice. You are correct about one thing, Herr Professor, the music is astoundingly beautiful"

"How did you learn of Triplett?" said Nieting.

"I don't know, from a poster perhaps."

"How did you get to Watts?"

"I went with friends, naturally, musicians that I knew or rather that Snellman knew from here, from Venice. Oh, you must hear BAD perform if you get the opportunity. I was able, or should I say, Snellman was able to speak with Mr. Triplett after one performance. This was several years ago, I think. He was an exceedingly charming man, brilliant, earnest, an inspiration. Why so crestfallen, Herr Professor? I would expect you to welcome additional insight into your subject."

"Snellman, please do not affect a snug tone," said Nieting. "I will not tolerate triviality. What else do you know of Morris Triplett?"

Snellman's eyes misted as he answered.

"Herr Professor, we are comrades," he said. "I shall give you everything. I shall pour my heart out to you. Where to begin? Yes, black music is truly marvelous. I have enjoyed Jazz very much since I've come to this country. It seems to me you are not mistaken. Mr. Triplett and his colleagues are truly a treasure. To this degree, I concur, your analysis is sound."

"To this degree?" said Nieting. "Really, Snellman, to what degree?"

"What you've stated is true only as far as it goes," said Snellman. "There is nothing to indicate that the music will be used for political purposes or that BAD will vanquish the whites."

"You speak like a child, Snellman" said Nieting.

"Do I look like Snellman?" replied the poet.

"No, you look like a filthy Zarathustra," said Nieting.

"And you, professor, look like a used car salesman."

"Used car salesman?" said Nieting.

"Precisely," said Snellman. "That is, a symbol of dishonesty, shoddiness, pettiness and vulgar self-interest."

"Explain yourself," said Nieting.

"You are an egoist, Professor," said Snellman, "You have indulged your fancy in ways you never would have tolerated from your students. You are making a great mistake, one that will waste years and either disenchant you to the degree that you abandon your profession or you will become exactly what you say you despise, a peddler of the black man's goods for you own advantage, a thief, as you correctly termed it."

"I am shocked, Z," said Nieting. "Your words are not well considered. Your condition has caused you to speak irrationally."

"I am speaking to you as a brother," said Snellman. "I have had experience in such endeavors as you have undertaken."

"Your experience is quite transparent, Snellman," said Nieting. "You are a drug addict. A junky, according to the owner of your last residence. I do not believe in avoiding truth. I refuse to ignore the obvious. I don't care how sordid it might be."

"You are a fool to think you've nothing to learn from a junky, Herr Professor," said Snellman. "I assure you, I have made the same mistakes you are making. I also had a pretext for coming to America. You pursue this song like a man after diamonds and gold. What is there to warrant such desperate pursuit? Or, is it you being pursued?"

"I am here as a trained anthropologist is search of a cultural artifact. I have no idea to what you are referring."

"Perhaps what you say it truthful," said Snellman. "I too came to America to do important work. Before I came here, I saw nothing to gain from residency at an American university, even a prestigious university. Everyone at home said it was a great honor and a stepping stone in my career. Fuck careers, Nieting, fuck careers. Artists don't require stepping stones. I came here because I wished to learn of the indigenous natives of North America, the so called Indians. I wished to attain their secrets. I wanted to possess their wisdom and knowledge."

Snellman shook his head wearily, appearing lucid for the first time.

"I came here to purge myself," he said. "I came here to learn to live a spiritual life. The Chumash possess truth gained through great suffering. I wanted what they had. In Berkeley I sought out anyone with knowledge of indigenous American culture. Of course, I was directed to the Anthropology department. At that time, Kroeber had recently died. He'd created the most renowned center for the study of indigenous North American culture in the world at the University of California. You know Kroeber's influence. He dominated the field. I wanted knowledge. Yet, I was struck at the absence of Indians, not only in the department but in the institution at large. They were not a presence in the place dedicated to their study. Imagine, the professed study of a people that in no significant manner involves the people to be studied beyond mere subjects? Clearly, this could not yield the results I desired. I struck out to find what I was looking for. I contacted Indians living in the Bay area and when I traveled to Los Angeles I became associated with a group of individuals. They were Chumash people. They'd formed a collective and administered a small clinic and meeting place in a destitute area of Los Angeles, a part of town known as Skid Row where many of their people lived.

"I made some very good friends among these people. I was well thought of, regardless of my insufferable attitude towards their culture, which was chauvinism, purely and simply. In my exuberance, I presumed to understand their inner most selves, their culture, better than they. My closest friends among the Chumash listened to my ceaseless hypothesizing, my grotesque poeticizing, at first with good natured tolerance, until finally they saw fit to set me straight. This was an act of love, I assure you, one that I shall always be grateful for.

"I lived in an apartment in East Los Angeles at the time and through my research came to the conclusion that a native village once existed on the same location. This was quite exciting and extremely fateful. I could sense the presence of these ancient Indians and from the feelings I picked up, very intense feelings, quite directed, I began to compose new poems from the voices of certain members of the tribe. A shaman and an old woman, and several times a sick child spoke through me. This writing was transcription and nothing more. I wrote what I heard. One piece contained a dozen voices interacting in a ritual. You'll laugh, but I did not question that the voices spoke German. It seemed normal to me because I did not speak Chumash. I am not an unintelligent man, yet I was sure their spirits were speaking through my body. The writing poured from me. The wisdom of the work far exceeded my understanding of the subject. My Chumash friends were not impressed. In fact, they were deeply offended. However, my enthrallment and sense of privilege continued to expand. What did I need of my friends' knowledge, when I was now privy to the knowledge of their ancestors? What these people owned was mine for the taking. I never would have believed that I would take on so easily, so unknowingly, the privileges of being a white man. I even labored under the strange conceit that I did not possess the racial complexes, the illnesses of white America, yet I exhibited the illness with an intensity that blinded me to my behavior. I never questioned myself, not acutely enough. Old brother Nietzsche would have been disgusted. The game ended when my friends confronted me with a rather exhaustive list of reasons my writings were in no way connected to the spirits of their ancestors. They'd collected an irrefutable list of points of fact, flaws in my story that I'd ignored out of an over oxuberance of self-interest.

Unfortunately, I argued with my friends. The argument became angry and they began to leave in disgust, one by one. Finally, in an effort to break off the debate and extricate myself, I announced that my Indians were of another tribe unknown to my friends. I declared that my Indians were my business and that they could take their Indians and I would take my Indians and we would all go our own way. There was even an implication, quite intentional in the heat of battle, that perhaps my friends lacked true authenticity, were not, in fact, really Indians.

"Yet when I suddenly heard the sound of my own voice saying these things, spewing the painfully typical logic of the colonizer in the particular manner of phrasing that I'd spent decades perfecting, I fell to the ground. Collapsed. It was curious. My body dropped to the floor. I hadn't fainted, rather I'd knocked myself off my feet, struck by my own words as with a hammer. In a flash, everything became clear. It truly was a flash, like a giant flash bulb pressed before open eyes, white light and a blow to the head. I saw myself as I truly was.

"The few of my friends who hadn't fled rushed to me and pulled me to my feet. There were no words exchanged beside my simple utterance, 'you are correct. I am sorry.' I walked from the room and never returned. From time to time, I encounter a few of my old colleagues on the beach. Our relationships are for the most part cordial, if not sympathetic. I think they respected my decision to recant, which is what I did. Hence forth, I've left the defining of others' souls to themselves. The black man has no need of your assistance, Herr Professor. You are an interloper, an adventurer, a man seeking the best investment, a white man."

"This is untrue, Snellman," said Nieting, "and quite unfair. You know nothing of my work."

"Beware, professor, you have drunk the magic potion of whiteness. It is most difficult not to be made drunk with it and the addiction is as insidious as a narcotic. I willingly gave up everything in order to kick. It was the only way I could be sure I was clean. You too will lose everything. You won't heed my warnings, I think. You are pig headed. Lost children cannot afford to be pig headed."

"Lost children?" said Nieting. He heard Emil cackling and turned quickly towards the front door. No one had entered or departed the cafe since he'd arrived. The girl writing in the notebook rose casually, waved at John and walked out of the café.

"Have you any money?" said Snellman. "I can fix you, if you'd like to join me. We can combine our resources and each benefit. Hans is a dependable friend. There are worse circumstances than scuffling at Venice Beach. Leave the black man to decide his own fate. To him you can only be an impediment. We are what we are. Join me, Herr Professor."

"Good God, Snellman," said Nieting. "Are you asking me to become a drug addict?"

Snellman jumped to his feet as John rounded the corner of the counter and headed towards him.

"Addiction is a relative term," he said. "We must practice acceptance."

"Okay boys," said John, gathering up the cups. "I've listened to enough of your bullshit for one night."

"We were just leaving," said Snellman. "We are going to the Lafayette. The coffee there is superior and they have pie. Come, Herr Professor, you were asking for my critique on your forthcoming book. I am sure I can assist you."

Nieting walked out of the Venice West Cafe into the night of Ocean Front Walk with Snellman on his heels. Outside, Snellman grabbed his arm and held him fast.

"You misunderstood me, Herr Professor. I simply offered to fix your problems. I offered to be a colleague."

"I have no need of a colleague," replied Nieting.

"What will you tell Hans? He mustn't desert me."

"I will tell Hans the truth."

"What does that mean? What is your truth? I'm afraid it differs from my truth. I was not forthcoming earlier. I do have new work. I've written an entire volume, new poems on my life in exile. Han's must continue to sustain me. This work is my crowning achievement, the best of my career. It must see print. It was written specifically for German youth, to assist them in the remaking of German society. I can show you. I have the manuscript hidden nearby. You will be delighted."

Snellman's eyes shifted from Nieting's face to something over his shoulder and followed it until three people emerged to the left, a man walking in the center, who stared at Snellman strangely, and two others crowding around the man like children pleading for candy.

"I shall see you again, Herr Professor," said Snellman. "Your trip to America would be well rewarded by your collaboration in the publication of my new work."

He turned and moved quickly after the three people.

"You'll return, Herr Professor. I'll make it worth your while. I have letters too, dozens of them that you can deliver to Hans or perhaps publish yourself."

Snellman ran, raising his boney knees and pumping his toothpick arms, the great mass of hair on his head flopping up and down like a hat that might fly away at any moment. When he fell in with the three, the man in the center glanced back without expression and continued on. The quartet turned off of Ocean Front Walk and out of sight.

◆ ◆ ◆

Friday morning, Suzette Auger called for the Disneyland limo for the second time in two days. Her husband had complained of fatigue, yet insisted on going to work. She'd tried to convince him to stay home and he would not have it.

"I can't let those two old men try to carry things without me. I might be the cause of someone's death."

"Oh stop it, Jean. That's nonsense."

Auger had laughed, telling Suzette he was only teasing. He assured her the weakness would pass, but he did not tell her about the strange ailment that not only prevented him from sleeping but tormented him with dreams when he did manage to drift off. Far worse, he'd seen visions while awake, his life playing out before his eyes. He was struggling for his sanity, yet his wife knew nothing of his suffering. At first, Auger suspected the German journalist of somehow triggering something in his mind. Those damned questions about his family. But, the German hadn't asked any questions. Auger had volunteered the information. There was the fatigue as well, ever since the last show at Disneyland the previous day, before he'd even met the German. He believed it was the excessive heat and going overboard in the performance that had wasted him so, chasing Goofy around the deck of the Mark Twain, thrusting his slide at him so he jumped in the air to avoid being hit. The crowd loved the routine. Auger had simply pushed himself too far. He hadn't felt right since.

Watts was in flames. It was all over the newspapers, television and radio. Auger watched the footage on TV before going to bed Thursday night, black people taunting and threatening police, and first thing in the morning he turned it on again. Suzette scolded him, saying his interest was morbid and not good for his health, but Auger insisted the scenes of violence had no effect on him, had nothing whatsoever to do with him. He didn't tell her that as he lie in bed the night before, thoughts of the violence in Watts filled his mind, juxtaposed with the reveries of his youth. Uncontrollable images of the past, things he'd believed he'd banned from his memory years ago, things he didn't know happened at all swirled amidst scenes of burning cars and helmeted police scurrying under a rain of sniper fire. The experience was exhausting. Nevertheless, just before noon on Friday, Auger hauled himself up at the sound of the doorbell and answered the door, grinning sheepishly as he motioned to the driver to carry his instrument case. *I won't get anywhere giving in to this thing,* he thought. *That's for damned sure.*

On the ride to work, Auger fought off sleep, fearful of where his dreams might take him. Yet, TV images of Watts ran through his head, crowds of black people fighting police, Chief Parker blaming communists and civil rights fanatics for instigating the rebellion, and white people, some of them his neighbors, crowding gun shops, arming against black revenge. He fidgeted in the seat of the limo nervously tapping his instrument case even as he struggled to keep his eyes open. When the car reached Disneyland, Auger crawled out the door as the chauffeur carried his instrument to the golf cart waiting to transport him to the outdoor stage where the Young Men of Jazz were scheduled to perform. When he arrived backstage, Johnny St. Cyr and Paul Barbarin were busy unwrapping an order of Mexican food. The two men hurried as they worked, peeking into the orders to see what belonged to whom, opening tiny containers of salsa and placing napkins and plastic utensils on the small circular table. Neither man greeted Auger as he entered, except for a raised eyebrow of anticipation from Barbarin and a wink from St. Cyr.

"Seeing that this is our last week here at Disneyland," chuckled Barbarin, "it'll be a while before we get to eat *Mexico Lindo* again. I know we do it every Thursday, but I figured there wasn't nothing wrong with doing it two days in a row. Just don't tell my wife."

"Who gets the Chili Relleno?" said St. Cyr.

"That's Auger," said Barbarin. "It's been six weeks since we been doing this and Auger ain't had but one thing each time and you can't remember Chili Relleno?"

"Just one thing I got to remember," said St. Cyr. "Carnitas Buritto con salsa."

St. Cyr and Barbarin slid into their seats and started to eat, neither man noticing Auger drop into the chair or his unusual lack of enthusiasm for the weekly ritual until he tossed his fork into his plate and clutched his forehead.

"What's the matter, Jean," said St. Cyr.

"Two days of this spicy food is too much for him," said Barbarin.

"It's ain't the food," replied Auger. "I just don't feel like playing no more. That damned horn takes too much muscle, too much wind. I'm too old for this."

"What are you talking about?" said Barbarin, emptying a container of hot sauce on a pair of enchiladas.

Auger held his head in his hands.

"I was supposed to talk to a writer today, a professor," he said, "a German boy. But I don't think I can do it."

"What's he want?" asked St. Cyr.

"He wants to know about Buddy Bolden, I guess," said Auger.

"They ought to pay for that god-damned information," said St. Cyr.

"I don't feel good," said Auger. "I been having thoughts lately."

"What kind of thoughts?" asked Barbarin.

"About my folks mostly, back home. And I didn't sleep last night. The little I did get was nothing but dreams, wild dreams. Some of them were about the old days."

"I know what you mean," said St. Cyr. "One time after we ate this food, I went home and dreamed of Joe Oliver. We was playing and Joe kept shouting how I had the time all wrong."

"No," said Barbarin, leaning back and laughing. "What did you say back to him?"

"Nothing, that was it," said St. Cyr. "He was cussing and I couldn't get it right, couldn't please him, then just woke up. It was good to see ol'Joe though."

"Amen," replied Barbarin.

"I can't work today," said Auger. "I can't keep my eyes open."

"Probably that mess over in Watts is on your mind," said Barbarin. "I know I lay there last night, just thinking about it. Don't know what time I got to sleep."

"No, that ain't it," said Auger. "That don't affect me no way."

"What do you mean, it don't affect you?" said St. Cyr. "Those are your people down there."

"Like hell they are," said Auger. "Marquette Frye ain't shit to me."

"Hell nothing," said St. Cyr. "You know how many of those folks come from Louisiana? Shit, first place you played in Los Angeles was the Cadillac Café on Central Avenue. You used to live right down there on Alameda in your little chicken shack. I used to come visit you. Those Negroes used to buy your damned chickens. Don't tell me they ain't your folks."

"I'll tell you what I please," said Auger. "My folks never rioted."

"C'mon Jean," said St. Cyr. "You know what it's like down there. There ain't no damned jobs. Schools ain't worth shit. Nothing for the kids but the street. It's been a powder keg waiting to blow for a long time now."

"Besides, the police were involved," said Barbarin. "You know how they did that boy Frye. You know how the police do."

"No, I don't," said Auger. "I ain't got nothing against the police."

"You don't?" replied Barbarin, raising his brow. "That's one damn thing that hasn't changed from back home."

"That ain't true," said St. Cyr. "Police are far worse out here. You know, they recruit'm out of the South. Can you imagine that? I seen the flyer they use to recruit. My god, that Chief Parker ain't no better than a common criminal, a god damned thug. He hires crackers with experience whupping niggers' asses. I just hate to see those folks tearing up their own neighborhood. I got a mess of cousins out there, too. This is serious business."

"For Christ's sake, don't blame Chief Parker," said Auger. "I know that nigger Marquette Frye. I know the type. He got his mother brawling out on the street. That kind don't care about nothing. Always drinking and taking dope, chasing pussy. They don't know how to work. They don't respect work, so they don't respect themselves. Look at us. We come from poor folks and we made our way out of it."

"We was blessed with this music," said St. Cyr, "besides being in the right place at the right time."

"Bullshit," snapped Auger. "I'm here cause I worked myself here. You don't get nothing, you can't *have* nothing you don't work for. No welfare check, nothing. The police need to clean that mess up down there. Beat some ass and slap some of those niggers behind bars."

The men ate in silence for several moments until St. Cyr shook his head and said, "I don't know, Jean."

"I know," said Auger. "I know real good."

Again, the men ate without speaking, until Barbarin broke the silence.

"Auger don't know a god-damned thing," he said. "He never had any hard times. He grew up on his uncle's plantation. His folks was rich."

Barbarin winked at St. Cyr, who looked back sternly, shaking his head, signaling him to back off. Auger jumped to his feet and the folding chair flew as he staggered backwards.

"Motherfucking hell we was," he shouted. "Don't tell me we was rich."

"Calm down, Jean," said St. Cyr. "Paul was only giving you a hard time. He knows you had it tough, just like everyone else."

"Barbarin don't know shit," said Auger. "None of you niggers know shit."

"Tell him, Paul," said St. Cyr. "Tell him you was only kidding."

Barbarin shoveled a fork of food into his mouth and waved Auger off.

"Ah, I ain't telling him nothing."

"God damn it, tell the old man before he drops down dead right here."

"He'll be alright."

Auger trembled, pointing his finger at Barbarin.

"I sure as hell don't need you to say a god damned thing."

"Go on home, Jean," interrupted St. Cyr. "Take the day off. You said you was tired. Come back when you're rested."

"None of you know shit," said Auger. "Never did know shit."

St. Cyr and Barbarin watched Auger grab his instrument case, soiled napkin stuck in his collar, hands quivering, head shaking with rage, and storm from the room. Outside, the sun hit Auger like a fist and he faltered, weaving for several steps, then racing forward dragging the instrument case to the golf cart still parked on the path. He tossed the case in and climbed aboard, shouting for the attendant who exited a nearby restroom frantically zipping his fly.

"Get me the hell out of here," said Auger. "God damned fools don't know nothing. Not a god damned thing. They don't know how those trouble makers operate. I know those types. I know the Robert Charles type. Riding round in beat up cars, drinking wine day and night, looking for handouts, always waiting for someone else to do the work or ready to hit some poor bastard over the head and take what little he got. I know Robert Charles' type."

In the parking lot, Auger moved shakily from the cart to the Disneyland limo, still ranting about the trouble makers and criminals who started all the problems in Watts.

"God damn Robert Charles and his brother. They got their mother out in the street, head full of curlers, wearing a god damned raggedy night gown, cussing and fighting with the police. You think I got sympathy for that thing? They're a disgrace, pure and simple. They ain't even human. They're animals. No one can tell me different."

Inside the limo, Auger tried to catch his breath. His hands shook, even his head was shaking and his grey hair hung down over his eyes. There was nothing he could do, nothing was within his control. He was merely a speck of detritus caught in the wind. His mind had gone wild, haywire, like it was separate from his body, like the two had been severed, ripped apart and were falling further and further away. He wiped his face with his hands and water splashed. He leaned his head back and drew a long breath as the driver wheeled through the Disneyland parking lot towards the freeway north.

♦ ♦ ♦

It was unusual for Auger to be wearing his pajamas in the late afternoon. He sat on the edge of the couch in the recreation room of his Brentwood home. His eighteen year old daughter Celine sat on a patio chair outside an open sliding glass door next to the pool reading a Beatles' fan magazine. Auger rose and changed the channel of the television, searching for the latest news bulletin. Suzette called from the other room.

"I hope you're not angry that I phoned that German writer back and rescheduled. It's best that he comes here, don't you think? Since you aren't up to going to Disneyland, I mean. Are you mad, sweetheart?"

"I just don't want to talk to no writer," said Auger. "Why the hell should I give him anything? He ain't looking to give anything back, I promise you that."

"There's nothing wrong with a little press," said Suzette. "That's what you've always told me. Besides, you never know when we might take another trip to Europe. Why not pay for it with a few concerts? Who knows what a little publicity can get us. Wouldn't you love to take Celine to France, Jean? We really should do it. I think we owe it to her."

"I guess you're right. If you put it that way. Just check with me next time. I might have had something else going on."

Auger clicked the channel again and the TV barked, "Among those whose cars were damaged was Supervisor Kenneth Hahn. . . Several officers were treated at Central Receiving Hospital for wounds received . . ."

"Damned thugs," said Auger, "hoodlums is what they are, doing all that damage. They say they want jobs. It ain't jobs they want, they want the government to hand them a living."

"I agree," his wife called from the other room. "I heard on the first of every month the liquor stores in the colored neighborhoods have lines out the door. Then you read about the children being malnourished. It makes me sick."

A commercial came on and Auger switched the channel again and a black boy appeared, standing in front of a microphone surrounded by men in suits, speaking to a black audience apparently at some kind of community meeting.

"I was on Avalon last night," said the boy. "Tonight is gonna be another one, whether you like it or not. Now, they're after white people. They gonna congregate. They gonna caravan out to Inglewood, Playa del Rey, and every place the white man is. We gonna do the white man in."

"God damn it," said Auger. "They're gonna cause the rest of us to go out and get guns."

"Don't even mention getting a gun, Jean," said Suzette. "You know that kind of talk upsets me."

"I was just saying," replied Auger. "Other folks might get guns."

"Well, please don't just say," said Suzette. "It's nerve wracking enough without that. Those people are savages, uncivilized savages. No one knows how far they'll go. I refuse to think about it."

Suzette came into the room, moving in front of Auger as he reached for the dial. She squeezed his shoulder and stood between him and the set, gently patting the back of her freshly cut Bob haircut and giving a cute curtsey. Her close fitting pink slacks, slit at the ankle showed her youthful figure.

"How do I look?" she said. "Do you like the cut? Eloise says it's too young for a woman in her fifties."

"Nonsense," said Auger, grabbing his wife around the waist. "Tell Eloise she's too old for a woman in her fifties."

Suzette giggled.

"I will not," she said. "Celine, sweetie, get your things. We have to leave now or we'll be late."

Auger rubbed his face with the heels of his palms and yawned, watching his wife as the television blared behind her.

"A blaze has been reported at Olympic Blvd., the first fire north of Interstate 10. Chief Parker . . ."

"Celine and I are going now, Jean," said Suzette, nearly shouting, "You'll have the whole house to yourself. We'll be at my sister's in Santa Monica."

"Maybe you shouldn't go to Santa Monica," said Auger.

"It's a thousand miles from Watts," said Suzette.

"They got nig . . ." Auger stopped and eyed his daughter watching him. "They got bad neighborhoods right there in Oakwood."

"We're not going near Oakwood or Venice," said Suzette. "My sister's neighborhood is safe, Jean. Stop this. Get some rest, please? You have an appointment tomorrow with that journalist and you want to be at your best, don't you? Just think, darling, we only have a few days until Duke comes in and the summer at Disneyland is over and you can get some real rest. We'll go to Hawaii just like we planned. Don't think about those animals down in Watts. That's why we have a police force. That's why we have Chief Parker. None of it can touch us, Jean. Just rest, do you hear me?"

"Yes, I hear you," said Auger, leaning around his wife to look at the television set.

"And don't sit around watching the news all afternoon," said Suzette. "It'll only get you riled up."

"I won't," said Auger.

"Promise?"

"Yes, I promise."

"All right then," said Suzette. "I hope you mean what you say, Jean. I really do. Come Celine, let's go visit cousin Angie."

Suzette kissed Auger and his daughter Celine kissed him as he embraced each in turn. In a moment he heard their footsteps outside and then the car start. The TV screen showed the contorted face of a black woman berating the camera.

"Them folks are mad, all right," said Auger. "Look at that black bitch, will ya. She ain't been out of the fields six months, I bet. They got no idea the trouble they're causing themselves. White folks'll arm for sure. The ones that ain't armed already, sure enough will now. Who could blame them? Things'll be tougher on everyone. When a nigger does wrong he makes it tougher on everyone. Those blacks don't understand how much work it takes to make it or else they wouldn't be putting everyone else in jeopardy. All the colored folks who do right and work for everything they got stand to lose by it. When the whites get mad, they'll be hell to pay."

Auger sprawled into the soft cushions of the couch, rubbing his eyes with gnarled fingers.

"Can't shake this feeling, so damned weak. Can't let myself sleep cause I'll have those god damned dreams."

His eyes closed and he dropped off, arms spread across the back of the couch as though he were gesturing to a full house of grateful fans, mouth gaping as if shouting his appreciation for their unbounded love. He slept, and he sure enough dreamed.

Night. He is trying to make his way home from Disneyland. Brentwood is nearby, in the direction he's walking, yet every turn brings a street he's never seen. The streets have New Orleans street names, Dryades, Clio, Erato, Saratoga. Then he's running on Hollywood Boulevard. He reaches the intersection at Hollywood and Vine. Spotlights flash off the low clouds. To the west on Hollywood Blvd., blinking Klieg lights illuminate Grauman's Chinese Theater. There must be a premiere. There must be press and movie stars there, all kinds of celebrities. He might know someone. Maybe Orson is there. Perhaps he can catch a lift home to Brentwood. There are hundreds of tourists in front of the theater snapping pictures, gapping dumbly at a juggler, staring into each other's faces looking for movie stars. All the people are white because the crowds at Graumans are always all white. There is gunshot inside the theater.

He says, "Must be a cowboy movie or maybe a war movie, maybe Audie Murphy." Louis Armstrong is there, wearing a tuxedo, the shirt open at the collar like he just got off work. He says, "they're executing niggers in there. Fire bugs picked up in Watts." A volley of gun fire explodes and white smoke pours from the front door. Mantan Moreland stands next to Armstrong. He say's "God damn them, they're killing niggers again. Just like back in Louisiana, ain't it Auger? We best get down to Central or we might be next." Armstrong says, "They call this the Fourcourt of the Stars, don't they? Well, Pops is a star. Ain't nobody gonna bother ol'Sachel mouth." Auger shakes his head, gesturing to Moreland and Armstrong to back off, don't come near. The ushers are pointing at them and whispering. Auger pushes through the crowd and on to Hollywood

Blvd pursued by a group of white tourists. He ducks into an alley across the street from the Jade Supper Club. The place is closed and he won-ders where all the movie stars are who always come to see him perform. The mob is searching for Negros and the alley is crowded with children. Auger can't squeeze in, half his body sticks out. He is exposed. His horn glows with the light from the spotlights at Graumans. Stonewall and Chiff Matthews huddle in the darkness. He sees Raymond and Rabbit and Foster Lewis, all the children from Pine Grove Plantation. The alley is packed with kids hiding from the rampaging tourists. An old woman tells the children to be silent. Stonewall whispers, "it's Aunt Luzinda," as she pulls the children back into the alley, shepherds them and they run to her, leaping into the darkness through an opening in the wall, like a door-way, a portal through the clouds. Auger is an old man and can't move fast enough. His horn is wedged at his feet, tripping him up, and the old woman doesn't see him or refuses to look. The tourists hear the noise of the children scurrying and charge the alley. Stonewall turns his head and looks blankly at Auger just as the woman's hand pushes him through the dark portal. She looks at Auger and smiles sadly. The tourists circle Auger like wolves and beat him, knock him down with a blow to the head and kick him from all sides. A man runs from the alley carrying Auger's horn, playing Auger's Creole Trombone with perfect facility. He sees his daughter, Celine, through the crowd, standing on the sidewalk weeping and calls out, "don't cry darling, this is only a dream. Daddy's not really hurt." The child is repulsed, shakes her head in disgust and he realizes she is weeping because he is a colored man.

Auger opened his eyes in the sunlit recreation room of his Brentwood home, the silent television flickering images of a smiling white man and white ventriloquist's dummy, each with a blackened eye and lit cigarette dangling in their mouths and the words *We'd Rather Fight Than Switch*, flashing the screen.

◆ ◆ ◆

Sleep did not come easily to Auger that evening. He lingered in the darkened living room, nervously listening to the rustling sheets from the bedroom until Suzette called out.

"Jean darling, come to bed. I'm waiting for you."

"I'll be along in a minute, baby," said Auger.

His hands shook with exhaustion, yet he knew if he lay down he might not sleep and if he did sleep he would open himself to attack from whatever it was causing him to see the terrible things he couldn't stand seeing.

"Sweetie," said Suzette. "Come along so we can talk for a few minutes. I'm tired. I don't want to fall asleep until you're here."

"Coming baby," said Auger.

A creaking in the house from the dark somewhere behind Auger startled him and he headed quickly to the bed where his wife lay waiting. His eyes searched in the blackness as he looked over his shoulder.

"Deslonde?" he whispered. "God damn it, not that."

"What did you say, sweetie?" said Suzette.

She held back the covers and Auger climbed into bed, then she sat up and straightened the sheets, covering them both snuggly.

"That's much better, isn't it," said Suzette.

"It sure is," said Auger. "I'm one lucky boy to have a wife that makes such a clean fresh bed up like this."

Suzette giggled.

"Oh c'mon, Jean."

"No, I mean it," said Auger. "This is the next best thing to heaven and I get to sleep with an angel too."

Suzette kissed her husband on the lips and nestled her head on his shoulder.

"Jean?" she whispered.

"Yes, darlin."

"I've been doing some thinking lately."

"What about, darlin?"

"I've been thinking about the way we live."

"What do you mean?"

She took a deep breath.

"Okay, here goes," she said. "I guess all of the trouble with the coloreds has got me wracking my brain for some way to just escape it all. For good, I mean."

"Go on," said Auger.

"It's got me thinking about Hawaii," she said. "Our vacation is only a couple of weeks away. You know how much Celine loves it over there. She's so excited, so happy. It's great to see. She's a happy teenager, Jean. We should be proud of that."

"I know . . ."

"Shhhh . . . let me finish. I've been thinking about our lives. Living in the city isn't getting any easier and now with riots, it's become unbearable. Believe me, I'm not bringing anything up. Who wants to talk about that? I feel too good right now to do that. I'm tired. Good tired. I'm comfortable for the first time in days. I'm with my family, with my husband who I love with all my heart. My little girl is safe in her room. I've just been thinking a lot about this. . . "

"Tell me what it is, sweetheart. What's on your mind?"

"Let's not just vacation in Hawaii this year, Jean. Let's look for a house when we're there. Let's find ourselves a dream house. I think we should sell this place. Let's leave all of this behind. When are we gonna do it, if not now? We're set up well enough for you to finally retire in style. I don't mean give up playing completely. Play when the spirit moves you. We can afford that now. All the troubles with the coloreds has made me realize that sometimes you just have to make a move, do what's best for us. I know you haven't been feeling right lately. You can't go on like that. We have to find a place where we'll be happy."

"I think you're right, darlin," said Auger.

"You're kidding, Jean," said Suzette.

"No, I think you're right. My head's been filled with so much business lately. I don't mean that god damned mess down there. Business, I been thinking about the music business and how I've just about had enough of it."

"I can't tell you how happy that makes me to hear you say that."

"Well, I'm saying it. I just didn't put the rest of it together. I guess that's why I have you, to point out what's right in front of my face. You know, I feel better now. I think that's why I been a bit down. Too much on my mind. I didn't think I could finish the week with John and Paul, but now I think I can. We're gonna live in Hawaii."

"As easy as that?"

"Why not?"

"That's right, why not?"

Suzette rested her head on her husband's chest and he stroked her hair.

"In the morning," he said, "Before that writer fellow shows up, we'll talk about how to go about this, maybe call the real estate agent, you know, test the waters and see what the markets' doing. I hear folks are getting pretty good prices nowadays."

"Particularly in exclusive neighborhoods like ours," said Suzette. "Oh Jean, I can't tell you how happy I am."

"Well, you got quite a job ahead of you, packing, moving all our belongings, furniture, and all. We'll be starting over again in Hawaii. It won't be easy."

"It'll be a breeze, Jean, a breeze," said Suzette.

"You get some sleep, love."

"That won't be a problem now, Jean," said Suzette, yawning. "We can tell Celine in the morning. She'll be beside herself. I love you, Jean."

"I love you too, sweetie."

Suzette closed her eyes and sighed sweetly. Moonlight streamed through the glass of the patio door, illuminating her face and hair against the white pillow. Auger watched as she slept then slipped from her embrace and stood over the bed gazing at her. The straps from her nightgown had slipped down and her naked shoulders glowed in the light, her breasts half exposed looked like the luscious flesh of a young girl. She truly was the vision of an angel to old Auger. He slid the glass door open and stepped outside onto the patio. The pavement, still hot from the intense heat of the day, warmed his bare feet. The moon, perched above the tops of the eucalyptus trees was more clearly visible than he'd ever remembered seeing in LA. The stillness of the night seemed to be coming from inside of him.

My life is good, he thought. *I've always been blessed and the blessings always kept coming, getting better and it's still getting better. I don't know how I deserved all this, deserved a beauty like Suzette.*

Lights from the bottom of the pool shinned through the shimmering water. Celine had forgotten to turn off the lights and filtration system when she'd finished playing in the pool a few hours earlier. Auger walked around the edge of the pool to a switch on the side of the house and turned it off.

If old Stonewall and Chiff could see their old pal Auger, what would they think? Here I am, wearing fancy pajamas, strolling round my own built-in swimming hole. I don't know if they'd believe it was me. They'd say I paid a month's salary to set it up just to fool them. They sure was good boys. I don't know why I been so wrought up lately. Our lives wasn't so bad. Life in Louisiana was tough, but we had a lot of love, a lot of good memories

Auger lowered himself onto a chaise lounge next to the pool, put his hands behind his head and gazed at the moon.

I don't know why all those bad memories come on like that . . . all that craziness, silliness, foolish ideas . . . most of it was plain lies . . . and now it's gone, thank goodness . . . how sweet my girls are . . . what a sweet life I got . . . I'm smart enough to know it, too . . . I know how blessed I been . . . and I'm smart enough to know everything I ever had come from the music . . . it all come out of that trombone . . . and the man most responsible was Buddy . . . he gave us all so much . . . and that's a grand thing to remember . . . that's a good memory . . . Buddy Bolden is a treasure in my heart . . . he was a real sweet man . . . a great man.

The surface of the pool was aglow with moonlight rippling from the filtration system and Auger saw Bolden there. Mr. Buddy Bolden, hair cropped close, a thin line of a moustache on his upper lip a la Charlie Galloway's barbershop, gripping his cornet over his breast like a peace pipe, deadpan, dignified, thick healthy jowls of a man who loves to eat and drink, powerful neck, great broad chest capable of wind enough to nearly tear a horn apart.

My god what a man . . . What a man he was . . . He had no idea how much he was giving and he didn't hardly get nothing for it . . . not compared to what we all got out of it . . . he just gave so much to all of us . . . We're all of us Buddy's children. Them ain't bad memories. Those are good things to look back on, a treasure I'll keep till the day I leave this earth.

Auger was no longer afraid. He wanted to reach down into the water and shake Buddy's hand, welcome him back home. He chuckled.

I got a lifetime of beautiful memories. I might even write a damned book. Hell, Bigard done it. Pops done it. Duke done it. That's probably why I been feeling so strange. All that life inside of me needing to be told to the public, liked to bubble up and out, come out all distorted and such, because I ain't done what was needed. There's money in telling your story, if you've lived the kind of life I did.

"That's it," he said. "I'll retire to Hawaii, write my story and make a million dollars."

Maybe get Orson to make a movie out of it. We'll get Montgomery Cliff to play me, or maybe that young fella Tony Curtis. Auger smiled broadly. *Shirley MacLaine can play Suzette. Why not? They're both dancers. Wouldn't that be sweet?*

The old man mused for several moments on the beauty of his life and the endless possibilities still open, the money to be made, even the music yet to be played, then returned wearily to his wife's side where he slept soundly, dreamlessly, for the first time in days.

Saturday, August 14, 1965

Nieting set out from the Imperial Highway Motor Lodge around noon and drove through the smokey streets of the city. The car was packed with his camera and recording equipment and his rucksack contained his notes and list of questions to be asked of the most important informant of his life. The excitement of the events in Watts was nearly unbearable, yet Nieting felt self possessed if not quite calm. In fact, with the absence of Emil, he felt nearly sane. He found Auger's house at the end of a rise on a long street that curved like a bow. It was a large home modeled after a French farm house with a steep roof of wood shingles. There were bay windows with louvered shutters extending across the front and ending at the heavy wooden entrance door. The path to the door ran against the louvered windows behind a line of several small Jacaranda trees, a Banana tree, and a bed of ferns and tropical shrubs that screened the front of the house from the street. A perfectly manicured lawn ran to the sidewalk and a grassy parking strip with two tall palm trees. Eucalyptus trees crowded above the roof from the back yard creating a sense that the house was situated on the edge of a dense forest and the rustic French farmhouse part of a surrealistic fairy tale landscape.

Inside, Auger sat on the edge of his bed and buckled the straps on his leather sandals, his eyes riveted on a portable television flickering with images of Watts burning. His life had changed instantly the night before when he and Suzette agreed to leave Los Angeles and retire in Hawaii. Nevertheless, the violence in Watts continued to consume him, in spite of his efforts to put it out of the mind.

On the front steps, the door to Auger's home opened and Nieting was greeted by a buxom woman with bright blue eyes and dark brown hair cut short. She was lovely in an ankle length sun dress, snug at the waist with thin straps over tanned shoulders. He would have thought her to be a servant except that she was clearly a woman of means, or she might have been Auger's daughter, except that she was larger than Auger, who was a petite man. And, she was white.

"Hello Professor," she said. "I'm Suzette. I'm Jean's wife. Please come in."

The woman seemed to have a slight French accent, perhaps worn away by many years in America. She must have been excessively youthful for her age if she were married to old Auger. She was a bourgeoisie through and through, slick and refined. Nieting's surprised look seemed to please Mrs. Auger. She smiled as she led him into the living room. The room was bright with large windows covered by white drapes glowing with sunlight. Towards the back of the room were sliding doors overlooking an outdoor patio and a swimming pool of shimmering blue.

"You know, we have quite a few stars living in our neighborhood," said Mrs. Auger. "Marilyn lived right down on Fifth Helena until the night she died. We lived here at the time and it was terribly sad. That was almost exactly three years ago. Fred MacMurray is a neighbor and Bill Bixby. Do you know *My Favorite Martian*?

"Pardon me?" said Nieting.

"Of course you don't," said Mrs. Auger. "How silly of me. Parlez-vous Francais?"

"I'm afraid not," said Nieting, lowering his gear to the floor. "Enough to find a good meal perhaps, but no more."

"That's alright," replied Mrs. Auger. "That's ten times better than most Americans. People here speak one language and that's it. I was born in Paris, but I've been in the States so long, it feels like another life. I'm glad my father brought us over, though. Life has been pretty wonderful here. Even with the blacks behaving like they are. We're all kind of nervous, you know. I'm a nervous wreck. It's terrible what the blacks are doing, don't you think?"

Nieting slipped the camera strap from around his neck and motioned to a coffee table in front of the couch.

"May I set up my recorder here?" he asked.

"Of course, and you can pull that chair over if you like, and please, call me Suzette. Jean will be here any minute. Make yourself comfortable. Would you like a cool drink? Lemonade or something?"

Nieting hesitated. It struck him that Auger might be up to one of his tricks just as he'd tricked the tourists at Disneyland when he pretended to be an Uncle Tom entertainer. The woman might not be his wife at all. She might be an actress hired by Auger. He gave a half smile, flashing his eyes in subtle recognition that he knew something was up.

"Lemonade would be very good, thank you," he said.

Suzette cocked her head like an uncomprehending Cocker Spaniel and smiled.

"You'll be cool as a cuke in no time," she said, "Isn't it wonderful? Its central, every room in the house is as cool as the next. Jean had it put in last year."

She walked from the room and Nieting proceeded to set up the tape recorder. He could hear Auger's voice from another room and a voice blaring from the TV, "we gonna come down there tonight, where whitey lives, we ain't gonna burn up our own neighborhood no more." Someone moaned. It must have been Kid Auger. Then the TV went silent and Nieting heard the woman whispering.

In the bedroom, Auger was perched on the edge of his bed, engrossed in the television news when Suzette came in. She halted in front of the mirror with her body half turned and examined her backside.

"When you said this guy was German, I didn't realize that he was a Jew" she said. "I didn't think there were any of them left over there."

"How would I know what he is?" said Auger. "He said he was from Berlin. Besides, I don't care if he's Hindu. I been interviewed by all kinds."

"Just saying, Jean. I didn't realize he was a Jew, that's all. He looks a bit desperate if you ask me, kind of agitated."

"Oh he's just a puppy dog," said Auger. "Though, he *was* kind of serious the other day, nervous too, you're right. He had stars in his eyes, much as I hate that kind of thing. He'll be alright. I'll tell him a few stories and he'll be satisfied. How do you know he's a Jew anyway?"

"I can tell these things, Jean," said Suzette, clearly annoyed.

The TV blared, "we gonna come down there tonight, where whitey lives, we ain't gonna burn up our own neighborhood no more." Auger moaned.

"And why are you still watching that nonsense on TV?" said Suzette. "Please Jean, you're upsetting me with this constant fixation. And that guy gives me the jitters too. Jews always have ulterior motives. He was sweating like a pig when he came in or should I say like a rat?"

"Oh c'mon sweetheart. It's hot as an oven outside. Anyone would be sweating."

"You're right. I'm sorry daddy. Last night I thought all this anxiousness was behind me. I suppose it won't go away until we put 3000 miles between those niggers in Watts and us. Sorry for the ugly talk, Jean. I'm just so tired of it all. I just want to get away."

"Let's get this interview over with so we can get back to planning our future. Besides, a little press is always a good thing. I won't give too much away either, just enough so he wants some more. Always save the best. Always hold something back. Make'm hungry for more. It ain't much different from playing music. That's the way I've always done it.

"You can count on me," said Suzette. "I'll go get the lemonade I promised our friend."

In the living room, Nieting stepped to a wall decorated with framed photographs scrawled with dedications from musicians and entertainers, mostly Negroes. *To the Kid, Everybody's Daddy, Your Friend, Louis.* There were shots of Orson Wells, Lana Turner, Bing Crosby surrounded by a score of photos of black faces. Below the pictures was a phonograph and a rack of long playing records. A Hot Creoles LP lay on the turntable and the empty sleeve with a picture of the young Kid Auger sat on the top of a small bookcase. Nieting had never seen the photo on the album. He ran his fingers over the glossy cover, jumped nervously at the sound of movement in the back of the house and resumed setting up the recorder, picking up the morning issue of the *Los Angeles Times* from the coffee table.

EXTRA – EIGHT MEN SLAIN; GUARD MOVES IN

He folded the paper and placed it on the lower shelf of the table and ran the electric cord to a wall socket next to a large television. A portrait of a young girl in a gold-colored frame sat on top of the set.

Suzette appeared pushing through the swinging doors from the kitchen, carrying a tray with a pitcher of lemonade and three high-ball glasses filled with crushed ice. Kid Auger followed behind her. For a moment, Nieting didn't recognize him. He was a different man from the one he had spoken to two days before. He was dressed in a loose short-sleeved cream-colored silk shirt, open at the neck, with large lapels, a pair of white linen trousers and leather sandals. He reminded Nieting of a wealthy South American planter or a famous retired bullfighter. Auger stretched his hand out to Nieting.

"Oh, I see you've found my little home. Good of you to visit. Sit please. We're away from the heat in here. Though you know, where I come from the humidity is far worse than this. It never gets that bad out here."

Auger sat on the couch and sank into the soft cushions. He casually stretched his arm over the back of the couch and gently stroked the bare shoulder of his wife with the tips of his fingers. She sat on the edge of the cushion with her arm extended back for support. Nieting sat on a wooden chair directly across from Auger and his wife.

"I want to thank you, Kid," said Nieting, "for allowing me into your home. Before we get started, I must tell you how important you have been in my life. Today's meeting is far more than an interview for me. I realized this just recently, strange as that may sound. I am not speaking now as a journalist or as an anthropologist. I am speaking as a human being. Ever since I was a child, I believed that you spoke directly to me. I know that you saved my life, literally. I would be dead for many years if it hadn't been for you."

"My word, Jean," said Suzette. "Did you hear that? That's the most touching . . . "

"Well, I didn't do anything," said Auger. "Sometimes folks feel those things, especially young folks. All I do is play music, but thank you young man. We best get started, don't you think?"

"Of course, Kid." said Nieting, pressing the start button on the recorder.

"So, where did you say this article would be published?" asked Suzette.

"The article will be published in a journal in Berlin called MerzKraft," replied Nieting. "The readership is quite advanced and accustomed to challenging work. It is the perfect platform for your husband to speak from. I believe his insights will have a profound impact on the events transpiring around us today, as we speak."

"We'll I'm dying to know what you mean by that," said Suzette. "But I'll be quiet and let you get on with it."

"I am speaking to Kid Auger in Los Angeles, California, on August 14, 1965. Kid, may I ask you, what year were you born?"

"I have to check the encyclopedia to find it," replied Auger, turning towards his wife with a smile. She broke into a piercing laugh that surprised both men. Auger gently squeezed her shoulder and winked reassuringly.

"You are a Creole from New Orleans, is that correct?" said Nieting.

"No, I come from the country, a place called Pine Grove Plantation in LaPointe, Louisiana, bout thirty miles out in St. Johns Parish"

"Oh, you were raised on the plantation?"

"Yes, born and raised."

"Did you work in the fields picking cotton?"

"No, Pine Grove was a sugar plantation. We grew sugar cane. I worked in the fields and I worked in the mill. Didn't like it very much. I was just interested in the music, ya know."

"Were your ancestors slaves?"

"No, my daddy was a Frenchman, come to Louisiana when he was fifteen years old."

"Jean is the only one in his family with dark skin," said Suzette.

"My folks never did speak English," Auger continued, leaning forward and taking a glass of lemonade from the table. "I never learned to speak it until I was nearly eight or nine."

"Jean speaks French, real Parisian French," said Suzette.

Auger sipped the iced lemonade and placed it back on the coffee table.

"Do you remember Bolden?" asked Nieting.

"Oh yes, I remember Buddy Bolden."

"Did you hear him play?"

"Yes, on more than one occasion."

"When did you first hear Bolden's music? Do you remember?"

"First time? He was blowing out the door of a baggage car at LaPointe Station. They was advertising a picnic. He and a group of men. I heard Buddy's horn and went running. It was quite a day."

"Do you know where Bolden learned his music, who influenced him?"

"He learned all over, anywhere he could, like we all did. He got ideas from the Baptists, you know, the Holy Rollers and fixed it up his own way, put his own style to it. He followed the brass bands, Excelsior, Onward and so forth, old man Barbarin and such. There was music all over the streets of New Orleans, country folks, city folks, Frenchmen, Spaniards, Americans, even Choctaw Indians, hell even Chinamen. He stole every-thing thing he could get his hands on. We all did that way."

Suzette sat nestled beneath her husband's arm intently following Nieting's every move.

"Did you ever actually meet Bolden?" asked Nieting. "Did you ever speak to him yourself?"

"Oh yes. I come to the big city looking for Buddy. I run away from home just to join his band. I found him finally and we had quite a time together. I was still just a boy then."

"Was it common practice to employ children to work with grown men?"

"Oh, it wasn't terribly unusual. Buddy was a real gentleman, you know. If he knew your folks was the worrying kind, he'd pick you up and deliver you home at the end of the night, or someone would if Buddy got too drunk."

Auger and Suzette rocked with laugher as Suzette playfully slapped his forearm.

"That's terrible, Jean," she said.

"I know Bolden was a Jazz man," said Nieting, "and that improvisation was crucial to his work. Did he compose music also? Do you remember any of his tunes?"

"Well, *Make Me a Pallet* is an old favorite and it comes from Buddy. We still play that one today. There are others too."

"I see. I'd like to get back to that question in a moment. In the meantime, can you describe Bolden's physical appearance?"

"He was a good looking brown skinned fella. Wore his hair short with a nice part shaved in and a neat little mustache shaved on his lip like a line, ya know? Charley Galloway was a barber. He kept all them boys looking sharp. They dressed different from most folks, talked different, man they was all their own style. And of course, plenty young folks followed'm in all that stuff. Just like youngsters follow the styles today."

"Some American critics have written that Creoles in New Orleans looked down on American blacks. Is that the way you remember it?"

"Oh no, we was all together," said Auger. "Me and Joe Oliver, like brothers. I hired Louis to play in my band before Fate Marable did. We was all New Orleans men. Bolden played with Baquet, Tio, Picou, they was downtown men. Creoles. Hell, I always lived uptown. Never did live downtown."

"Right," Suzette shot in. "We want to be as far from those people as we can get."

Auger took his wife's hand in his and gently kissed it.

"Sorry, sweetie," she said to her husband, then, looking at Nieting she said, "I'm a bit wrought up. It's this terrible thing with the coloreds. They act like wild animals. I can't imagine what they want. Why they're so full of hate."

"Some folks never do respect the law," said Auger. "It ain't like the old days."

"In Lomax's book on Jelly Roll Morton," said Nieting, "both Morton and Big Eye Nelson talk about a disturbance in New Orleans, a race riot. I discussed this with Wilson Pinot in New Orleans recently."

"Is that right?" said Auger. "I was real sorry to hear of his passing. I got to thinking when Johnny St. Cyr told me the news. I've known him for over sixty years. Seems like my old friends are going away so fast."

"I hadn't heard he'd died," said Nieting. "He was a good friend of mine also. A very fine man. Quite dedicated to his people."

"He was a good boy, ol'Raoul was," said Auger.

"The last time I saw him was only a few weeks ago," said Nieting. "At the time he described the death of his father. Perhaps you remember the events he referred too. He said the year was 1900 and that a Negro named Robert Charles was involved in an incident that resulted in a race riot?"

"No sir," said Auger. "I believe I may have known something at one time, but that was many years ago. Sometimes memories just drift away. You see, I lived in the country at that time. Now, let me see, 1900, that was the year Louis was born. He used to tag round after my band. He followed Joe Oliver around too. Ragged little barefoot boy."

"Was Robert Charles a musician?"

"Yes, I believe he played trombone. Dressed real nice. Always wore a hat."

"So, Robert Charles was a musician. According to Morton, he was a newsboy, yet I was told in New Orleans that he was a political man, probably a nationalist and that he killed a lot of white people."

Suzette gasped and covered her mouth with her hand. Auger gently patted her knee.

"I have no idea," said Auger.

"No idea?" said Nieting. "I see. Now, getting back to Bolden . . . can you to tell me about Buddy Bolden's music. Who were his audience? Who did he play for?"

"Buddy played for anybody, for everyone. But mostly, it was the sporting people loved his music real well. He played that type of blues, you know, that the rough type went for. Gamblers, you know, pimps and their gals. Oh, the working gals loved Buddy."

"Was that in Storyville, the red light district?"

"Yes, in the District. Other places too. He played all the halls and you would see him in Lincoln Park. He played anywhere folks would pay."

"When you say sporting crowd, you mean poor people?"

"Not all of those folks was poor. Some of those pimps wore diamonds would choke a horse. They pull out a roll of cash thick as a five inch pipe."

"But there must have been common people, too. How many pimps and prostitutes could there have been? There must have been common people among his followers and they would have been poor Negroes."

"Oh there was a fair amount of pimps and such. This is New Orleans we're talking about. But, there was all kinds too. There was places all the longshoremen used to go. Some places was lower than others and some places the folks didn't want to hear Buddy play those blues at all. They thought it was too racy, too low class, too rough, ya know? So, Buddy would play waltzes, schottisches. He could be gentle and sweet when he wanted to."

"Did you play those rough types of venues?"

"Yes, I played them all."

"Did the white people get to see Bolden perform?"

"Sure, why not? We used to parade all over the city and anyone could see what we was doing. Now, Buddy didn't do that so very much but he was in the park all the time. You couldn't help but hear."

"He was a real community man," said Nieting. Isn't that right?"

"Oh, he was a community man all right."

Nieting beamed.

"I appreciate your saying that," he said. "Some people today think of musicians as purely entertainers. They don't see that artists are really human beings with connections to communities. Music is much more than just a good time. Often musicians are the only true chroniclers of the peoples' experiences."

"That may be so," said Auger. "Entertaining is good enough for me. That's what I get paid for."

"Surely you have more responsibility than that," said Nieting.

"What kind of responsibility?"

"To your community," replied Nieting. "It is the role of the artist to embody the spirit of his people, to express their thoughts and feelings. Just as the African Griot transmits the peoples' history and experiences through his art, a musician plays for the benefit of the masses, not say, for a club owner or a record company. A musician belongs to his people."

Auger waved his knobby forefinger at Nieting.

"You know, the thing that bothers me about all this Africa talk you hear nowadays is this. Our music got nothing to do with Africa. How could we have got it from Africa, when they don't even have it today? No, that's somebody else's story. It ain't so. Our music is one hundred percent American."

"Jelly Roll Morton claims Negro Jazz was influenced by European Symphonic music, Opera, etc," said Nieting.

"Oh yes, that's true," said Auger. "You hear something of just about everything in there. We took whatever we wanted, whatever we liked or thought the people might fancy and made it our own style, jazzed it up. We made it something different. You can hear that Spanish beat in there, actually that's where it really started in New Orleans, but people don't know nothing about that. Hell, you can hear Indian drums in our music.

If it ever lived and breathed in Louisiana, we took it into our music. That's what I call one hundred percent American."

"Precisely," said Nieting. "Music is an expression of the people, not a mere entertainment, and as one gifted with this collective knowledge, you have a responsibility to those who gave you the music."

Auger didn't respond to Nieting's statement. He simply cleared his throat and waited for the next question.

"Do you know *The Robert Charles Song*?" asked Nieting.

"No, can't say that I ever did know that one," replied Auger.

"Morton claims that it was a highly controversial social commentary and was suppressed by the authorities."

"Is that right," said Auger. "I wouldn't know."

"You've stated that Bolden was a community man, that he was closely connected to his people."

"Yes, Buddy was like that. He did play for his people."

"But not just to dance. It was more than that."

"What's wrong with dancing?" said Suzette.

"There's nothing wrong with dancing," said Nieting. "I didn't suggest that there is anything wrong with dancing. I mean, the music is more important than a party."

"I don't know what you mean," said Auger.

"Would you say your music has more importance than entertainment?"

"No, like I said," replied Auger. "I just want to make folks feel good. I guess you'd call that entertainment."

"But, the music was created as an act of resistance, don't you think? It is a means of survival, really. It was created by Negroes as a weapon against a system that is based on the premise that they are a natural resource to be expended for the benefit of the dominant group."

"You got me on that one," said Auger. "Folks just didn't think of things in that way."

"What do blacks have to do with it?" said Suzette.

"I don't even know what he said," said Auger, "but I'll tell you what, people want to relax after a hard day's work. They want to stretch out a bit. They want to dance, make love to their sweethearts, have a taste of this or that. I don't know what that mess is you was just saying. Sounds like a bunch of nonsense to me."

"Okay, okay, do you think the white tourists you perform for at Disneyland care about Negroes?"

"Negroes?" said Suzette. "What is he talking about, Jean?"

"This is Negro music we're discussing," said Nieting. "Shouldn't it be performed for the benefit of Negroes?"

"You have us mixed up with the Supremes," said Suzette.

"I told you two days ago, I ain't interested in agitators," said Auger.

"Yes, you did," said Nieting. "I understand that you are an entertainer. How come you don't entertain Negroes?"

"I entertain everybody."

"I didn't see a single Negro at Disneyland other than the Young Men of Jazz."

"I don't take tickets, I play music."

"What the hell are you getting at?" said Suzette.

"Now, sweetie," said Auger. "Let's don't get upset."

"No Jean," replied Suzette. "I want to know the point of all of this talk about blacks. This guy claims he's some kind of professor and he wants to write an article about Dixieland Jazz. What do blacks have to do with Dixieland Jazz? What do you want from us?"

"What do blacks have to do with Jazz?" said Nieting. "I'm glad I have that on tape."

"Turn that god damned thing off," said Auger.

Suzette shot back, "I said Dixieland Jazz. Don't you dare twist my words. Where do you get off coming into my home under false pretenses? You're supposed to be here to do an interview, not distort the things we're saying."

"What do Negroes have to do with Dixieland Jazz?" said Nieting. "Any comment, Kid? As a Negro, do you concede authorship of your music to the white man?"

"Don't you dare call him a Negro," said Suzette. "You have no idea who you're talking too. Who gave you leave to come here and insult us? You're a rude foreigner is what you are. A god damned Nazi."

"I am Jewish, madam. I assure you, I am no Nazi."

"I figured that one right," said Suzette. "Of course, you're a Jew."

"Sweetheart," said Auger. "Don't get yourself excited over someone like this. It isn't worth it."

"I want him out of here, Jean. Pack up your things and get out."

"You'd best listen to the lady," said Auger.

"I have everything I need, thank you," said Nieting. "I'll be quite pleased to leave."

"Go Hymie, go on for god's sake," said Suzette.

Nieting yanked the recorder cord from the wall and quickly gathered his equipment as Auger stood and waited patiently, finally taking Nieting by the arm and escorting him to the door. Strangely, Auger nodded almost reassuringly, opened the door for Nieting and stepped out, closing the door behind.

"Now, listen to me, son," said Auger. "You don't seem like such a bad young fella. I don't know how you got so full of yourself? Let me give you a few words of advice. You shouldn't be judging things you don't know nothing about. I think you're right about Buddy, though. He was nothing if he wasn't every bit a part of those folks he come from. But, all your college professor words don't mean a god damned thing. You talk like you own Buddy. From where I sit, that means what you say is bullshit. Even if you did say something true about Buddy. He did play for his people. He did help folks survive with his music. I forget myself sometimes just how much he gave. Lately I been remembering a heap of things I ain't thought of for a long time. But that don't make no difference. I think you'd better leave before my wife gets really mad. Believe me, you ain't never seen anything like it."

Emil giggled and peeked from the bushes. Nieting scowled at him.

"Look Kid," he said. "Time is short. I'll go straight to the point. I was hoping you could direct me to some information. I'm searching for a song, a song written by Buddy Bolden and repressed by the white authorities. The song may be lost to history if we do not act. I was told of the song by several of Bolden's colleagues. They believe the song would be of great importance during this revolutionary period. As a Negro artist, you can be of great service to the Revolution. You are desperately needed in our search to recover Bolden's song, *The Robert Charles Song*. I'd hoped to discuss this with you calmly and in greater detail but our talk didn't go as I'd planned. I do apologize for my behavior, but that is of no importance now. My car is parked not far from here. Come with me now. We'll go to Watts and join the rebellion. Come with me now, Kid. It would be the crowning gesture of your career, your art transformed into action, revolutionary action. Recovering Bolden's lost song would be a glorious way to sum up your life and work?"

"You're not the listening kind, are you," said Auger. "You must get punched in the nose a good deal. Is that right? Seems to me like it must happen fairly regular."

"Please, Kid," said Nieting. "You and I possess a greater connection than you realize."

Nieting grabbed the old man's hand between his and held it to his heart. Auger pulled back and Nieting held him fast.

"My god, man," said Auger. "Straighten up."

"I beg you, Kid," said Nieting, "You must consider my request," and Auger slapped him across the face with his free hand.

The slap caught Nieting square on the jaw from ear to mouth, splashing sweat onto a jacaranda tree. Auger wiped his hand on his white trousers. The force of being struck stunned Nieting. The old man had halted a terrible rush into some kind of chaos. The blow had sobered him. Auger had saved his life once again. Nieting cracked up like the two were actors filming a scene in a movie and the director just called "cut." But, there was no movie and the old man frowned and said, "Get out of here, boy. I don't want to have to fuck you up."

The door opened a crack and Suzette peeked out.

"Jean, Paul's on the phone. You need to come hear what he has to say. Right now, Jean."

"Barbarin?"

"Yes, he wants you quick."

Emil whispered from the bushes, "Let the old fraud go, Valentin."

"Shut up, will you?" said Nieting.

"Wait a god damned minute, boy," said Auger. "Don't you talk to my wife like that. I'll slap your face with my closed fist next time, you two bit motherfucker."

"Now you've done it," said Emil.

"I said shut up, leave me alone."

Nieting shouted into the shrubs as Auger quick stepped into the house, slamming the door and turning the dead bolt. Suzette peeked from behind the curtain in the window, then disappeared.

"Valentin, calm down," said Emil. "I pray this is the final shattering of your faith, the final myth obliterated. You don't need that old fraud Auger. You're rid of him. There's no need to deny the truth any longer. Finally, you've succeeded in burning all your bridges. Good work. Do you hear me? It doesn't matter a whit where I've come from, does it? I'm your only friend now."

Emil put his arm through his son's and the two hurried down the path.

"You really should consider your options, said Emil. "The most reliable option you have is ending this fiasco now. It isn't quite so difficult as you might think. I can show you how to do it. There is great comfort in death. Valentin?"

Nieting reached for Emil, intending to push him to the ground but he was nowhere. Nieting ran as Emil shouted after him.

"You've no one left but me, Valentin. I'm your father. Come here you naughty boy."

Nieting sprinted down the sidewalk, somehow thinking he could out run his father. He reached the car and sped off, taking the first turn on two wheels. He blew through a stop sign, nearly side swiping a private security patrol car turning off Fifth Helena, then jammed the gas and the car shot forward in a shrill screech. He shook his fist at the car radio at the sound of Chief Parker's voice.

"Don't let my father's remarks confuse you," shouted Nieting. "We shall struggle, collectively or singly if need be, until victory comes."

Nieting took the curves on Sunset like a race car driver, finally reaching the 405 freeway where he opened the little sedan up, rattling to a hundred mph and reaching the Venice exit in minutes. The exit sign came up fast and the car nearly flipped off the ramp when he hit the breaks, skidding to a halt in a cloud of burnt rubber within inches of a car waiting at a red light. When the light turned, he maneuvered past the car in front and burned rubber again, driving like a madman west on Venice Blvd. He laughed as he ran lights to the sound of sirens, pursuing him, they must be pursuing him, yet he didn't give a damn. The days of caution were done. He opened it up on Venice Blvd, passing other vehicles like they were standing still. He was untouchable. To hell with Kid Auger, the peoples' rage was unleashed and their will was irresistible.

Red lights were spinning ahead as he approached Lincoln Blvd. Police cars were everywhere. He slowed into a line of traffic funneled single file between a gauntlet of police cars directly in front of the LAPD station on Venice Blvd. The lawn in front of the station swarmed with officers brandishing shot guns, pushing a line of Negro men through the front door of the jailhouse. The rebellion was spreading and the reaction was fierce. A helmeted officer shouted into a bullhorn to the cars in the street to move through to let patrol cars pass just as Nieting bent to look out the passenger side of his sedan. He watched a cop pull a man from the line, crack him repeatedly over the shoulders with a club and kick him when he went down. The cop in the street shouted at Nieting to get moving and he froze as he watched the cop next to the station beating the Negro. He thought for a moment, from the man's build, that it must be Rene. A club slammed the hood of Nieting's car. "Move or I'll split your fucking head open." The stick bounced on the hood and Nieting hit the gas and the break simultaneously and the car lurched and stalled. He fumbled to start the engine as the cop cursed and when it finally turned over he drove on, taking a right onto Washington Blvd all the way to Main Street where he made a left onto Brooks Avenue towards the beach.

He parked near the ocean to the echoing sound of sirens and gun shots. The Revolution had truly begun. Ocean Front Walk was deserted. There were no old people in front of the synagogue. The storefronts were locked tight. He turned onto Dudley Avenue. The Venice West Cafe was closed, yet Nieting saw figures moving inside through a crack in the wooden door. On Ocean Front Walk, the pagoda where Rene sat the day he and Nieting first spoke was a void where the pulse of the drum had been. A helicopter with the markings of the LAPD swept fast and low over the beach. Nieting looked from under the roof of the pagoda, watching the pilot watching him before the copter veered hard left over the streets of Venice. Nieting paced the pagoda. There wasn't a human in sight save for a tiny speck moving in the distance on the sand beyond the synagogue. It seemed as if everyone had fled except for the solitary figure hiking across the sand. Whoever it was hoisted something onto his back and stepped onto Ocean Front Walk. Nieting sprang into the path, blocking the sun from his eyes with his hands. It was a man, definitely dark skinned, a Negro perhaps. He walked rapidly in Nieting's direction until finally the face was discernable, horn rimmed glasses and sparse goatee. It was Rene, moving fast, hurrying somewhere. Nieting rushed forward, stomping his feet with joy, waving his arms, shouting, "hey man, man!"

Rene seemed to recognize Nieting jumping up and down on the path and waved him off and when he reached Nieting he slapped his hands away and shoved past as Nieting trailed after, talking as he ran. "I met him, man." said Nieting.

"What the fuck?" said Rene. "Met fucking who, man?"

"Kid Auger. I met Kid Auger. You were correct. He's a fucking Uncle Tom."

Rene looked straight ahead as Nieting dogged his steps, breaking into the conversation of two days before.

"He's become some kind of super patriot," said Nieting. "The things he said were fucking wild, man."

Rene halted and lowered the drum to the pavement, shaking his head as Nieting continued chattering.

"How could a Negro speak like that?" said Nieting. "He's amazingly light skinned, you know. He doesn't even look like a Negro."

"Look man," said Rene. "I don't have time for tourists. I got business to take care of."

"Yes, I understand," replied Nieting. "I do as well. We both do. I wanted to ask you, will you come with me to Watts? It's imperative that I meet your Triplett now. I could use a guide, more like a research assistant, really. I'd be happy to pay you."

"You'd be happy to pay me?" said Rene. "Can you fucking imagine that?"

He scratched his head and laughed, then pushed a clenched fist in Nieting's face and Nieting still would not perceive his contempt.

"You want me to be your Man Friday?"

"Man Friday?' said Nieting. "Certainly not. I was inviting you to join me, to be my comrade."

"You're in over your head," said Rene. "You'd be real smart for you to fly back to wherever the fuck you come from."

"Why go back now," said Nieting, "When I'm so close to completing my task? I'll go back when my work is completed. The Revolution in Watts is the catalyst that will release the truth I seek."

"This isn't your business, whitey," said Rene. "You don't know shit about what's going on here."

"Nonsense," said Nieting. "You know who I am. We spoke just the other day. We agreed on many things. You said, 'I like how you think' and you invited me to Watts to meet Triplett."

"Bullshit," snapped Rene. "I never invited you anywhere. You don't hear a god damned thing but what you want to hear, white motherfucker."

"But, I'm not white," said Nieting. "I'm a European of goodwill, a friend. You'll need allies, thinkers and writers. You'll need men who can articulate to the world the nature of what you are doing."

"Get fucked, whitey," growled Rene, slinging the drum bag over his shoulder. Nieting lunged forward, grabbing Rene's forearm. Rene yanked his arm free and pushed Nieting to the ground.

"You do that again and I'll kill you, motherfucker."

Nieting stared at Rene, as if he couldn't comprehend his actions and the look annoyed Rene further. He picked Nieting up by the shirt and dragged him onto the sand, pushing his ass with his foot, and when Nieting flipped onto his back Rene straddled him and pressed his heel into his throat.

"You understand what I'm talking about?" said Rene, dropping his knee into Nieting's chest, thrusting his full weight down and clutching Nieting's chin in his fist and shoving upwards. "You dig, motherfucker?"

"Alright, man," said Nieting. "I dig. Yes, I dig. Let me up, fucking let me up."

Rene released Nieting's face and held him pinned with the weight of his body.

"Look man," said Rene. "I don't want to hurt you. I got nothing against you."

"Then let me up, for Christ's sake."

"I got nothing *for* you for either," replied Rene, "Go back to Germany before you get yourself hurt."

Rene rose up, shaking his head, repositioned the drum bag on his back and strode down the walk, not turning when Nieting called after him.

"Rene, wait. Please Rene. Forgive my forwardness. We can talk, Rene. Rene."

Rene disappeared around the corner of Dudley Avenue, knocked on the door of the Venice West Café and miraculously the door opened and he went in. Nieting walked after him and watched him go inside. He ran to the café and peered in through a crack in the door. The room was dark, but a light shown from a back room. Nieting pounded the door and shouted for Rene, then kicked the door and walked back to Ocean Front Walk.

"Black bastard," he said. "He doesn't realize the opportunity he just walked away from."

Emil laughed. Nieting banged his forehead with the heel of his palm and the giggling persisted. How could it be a creation of his mind? He pounded his head again. The sound was not inside of him, it was coming from the outside. Emil's voice was real. It wasn't simply a matter of being insane. The voice existed.

"This could be like old times if you would behave yourself," said Emil.

He was nowhere. It was just his voice again. Nieting turned full circle. "What do you mean?" he said.

"We used to listen to Kid Auger together, didn't we? You remember. I indulged you terribly. I allowed you to play that recording again and again."

Nieting held his head in his hands.

"Yes," he said. "We played it to drown out the sounds of mother and the men torturing her. I remembered just last night. She was dead, yet her voice came to me. We played the Hot Creoles to silence her. You refused to allow me to take my own life. You told me you'd play the song again if I wouldn't try to hurt myself."

"You're a grown man now, Valentin. Suicide is your right."

"Not that again?" said Nieting.

"Please Valentin, don't be so melodramatic. I find you terribly depressing when you get into these moods."

The surf pounded the shore fifty yards off, exploding, hissing and rushing back down the slope of sand as if the ocean were vomiting and swallowing back its bile. Again and again, the thud of ocean hit and the retreat sizzled and behind its rhythm a trombone was pumping, swirling like white water. Kid Auger was playing just as he had years ago to soothe little Val. Nieting shouted at the horizon.

"Your partner has returned, papa. Your alter ego is here to make the music for my demise. Did you send for him?"

"Don't blame Auger on me," said Emil. "Just another nigger minstrel as far as I'm concerned. It's you who insists upon acquiring heroes."

"Why must I die, father?" said Nieting. "Why do you ask me to murder myself?"

"You know full well, Valentin," replied Emil. "There is nothing more obscene that a child's suicide. It could not have been allowed. But now, you are a man, Valentin."

Emil stood a few paces away, his plaid trousers coated with sand. His face was serious for once, sorrowful. He slowly raised his arm and pointed upward and Nieting cowered as he followed his father's finger. The sky was black with aircraft, American bombers wing to wing, nose to tail, a curtain crawling across the blueness, shutting out the daylight, the rumble of a thousand B-52s crowding overhead below the gray clouds, each monster eyeing him, peering inside his body. His flesh was truly haunted. Emil was right all along. Auger played just like the old days, the long sweet line of a lament so gently modulated that Nieting crawled beneath the bell of his horn and watched the sky swarming with metal insects. He crouched next to the sea, shielded by Auger's horn as he had a hundred times before. He'd always been pursued by evil, by menacing shadows, by the unspeakable or at least the unspoken.

There were Negroes congregating on Ocean Front Walk. He saw a dark skinned man, shirtless and muscular, speaking to a woman, then several more men. They were watching the sky, pointing at the endless black rug of warplanes. The woman standing among the Negroes was white. She was far off yet her face was visible. She was his mother. He believed he'd never seen her so young before. Her body was robust like Nieting's young female students back home, happy, playful, innocent. The cheeks of her face were rosy and full, not opaque, bloated, stretched over blue veins and pathetic bones, the sad mottled face of his memory. She touched the Negro's arm, apparently explaining the meaning of the war planes, suggesting that they take cover in a bomb shelter. Her blonde hair lay in streaks on her shoulders, glowing like gold against the grayness. Her eyes turned towards him as the Negro put his arm around her waist and led her into an alley. She looked over her shoulder at little Val, talking all the time to the man, finally stopping and staring directly at him, smiling and disappearing. All of the Negroes retreated into the alleys as convoys of tanks and military trucks filled with solders and hauling giant cannon rumbled onto Ocean Front Walk from the north and south, Americans and Germans halting face to face and Russians coming from the east up Westminster Avenue. The three armies met in a standoff, poised to destroy one another, twitching like reptilian behemoths subject to nothing more than muscular impulse. The southern sky flashed with the fire of bombs and the distant rumble of the explosions intensified. The sky was black with death machines. All at once, the soldiers spotted Nieting on the water's edge, hundreds of them, Americans, Germans, Russians charged onto the sand, racing to reach him first. Then, the hordes halted en mass and stared as a bomber exploded over head and tumbled into the sea.

An avalanche of white water poured onto Nieting's back, knocking him to the wet sand and dragging him along as it ran back down the sloping shore. As he gained his feet the current pulled him down and held his twisting torso until it vomited him onto the shore. He crawled up on dry land and lay on his back gasping for breath. The sky was clear. Ocean Front Walk deserted. Nieting crouched on the sand and rubbed his chin, wincing at the sting left by Rene's boot heel. A police helicopter buzzed the shoreline over his head, cutting left over the embattled ghetto of Venice.

◆　◆　◆

7 p.m., Imperial Motor Lodge

The television spewed images of the rebellion incessantly as Nieting paced the floor of the motel room. Triplett was in there somewhere. He was inside the pictures flickering on the screen, near the flaming buildings and advancing police phalanxes. He knew the jeering crowds and they knew him. They were his people. Perhaps they were Nieting's people as well, or would be once he'd given back the gift, saved *The Robert*

Charles Song the prison of White Supremacy. Self-knowledge was the gift he was offering. The conduit between Dr. Nieting and the people would be his informant, Morris Triplett. Auger and Rene were no longer viable resources. It was as if fate had dropped Triplett into Nieting's lap. He was right there, inside the tube, in Watts, inside the Revolution. Nieting saw him in his mind, looking like the grand marshal of the Olympia Brass Band, broad chested, gray haired, dark brown, somber, except that Triplett would wear glasses, gold horn rims like an intellectual might wear. He saw the musicians assembled somewhere in the riot zone, waiting for all the members to arrive, counting heads, receiving intelligence from the streets, strategizing, considering how best to be useful to the people in the time of action.

Nieting had stopped pacing without realizing it. He snapped out of a trance to find himself starring into the brown blanket on the unmade bed. The lone figure of a cockroach moved slowly, traversing the vast hilly desert of covers like a human lost on the surface of a strange planet. Nieting had an aerial view of the solitary creature working its way out of the wilderness. He yanked the blanket and an earthquake twisted the landscape and the bug scurried furiously. When it had almost reached the edge of the bed, Nieting pounded the mattress with his fist, sending it back into the swirling cavern in the center of the brown blanket. Again, the tiny creature took off, moving so fast this time it made the side and disappeared over a jumble of sheets. Nieting dove onto the bed, sprawling to see where the roach might have landed, finding nothing except the filthy carpet scarred with cigarette burns and strewn with tiny bits of debris.

"My god, what determination, what will," he said. "Unrelenting resistance. The spirit of the cockroach is the quintessential characteristic of a successful insurgency. I must manifest the same primal drive if I am to recover the lost song. I must proceed to Watts immediately. I must make contact with Triplett."

He bounded off the bed and scooped up the book of maps lying on his rucksack next to the door. He flipped through the index of street names, running his finger across columns of listings. The first map in the book showed all of Los Angeles County divided into one-inch squares. There was no reference to Watts. He rifled through the pages as a breathless reporter on the television described events in the battle zone.

"The mob has moved a block down the street and set fire to a large surplus store that was looted just a short time ago. The fire department is headed towards the area. You can hear the sirens approaching from Avalon and Imperial Highway . . . "

"Imperial Highway?" said Nieting. "I'm sitting on Imperial Highway. Imperial Highway and Avalon? How could I not have realized this before?"

He checked the index for Imperial Highway and found the intersection on page 59. The word Watts appeared on the map, right there, miraculously, inches away from the airport, fourteen and one quarter inches to be exact, extending from page 56 to 59. Nieting flipped frantically through the book for the scale. The map placed Watts just over seven miles from the airport, seven miles from Nieting's motel, a straight shot up Imperial. The Revolution was a mere minutes away. He tossed the book onto the bed, rushed out the door to the balcony and stepped up onto the railing, pointing his nose eastward and inhaling.

"I can smell Watts burning."

It was 11:30 PM when Nieting started out to join the Revolution. He drove east on Imperial Highway and within two blocks of the motel the air was thick with smoke. Pink light danced on the low clouds of the eastern horizon. The streets were deserted except when a police car shot past with lights spinning but no siren. The car passed in a flash like a bullet shot into the night sky. Nieting pulled to the side as the light shrank into the distance. He waited in silence for several moments and drove on. The very idea that Watts and Triplett had been so near since Wednesday, since the first moments of the rebellion seemed prophetic. His hands quivered on the steering wheel. The idea of the people of Watts engaged in the battle for liberation was nothing less than the mystical fulfillment of the inevitable. Perhaps *The Robert Charles Song* would be released from the collective mind of the Negro by the great conflagration. When the forces of repression cracked beneath the fire of Revolution the song would break free. Robert Charles would be present just as the old men, Randall Marquette and Wilson Pinot had hoped. Nieting must also be present. He must be there to shepherd the gift to its rightful heirs. He felt a sense of calm as he watched a California Highway Patrol car approach in his side mirror, red light spinning as it sped past.

When Nieting halted at a stoplight at Main Street and Imperial, the intersection two blocks further on was illuminated like the entrance to a stupendous amusement park. One block further, just off San Pedro, the street was jammed with vehicles and people moving, scurrying like the roach on the motel bed. Beyond the intersection fire blazed, the flames reaching into the night sky like hands groping and the black smoke gushing in thick swirls against the red phosphorescent clouds. It looked like hell, but hell turned upside down, a hell of glorious release, of freedom, a hell where hell meant heaven or the road to heaven; it was the destruction, the tearing asunder of evil. It was the white man's hell. The sight was glorious. Nieting couldn't believe his eyes. He parked the car, checking the map under the glove compartment light, running his finger along Imperial Highway, over Hoover Street to Main Street to San Pedro Street, stopping finally at Avalon Blvd. He'd reached the front lines. He moved forward cautiously, keeping to the shadows. He crossed quickly through the brightly lighted intersection of San Pedro, hurrying past a Shell gas station and crouching like a commando as he skipped over railroad tracks. He halted half a block from Imperial and Avalon and gaped at the scene – charred automobiles lying dead on their backs, massive fire trucks parked haphazardly and police cars wedged like covered wagons. He jogged through the intersection to the east side of Avalon. It was like the earth suddenly split open on the other side, revealing another world, an image so violently abrupt and stark, Nieting nearly fell in the street. There, beyond the chaotic jumble on the corner were the crowds, the Negroes of Watts, massed just beyond the reach of the police, silhouetted by the red glow of burning buildings. Nieting's throat tightened and his eyes filled with tears. The spectacle was overwhelming. There appeared to be thousands of people assembled, watching and jeering as young men and boys close up hurled stones and bottles at the police, taunting and cursing, retreating when the police advanced swinging their clubs, then returning as the cops moved back to the safety of their ranks. Children darted back and forth slinging projectiles and fleeing as the police counter-attacked. Nieting wept, overcome by the heartbreak of it, the breathtaking distance, the chilling estrangement, the irreconcilable separation, the hate that existed between the Negroes and whites. It was all too much, beyond his capacity to withstand. Yet, it was what was needed. It was what must occur. It was catastrophic. It was unnerving. Nieting steeled himself.

"You there, halt. Stay were you are."

A helmeted cop wielding a club spotted Nieting and was coming towards him.

"What the hell are you doing in this area? You want to get yourself killed? Don't move. Stay right where you are. I said, don't move, god damn it."

Nieting froze. The cop's club twitched like a nervous appendage.

"I said don't fucking move."

Nieting instinctively raised his arms.

"Don't move, god damn it."

The cop appeared to cock his stick just as a siren blasted, then he halted as a patrol car followed by two civilian vehicles rolled between him and Nieting. The entourage came to a stop behind the barricaded intersection and the cop, forgetting Nieting, jogged to the head car. Nieting scooted after the cop, reaching the last car as four doors swung open and white men in civilian clothes alighted, one carrying a camera. They were reporters. Nieting fell in, unnoticed, as they flocked to the second vehicle and four Negroes in civilian dress disembarked. The Negroes didn't appear to be police officers. One of them wore denim overalls and carried a bullhorn and the others were dressed casually, as if they'd been called unexpectedly from their homes. They stood together as an LAPD Sergeant strode up. Nieting slipped away from the reporters and moved next to the Sergeant. He huddled shoulder to shoulder with the white cop facing the Negroes as the reporters looked on. The driver of the patrol car pointed at one of the Negroes, the young man in overalls.

"Sergeant, this is Dick Gregory," he said. "Downtown says he can speak to the crowd if he wants to."

"Dick who?" said the Sergeant.

"Dick Gregory," replied the driver.

"The colored comedian?" asked the Sergeant.

"Yes," said the driver.

"What the hell good do they think he'll do?" said the Sergeant and one of the Negros interjected.

"Sergeant, my name is Assemblyman Dymally."

"I know who you are," said the Sergeant and Dymally said, "Mr. Gregory is well known to these people. It's worth a try to see if he can have some effect. We have the Chief's assurance that you'll cooperate."

"I understand that," said the Sergeant. "I don't think you understand what's going on down here, Assemblyman."

"We know god damned well what's going on," said one of the Negroes.

"Calm down, Cleveland," said Dymally. "The Sergeant is going to accommodate us. Those are his orders."

"It's all right with me," said the Sergeant. "It's your ass, Mr. Gregory."

"It's my ass alright" replied Gregory. "Let's get going."

"We'll form a perimeter and you follow behind," said the Sergeant. "You have the bullhorn. You can make your statement as we move up Imperial."

"No way," replied Gregory. "I need your men to stay back. Walking behind a bunch of cops won't do any good."

"That mob is pretty god damned mad," said the Sergeant. "I don't think they want to listen to anyone. Your being colored might not be a guarantee that you'll be safe."

Gregory replied, "I was told I'd have leeway to do this thing."

"This is coming from Downtown, Sergeant," said Dymally.

"I know where it's coming from," replied the Sergeant. "If you want to do it, it's fine with me. Like I said, it's your ass."

"I'll take care of my own ass," said Gregory.

"We'll be glad to stay behind you then," said the Sergeant. "I assume you gentlemen want to accompany Mr. Gregory."

"That's correct," replied Dymally.

"We'll give you plenty of room then," said the Sergeant. "Go ahead, you're on, Mr. Gregory."

Dymally placed his arms over Gregory's shoulders. "This way, Richard," he said. The four Negroes walked through the jumble of fire trucks and burned out cars, three of them whispering to Gregory like he was a prize fighter and they his trainers. A cop in a white helmet, clutching a shot gun grimaced as Gregory moved past.

"Me and the wife saw you in Reno last year," he said. "I really like your act, Dick. Real funny stuff. I'm telling you this for your own good. Don't move too close to that mob."

Gregory looked to the side for the voice and his eyes met Nieting's eyes. He seemed about to say something, as if he thought Nieting had spoken, but he did not reply. He simply surveyed the scene, the unattended fires crackling, shaking his head. He made straight for a section of the crowd standing behind a line of police stanchions along the curb on Imperial like they were waiting for a parade to pass. The rest of the party followed as he began speaking into the bullhorn.

"Get off the streets. Go home. You're putting your wives and daughters in harm's way. Take them home and get off the streets."

Someone in the crowd yelled, "Hey, you gigging in town, baby?"

"No man, I just came in to see you," replied Gregory. "Someone's gotta say this. It ain't in our interests to be out here. Someone's gonna get hurt. You all just burning down your own neighborhood."

"Don't be coming in here telling us to go home."

"Yeah, we don't want none of that bullshit."

"We don't want none of Martin King's bullshit neither."

"We want what we got coming."

"We're gonna take what we got coming."

"Tell some jokes, man."

"Hey baby, this ain't Beverly Hills. You take a wrong turn?"

"No, I didn't make no wrong turn," said Gregory. "I'm here for you."

"Then throw a brick, baby."

"Throwing bricks won't help nothing. We're just putting our women at risk with all this fire power out here. All these kids out here, it ain't safe for them. I'm asking you to go home before somebody gets killed."

Gregory moved closer to the crowd, pleading for them to disperse as Nieting edged closer as well, finally coming within an arm's length of the stanchion. All eyes were on Dick Gregory. People bantered with him, some good naturedly, some angrily, some kidding, some earnestly debating the logic of leaving the streets. Nieting looked at the people along the fence, studying the faces until he came eye to eye with a man standing not five feet away. He was very black and his face shined with sweat. He returned the stare, examining Nieting intensely as if something about him was deeply troubling, or perhaps he too was conducting a study and Nieting was an object of observation.

Nieting blurted out, "Hey man," and the man looked surprised and stepped up to the fence, inches away. "I'm looking for Morris Triplett. Do you know him?"

"What do you want with Morris?" said the man.

Nieting gasped at the response.

"I'm a friend," he said. "I've been sent here by a colleague of his. I have important information that Mr. Triplett needs, that he must have."

Nieting leaned over the stanchion and moved his face close to the man and whispered.

"I'm not with the police. I merely joined them as a means to contact Morris. I'm sympathetic to your cause."

The man nodded his head slowly.

"Can you bring me to him?" asked Nieting. "Or get word that I would like to speak to him regarding issues of great importance to the struggle?"

The man looked into Nieting's face.

"I'm not connected to the authorities," said Nieting. "I'm not a police agent or any such thing. I am an ally, I assure you."

"Sure, I can get you together with Morris," said the man. He continued to stare deeply into Nieting's face.

"Fantastic," said Nieting. He had to restrain himself from leaning over the fence and embracing the man.

"Be here tomorrow," said the man.

"Tomorrow? You'll introduce me to him tomorrow, you say? When? What time?"

"It don't make no difference what time. Any time. Be here when all these police is somewhere else. Just come by tomorrow. I'll find you. Someone will find you. We'll give you what you want."

"What is your name? I don't mean to intrude, but knowing who you are would be very helpful. As I said, I'm not affiliated with the authorities. How will I ask for you?"

"Just be here. We'll find you. We'll be looking for you. That's all."

"But what time? We should be more definite, don't you think?"

"We'll make sure we find you. Just be here, that's all."

"I'd be more comfortable knowing who I am speaking with. I'll have no way to ask for you otherwise."

The man's face hardened for a moment and then he spoke.

"Ask anyone for Soul Brother Number One," he said, "and you'll be brought straight to me. Got it?"

The man grinned and his eyes sparkled.

"Yes," said Nieting. "Very good, tomorrow then. Thank you, Soul Brother Number One. Tomorrow."

The man never relinquished his connection to Nieting's eyes as he backed away, moving mysteriously into the crowd and disappearing into its depths. A woman to Nieting's right, wearing a house dress and curlers shouted past him, "Don't come down here and tell us lies," and Dick Gregory answered, "I ain't telling no lies. I don't want anyone to get hurt. Get your children off the street."

Shots rang out, popping like firecrackers and Gregory staggered, grasping his thigh and spinning around. The police and the reporters and the Negro officials scattered as Gregory made for the doorway of a one-story brick building. The crowd surged, not moving forward, rather seething, expanding and contracting like the ocean in a dream, pushing and pulling. In seconds, the street side of the fence was clear as the cops retreated, taking cover behind the patrol cars. The crowd at the stanchions remained immobile, immovable, possessing an unexplainable certitude that Nieting could see, borne of the awareness of their collective mass and the palpable weight of their anger. This was just what Nieting was looking for, another glimpse at the spontaneous power of the people. They writhed like a great snake – Triplett would be the snake charmer, the man who knew how to direct the irresistible force of the peoples' will. This knowledge swelling in Nieting's breast made him invincible. He was the only person on the street side of the stanchions who failed to take cover. He stood alone in the center of the street, fully aware of where he was and to his mind, safe. He was sure the Negroes of Watts would do him no harm. He looked at the men huddling for cover then turned to the hundreds watching Gregory and the thousands swarming down Imperial Highway, silhouetted by hell-red fires. Nieting felt like he was peering at the image of all humanity, all oppressed peoples, all of the abused, the shunned, maltreated, the unheard – they were the unheard making themselves heard at long last. They were the most powerful force on earth.

"Get down, you god damned fool." A policeman crouching at Nieting's side pulled him onto the pavement, forcing him to his knees and yanking him by the shirt towards a fire truck. When they made it behind the truck, the Sergeant shouted at Nieting, "you god damned son of a bitch, you're gonna get my men killed."

The cop dragging Nieting yelled, "Oh shit, Sergeant, look at that nigger now. He's out at the fence again."

Dick Gregory stood at the stanchion surrounded by the people, the left leg of his denim overalls slick with blood, speaking to a man holding a .22 caliber rifle. When the police advanced, Gregory waved them off and they halted. He conversed with the man holding the rifle, surrounded by children who had ducked under the stanchions and gathered close around him. He shook hands with the man, who quickly disappeared into the crowd as Gregory limped back to the police line.

"He apologized for it, the brother apologized," said Gregory. "He promised he'd go home. Get me to the motherfucking hospital, will you?"

Nieting was up off the ground in an instant, following along in the pack of reporters as Gregory was whisked behind the perimeter where two medics quickly examined his leg and lowered him onto a stretcher. Nieting jogged next to the stretcher as if he were a doctor or close friend as attendants moved Gregory to an ambulance, but he continued across Avalon and back down Imperial Highway, hurrying along the darkened street to where his car sat in the shadows. He unlocked the car door as the ambulance carrying Dick Gregory screamed past into the darkness.

As Nieting cruised beneath the Harbor Freeway overpass, away from the wailing sirens of Watts, a convoy of National Guard rolled past in the opposite direction. His hands shook as he slumped in the driver's seat and looked straight ahead. The presence of the soldiers crawled over his flesh like the icy hands of a corpse. The streets of Berlin were outside of his car now, the once broad avenue where he grew up reduced to a maze of rubble below the jagged shells of buildings. He stared straight ahead, feigning innocence, as if it were natural that he be on this street at this time, struggling to contain the terror as he had many times before when soldiers passed. German soldiers, Russian soldiers, American soldiers, weapons resting on their hips, the great machine guns mounted on jeeps reposed like flesh eating prehistoric birds. Nieting remained in Berlin until the last truck rolled by, then continued very carefully down the palm lined thoroughfare of Imperial Highway to his room, to prepare for the Revolution.

♦ ♦ ♦

Amazingly, after the unwitting mistake of allowing a madman into their home, a man who threatened them with wild statements and insulting accusations then fled, dashing down the street arguing vehemently with himself, and after Barbarin's phone call warning Auger to watch out for the German who had assaulted a baby in a stroller at Disneyland, a warning which Auger heeded, calling the security company and alerting them to the intrusion into the neighborhood of a dangerous criminal, the Augers remained light hearted. They were moving to Hawaii. Nothing could touch the excitement of it. For a brief moment, Suzette secretly marveled at how quickly she'd gotten over the episode. She was proud of her resiliency. After all, the madman wasn't her problem, he was his family's problem. To Suzette, he was simply another nut one encountered in Hollywood from time to time. It wasn't uncommon for celebrities to be pursued by unbalanced fans. It was the nature of show business. That they were moving to Hawaii put everything else in perspective. There was so much to be done. The real estate agent was due to arrive at their home shortly.

When Auger told his wife he was writing a book telling the story of his life she was thrilled to no end. He'd always been a resourceful provider, always understood how to maximize benefit from every aspect of his talent. A book could mean a movie. The future looked bright. The dismal question of the coloreds would be half a Pacific away once they arrived in Hawaii. The Augers would resume living the good life. Suzette danced around the house straightening up for the real estate agent. She called Celine home from a neighborhood girlfriend's house, not that she was overly worried about the madman, but to be safe. Celine sat on the couch snuggled next to her father as they watched her mother dusting, placing a vase just right on an end table, slipping the Hot Creoles LP back into the sleeve and into the record rack, dancing as she worked, gliding over the carpet in ecstatic swing moves as her husband and daughter laughed and made comments. The release of tension, the exhilaration, the letting go was joyous. They chattered and giggled and teased, poked and caressed one another with exaggerated abandon. Finally, the three embraced in a fit of hysterical laughter that might never have ceased escalating had not the real estate agent had arrived. Suzette answered the door. She was on. She introduced the agent to her family and began the tour. Auger stepped away and strolled lazily around the pool, raising his face to the hot sun. In moments the sound of the Beatles boomed from behind Celine's closed bedroom door.

"Celine, honey," said Suzette. "Turn the music off until Estelle and I are done talking about the house. Thank you, baby."

Suzette's voice was full and strong, the sound of her happiness was palpable and Auger was responsible for it. Everything had been restored. He was back where he belonged. Not only had the strange ordeal ended, but he'd come away with more than he had before. He realized the beauty of his past now, the value of it, the actual lucre it would produce as well as the sweet nostalgia contained in the very stuff of his life. It was all his again and he intended to make the most out of it.

I'll get me one of those tape recorders, he thought. *Nothing too big and fancy. They must make small ones. I'll speak my story into the machine, then get some writer to type it up and help organize the pieces. It'll be about all the things I been through, the people I've known. Why the hell would I give what I know about Buddy to some stranger when I can write the story myself. I know Buddy would have wanted it that way, one of his own telling his story and getting the benefit from it instead of some greedy bastard who couldn't really understand what it all meant anyways. Good ol'Buddy. He sure did help folks survive, helped me survive. That punk was right about that much. But that god damned song he was going on about. Can't no one on this earth tell me I remember things that never did happen. I don't know no song. Wish I did. I could use some new material right about now. Where do people get this stuff from anyway?*

"Jean, darling." Suzette called from the house. "Celine, come out of your room, sweetheart. Come into the living room. Jean, I've got to tell you what Estelle said. Come inside quick. Estelle is a real sweetheart. I have to tell you what she said. I have great news."

Real estate in Brentwood was at a premium. What news could have been better? The future truly was exciting and it was rushing headlong at the Augers. The past however, would not disappear, regardless of what the old man told himself. It would not let him live in peace. That song. What could the mad German have meant? Where did he get off making such things up? His words kept coming back into Auger's mind. Could there have been such a song? Something was lingering inside of him, something frightening. He sat in a chaise lounge next to the pool as Suzette skipped about inside the house, singing gaily as she straightened the place up for prospective buyers and Celine sang along to the Beatles behind the closed door to her room. Auger's gut tightened. He looked up quickly when a bird rustled the leaves of an Orange tree. *Deslonde?*

"Please not now," he whispered. "Not with my girls at home."

He clutched the aluminum frame of the chaise lounge as if someone might try to forcibly remove him, might try to make him go back, to re-member things he did not want to know, things that did not happen. The water rippling in the pool sparkled under the hot sun and Auger's mind rippled behind his eyes like aqua blue water reflecting light, undulating, merging inside and outside into a serene stillness, drifting irresistibly, floating freely . . . the only thing little Jean was conscious of were the gun shots. There were several before he'd fully awakened. The shots sounded far off until his eyes opened in the pitch dark. The explosions seemed close by then, just outside in his sister's backyard or perhaps in the yard of a neighbor. Could it be the policeman Trenchard come to get him? Another shot sounded and five more in rapid succession, dull thuds reverberating inside Jean's skin. Then, there was stillness. Had no one awakened? He lay in bed dozing restlessly, tossing for the few hours left before daylight and awakening in the brightness of the little room to the sound of his sister moving in the kitchen. Perhaps he'd dreamed the shots, after all. Surely, she would have heard them. He wouldn't ask her about it. The last thing he wanted was his big sister meddling in his busi-ness. He didn't say a word to her that morning, he simply walked out the door determined to find Buddy Bolden.

Jackson Street was shaded from the morning sun by the roofs of houses as Jean walked to the trolley stop. At Magnolia Street, he head-ed for the red sign with white frosted letters of the Clio streetcar line. The trolley was empty when it rolled up to the stop. Jean hopped on board, dropped a nickel in the box, the motorman rang the bell, and the car jerked forward. Morning commuters crowded on at each stop, quickly filling the train as it moved through the Poydras/Rampart commercial district towards Canal Street. Jean sat facing the aisle with his back to the window, opposite a row of open newspapers with the banner headline strewn in front of him down the line.

New Orleans Daily Picayune
TWO POLICE VICTIMS OF AN ASSASSSIN'S WEAPON.
Robert Charles, the Negro Who Escaped After Wounding Officer Mora
Tracked to His Lair and Murders Captain Day and Officer Lamb, While Their Fellow Officers Found a Safe Hiding Place

A stout man with a large mustache sitting next to Jean noticed him reading across the aisle and offered him his newspaper. Jean recoiled. The man did not seem to realize that Jean was a colored boy.

"Go ahead, take a look," said the man, "I read it already. It amazes me how brazen these niggers are nowadays, killing officers of the law."

Jean declined the man's offer with a meek head shake as a man across the aisle answered.

"You know, that nigger stood down three of those police. They say the corporal's name is Trenchard and he and the other two are cowards. The force is charging them. They was afraid to take the nigger."

"Captain Day wasn't no coward," responded the man next to Jean. "He was as brave as they come and he was gunned down in cold blood."

A man holding an overhead strap and standing at the rear door of the trolley said, "You don't know the half of it. I heard them shots last night. I live over on Fourth Street, up the block from where that nigger did the murdering. I heard the shots. Must have been around 3 a.m. or so. I fell back to sleep, but around six this morning I went over there. I seen Captain Day's body laying on the ground all shot up. And the other one, Lamb was a few feet away. A coward's a coward and I hope Trenchard gets all he deserves, but I'll tell ya, this ain't no regular nigger. This is one insane nigger. He got no human feelings. There's a crowd outside his place right now. Those men won't leave. They think he's still hiding in the neighborhood. God help the darky that wanders onto that street."

"God damn Robert Charles," said the man next to Jean. "It's niggers like Robert Charles gets the decent darkies stirred up. They say Robert Charles hates white folks."

"Decent darkies?" said another man. "Well, hell, there ain't no such a thing if you ask me. Some folks say this is just the tip of the iceberg. They say the niggers is planning to take control of the city."

"There was two of'm last night, as I understand it," said the man clutching the overhead strap. "Charles was the smart one. They got the other over in the Parish Prison."

"I don't know what it will take to make these niggers understand this is the white man's country," replied the man next to Jean.

"Passing the Star Car bill would help," said another man, pointing towards the front of the car at a black man and woman sitting side by side.

"Yes," said a woman sitting on the other side of Jean, "it would be much more convenient to ride without that god awful stink."

Jean saw the two blacks stiffen at the woman's words. He could see the back of the man's beige suit and the woman's yellow dress with a high mesh collar, shoulders that puffed out and long sleeves that ended in lacy frills. She wore her hair up and pinned under a flowered hat.

"You can put a suit on a monkey," said the white woman, directing her voice towards the couple, "but it's still a monkey."

"And we don't want no stinking monkeys on our trolleys," replied a voice in the front of the car.

Jean huddled quietly, pressing his knees together and sinking as deeply into his seat as he could.

"They are killing peace officers, now," shouted a man. "When will someone put a stop to these niggers terrorizing the streets of this city!"

Shouts of approval sounded all over the crowded streetcar as the black man in the suit rang the bell to stop at Felicity Street. Seeing the front entrance blocked, he and the woman began to move towards the back door as passengers cursed them. Suddenly, the front of the women's dress was spattered with brown spit. She cried out and her companion stopped and turned just as fists came from every direction, knocking the man to the floor. He jumped to his feet and grabbed the woman by her wrist, pushing his way toward the door, past Jean, as several more blows landed on his face and a hand reached out and tore the hat from the woman's head and tossed it out the window onto the side of the track. The passengers applauded as the man and woman jumped from the trolley before it came to a full stop. The couple stood trackside, staring at the departing trolley and the jeering passengers as it sailed toward Canal Street.

Jean closed his eyes and sat against the frame of the open window thinking of the man who was the cause of all the trouble, Robert Charles. He heard Buddy's conversation on the street of four days earlier for the first time. Robert Charles was Buddy's friend. Robert Charles, whom all of white New Orleans despised, whom they would kill if they could, whom they would kill sooner rather than later. This is how things were. There was no doubt that Robert Charles was a dead man. Jean stared at the floor, afraid to raze his eyes for fear of being recognized as a colored boy.

At Canal Street, the trolley emptied and the people who only moments before had mercilessly thrown blows and vile curses at the couple disappeared into the thriving business district. Jean walked up Canal to Franklin Street, to the Big 25s and hung around for several hours watching for Buddy but he didn't show. The boy knew Bolden wouldn't be there until night but had hoped somehow he might show up. He decided it would be best to get off the streets until dark. It was dangerous in daylight. Perhaps after dark he could move around without being noticed.

He arrived back at Canal and Royal just as the Clio streetcar reached the stop and bounded onto the back of the car. The car pitched forward through the chaotic jumble of traffic as Jean huddled on the back platform. Inside the streetcar, the name Robert Charles sounded again and again, spit like a curse; cocaine fiend, morphine addict, black brute, cold blooded murderer, hater of the white race. He was a sharp dresser who always carried lots of cash and bullied dim witted darkies into contributing to his anti-white conspiracies. Was he a full blooded nigger or a half breed? Some claimed he was a Cuban looking black, a mentally defective mulatto, a sexual pervert, a vicious animal. He shot Captain Day five times as he lay dying for no reason other than blood lust.

"The darkies know where he's hiding, as much as they deny it."

"If it comes to it, we'll kill every last one before we give our city up to that element."

"This is still a white man's country, god damnit. If its race war they want, you know who'll come out on the short end."

The voices in the trolley cut into the air like razor thrusts and even as Jean tried to shut out the words, he couldn't help hearing the sounds, like a dream of something evil lurking in darkness just behind one's back, unseen, yet whispering incessant threats. Jean fled the train at Clio Street, four blocks short of Jackson. He headed up Clio and at Dryades Street turned towards his sister's house on Jackson, but halted at the sight of hundreds of white men traversing the thoroughfare. Some of the men flashed guns and others passed bottles as gangs of boys ran in packs through their ranks. They were there for Robert Charles. Jean backtracked to Clio and walked a block further to Rampart before cutting over to Jackson. When he hit Jackson Street, the houses of Celine's neighbors appeared safe and calm.

Two men raced past as he closed the gate to the little garden in her front yard. One of the men wore a long raincoat and clinked as he trotted, speaking loudly to his companion, neither noticing Jean as they went by.

"God damn it's hot and I got twenty half pints stuffed inside this coat. I'm suffocating in here. But, I'll feel nice and rich after I pass out all this whisky. Those boys over to that darky's place must be plenty thirsty by now."

Jean crouched in the garden until the men turned left turn on Willow Street.

Later that evening, after his sister and her family had gone to sleep, Jean slipped out the window of his room and headed towards the Big 25s

Club. Mist rose in the darkness outside of his sister's house covering the street lights in a dull glow. Over the rooftops against the eastern sky, light flashed off the clouds accompanied by a low rumble like thunder. All else was still and dark except for the muted light from street lamps nervously buzzing. Jean watched his sister's place for signs of movement but all was still. The strange flickering against the black sky crept along the underside of the clouds, moving like candle light dancing on a wall and seemed to be coming closer. Finally a light flashed down Jackson Street for a split second, ten blocks away at St. Charles Avenue like the light in a lighthouse spinning. It appeared again like a star tumbling in the street and was moving in Jean's direction. The strange brightness filled the street like molten metal flowing through the veins of the city.

Every house in the neighborhood was dark despite the strange noise steadily rising, moving, spiking shrilly then settling into a low steady rumble then spiking again. Within moments he heard the voices, muffled at first, the thousand disparate voices of the beast, shrieking, howling, wailing separately, distinctly, yet inseparable, a single irresistible force. He watched, curiously, forgetting for a moment the urgency of his escape and that he had so far to go to get to the 25's. The size of the point of light grew ever larger and the rumble of the storm intensified until finally two blocks off at Freret Street, the physical substance of the beast became visible, a wall of men rushing through the intersection, hundreds of torches trailing thick black smoke, clubs, pistols, rifles, held aloft. An indistinguishable mass of men swarmed, surging chaotically yet directed by something, some desire, some lust they all held in common. Jean turned on his heels, took one last look over his shoulder at his Celine's house and swung back around into the huge faces of two horses hitched to a large wagons. The horses reared their heads as Jean jumped from their path and the driver pulled the rig by, blocking the path of the mob. A man next to the driver held a pistol and the driver admonished him when he saw it.

"Put that damned cannon away. Get it out of sight and don't touch it again. You want to start a shooting war?"

244

"No sir," replied the other. "I'll stash it under the seat."

The eyes of the driver passed over Jean, but did not see him. He stood in the cab and waited, facing the onrush of men, waving his arms desperately as if he intended to contain flood waters with his hands. When they reached him, the mob halted, miraculously, weaving at the man's feet like a giant drunkard, thousands of eyes wide with madness, staring dumbly as the man shouted over their heads.

"Please, you must not go any further," he said. "You must disperse and return to your homes. You are dishonoring our city."

The thousands roared and moaned, cursing with one voice and the man in the wagon reeled as though resisting the winds of a hurricane. For a moment, the impasse seemed frozen in time, the man in the wagon standing upon a cliff above the roiling sea, the cauldron of hate swirling below, he balancing with his legs spread and arms wide like Moses beseeching God. One would have expected a great howling wind to part the sky and an angry god to appear and smite the mob, yet the air was dead, thick with humidity and the stench of decay. A man stepped from the crowd and handed a lit torch to another and jumped onto the back of the buggy, signaling to the mob for silence. He was a large man with a sweat stained shirt and disheveled hair. He reeled as if he were drunk and stumbled when the horses stirred but regained his balance and shouted at the man addressing the mob.

"Who the hell are you?"

"My name is St. Clair Adams," came the reply. "I am an attorney in this city for twenty years. You must listen to what I have to say." He shouted into the face of the beast. "You must allow the law to take its course. The Negro will be brought to justice. You must not take the law into your own hands."

Countless voices spit back.

"God damn the law."

"The law is too slow."

"We are the law."

"This is the law."

"The people are the law."

"This is our will."

"Our will is the law."

Thousands more voices cursed, spewing incomprehensible drunken rage, unexplainable mirth, cold blooded sadism, vacant perverse fascination, an avalanche of noise. St. Clair Adams stamped his feet in the cab of the buggy and the horses started, one shrieking and straining as the man next to Adams leaned on the reigns and tried to calm the spooked animals.

"I implore you men," said Adams, "do not destroy the good name of our city. Do not dishonor New Orleans by an act of irrational passion that the rest of the nation will behold with contempt."

The mob howled like jackals with cancerous bowels, unearthly, and the man that had climbed into St. Clair Adam's buggy waved his arms and others on the ground barked at the men to be still so he could speak.

"I am no attorney, gentlemen," shouted the man. "I am the Mayor of Kenner."

Again the noise swelled until someone fired a pistol into the air and the racket lessened enough for the man to continue.

"I am from Kenner, gentlemen, and I have come down to New Orleans tonight to assist you in teaching the blacks a lesson. I have killed a Negro before and I am willing to kill again. The only way you can teach these niggers a lesson and put them in their place is to go out and lynch a few of them as an object lesson . . . that is the only thing to do. Kill them, string them up, lynch them. I will lead you if you will follow."

The man climbed down from the buggy and took back the torch as someone shouted, "That's telling'm Mayor Cowan."

"On to the Parish Prison," shouted Cowan, "and lynch Pierce."

The earth shook and Jean cowered in the gutter as the mob thundered its approval, stomping and shouting and shooting guns into the air. A man rushed forward and slapped the rump of one of the horses and the buggy jerked from the path and the river of men surged past his sister's darkened house. Jean looked at the house one last time and stepped towards the 25s.

He ran on Robertson Street, away from his sister's house as the mob slithered behind him on Jackson, swinging en mass a block up onto Magnolia. Jean hurried on, peering between the houses as the mob moved parallel to him on the next street. There were men on Freret Street, as well, one block before Robertson, moving parallel to Jean on his right. He could see the torches and the men running as he looked past the houses and through the yards. Thousands of men moved on all sides, to his left and to his right and behind on Jackson. When he crossed Calliope Street, the mob was still there on both sides, wild and chaotic, glowing in the torch light and disappearing behind the houses, the sound magnified as it echoed through the backyards.

At New Basin Canal, the mob on Magnolia turned left towards the Clairborne Avenue Bridge and the Parish Prison and Jean cut right towards Rampart Street and the 25s Club. Hundreds of stragglers from Freret Street moved past him trying to catch up to the huge mass turning from Magnolia. The street was crowded and Jean slowed up to avoid colliding with the oncoming bodies. He'd been keeping to the side, seeking cover in the shadows and was suddenly enveloped by a group of young men striding towards him. One of them called out, "Hey you, boy. What's your name?" and Jean halted but did not look in the direction of the voice. The question came again, angry this time, and before Jean could speak a voice answered from among the overgrown hedges in the front yard of a nearby house.

"Who wants to know?"

A man stood in the darkness as if trying to avoid being seen. Jean hadn't noticed him, not ten feet from where he stood. Several of the men rushed across the street.

"I said, what the hell is your name?"

The defiant response was taken as an affront or a challenge and the tone of the man in the yard changed as the men reached him. He held his arms in front of him with his flat palms facing the oncoming gang.

"Wallace," he replied.

"What's your first name?"

"Wallace."

The entire gang laughed and crowded around the man as Jean edged beneath a low hanging Willow tree.

"Wallace Wallace?"

"No, Wallace Sabatier."

"Hey, you look like a nigger. Fellas, we got ourselves a nigger."

"I ain't no nigger."

"Hell you ain't."

"I don't think he's a nigger."

"Hell he ain't"

"He's a darky sure as shit."

"I ain't, I swear it. I'm white as you are."

"Let's have a look at you, boy."

The men closed in on Sabatier, the largest of them grabbing him by the collar and dragging him across the street to the canal side where he held him beneath a streetlight as the others danced about gleefully, then shoved in close for a better view.

"No, he's white alright."

"I'll be god damned, you're right."

The large man put his arm around Sabatier's shoulder in mock affection and gave him a hearty shake.

"Okay Wallace Wallace," he said. "We're nigger hunting tonight. You coming with us or you some kind of nigger lover?"

"I'm going with you all."

The men cheered and slapped Sabatier's back and one saw Jean's legs beneath the tree across the street.

"Hey you, come on out so we can get a look at you."

Jean obeyed, emerging from the curtain of Willow branches into the light.

"Come here boy, we need to talk to you."

"Is that boy a nigger?"

"Naw."

"I'll bet he is a nigger."

"He's just a youngster. I want me a real black one."

"Come here boy. You a darky?"

"What are you anyway?"

"Ah, let's get going. We're missing all the action."

Jean sprinted from the yard, down the center of the road, passing stragglers who looked after him curiously. He could hear the gang of men laughing.

"You see the look on Wallace Wallace's face when he thought we was gonna string'm up?"

"Let's go Wallace Wallace."

"They're gonna lynch that nigger at the Parish Prison. We better get moving or there won't be nothing left when we get there."

"Ah, let's find our own darkies."

"Hell no, I want to see the barbecue."

Jean hit the curve at Rampart at full speed, running past the end of the New Basin Canal and on towards Canal Street. He ran block after block on the empty streets. The vast thoroughfare of Canal was deserted when he reached it. There were no trolley's lined up, no horses crowding, no human beings hurrying, only the high canyon walls of buildings and silent billboards and the slapping of his feet on the road bed. When reached Franklin, he cut right and in moments reached Customhouse Street.

The Big 25s Club was fully lit when Jean reached the intersection. Two colored men stood outside conversing as Jean hit the sidewalk running and pushed through the swinging doors. He slid to a stop on the sawdust floor and no one raised an eyebrow or even noticed him. There were only a few people in the place and all the faces were black. What was happening out on the streets was not happening inside the 25s. Just as he'd thought. Buddy wasn't afraid of anything. Jean was safe in the

25's. Wherever Buddy was it was safe. The 25s was a long rectangular room with a bandstand at one end and a bar at the other and a dozen small round tables scattered about. There were no more than ten people in the place and they were quiet, relaxed, almost dozing. There were three musicians on the bandstand, but Bolden wasn't among them, and several people huddled at the bar. Jean recognized a man on the bandstand sitting in a chair strumming a guitar. *That's Galloway. I seen him in La Pointe when I heard Buddy that day.*

Galloway spoke over his shoulder to a boy no older than Jean, clutching a bass fiddle. "Hey Pinot. You got to push harder tonight. I don't want to be waiting for you no more."

"Leave the boy be," said a man leaning back in an old rickety chair opposite Galloway, carefully examining the keys to an accordion. He spoke to the boy holding the bass on the bandstand. "Don't listen to what ol'nasty Charlie Galloway say."

"I just told him, don't be sleeping back there, Henry," said Galloway.

"The boy ain't sleeping," replied the accordion player.

"Buddy," shouted Galloway, "C'mon up and play some god damned music."

He yelled across the room to a man with his back turned, standing at the bar between two women sitting on barstools. The man's shoulders were broad and his head bobbed as he talked to the women, then dropped back as he drained a shot glass. He glanced over his shoulder when Galloway called again and Jean saw his profile. It was Buddy.

"God damn it, Buddy," said Galloway.

Jean walked across the room, reaching Bolden just as he hoisted another shot glass to his lips. He blurted out, "Hey king, my name is Jean Auger and I'm here to join your band. I play the best trombone in St. John's Parish."

Bolden looked at the boy as if through a haze, studying his face, bleary-eyed and squinting, weaving slightly, his mouth poised as if he intended to shout a greeting the second he could figure out who he was talking too. His eyes lit up at the mention of a trombone.

"Boulboul?" said Bolden, "Picou's man, Boulboul. You speak American, Boulboul? Eh? No matter if ya don't. Picou say you play those low down blues just like Buddy like, only with that Cuban thing, hot meat sizzling on the fire, spitting grease. Bouboul?"

Bolden rubbed his eyes and poked one of the women sitting at the bar as though she might help him understand, but she shrugged her shoulders. Bolden's great happy lit up grin suddenly collapsed into a dark bitter frown.

"Bouboul sposed to be a grown man."

Bolden pounded his fist on the bar.

"You ain't nothing but a god damned kid," he said.

He pulled himself up and staggered towards Jean, grabbing him by the back of the neck and shoving Jean towards the door.

"I don't take no children in my band," he said. "You got to be a grown man to play with Buddy Bolden."

"Buddy," yelled the accordion man, "god damn it, get on up here and let's get to going."

Bolden ignored him as he steered Jean by the neck, pushing him towards the street.

"If I catch you around here again," he said, "I swear I'll turn you over to them cops. You won't never see your folks again."

The women laughed as Jean shrunk under the pressure of Bolden's gripe. He struggled not to fall as Bolden thrust his arm out, propelling him past the swinging doors onto the wooden sidewalk.

"God damn it Buddy," shouted a voice from inside. "You drunk? God damn it, you are drunk."

"I ain't drunk," came Bolden's voice, then a blast of his cornet and gasps and a woman's voice pleading, "Oh, Buddy, play me those blues."

Jean wandered across the street and stood at the entrance of an alley in the shadows and sobbed, wiping his wet face with his forearm. There wasn't a soul on the streets around the 25s, all the bars were dark and the doors and windows sealed tight. Jean crouched in the alley listening to the voices inside the 25's shouting encouragement as Bolden blew a series of notes, bringing his foot down on the wooden floor with each beat, his friends shouting, "yeah," each time his foot landed. All the buildings in the neighborhood were shuddered and the streets were deserted except for the lights inside the 25s. Jean huddled close to the side of the alley, watching the distended shadows of the two women inside the 25s dancing on the sidewalk outside the front door.

The sounds of voices and gunshots echoed through the streets like Mardi Gras, drunken revelers shrieking and howling, yet it was the sound of murder, not the sound of celebration. He lowered himself down close to the ground, fixing his eyes on the lights of the 25s and lay in the dark shivering as the sound of voices and of men running, their feet pounding the road like horses stampeding, came closer. He could feel the earth vibrating. There was a child whimpering back in the alley and a rustling and whispers of, "be still, be still." Jean saw the outline of several little heads pressed against the plank fence.

They came down Customhouse, a hundred strong, charging onto Franklin, waving pistols and clubs, swarming like moths to the light of the 25s, straight to the front entrance, bursting past the swinging doors, firing shots, falling over one another, trampling each other. Jean heard the screams of the women inside. He heard wood smashing and the sickening thud of gunshot, again and again, a massacre, murder, flashing light as a black man ran out onto the street and disappeared pursued by a gang of white men. Wallace Sabatier burst out of the 25's, howling with a twisted face, clutching a stick, then ran after the ones chasing the fleeing black man. Another black man, tall and gangly, flew out of the door of the 25s through the white mob so fast they didn't notice him until after he was past. He came directly for the alley where Jean was and when light from a torch flashed into the alley and the black man saw Jean and the other children hiding there he reversed direction, slipping through the mob miraculously, leaving the alley behind in darkness and silence. White men poured from the 25s, one swinging a pistol over his head and shouting "There's more in the alley."

"Niggers in the alley," came a reply as men ran right and left to cut off escape from both sides.

There were more shots as the white men milled about impatiently. The 25s was dark and quiet. All that stirred inside were clouds of smoke swirling out the entrance.

"They got one over on Villere," someone shouted.

"Let's go, before they kill him."

"I just came from Villere, I want a fresh nigger of my own."

Within moments the street had cleared and all was still, yet the echo of the violence seemed to hang in the air.

"He's dead," whispered Jean, watching the single door left on the hinge swing back and forth and inside nothing but dust and deathly silence. The children behind Jean bolted from the alley, little heads bent low, moving in single file close to the buildings and out of sight.

"Buddy's dead," said Jean.

Jean pressed his hand over his mouth to stifle his sobs. Bolden was dead. It happened so quickly, an instant severing of life. Death swooped in, plucked its prey and took flight. Just like that, Buddy was gone. There was no use crying. Jean had to get home. He had to get back to his sister's house. He followed the path the children had taken, moving close to the buildings and running crouched over. There was no one on Canal, yet Jean moved stealthily, scurrying where there was the least light, creeping through the business district, staying low, keeping away from open spaces. When he hit the residential streets west of Poydras, he moved beneath trees and next to hedges, lingering in the shadows at any sign of movement.

Buddy's dead.

Several times he saw gangs of whites and each time he hid behind a bush or tree until they'd passed. At Celine's house, he climbed through the same window from which he'd made his escape. The house was still dark and quiet. He undressed quickly and climbed into bed and lay there trying to shut out the distant sound of gunshot from the streets of the city.

When his eyes grew accustomed to the darkness, he saw Celine's figure at the open door. She seemed to realize that Jean had noticed her presence and gently pushed the door closed.

Sunday, August 15, 1965

Never before had Nieting's pen moved so swiftly, never had words flowed as directly, without the mediation of second thoughts or corrections or clarifications, everything spinning like gold thread out the tip of the ball point onto the clean white sheets. It came as a single act of thought, so ripe for birth it popped out like a perfect painless delivery and lay on the page looking up at him, a flawless, pristine symmetry come straight from his body. When the rush of words ceased finally, he raised his eyes to the sunlight rimming the top of the door to his room and blocked the glare with his hand. A man on the television announced the time. Nieting had been writing all night. His chest was heavy with the residue of the great emotion he'd ridden on the long journey inward. He'd been inside a thought process, cascading with the logic, dancing gracefully as the implications unfolded revealing deeper and deeper meanings. For hours his mind had been one with his body and his hand had formed it all into a meticulous painting, or better, a photograph with every detail razor sharp on the surface yet etched so deeply the image seemed to descend into eternity. It was a manifesto he'd composed, a manifesto in the tradition of the great manifestos, Communist, Futurist, Surrealist, Manifeste Dada, and now a manifesto for musicians, revolutionary musicians, Negro musicians.

"That's it," said Nieting. "Manifesto for Negro Musicians."

He stood up next to the night stand where he'd written, knocking the table and scattering the pages across the dirty carpet like treasure spilling over the floor. He stepped over the pages.

"If Mr. Triplett prefers, I'll change the title to *Manifesto **of** Negro Musicians.* They can take it for their own. We can share authorship or call it a collective document. My name needn't be mentioned at all."

Nieting hadn't slept for nearly twenty four hours yet felt invigorated, joyous, complete. He swung the door open and light rushed in chased by suffocating heat. Nieting began to sweat. The temperature would be stifling again, yet for all the heat and light, the pages on the floor burned brighter and hotter. Nieting wrapped his arms around himself and grinned.

He ran down the stairs to the parking lot in his bare feet, skipping over the burning asphalt, shielding his eyes against the glare and grabbed a copy of the L.A. Times from the vending machine and hustled back to his room. The television was on, had been on all night, yet Nieting had been oblivious to it. Now, when he entered the room, he was met by a reporter's voice broadcast from the streets of Watts, speaking rapidly, hyperventilating as if all hell was breaking loose around him.

"A white deputy sheriff and three Negroes were killed by gunfire last night shortly before National Guardsmen moved into the area where riots raged for the third straight night. A huge section of Los Angeles was virtually a city on fire as flames from stores, industrial complexes and homes lit the skies. Several more people were shot during the night, as Negro mobs fought bloody battles with police, looted stores and set fire to scores of buildings. Sniper fire and uncontrolled flames are being reported over a widening area. This morning, the violence has reached nearly to City Hall from south Los Angeles at least 10 miles from where it all started. Well over 200 people have been injured in last the three days, including more than 30 peace officers. Deputy Sheriff Ronald Ernest Ludlow, 27, was shot in the stomach at Imperial . . . . "

Nieting was breathing more heavily than the reporter. He raised the L.A. Times and the front page screamed into his face;

RIOT SPREADS, 4 KILLED, GUARD CALLED
Scores of Fires Rage Unchecked
Eyewitness Account: "Get Whitey," Scream Blood-Hungry Mobs
Anarchy Must End - editorial
Racial Unrest Laid to Negro Family Failure

The paper shook in his hands, so he dropped it on the bed. He felt his stomach rising and rushed to the toilet and fired a volley of vomit into the bowl as he retched and coughed. He sat on the linoleum floor wiping his brow with a wad of tissues and chuckled. He thought of the previous evening and the masses of Negroes and how Soul Brother Number One had somehow picked him out of the crowd like he knew Nieting was deeply involved in the struggle. Soul Brother Number One's face was taut, the lines chiseled like a mask of coal shining with the reflection of fire and his eyes shown viscous red.

Afterwards, Nieting had devised a plan. It had come to him during the night. He would go to Watts in the light of day and find Triplett. If Soul Brother Number One was able to do as he claimed and find Nieting amidst the chaos, then all the better. Nieting was equipped now. He was in possession of an offering, a gift more potent than military firepower, more illuminating than any tactics or strategy. *The Manifesto of Negro Musicians* would become synonymous with the rebellion of Watts, intertwined forever with the great rising as would the major accomplishment of his life, the recovery of *The Robert Charles Song*.

It was a morning of brilliant sunshine in Southern California. Even with the dusty veneer of smoke it was a travel agent's dream, a Mecca for vacationers. Nieting donned his shades and lingered on the motel balcony. He felt a stillness, a calm borne of inner certainty and even of faith. Very slowly and with great deliberation, he packed his gear, the recorder, the camera, the notebooks, the files, carefully folding the manifesto and placing it in a front zippered pocket of the rucksack and carrying everything to the car.

The little sedan puttered as Nieting accelerated through the sparse Sunday traffic of Imperial Highway, the sparse Revolution-has-come traffic, the road ahead open like arms beseeching. He sailed toward the gray smoke enveloping the interior of south Los Angeles as a commentator spoke over the radio.

"Negro comedian Dick Gregory suffered a gunshot wound in the thigh as he went to the riot area last night in an attempt to calm the mobs.

Gregory, a hero of the civil rights movement, met with other Negro leaders Friday in an effort to seek a solution. But, the voices of reason were drowned out by the surging sea of hatred directed at the police and Caucasians . . ."

The words of the commentator did not anger Nieting. Such statements could no longer distract him. There was a stillness inside of him, like a warrior might attain or a man willingly going to his death for truth. He'd passed the point where anger was a requisite to action, amazingly, in perfect synchronicity with the Revolution. Victory was inevitable now, he and the Negroes had reached the great transformation where the only pursuit of significance was the pursuit of truth. The act of destruction had become one with the act of creation. Nieting had expressed this state perfectly, albeit in preliminary form, in the manifesto he would deliver to the hands of Morris Triplett. Only the future existed.

A beer jingle on the car radio and then a voice.

"Chief Parker stated last evening that the root cause of the disturbances is the activity of so called civil rights leaders and outside agitators and their constant harping on the social and economic conditions of the Negro."

Chief Parker's voice jumped from the dashboard with a shrill twang.

"If you tell people long enough that they're disadvantaged, that they're not receiving their fair due, and that it is alright to break the law, it should not be surprising when they lose all respect for the law."

Nieting laughed as though the Chief of the Los Angeles Police Department had delivered a punch line to a joke, an absurd joke, hilarious black humor. The Chief's remarks betrayed such vapidity, such ignorance, it was cretinesque, devoid of sense, a desperate pack of lies. An electric current ran through Nieting's body, animating reality to a level of clarity he had never known before. It was exhilarating. It was the power, the force of the Revolution. The spirit of the revolt of the Negroes of Watts was palpable. It was alive in the very air. It was an animal with breath of fire. The beats of its heart were African drums. Mere proximity to it could alter the course of one's thinking, of one's life. Nieting had never felt as alive, never so clear. The thought of the *Manifesto Of Negro Musicians*, the fact of its existence, its inextricable unity with the Revolution, its birth through the medium called Dr. V. Nieting, manifested in an extended rebel yell out of the window of the car.

Nieting regained his composure when an elderly Negro man on the southwest corner of Hoover Street and Imperial Highway shook his fist in response to the scream. The man's face contorted as he shouted an inaudible reply, so enraged he knocked the hat off his head jumping into the street as Nieting drove past. The man's reaction puzzled Nieting. True, he'd given a rebel yell, but he'd always used it ironically, as a reversal, as an anti-rebel yell.

Chief Parker chimed in, "the so-called Negro leaders are no leaders at all." Nieting slapped the radio button and Parker disappeared. He slowed behind a line of cars at the intersection at Main Street and Imperial. The street was blocked with a makeshift barricade of two garbage dumpsters and miscellaneous debris manned by a half dozen helmeted California Highway Patrol officers armed with shotguns. He waited as an officer spoke to the driver of the first car and another cop signaled the rest to turn around and go west on Imperial. As the other cars became embeshed in a jumble of u-turns, Nieting propped the book of maps on the dash board and perused the options.

"Central Avenue is a good place to begin, he said. "According to my sources it is a traditional meeting place for Negro musicians, a legendary street. Auger worked there before the war. It would be the logical spot to begin the search for Triplett. It is only three or four blocks east of Avalon. The closest street through is 108th."

He ran his forefinger across the map and tapped his destination.

"Central Avenue is right there," he said.

Nieting could feel his body, every nerve, every sinew, vibrating with certainly, with clarity. He swung the car northbound onto Main Street and jammed the gas as officers ran into the street shouting for him to halt. He heard the policemen's voices and although he couldn't discern their words, he knew they were words of dire warning. He knew the cops would fire their weapons. The tires screeched and the car swerved to the booming thud of shotguns discharging and the metal clanging of pellets sweeping like sheets of hail across the rear of the car.

"I've been fired upon by the state," shouted Nieting. "I am inside of the Revolution."

Instantly, images, words, disjointed phrases flooded his brain in a speeding blur, but for once did not bring chaos, rather everything was taken in, organized in unquantifiable flashes, gathered in his flesh; his mind and body were one, acting in perfect concert. To exist in the utmost realm of excitement and yet remain so quiet within, to witness reality moving at quantum speed, so fast time stands still, was a vindication for a life time of suffering. The past had been jetisoned in the act of revolt, left in the dust with the cops. He knew the description of the car and the license plate number were being broadcast at that moment. They'd have mistaken him for a white, perhaps a racist from some nearby white community, embattled, striking back, seeking to enflame the situation further. The authorities would have completely misread him, misunderstood who he was. He mustn't be arrested. To be captured would be a disgrace. He would become a laughing stock. The manifesto, the only copy of the manifesto would be confiscated. It would never see the light of day. He would be held incommunicado, if not murdered at once, executed on the street by the police. It was imperative now, irrevocably so, that he find Triplett immediately. He must pass the manifesto on, if he did nothing more.

In less than sixty seconds he reached 108th street. The road east to Central was blocked by a contingent of L.A.P.D. officers, who watched Nieting sail past. One officer shook his head and waved him towards a side street to the west. Nieting would not be turned back, not by policemen, even if they did fire weapons at him, even if they did shoot his car in the back. Instead, he continued north, pulling over after a couple of blocks to read the map for another route to Central Avenue.

There were crowds up Main Street, hundreds of black people milling in the street. Nieting stopped the car and watched as the crowd scemed to stir. Then instantly everyone bolted as if a starting pistol had been fired, crisscrossing each other's paths as windows shattered and men, women and children poured into several large storefronts. The perpetual sound of sirens seemed to be coming nearer as people emerged from the stores, arms loaded with goods and others passed them on the way inside in a wild festival of appropriation. There was an explosion further up the street and people cheered. Flames shot up and the smoke rose along the northern horizon beyond the ecstatic masses. The sirens were suddenly very near causing some people to scatter as others continued working furiously emptying stores. Black clouds of smoke crawled over the pavement like an amorphous predator, swallowing the people, the street, the sidewalks and finally Nieting's car. He tied a handkerchief over his mouth and eased the car through the crowds into a stretch of Main enveloped in flames, finally stopping and ducking down, unable to move. He peered up through the windshield into a swirling black belly of smoke and saw flashes of blue sky stabbed by daggers of red flames. His body trembled uncontrollably. Nieting had been here before, inside the conflagration. He cowered on the floor as the smoke groped the car, spreading over the body like a burning tongue.

He sat up and lightly pressed the gas pedal, feeling his way through the grayness. Both sides of the street were aflame and there were no firemen in sight, only the unending whine of sirens coming from all directions. The street was littered with all kinds of debris, shoes, baby cribs, clothing, air conditioners, bottles, bricks, but the people had moved on. Nieting wept as he maneuvered through the refuse, slowly ranging back and forth from one side of the street to the other, avoiding the busted fetishes of the old order. He'd traveled on burning streets before, in some other life, except then the piles of junk were interspersed with piles of human flesh. Nieting shouted at a boy sprinting past the face of a building as the façade twisted and crashed in flames, scattering red embers that pursued the boy as he fled. He shook his head violently as the streets of Berlin burned before his eyes, finally raising his glance to the head of a palm tree against a swatch of blue sky. The vision of Berlin vanished as the smoke cleared enough to see the street sign at 103rd. He turned right, creeping around the corner, passing a cop car flying by with red lights spinning. War. It was war. Did any man relish war? Wars were all the same. One must endure it for the people, an unimaginable intensification of suffering for an end of suffering. Creative destruction was just. War would end forever with the triumph of the Revolution.

Nieting drove east on 103rd street, finally coming to a stretch of small neat houses with front yards of lawns with people talking, lingering on steps and in driveways, a rather relaxed scene, in as much as the world was being turned on its head at that moment and gunshots and the sirens of eternity, the chaotic racket of war reverberated in an unending stream of sound that permeated everything. Heads turned with surprised looks as Nieting drove by, fingers pointed, people yelled to one another, some running into his rear view mirror, then an object bounced off the hood of his car and children in bicycles struggled vainly to keep pace. They had no way of knowing the driver was Dr. V. Nieting or was author of the *Manifesto of Negro Musicians*. Their hostility, if it was hostility, only children had thrown projectiles after all, was directed at a strange car driven by what looked to be a white man. Nieting sped up 103rd towards Central, but not out of dread of the people, nor out of fear. Until he reached Triplett, the danger of being mistaken for a white was unavoidable. The real danger now was the authorities. He'd fled the police, had been fired upon, had defied the paramilitary. He was fleeing the state, hurrying to the bosom of the Negro people. They roared at him and he gazed at them adoringly. They would be his people soon. He would restore the gift of *The Robert Charles Song* back to them. He would be their philosopher. They would all be family in the Revolution.

A woman emerged from the front of a small duplex cottage catching the screen door behind a child bounding out. She stepped onto the step just as Nieting came parallel to the property. She was beautiful in a pair of short shorts and a snug tank top, her legs long and chocolate brown, her breasts full beneath the light cotton shirt, her face an angel's face. She looked at Nieting as he looked at her, both gazes frozen in time. Once again, everything was clear to Nieting. One must create a new world for the children, for the love of humanity's most vulnerable. This was what he was fighting for, that there be no more orphans of war, no more DP camps, no more lost children. Solidarity is forged in action, love is the byproduct of Revolution. The woman frowned with disgust and Nieting swooned. How beautiful the people on 103rd were, how natural and child-like they appeared in the privacy of their lives, lingering on their front lawns, laughing, gesturing. Nieting was a part of them already.

Fires raged north and south at San Pedro at 103rd Street. People dashed from storefronts, arms loaded with goods, pushing overflowing shopping carts, hauling appliances on dollies amidst a tangle of fire hoses and desperate firemen. Small children darted about like gnats, dragging boxes, clutching radios, a man rolling a rack of clothing still on the hangers, people pushing shopping carts filled with groceries, hauling cartons of canned goods. At the corner of Avalon Blvd. he stopped the car and wept uncontrollably. He saw the burned out streets of Berlin where he'd wandered as a boy. Nothing was untouched, not a single structure had been spared. The boulevard was leveled for what appeared to be blocks running north and south. It looked like the scene of a massive aerial bombing. Nieting's heart swelled. No one could understand the suffering of the Negro as he did, perhaps not the Negroes themselves. He swore then and there, in a little prayer-like vow, whispered with closed eyes and tears flowing, that he would dedicate the rest of his life to the liberation of the Negro. He vowed to pursue the Revolution until his death. Then he wiped the tears away and breathed deeply. A Negro man lay face down near the curb, his back a swamp of red gore.

Ahead on the corner, two Negro men stepped into the street and waved Nieting south on Avalon, nodding and gesturing to him to come forward. They pointed up the boulevard, motioning for him to go that way. Nieting grinned sheepishly and nodded as if he grasped the exact import of their message. Another man yelled something to the men on the corner. He looked like Soul Brother Number One. He turned his head towards Nieting and nodded affirmatively, pointing down Avalon.

"Soul Brother Number One," said Nieting. "My god, it's him. It is a miracle, I swear it, it is a miracle."

Nieting hit the horn and began to pull over but the man waved him forward.

"Soul Brother Number One is leading me to Triplett," he said, "Just as he said he would. Communication systems among the Negroes are far more sophisticated than I realized."

Two boys appeared suddenly, running on the sidewalk parallel to Nieting's car. They seemed to be chasing him. Nieting nodded at the boys, very formally. He considered inquiring as to whether they might know Professor Triplett, but hesitated. One boy appeared to smile as the other flipped his middle finger up and thrust it towards Nieting. Then the other hurled a stone and cracked Nieting's windshield.

"Silly boys," shouted Nieting. "You have no idea the mistake you make."

He stopped the car and the boys ran further up the street. They stood a half a block away and gestured for him to follow. He parked and got out of the car as the boys danced about, signaling to him to come along, one even holding his hands together like he was begging and the other stomping his foot like in a child's tantrum and pointing to the ground. There was something about the boys that was convincing, their insistence, the childish antics like a comic ballet but Nieting held his ground and continued observing. A car stopped near the two kids and several Negroes stepped out. One of them spoke into a two-way radio and another called the boys and they came to him. They were standing in front of the one structure on the block that had not been fired. The windows had been smashed and glass and the remnants of its sacking lay about the sidewalk. The man spoke to the two boys and they listened eagerly then bolted off. He'd clearly given them instructions. He walked to a pay phone and made a call, hanging up just as his comrades emerged from the storefront. They all got in the car and pulled from the curb at the moment the building came alive with the blast of flames that leapt after their car as they sped off.

Nieting leaned against the car and wiped his face with his forearm. The extent of the rebellion was overwhelming. It seemed to go on indefinitely, street after street, mile after mile. There was too much action spread over too large an area, too many forces rushing madly. If he were to reach Triplett, it would truly be a miracle. He held his head in his hands, unsure for the moment which way to proceed.

"What the fuck are you doing down here?"

He looked up into the glaring reflection of the sun off the twisted shell of a washing machine and another voice spoke.

"You want to get killed, boy?"

The voices came from the silhouettes of four people on the sidewalk obscured by the glow of sunlight.

"Get out of our neighborhood, whitey," said one of the figures. "You better get going or you're gonna get killed."

It was a teenaged girl speaking, they were all teenagers, two boys and two girls, staring at Nieting. He looked back dumbly, not comprehending their words.

"Hey, don't you speak English?" said a girl.

Nieting stared blankly.

"We don't want whitey down here," said the other girl. "You stupid or something?"

"Yeah," said a boy, "get the fuck out of our territory."

Nieting shook his head like a drunk trying to clear his mind and the children laughed.

"I'm looking for Professor Triplett," he said.

The four young people looked silently at Nieting.

"You don't understand," he said. "I'm not an intruder."

"Oh, we understand well enough," said one of the girls.

"No, you don't," said Nieting. "I'm not whitey, I mean, I am not a white man."

The four hesitated, looking at one another, then broke into laughter.

"He says he ain't white."

"Looks like a blue-eyed devil to me."

"No, I am no devil. I am looking for Soul Brother Number One. He can vouch for my credibility. He asked me to meet him today."

The children screamed with laughter, staggering, grasping each other.

"If you ain't white, what the fuck are you?" demanded one of the boys.

"I'm a European," said Nieting. "You see, I'm not a cracker at all. I'm from Germany."

"Germany?"

"Yes."

"So what?"

"You ain't nothing but a god-damned white man."

"We told you to get out of our territory."

Nieting looked around melodramatically, sweeping his hand over the devastated cityscape, then turned back to the teenagers.

"Your territory doesn't seem to exist any longer, does it?" he said.

One of the boys, a skinny kid in a white tee shirt skipped off the curb, walked straight up to Nieting and laid him out with a right jab. He had to thrust upward to connect to Nieting's jaw, but Nieting went down hard anyway, sprawling spread eagle on his back. He heard the sound of feet scurrying as he lay dazed in the street. He slurred, "the ignorance of the Negroes is appalling," then drifted into half consciousness. *Their ignorance,* he thought, *ignorance, their ig . . .*

There was no telling how much time passed when he was lifted to his feet by the front of his shirt. A badge on a man's belt passed his eyes as he rose up. The man wore civilian clothing, yet was apparently a cop. Three more of them emerged from a black car of the same make and model as the L.A.P.D. patrol cars Nieting had become so accustomed to seeing, unmarked, with a large spotlight mounted on the driver's side. They all wore civilian clothes with badges pinned to their shirts and side arms strapped to their hips. Two of the cops went straight to his car, checking the glove compartment where his papers were, pouring over the inside of the car, pulling the back seat out and dropping it into the gutter, rifling the trunk, going through all of his bags.

"What the fuck are you doing down here?" said the cop.

Nieting's head spun as the cops huddled a few feet away examining his papers. Finally, one of them walked back and handed the papers to Nieting.

"I asked you what your business is in this area."

"I am a reporter. I am on assignment for MerzKraft."

"MerzKraft?"

"Yes, officer. MerzKraft is the leading daily newspaper in Germany, much like your Los Angeles Times."

The cop jotted Nieting's words in a small note pad.

"Where are you staying in the city?" he asked.

"Imperial Highway Motor Lodge."

"That's a pretty low dive for someone from such a prestigious paper, isn't it?"

"Yes, I agree. I was quite disappointed myself. Clearly, the secretary wasn't able to discern the quality of the inn from the literature. She must have assumed it was substantially more convenient that it turned out to be."

"Right," said the cop.

The officers conferred out of ear shot. Their demeanor was strangely casual under the circumstances. They even laughed at several points during their deliberations as Nieting watched from the curb. *They are sure to know who I am*, he thought. *Perhaps I should attempt to escape. No doubt they recognize the license number. Running would be fatal. They would surely kill me. They would use my fleeing as their excuse to murder. There is no one on the street besides the police and myself. I am at their mercy.*

Without warning, the four cops loaded into the black car and the cop who'd hoisted Nieting off the pavement shouted from the driver's seat, "Get in that car and get the fuck out of here. Don't you read the fucking newspapers? You're a fucking reporter for God's sake."

They watched Nieting hurry to the sedan, load his belongings, leaving the back seat lying on the ground, and start the engine.

"Turn that thing around," shouted one of the cops. "Don't go south. Go up to 103rd and turn left. Don't let us catch you here again."

"We'll feed you to the fucking niggers if we lay eyes on you," said a cop. "Get the fuck out of here."

Nieting continued north on Avalon, watching the officers in the rear-view until they took off into a side street. He continued past 103rd, failing to make the left as the cop had commanded. He was driving away from the section where he'd met Soul Brother Number One. Yet Soul Brother Number One had been able to find him blocks north of where they'd first met. The Negroes were organized. Amazingly so. Below the chaotic rioting of the lumpen populace disciplined cadres were systematically at work. He'd seen the man with the two-way radio instruct the two boys in something. The one building on the street that was not burning burst into flames after the man made a call at a pay phone. A plan of action had clearly been consummated. They were a guerilla cadre, perhaps connected to Triplett's group. BANG could very well be the cultural wing of a group directly working in the armed struggle.

It was still a good bet that Triplett's headquarters would be on Central Avenue or that that would likely be the best place to pick up his trail. Nieting drove for three blocks, traversing streets of fire and pandemonium. What wasn't burning was being looted by mobs, hundreds, thousands rushing madly in a desperate carnival with no police or firemen in sight. The people emerging from shattered storefronts carrying loot of every kind did not appear to be revolutionaries, rather people desperately clutching goods, boxes of diapers, TV sets, HiFi's, clothing, the rewards of American freedom that remained beyond their grasp until this moment. Nieting cruised slowly through the streets as if no one could see him. Several times, people over laden with goods spotted him gaping wide eyed from his busted up sedan. A woman waved, as if Nieting were passing by in a tourist bus. Her arms were full of clothing, the tags and hangers bouncing as she booked across Avalon.

At Century Blvd, he turned right and in moments reached Central Avenue, the famed thoroughfare of Negro arts described by Oscar Worst. The conflagration raged on all four corners of Century and Central. There were no crowds of well dressed Negroes milling before glamorous nightclubs or chorus girls strolling to work as Oscar had described. There wasn't even a quiet storefront where a man like Triplett might hold court. He remembered Oscar once reading a news clipping describing the Negro movie actor Mantan Morlan driving a yellow Cadillac down Central with a lepeord in the back seat with a jewel studded collar and a silver chain. Now, the legendary avenue was at the heart of the battle. There were fire trucks there, but no firemen in sight until Nieting drove past the two engines parked nose to nose and saw the broken out windshields and the firemen huddling, ducking snipers' bullets. The street was flooded with water as the buildings burned. Flames spit forth and the walls of what appeared to be a supermarket collapsed, spewing dust and debris in a hot swirling gust, obscuring everything for half a block. Nieting moved through, bouncing over the fire hoses as a brick hit the left fender of his car and skipped end over end across the hood.

He swung south onto Central into a fiery maze and hit the brakes. Several blocks away a sea of spinning red lights was sweeping northward towards him, driving a mob of hundreds in its wake. Nieting hit the gas hard and shot into a reverse U-turn and headed north, away from the oncoming authorities and the mob. He watched the flashing lights in the rearview mirror. At 87th street, just south of Manchester and Central, he lowered his eyes from the mirror to the street onto a huge mass of humanity jamming the thoroughfare. If he hadn't looked down at that moment, he would have rammed into the crowd. People were running in every direction, frantically hauling goods or rushing empty handed into storefronts. There was no doubt in Nieting's mind that he had been noticed by the Negroes, yet he remained unmolested. This was proof that Rene was correct when he stated that Nieting wasn't a white man. Complexion was meaningless. After all, there was an endless variety of skin shades among the Negroes themselves. Besides, the people knew his status because they sensed it. How else could he be witnessing such a scene, a scene no white man should ever witness, not from the inside as he was. The Negros worked like an army of ants. They seemed so self directed in the chaos, like everyone knew just what their job was and was executing the assignment with a mad fury. Nieting was sure he was safe now. These people were living the Revolution. No one had time to worry about a man who merely appeared to be white. How could anyone privy to this spectacle possibly be truly white? There was an intimacy to the scene; raw, unbridled emotion, unleashed rage, unrestrained lust for the material fetishes so relished by the whites set loose in a frenzied expression of desire. It was a ritual of destruction, a symbolic taking back of collective spirit, albeit in the form of consumer goods. It was a private affair, personal, shameful in its excesses and the abject release of all restraints like the intimacy between lovers. Nieting felt a closeness to the Negros such as one can only know through the collective experience of a great spiritual suffering. Suddenly, a thud and the sound of glass shattering, chips raining into the back of Nieting's sedan. On the left a group of Negroes charged as a woman in the lead, shouted "kill him, kill him, kill him." A hand reached in a grabbed the rucksack. The tape recorder and camera in the back were gone. The front passenger window exploded and Nieting jammed his foot on the gas knocking a man to the ground as he careened north on Central. Stones and bottles poured onto the car as Nieting sped through the crowds, swerving wildly to avoid debris, a washing machine in the center of the right lane, another car capsized, objects landing all around as Nieting pushed the car in a blind panic.

At 82nd street, he lost control of the car, careening into the carcass of an overturned, burned-out police car. The vehicle stopped short on impact and Nieting cracked his face against the steering wheel. He was stunned, yet pushed the door open just as the angry crowd reached the car. In an instant there were hands all over his body, pulling him out of the driver's seat, reigning blows, pummeling him with fists, sticks, and feet. Someone wielding a razor thrust the small shining blade at his legs, rending his trousers into bloody ribbons. He slumped against the car, fell to his knees, was knocked sideways to the ground as the assailants worked furiously at his body. Then, the beating suddenly ceased. He felt the pavement of Central Avenue vibrate as the crowd retreated all around him like a stampeding herd. He was barely conscious. Someone was going through his pockets. They took his wallet, belt, passport and one of his shoes before they ran off. Someone tore the shirt off his back and another kicked him in passing. He knew that the mob was gone because the street quit shaking with their pounding feet. He dragged himself up and took off in what seemed to be the opposite direction of the crowd only to find himself suddenly in the ranks of the 18th Armored Calvary, Burbank Unit. There were American soldiers everywhere.

He shielded his eyes with both hands from a blinding light in the street. The light wasn't a reflection from the sun or the inferno of buildings. It came from the double yellow line in the center of the street. It was alive, buzzing, smoldering. At first, it was a hotwire vibrating, then a fast stream of molten gold. He hadn't paid attention to the lines before. All L.A. thoroughfares had those lines. He'd no reason to look closely until now. He could feel a magnetic force emanating from the lines, pulling the body in, clamping the torso like a tram on tracks. Instinctively, he acquiesced to the pull, keeping his feet within the double line as he ran between the right and left lanes of Central Avenue, between the convoy of jeeps with machine guns mounted and trucks crowded with troops with bayonets drawn, soldiers walking, watching the roof tops with rifles resting on their hips and bayonets glinting in the sunshine. They couldn't see him running, flaying his arms about, because he was invisible behind the magnetic force of the double yellow lines. If he kept within the force field they would not see him. He ran on the line as on a tight rope strung above an endless abyss, watching the convoy rolling northward. He saw Russians among the American soldiers, god damned Red Army, blood thirsty Asian faces, rapists, torturers. They were there to get his mother, to torture her. He couldn't bear thinking of what they would do to her, what they were doing now, piercing her, destroying her again and again; she endured the torture for him, to keep him alive, to rescue him, her son, her boy, her little Jew. The Americans would take what was left. She would submit to them because of him, for money to feed him, as she had submitted to the blackmail of her Nazi pimp, to hide him, to hide her little Jew. There were SS on the sidewalks, running parallel behind the Americans and

Russians, the red arm bands with the immaculate black swastika in a field of pure white flashed between the cacky green uniforms of the soldiers. They could see him in spite of the shield of the double line. They were wise to him. The charade had come to an end. He tripped over his feet and sprawled on his naked chest on the concrete road bed. He covered his ears against the rumbling of tanks and the hum of the aircraft, bomber squads blackening the sky, as he tried to melt down into the lines and travel along the track to another part of Berlin, to the Haberstrasse where he lived with Uncle Max and Heinrich. They would protect him. He stiffened his torso, thrusting his arms forward and stretching with all his might to keep every bit of his body within the force field. The electric current burned his flesh as it carried him forward with incredible speed. He shook with the velocity, the sheer force of the trajectory and steeled himself against the pressure bearing down on his body.

When he raised his head, he was in Los Angeles. The rear of the convoy was growing smaller as it moved north on Central Avenue. Several blocks to the south, sun reflected off the white helmets of the LAPD, the line of shot gun totting cops strung across the street, marching in a second sweep northward behind the National Guard. Negroes began to emerge from alleys and peek from doorways.

"Look, there's motherfucking whitey."

Nothing had any meaning for Nieting. It was all a movie he could only watch, not participate in, even as several men lifted him to his feet, dragged him to the sidewalk and slammed him face first against a brick building.

"Kill the motherfucker."

"James Carlton, take your hands off that man."

"He's whitey, Mrs. Minnifield. He deserves what he's getting."

"You don't deserve to be no murderer. I said take your hands off him."

"You heard Mr. Minnifield, let that man be. You're not a killer."

"Your people didn't raise no animal, Little John. Your folks raised you better than that."

"I know they did, Mr. Minnifield, but we fighting back now. It's whitey's turn to take it."

"You best get off this street before the cops get much closer."

"They're shooting to kill."

"So are we."

"Kill that white motherfucker."

"Get moving."

Nieting collapsed onto the sidewalk, vaguely aware of the figures, a woman and a man, standing over him. He lay at their feet, at their backs, the conversation trailing off in his consciousness. He was inside of a building. The man and woman carrying him were elderly, one on each side, holding him up by the arms until he regained himself and walked silently up a flight of stairs.

"You'll be able to rest up here for a minute," said the old woman. "Just till all those black folks get off the street and those police get here. They won't harm a white man."

"The police are coming fast," said the man. "We could have left him down there. He would have been all right."

"We couldn't give those boys the chance to do wrong," said the woman.

"You're right," said the man. "But I don't know how in god's name he'll ever get out of here. Mister, I just happen to know those youngsters. If we hadn't shown up, you'd be a dead man. I'd hate to have that on those boys' hands. You'll get killed if you go out on that street right now. You can't be sure those police won't get trigger happy either."

The couple guided Nieting down a short hallway to a door which the old man unlocked.

"I'm Laurence Minnifield," he said. "This is my wife Barbara. What's your name, son?"

Nieting couldn't answer.

"I think he's in a daze or something," said Mrs. Minnifield.

"Must be in shock," said her husband.

The door opened only part way, blocked by a large television set inside and the old man had to push hard to shove the set back. A younger man stood by the window holding a rifle, peering out the lace curtains into the street. He appeared to be in his early twenties. He wore a white t-shirt and blue jeans and was sweating in the stuffy apartment.

"Damn it, Yusef," said Minnifield. "I told you to get that shit out of my house."

"That ain't none of mine," said the young man. "You got to talk to Georgie about that TV."

"I don't want nothing in my house that ain't been bought and paid for."

"Oh, you paid for it all right, Pops," said Yusef, "too long and too much."

"Get that gun and all your goods out of my house," said Minnifield.

"What you got whitey in here for?" replied Yusef.

"He ain't done a damned thing to be killed," said Minnifield.

"How do you know, Pops?" said Yusef.

"Don't you pay him no mind," said Mrs. Minnifield, leading Nieting into the apartment.

"You telling me to go and you got him up in here?" said Yusef, pointing at Nieting with the barrel of the gun.

"Put that gun up," said Minnifield. "I'm telling you to take your stolen goods and that gun out of here. You want to come back after that, you're welcome."

"Sit down over here, young man," said Mrs. Minnifield.

"For god's sake, don't sit him down on that chair?" said Minnifield. "He's got blood all over him."

"He's got to sit somewhere," replied the wife, "the poor man is hurt."

"Take the shower curtain down, then," said Minnifield. "I don't need to be cleaning this man's blood up for the next month just because I'm trying to be a descent Christian."

Minnifield was a tall man with long arms and slightly stooped shoulders. His hands were calloused and his right hand was missing two fingers. His face was kind and intelligent, ringed by patches of white hair around a bald spot on the top of his head. The man's kindliness sent a wave of longing rippling through Nieting's stinging flesh. He longed for Uncle Max. He longed for his father and for Kid Auger. He listened for Auger's horn and it wasn't there, only the husky voice of a Negro blues singer weaving in and out of the racket of war, thick with sadness, sweet sorrow, bitter irony. *"I had a dream last night, I was standing on 18th and Vine. I shook hands with ol'Piney Brown, and just couldn't keep from crying.* Nieting sobbed quietly. He didn't know if he were in the room or not. To not be there and still be witnessing the scene was no more implausible than being there. He noticed himself in a mirror, nearly naked in the small living room of an elderly Negro man and his wife. The only clothing on his body was a pair of shredded cut-off shorts that were a pair of trousers a short time before and one white sock black with blood. His legs and arms were bloody and his face and hair were slick with it. His chest was a field of slashes and scrapes, his eyes were white, wide, wild, flashing as if peering from behind a bizarre mask. He looked like one of the primitvie masks in Heinrich Menk's collection. He pointed at the image of himself and laughed. He could see Max and Heinrich behind him in the mirror laughing and poking one another with elbows. Max winked at little Val. He understood his thoughts. He understood his suffering. He had always protected Val and now Uncle Max understood how little Val had gotten where he was. He knew why he was here and the sight of him reminded Nieting of the work he had come to America to complete. He remembered his quest to recover *The Robert Charles Song* and the manifesto he'd composed. He recalled the reason that he was in Watts. He must find Morris Triplett. He must deliver the manifesto to him personally. Nieting held his quivering hands up in front of his face and examined them and grinned sheepishly at his hosts.

"Whoa," said the old man. "What hell was you laughing at? Ain't nothing funny going on here."

"Look at that weird smile," said Yusef. "He's gone and flipped his wig. Why you bring a crazy white man in here, Pops? You telling me to get out and you bring him in?"

Nieting hesitated. Yusef was correct, however, Nieting's madness was besides the point.

"You must forgive my appearance," said Nieting. "I am not crazy."

"Watch him, pops," said Yusef.

"Do you know a man named Triplett?" asked Nieting.

"What's that?" said the old man.

"Do you know a man named Triplett?"

"Triplett?"

"Yes, Morris Triplett."

"What do you want with Trip?" asked Yusef.

Nieting held his blackened face in his bloody hands.

"You do know him," he said. "I must make it to his headquarters. I must join his fighters. They will know who I am. They will recognize me. I have a gift for them, something valuable, necessary to the Revolution. They'll assist me, take me to safety. You must help me."

"Fighters?" said Minnifield.

"Mister, you got the wrong Morris Triplett," said Mrs. Minnifield.

"No, ain't but one Morris Triplett," said the old man, "and he ain't no fighter. Not that kind of fighter. Who the hell *are* you, boy?"

"You brought the god damned FBI up here, Pops," said Yusef.

"What?" said the old man. "You LAPD? Still harassing those musicians in the midst of all this mess? You got your eyes on the wrong folks as usual. Still got time for this petty bullshit. Morris Triplett's fighters? Good god, what'll the white man come up with next? I've known that man and his family for longer than twenty years and never, I mean never seen or heard him do anything with no guns. He don't hurt nobody. He's a damned teacher is what he is. You all should be giving him awards for taking youngsters off the streets, finding children with talent in all the misery down here."

"I swear I am not affiliated with the authorities," said Nieting. "They've fired their guns at me several times today. They realize I am here to assist the Negro people. They recognize that I am a danger to them and they are correct in this."

"I'll be god damned," said Minnifield. "That son-of-a-bitch Klansman Parker is right. Outside agitators have come into our community. You ain't wanted here, mister. You come in here to manipulate our people. You want a piece of the pie like all the whites."

Yusef cackled.

"What makes you so dangerous to whitey, whitey?" he said.

"I am a kindred soul to the Negro people," replied Nieting. "I understand their interests and the interests of all oppressed people. I have information that is essential to the struggle. World-wide solidarity is required now as never before."

Yusef snapped back, "Solidarity with the white man don't mean but one thing, business as usual. White man always calls the shots, whether you call yourselves communists, Christians, liberals, it don't mean shit."

"You're damned right," said Minnifield. "I might have been tempted to leave you out on that street if it wasn't my boys about to kill you. It wasn't your blood I was trying to save, it was your blood on their hands."

"It's too late for that, Pops," said Yusef.

"To hell it is," replied Minnifield. "You can't win nothing by falling as low as the white man. You don't give up your decency because the white man lost his a long time ago."

"I must agree with your son," said Nieting.

"He's my grandson, mister," said Minnifield. "No son of mine ever . . . "

"I agree with your grandson, then," said Nieting.

"Oh, you do, do you?" said Yusef.

"Armed resistance is a necessity," said Nieting. "I don't believe the white man will give up power freely. The tendency of Western man is to seek power, not relinquish it. The difference today is, the Negro is no longer in the asking mood. He's ready to take what he has coming to him."

"You see them machine guns out there?" said Minnifield. "You're telling our young men to go up against that?"

"I am telling you, it is necessary today to resist with force of arms," said Nieting. "The white man cannot win another war on the ground. His days of military victory are over."

"We know Brother Malcolm's words, Whitey," said Yusef. "You don't have to go quoting to us."

"You'll have to do better than that," said Minnifield. "Malcolm never told us to go up against machine guns. Only a fool uses bricks against tanks."

"I realize that you've heard these sentiments before," said Nieting. "However, I do have more to offer than mere repetition of another man's words."

"What do you have to offer, son?" said Mrs. Minnifield.

"I've composed a manifesto, a manifesto of Negro musicians."

"Please lord, don't let him say it," said Minnifield.

"I've composed a revolutionary document, a declaration of principle and a blue print for action. This is the reason I must find Mr. Triplett. Only he can assist in the recovery of the lost song."

"Lost song!" said Minnefield. "The man is out of his mind."

"Hey Pops," said Yusef, "whitey done wrote Trip a manifesto, just for him. Ain't that sweet?"

"Not exclusively for Mr. Triplett, I assure you," said Nieting. "The application is suitable for Negroes in other cities, as well. The fact that he and his organization, BANG, are in the revolutionary vanguard is the reason I've chosen them to be the recipients of my manifesto."

"BANG?" said Minnifield.

"I don't generally accept the idea of a vanguard," said Nieting. "I distain elitism, however, the leadership role of these men is incontestable."

Yusef slapped the butt of the rifle with delight.

"I think he means BAD, Pops."

"I'll be damned," said Minnifield.

"Hey whitey," said Yusef, "you mean the Black African Diaspora Ensemble, don't ya?"

"You poor unfortunate boy," said Mrs. Minnifield. "Where are your folks? They must be worried to death wondering where you are. Do they know how far from home you are?"

"My parents are dead, if that's what you mean," said Nieting.

"I figured as much," said Mrs. Minnifield. "You seem like such a sad boy."

"I'd be sad too, if I was him," said Minnifield. "With the problems he's got. Police looking for him and he don't stand a chance out on those streets and he don't have the sense god gave a goat."

"We got to get him out of here, Pops," said Yusef. "We don't need no white fugitive up here, especially an insane white fugitive FBI agent."

The old man glanced at his grandson.

"Get out of that window with that rifle, you damned fool. You got the barrel sticking outside."

An explosion and spray of shattered glass; a shotgun fired from the street into the Minnifield's second story window just as Yusef, heeding his grandfather's admonition, stepped back from the curtain. The force of the blast knocked the rifle from his hands, sending it across the room where it discharged a round into the ceiling. Almost simultaneously, the ground floor door of the apartment building down the flight of stairs flew inward, splitting down the middle and falling flat on the ground. The old couple froze as Yusef, with Nieting on his heels, flew out a rear door of the apartment. Nieting looked back as he exited in time to see a dozen policemen swarm into the room and the two old people thrown onto the living room floor. Yusef went down the back stairs fast with Nieting nearly touching him and at the bottom cut right, leaping over a plank fence. Nieting reconnoitered for a split second and went left, down an alley and back onto the sunlit street, out among the ranks of police as they scurried to seal off the building where the Minnifield's apartment was.

Nieting staggered on to Central, unnoticed among the cops, a naked madman with wild hair, bleeding, yet invisible. He watched the action; the two old people hustled out onto the street, surrounded by police-man, Mrs. Minnifield's eyes meeting his eyes with no sign of recognition, only confusion and terror, then the old man, face bleeding, hands cuffed behind his back, head pushed forward under the hand of a cop, the old couple disappearing in a sea of blue uniforms.

He found his car where he'd left it, scarred and beaten, the key in the ignition. It was high time to abort the mission. The car was empty except for a million shards of glass. Everything was gone. The tape recorder, the camera, the bags containing his clothing, all of his notes, writings, books, the manifesto were gone. He swept the glass from the driver's seat, started the car and drove a few yards to Nadeau Avenue and headed west through burning streets, through the battle zone, past Avalon to San Pedro, then south to Manchester through the fires of hell. He approached a road block at Manchester and Firestone manned by police officers and never slowed the car. He ducked when he crashed through a barricade of plywood as gunshot riddled the war torn sedan. Miraculously he escaped the hail of shot gun pellets and pistol shot. By the time he passed Main Street, the two left tires were in shreds, yet he gunned the engine when a group of Negros chased the slow moving sedan, hurling stones and curses. They all looked like Soul Brother Number One. They all looked mad. Nieting wheeled right at Broadway and Manchester into the thousand faces of the mob. The street was ablaze all around, fire trucks lying idle as the ranks of National Guard moved up Broadway from the south, machine guns mounted on jeeps, bayonets drawn, gas masks on.

When the sedan rolled to a stop, dead finally, Nieting accepted his father's words for the first time. The ghostly voice sounded audibly in his mind. *I'm all you have left, Valentin.* Nieting understood now that he was truly alone. *If only father were here. If only he were here.* The massive mob drifted north before the inexorable flow of soldiers and guns and clouds of tear gas and the smoke of the burning city. Nieting jogged in the ranks of the soldiers, yet no one paid any attention to his presence. He was nothing. He was a speck of dust, a dry cinder from a burned out building. Perhaps he'd died somewhere along the line and was watching from some Christian limbo. Perhaps Broadway led to hell. He ran along with the troops, even though he knew where they were leading. He knew their intent. The troops were his protectors now, escorting him to oblivion. They could have his mother. She would be their whore for eternity. She would suffer for all time to save her son. Each act of degradation would occur over and over forever. Her suffering would be eternal. He accepted her fate as a deal between himself and her tormentors. He would be her pimp. Perhaps he'd always been so.

He slapped at his mother's face and shouted, "Dirty bitch. You don't like it? Here's another one for you then."

The American soldiers grinned. They were satisfied now. Now, they would help him. The deal had been struck. The only question was whether they would insist upon taking him to the DP camp, to the section for unclaimed children or directly back to Uncle Max. There was no reason not to bring him home. He'd given her back to them. Certainly, they were escorting him to the apartment on the Habberstrasse. Block after block they marched. No one was disturbed by a half-naked child among the troops. It was a common sight in Berlin, ragged urchins chasing the throng of soldiers, desperately seeking shelter, begging food. Nieting was merely a lost child, of no consequence, an unexpected survivor, harmless, barely existent, yet he was safe finally. All that had been required was to give the whore up. He was joyous. She'd finally gone back to where she belonged. He and Uncle Max would never speak of her again. The enemy was clearly retreating although Val could see nothing but soldiers in front, behind, to the right and left. The road extended endlessly, little Val skipping in and around the American troops, pretending to scatter flowers in their path. He even managed to elicit smiles from the soldiers close by. The charred buildings seemed to undulate in the suffocating heat. Little Val marveled at the scent, so familiar it was delicious, reassuring, like eternal recurrence; he would be in his room shortly, perhaps he would spin Auger's record on the phonograph.

At Forty-first and Broadway, little Val's illusion of security was once again shattered, as it always was, as it always would be, by war. A sniper fired from a roof top and the troops scattered, returning fire, shouting, taking cover. Then, silence for a split second. The sniper was gone and the soldiers pursued like chasing ghosts. Little Val had remained perfectly still in the chaos, but when he bolted finally towards the cover of a burned out car, somehow he was no longer invisible. Soldiers approached him from every direction, training their guns, wheeling a huge machine gun muzzle mounted on a jeep top towards him with metallic clicks and rattling steel.

"I'm not the enemy," yelled Nieting. "We've made a deal. I've given you the whore."

The barrels of a hundred guns covered every bit of his body like eyes with razor sharp teeth ready to tear him to pieces, cold, cruel flesh eaters. Nieting dropped to his knees in supplication, thrusting him arms above his head.

"Don't shoot," he shouted. "Do not shoot. I am a white man."

A cop toting a shotgun ordered him forward. Nieting looked for the man's eyes. He wished to nod his acquiescence, to signal gratitude, but suddenly the cop was on the ground shouting to his comrades, sniper fire from the roof top. Nieting felt a breeze next to his ear and heard the cracking of gun fire and dropped flat on the pavement, turning onto his back beneath the broad expanse of blue sky. You couldn't tell the earth was hell if you looked straight up beyond the smoke and gas into the endless distance. He flexed his muscles with all his might, trying to raise his body up, ascend into space, but the burning pavement held him fast. He was stuck, rooted in the inferno. "Father," he shouted, "come to me now, please. I'll do anything you ask. I will be a good boy, father. Do not forsake me, papa, help me."

"Promise to be a good boy?"

"Yes, father. I promise to do whatever you ask. Stay with me now."

A great hulking torso moved slowly over Nieting, eclipsing the sun, a looming shadow descending and causing him to shade his eyes from the rim of blinding light. Triplett, Professor Triplett, broadchested with jet black complexion and snow white hair and beard, immaculate in his marching band uniform.

"Brother Nieting? So my friend, we finally meet."

"Yes, Comrade," said Nieting. "I'd thought all was done. I'm afraid I'd lost hope."

Nieting raised on his elbows as Triplett bent towards him, extending a large strong hand. Soul Brother Number One leaned to the side to see past Triplett's big frame. His appearance was hilarious, yet quite striking. He was dressed in the garb of a Mau Mau warrior. He smiled amiably and nodded to Nieting as if a play had ended and the actors had come out to introduce themselves. Soul Brother Number One winked at a man who suddenly joined he and Triplett, another cast member, this one in the uniform of a Nazi officer, his mother's SS pimp. He too nodded at Nieting as Triplett bent further towards him; there was a Nazi band on Triplett's sleeve, the black insignia of death. Triplett's eyes were red. His teeth were black. The dagger he slipped from a leather holster on his belt glinted in the sunlight as he lifted Nieting by the neck and thrust the blade deep into his belly, spilling his intestines onto the burning embers like writhing worms. Nieting cried out in agony. Emil stood on the sidewalk watching but did nothing. Nieting called to him for help and he merely looked back with a forlorn grimace.

Little Val ran across the street into his father's arms, jumping at the last minute and burying his face in his chest, hiding, as Emil enveloped him, speaking gently.

"Everything will be alright now, Valentin. Your suffering will end soon. I promise you that. Sleep now."

The boy sighed and slumped into the luscious bed of his father's embrace, but forced himself against slumber for an instant to look into his father's eyes.

"Where is he, papa?" asked little Val.

"Listen, Valentin," replied Emil. "Close your eyes and listen."

How sweetly Auger's horn quivered. The sound was like a delicate flower, a sorrowful kiss, a sweet embrace, stark as the truth, as Auger picked up the tempo, almost imperceptibly, so that one suddenly realized the sound dancing, bouncing joyously. Little Val laughed and laughed as Auger caressed him with his velvet tone. The sound was pure love.

The Pine Grove
Orchestra

Auger's eyes opened into the blinding sun, awakened by the click of a snare drum. He'd been napping in his bed. He was sure of it. Only he wasn't in Brentwood any longer. He was back there again, locked in his mind, unable to do anything but watch.

The Pine Grove Orchestra; five boys approached the La Pointe railroad depot hauling their instruments. The youngest was Rabbit, twelve years old, with a snare drum strapped around his neck. He tapped a halting march beat on the rim that seemed to grow progressively slower and more tired as the group drooped along the dirt road.

"Cut that god damned drumming," yelled Stonewall Mathews. He carried a cardboard guitar case with a broken handle tucked up under his arm. Rabbit beat the drum for several seconds then wisely ceased.

"And damn you too, Chiff," continued Stonewall, "quit going on and on. You're driving me crazy."

"I don't give a damn if I'm driving you crazy," said Chiff, grasping the back of his sweaty neck. "I should have watched her. I shoulda seen she was going away inside her head. She always leaves in her head first, says things that let you know what she's fixing to do. I didn't see it. I shoulda been looking closer."

"There wasn't nothing to see," said Stonewall, waving his hand in frustration. "And even if there was, no one can stop Aunt Luzinda when she gets something in her mind. No one knows when she's gonna have a spell."

Chiff turned to Jean and spoke as though pleading.

"We looked over every foot of Pine Grove as far down as Debord's farm. There wasn't a trace of Aunt Luzinda nowhere."

"When Aunt Luzinda don't want to be found, ain't no one can find her," said Stonewall, his voice becoming quiet. "No one knows the territory around here like she does. With all that sun, I just don't see how she could have covered much more ground than we did."

"Poor Aunt Luzinda," said Foster Lewis. He was a boney legged thirteen year old, lugging a tuba wrapped in a cloth sack on his back, hunched over dramatically, his face dripping sweat onto the dusty ground. "I spect she got tired out in all that heat. Probably fell in some bayou and drowned."

Chiff and Stonewall looked silently at the ground.

"Shut up, Foster," said Jean. "She's hold up somewhere, that's all. She knows every shack for miles around. Better than we do. She's all right."

"I don't know Auger," said Stonewall, softly. "But we all praying. Every day we praying. But, you know with the heat like it is . . ."

Foster blurted out, "Then why *we* got to go on the road? It's too hot to be on the road and they got white men all over looking for that nigger."

"Ah, that shit's all in the city," said Chiff.

"Hell it is," said Foster, "They're searching out in the countryside too. Even trains up north in Chicago and St. Louis. It's in the newspapers. I heard folks talking. What if that nigger did make it out of the city? What if we run into him? I don't want to be shot with no Winchester."

"Hell, he only kills white folks," said Stonewall. "He don't kill no niggers."

"How do you know?" said Foster.

"He killed ten police already," said Stonewall. "He's hold up with some niggers in New Orleans. Besides, I don't care where he is. If I meet Robert Charles, I'll shake his hand and join up with him."

"I don't want no part of Robert Charles," said Foster.

"I don't want no part of Robert Charles myself," said Jean. "But he's back in New Orleans, not out here."

"We can't go on the road with that nigger on the loose," said Foster. "And it's too damned hot and this tuba is too damned heavy."

"I ain't afraid of Robert Charles," shouted Rabbit, striking his snare drum.

"Hey Foster, you look like one of them Chinese coolies in the newspapers," said Raymond Brown. For a split second the boys looked at each other in surprise, then screamed collectively, falling over one another in a fit of raucous hilarity. Raymond's expression remained unmoved except for a tiny curling of the lip. He was fifteen and the oldest of the group. He usually kept aloof when the boys clowned. When he did deign to speak, however, the timing of his comments was sure to disarm the other boys and send the conversation careening in another directions all together.

"I ain't lying," he said. "Foster sure do look like one of them Chinese coolies they got in the newspapers, the way he's totting that horn up on his back."

Raymond carried his violin case tucked under his arm. Even in the draining heat he affected a subtly rhythmic gate, pointing his forefinger at Foster in sweeping dismissal. He wore his wavy black hair parted in the middle and slicked down to the side with a youthful never-been-shaved mustache running down onto his chin.

"Fuck you," growled Foster, and the boys screamed with mirth.

When the group entered the train yard of the LaPointe station the great black engine was gushing white clouds that dissipated under the burning sun as the passengers bound for New Orleans boarded the cars and a few wagons off loaded produce for the city into the open boxcars and others loaded up with goods from Baton Rouge and points between. The boys stood beneath the awning of the small white building housing the telegraph and dispatcher and surveyed the depot. Jean noticed a stout, red-faced man eying two wooden crates stacked inside the open door of a boxcar. He had long silver hair pushed back over a bright red bald spot on the top of his head and long shaggy side whiskers. He was sweating as he scratched his pate and smoothed his hair and looked dejectedly around the depot. Jean waved Stonewall after him and the two approached the old man, whose eyes lit up as the two boys came towards him.

"You niggers want to make some money?" said the old man.

"What you want us to do?" replied Stonewall.

The man leaned forward cupping his ear.

"What say?"

"What you want us to do," repeated Jean.

"I got to get them crates over to Beauregard Plantation, just east of Kenner. I need you to load'm on the wagon. They a bit heavy. My old heart ain't what it used to be. How bout it?"

"We'll load'm for you," said Jean, "for a ride as close to Kenner as you go."

"Kenner, you say?" said the man. "You got a deal. But you got to be careful. Those are expensive items up there. There's a carved cedar mantel for a fire place and some cedar handrails for a staircase. They come all the way from Charleston. Got to get them to Beauregard Plantation without a scratch or a crack or I'll lose the fee."

Jean and Stonewall motioned to the other boys and in a short time the two crates were loaded neatly into the back of the man's wagon.

"All right boys," said the man, "climb on in and let's get to going."

The boys scurried into the large bed of the wagon, laying the instruments down, except Rabbit who kept his snare drum slung around his neck. They perched on the crates as the man waved Jean into the passenger side of the cab.

"My name is Vic Latour," said the man, nearly shouting. "You boys musicians?"

"Yes sir," said Jean, "we the Pine Grove Orchestra."

"Eh?" said the man. "Come again. Musicians are you?"

"We're the Pine Grove Orchestra," said Jean, side glancing the others who he could see were all grins.

"From over yonder on the Pine Grove Plantation?" shouted Latour.

"Pine Grove Orchestra," bellowed Stonewall from behind, his hands cupped towards Latour's ear. The boys instantly stopped joking and came to attention, waiting for Latour to respond angrily to Stonewall's impudence.

"I understand," replied Latour, shaking the rein, then "Get along mule," as the wagon lurched towards the River Road.

"Now don't get me wrong boys," he yelled. "I ain't got nothing against music. Music is alright. Nothing wrong with music."

Latour spit into the road. His words came rapidly in a loud high pitched voice, earnestly, as though making a case.

"It's just it ain't good for a nigger if he ain't working hard, that's all. And music make a nigger lazy. See what I mean?"

Jean looked straight ahead, averting his eyes from Stonewall who was thrusting his middle finger up behind the old man's back as Chiff held his full palm over his mouth to stifle the laughter. When Jean's eyes darted back to Stonewall, he was standing in the bed of the wagon frantically pointing to his ear, mouthing "deaf, he's deaf." Chiff dragged him back down and Stonewall punched his arm and Chiff cried out, "shit, I told you, don't hit me." Latour didn't hear a thing.

"And then there's all them temptations," said Latour, scratching his grisly chin. "You boys are old enough to understand what I'm talking about. Whiskey. Women. I don't recall knowing a nigger could resist that. Some things is just best left alone."

Stonewall crouched behind Latour, mimicking him as he talked while Raymond sat with his legs dangling off the back of the wagon, oblivious to the others, lightly tapping his thigh to the beat of the music in his head.

"Besides," Latour blurted out unexpectedly, startling the boys in the wagon and making them contort in silent laughter, "You could get yourself killed. Reminds me of poor old Mack Merit. He was one of Major Strong's niggers. He used to play fiddle all over St. John's Parish, all the big farms. Even the white folks called ol'Mack. They didn't want none of that low down nigger stuff, mind you, just genteel things rich folks want to hear. Ol'Mack could do it all."

Stonewall reached across the wagon bed, grabbing his brother's arm, yanking his hand away from his mouth. Chiff pulled back, leaning into Rabbit who fell into Raymond nearly knocking him off the back of the wagon.

"God damnit, Rabbit," yelled Raymond, and the boys froze again, looking with wide eyes at each other until Latour began speaking and again they shook with stifled laughter.

"But ol'Mack started to loving whiskey too much," said Latour

He hesitated as if his words would have greater impact if he let them sink in. Jean looked at Latour as he spoke, nodding, then glanced back at the others and shook his head, signaling to cease their antics.

"So one night, Mack was playing in some nigger shack," said Latour, "over yonder on Demas' Plantation. He was working that fiddle real well, making all the girls feel good, too good I expect. They say some young buck, black as ink, figured Mack shouldn't be making his girl feel so damned good. He took his razor and cut ol'Mack up like a hog. Of course, all the niggers run off and left him to die there on the floor of that shack. Poor ol'Mack sure could play that fiddle."

Latour looked at Jean expectantly and Jean gave a polite nod. The old man appeared crest fallen at the lack of response to the story of Mack Merit's demise and drove the mules in silence, and the boy's, not knowing what to make of the white man's sudden sullenness, were quiet themselves. Just outside of Kenner, next to the railroad tracks, the road forked, heading east towards the Beauregard Plantation and south towards the lumber camps in the pine forests of St. John's Parish. Latour slowed the mules and the boys jumped from the wagon. The old man shook the reins and the mules pulled away, disappearing finally behind a bend in the road. At that moment, the Yazoo & Mississippi Valley Railroad train rattled by not more than thirty yards away from the road as it slowed for the stop at Kenner. A black man jumped from an open box car and ran along side before cutting toward the road and coming to a stop not far from where the boys stood, resting momentarily under the shade of a willow tree.

"Hey you all," yelled the man, and Chiff and Stonewall responded cordially.

"How you boys doing," he asked, bending over to dust off his clothes. "Whoo-eee, it's a hot one ain't it. You can't tell how hot it is on the train with the wind blowing, but get off and its like jumping into hell. Shit, it's bad. Where you boys headed?"

"Just south of town, Kenner, to work," replied Rabbit.

"Must be Kenner over yonder," said the man. "I don't go near Kenner. Folks say they don't like niggers they don't know over there. You all got to go through town?"

"Yes, sir," said Rabbit.

The man listened with a serious expression then slapped the dust from the front of his trousers.

"You boy's look like musicians," he said.

"We're the Pine Grove Orchestra," said Chiff.

"I can see you all are professionals. Look real good with them instruments. I bet you get the people to moving when you play."

"Yes sir," said Stonewall, "we know how to show'm a good time."

"Any money in that?" asked the man.

"We do all right," said Jean.

"Well, that's fine boys, real fine," said the man. "My name is Richard, Richard Ricks. I been to New Orleans this morning and had to get the hell out. Big trouble going on back there. Now I'm headed for Lutcher. Heard there's work in Lutcher. In the turpentine mill. My cousin say, if I get there today, the boss'll give me work so I caught me a boxcar."

Ricks ran his eyes over the group and smiled.

"You sure are a professional looking bunch, with them instruments. My god, is that a tuba in that sack? Makes me happy just to think of you boys playing music. Wish I could hear you sometime."

"Yes sir," said Stonewall, "we got to go now."

At Stonewall's words the others picked up their instruments and the Pine Grove Orchestra began a slow march towards Kenner. Ricks stood with his hands on his hips, watching as they moved off and shouted after them.

"Good luck now. Ya'll keep your eyes open." He sat on a large stone under the willow tree, removed his shoes and began vigorously rubbing his feet.

The dirt road to Kenner was narrow and dusty and riddled with stones and lined with brush. The group ambled slowly toward the town, Foster grunting and complaining under the weight of the tuba, the others ignoring him, too hot to respond with even a taunt or insult. After traveling a hundred yards or so, Jean glanced back towards the tree where Ricks sat. He saw two white men pointing pistols at Ricks, who stood with his hands over his head. One of the whites grabbed Ricks by the neck and thrust him to the ground, bent over him and pressed the gun to his head.

"Shit, look down the road," said Jean.

The boys turned in unison as the man standing over Ricks kicked him in the head and shoved the pistol into his face.

"This way," said Stonewall, scurrying off the road. The others followed quickly, hustling the instruments into the cover of the brush.

"What the hell they doing that for?" said Chiff.

"How we supposed to know? Just get down," replied Stonewall.

"They gonna walk this way, get down," said Jean. "Be quiet, get down."

The boys huddled in the brush until the two white men shoved Ricks past them on the road.

"Gotdamn Willie," said one of the men, "you gone and caught the nigger. You got Robert Charles."

"Thass the easy part," replied the other man, "Just dumb luck. Now I got to keep him from being barbecued until they come out from New Orleans to get him."

"That wouldn't be so bad," said the first man. "That's white justice, in'it? Hey Robert Charles, that's all right justice, in'it?"

"My name ain't Robert Charles, boss. My name is Ricks, I swear it, boss. I don't know no Charles, boss."

"Shut up, nigger," said the man, kicking Ricks in the buttocks as Ricks squealed in terror.

"Naw," said the other, "Willie Adams ain't never lost a nigger to a barbecue and this one is too valuable to start now. Wait till Mayor Pro Tem Cowans hears about this, hey John?"

"Yes sir, wait till mister mayor hears about this," replied the first man. "He'll be fit to be tied."

The boys lay motionless under the cover of the brush, scarcely daring to breath for a while after the men passed. Finally, Jean and Stonewall crawled up onto the road, looking both ways for signs of the men, then motioned for the others to come out.

"We got to get out of here fast," said Rabbit.

"They ain't after us," said Chiff. "We didn't do nothing."

"What that other nigger did?" snapped Stonewall. "You don't have to do nothing to get in trouble."

"We got a job to do," said Jean, "I don't want to go home without something to show for it. Besides, we're musicians, folks like us."

"We niggers," Chiff shot back.

"No," said Stonewall, squaring his shoulders up. "We can't give up a chance to make some money because of some other nigger's troubles. Let's go to town and see what's going on before we go all the way back home."

"I ain't going to town," said Raymond. "Did you hear that man say barbecue?"

"Look," said Stonewall. "We can send Auger into town. It was his idea to come here. And he's the leader of the damned band. And he's the brightest colored. Won't no one even know he's a nigger if he keeps it low key. He can sneak in, see what's going on and come back here. If it's safe we go make some money, if not, we go back home."

"No use wasting the whole day," said Jean. "Give me an hour. Take care of my horn. Robert Charles is in New Orleans. There ain't no reason they'd be fussing out this way. I'll go in, make sure things is all clear then come get you all. Then we go make some money, eh?"

"That's the plan," said Stonewall. "We'll be waiting down here in the brush."

Within a half hour, Jean was walking on a quiet street lined with wood framed houses with front yards surrounded by white picket fences and filled with flowers. It was nice street, the houses were well kept, but there were no people to be seen. Jean passed a cottage set right up a few feet from the road side with the front door swinging wide open. As he passed he looked through the house and out the open back door into the yard. There was no one around. He followed the street a short distance, finally reaching the center of town where he turned onto a broad thoroughfare, the main drag of the business district. The road was unpaved and filled with deep ruts. There were large houses and storefronts made of wood and several brick buildings, and everywhere Jean looked he noticed the absence of the people of Kenner.

Jean proceeded for another block, turning randomly onto the next street then halted abruptly at the sight of a large crowd milling around a train stopped at a railroad crossing and droves of people arriving from two adjoining streets. He felt a rush of panic and looked about quickly to see if he'd been noticed just as a crowd of young men came strolling towards him. They walked arm in arm as if on the way to a picnic or a ball game. Jean nearly screamed out as they neared him, realizing at the last moment that they were not after him but headed for the spectacle of the stopped train. There were people all around walking in the same direction towards the train. Jean fell in among them for cover, moving towards the mob gathering around at the railroad crossing. He moved quickly among the people, trying to disappear, blend in, praying no one would realize that he wasn't one of them. Everyone was turned towards the train like it was a stage, as if any moment a band of musicians might appear in the doorway of the boxcar and begin playing, just like Buddy Bolden had the first time Jean saw him. The doors to all the boxcars were open wide. The neighborhood swarmed with men carrying guns as the crowd around the train swelled. There was an electricity about the mob and Jean felt as though he were suffocating. It was the same as the city. The horror had followed him home after all. His body quivered at the thought of the vast mobs of New Orleans. They were all white men then, drunk and enraged, and boys; now there were women in the mob and little girls huddled under umbrellas and awnings, gaily watching the spectacle. Jean tried to be inconspicuous as he struggled to catch his breath, imagining everyone could see who he was and any minute cries of nigger would signal the end of his life.

A boy standing next to Jean shouted, "Looky, there he goes," pointing to the top of a box car at a black man running, crouching for cover as a barrage of gunfire burst from all sides of the train. Men near Jean fired pistols over the heads of the people on the street at the man running for his life across the top of the boxcar, jumping from car to car, racing towards the engine. He reached the first car under a hail of bullets, leapt into the coal tender then bounded into the crib. The engineer cowered, rearing back, and the men, pushing forward from the mob, rushed on board. Somehow the black man lept over them as they climbed into the crib. He appeared to fly over them, the crowd gasping as the man careened upward out of the train, finally hitting the ground as three white men rushed up. They grabbed the black man, who struggled free and took off over a picket fence and disappeared into a yard as a dozen whites bolted after him.

When another black man appeared on the top of a box car, a great collective gasp went up just as Jean turned and saw the man running. He jumped to the opposite side of the roof of the car and reared back, apparently looking off into a sea of angry whites, then he skipped back to the side where Jean stood. Shots rang out and the man crouched, then jumped into the crib where a white man stood waiting. The white man pressed the barrel of the shotgun against the black man's forehead as another white man bound his hands behind his back.

The crowd cheered and shouts of "lynch him," "get a rope," "burn the nigger," and "fetch the kerosene," came from all around as the black man was yanked from the engine.

"Step back," shouted the man with the shotgun, "Give us some room, we are officers of the law." He wore a badge and held the gun in the black man's back, pushing him ahead with the muzzle, causing the man to cry out at each forward thrust.

"Keep your hands off my nigger," he shouted. "I caught Robert Charles. Get back. I'll shoot the first man lays a hand on my nigger."

"I ain't Robert Charles," said the black man. "I'm Luke Wallace. I swear it. I don't know no Robert Charles."

"Hell you ain't Robert Charles," said the white man, slapping the back of Wallace's head with the barrel of the gun. He shoved the prisoner past Jean, who followed behind, through the opening in the crowd, then cut to the side of the street.

"There's another one," shouted someone and instantly dozens of guns opened fire on the empty boxcars. Jean edged away, moving backwards, keeping his face to the mob, when a hand gripped his shoulder.

"Watch where you walking, boy." A tall, thin-faced white man appeared to squint as he scrutinized Jean.

"You silly little fool," he said. "You trying to get killed? This ain't the place for any kind of darky. Get on out of here."

Jean was frozen as the man continued speaking to his companion.

"That's the wrong nigger Albert got there," he said, pointing after the man with the shotgun.

"What the hell you mean, wrong nigger?" said his friend.

"Willie Adams got Robert Charles right now over to the jailhouse. He already telegraphed New Orleans. They told him hold that nigger till they get here."

"That right?'

"Yes sir, I seen Robert Charles myself."

The man's friend grinned mischievously. "No matter," he said, "Ain't nothing wrong with a little nigger target practice."

"No they ain't," replied the man, turning towards Jean and winking. "Looks likes folks just getting started at it, far as I can tell."

Jean walked away from the two men and slipped into a group of boys, then ducked behind a horse tied to a post. There was a festive air on the streets now. He tried to move casually, staring at the ground as he back tracked down the street. When he made the corner he charged off as fast as he could. He sprinted in the afternoon heat, back past the neat rows of houses and flower-filled front yards at the town's edge, then past a corn field, then to the dusty road outside of Kenner, finally reaching a stretch lined with ditches filled with brush. He scrambled off the roadside and burrowed for cover beneath the bushes, careless of the thorns and dry branches that scratched his flesh as he pushed through. He grasped handfuls of dry dirt like he wished he could tunnel down, keep going and never stop, never rest again, never stop. Keep running, always. Never stop. Never stop. His heart pounded so loudly he feared the beating would give his hiding place away to the white mob. He curled up pretending to be a stone.

He listened for footsteps and the shouts of the crowd. He listened for the voice of the thin faced white man. *Damned little fool. Ain't no kind of nigger safe here.* He lay for a long time listening to the sounds of birds chirping and squawking. Finally, he remembered the Pine Grove Orchestra and crawled cautiously out of the brush. He looked toward Kenner, raising his hand to his eyes against the glare, squinting to see the army of whites, but there was no one. The road was quiet except for the birds. He took off towards the spot where he'd left his friends.

Within fifteen minutes he saw them standing in the road in a bunch, Stonewall and Chiff arguing, belly to belly, waving their hands about. He could barely hear their voices over the distance. Rabbit, snare still drum strapped around his neck, spotted Jean seventy yards away and shouted and the boys all looked at once then charged to meet him.

"What the hell took you so long?"

"We was getting ready to go home without you."

"We best get out of here fast," said Jean.

"What you mean?"

"They looking to barbecue as many niggers as they can lay their hands on. They just getting started at it."

"What?" said Stonewall.

"They shooting niggers," said Jean. "They calling for the rope, calling for the kerosene. They already got two niggers in jail. That one we saw and another one. It's only a matter of time till they . . ."

"It ain't gonna be me." said Chiff, shielding his eyes from the sun and peering towards Kenner.

"We can't walk back in daylight," said Raymond.

"We got no fucking choice." replied Stonewall. "We got to go."

"We could wait till dark," said Foster, his eyes swelling with tears.

"I ain't waiting for no god damned night riders to barbecue me," said Stonewall.

"We got to make our way to the river, said Jean, "Then walk the bank home. It's only a few miles."

Stonewall's voice rose into a shout.

"God damn it, Kenner between here and the river."

"I don't want to die," said Foster.

"We ain't gonna die," replied Stonewall.

"How we gonna get home?" said Chiff, holding his face in his hands.

They began walking down the road arguing, finally reaching the tree where they'd first met Richard Ricks.

"There's that nigger's shoes," said Foster, pointing to Ricks' worn out shoes still sitting under the willow tree where the white men had taken him.

"He don't need them now," said Raymond.

"How the hell do you know? said Chiff. "Maybe he broke and run from those white men. Maybe he made off. Maybe he needs them shoes real bad."

"No," said Jean. "I heard a white man say they got him in the jailhouse. They say his name is Robert Charles."

"Why we have to run if they got the nigger?" said Chiff.

"They want as many as they can get their hands on," replied Jean. "I swear I heard it said."

The five boys stood belly to belly arguing, waving their arms about and shouting into each other's faces until finally Rabbit, taking one of Ricks discarded shoes, tossed it onto the railroad track and sank onto the same stone Ricks had sat on and began to sob.

"I don't want to die," he said. "And we'll lose our instruments too. It took so long to get money to buy'm and now it ain't no use after all."

"We ain't gonna die, I told you," said Stonewall.

All the boys turned their heads at the sound of a wagon creaking and clanking and hooves clomping on the rock hard road and everyone except the sobbing Rabbit became silent as a wagon appeared around the bend of the road. Vic Latour stood in the cab frantically waving the boys towards him, shaking the reins, hurrying his two mules along.

"I was hoping I'd see you boys again," he said, not stopping the wagon. "I hear things is pretty hot in Kenner."

Latour ran his hand through his white hair and looked in both directions on the road as the boys jogged beside his wagon.

"Far as I can see, you all are sure enough innocent niggers," he said.

"Yes sir," said Foster, "we sure enough innocent niggers."

"We ain't done nothing but play a little music," said Chiff.

"Well, you sure are some unlucky niggers," said Latour. "White men been running these roads looking for Robert Charles' gang since before I left you off this morning. You all know that?"

"No sir," all the boys replied.

"They got that nigger Charles over in Kenner," said Latour, "but folks say he got a gang of niggers still running around. Stealing livestock and such. And they aim to get every one of'm. I was hopping to see you all, so I could warn you to keep off the road. I wish to God I could help you more, but this is real serious business. Wouldn't be the first time a white man got killed for helping niggers."

Latour rose off the seat and shouted, "If I was you all, I'd stay out of sight and off this road till after dark. Keep down low. Just stay low and wait for dark."

Chiff, Foster, and Raymond moved towards Latour's wagon as he snapped the reins hard and cursed the mules and the empty wagon lunged forward, bouncing over the ruts and moving off in a cloud of dust.

"Yes sir, you sure are some unlucky niggers," Latour shouted back.

The boys watched the swirling dust racing in the air like locusts swarming even as Latour's wagon rattled out of sight and the cloud was all that could be seen moving along in the distance. Jean wept as he watched the dust kicked up by Latour's wagon vanish behind a stand of trees. He heard Stonewall's voice speaking in a whisper.

"Don't *you* cry, Auger. I need you to help me keep these boys together. Don't you cry now."

Jean turned his back on the others and dried his face as they all sobbed openly, oblivious to anything except raw terror

"Get down into that brush," said Stonewall. "You heard that peckerwood, they running the road looking for niggers."

The boys hurried into the bushes, carrying the instruments, except for Foster who left his tuba behind. Jean lingered on the road with Stonewall for a split second, their eyes meeting, their glance acting as a kind of vow – no more crying, it was time to do something. Stonewall grabbed the sack containing Foster's tuba, slung it over his shoulder and followed Jean as he slid down a short gully. They moved through the brush in a line, away from the road, staying low, Jean in the front and Stonewall taking up the rear, stopping to rest beneath a group of trees out amidst a large expanse of scrub. They huddled beneath the dry bushes, panting, coated with dust and sweat and said nothing for a long time. There was no movement besides the fluttering of birds in the undergrowth. The boys were silent as the afternoon passed into shadows and finally the pitch blackness of a moonless night. Only once, just after dark, did they hear the sound of horses on the River Road, but no one said anything about it. They huddled in silence until Stonewall whispered, "Hey Auger, you think we should move?"

"Too dark," said Jean. His voice sounded as if his eyes were wide open. "We wouldn't know where we was going. Could end up on some peckerwood's back porch. We best stay where we are."

"How can we stay here?" said Foster. "We can't move in the daylight and we can't move in the dark? We'll starve to death or die of thirst. We got to move."

"I ain't going nowhere," said Raymond.

"Me neither," said Rabbit.

"We wait," said Stonewall.

"Foster's right," said Chiff. "If we stay in one place, they're sure to find us. We got to move. If we don't move we'll die here."

Chiff's voice broke as he spoke, ascending into sobs that rose suddenly into shrill weeping. The other boys tensed, not daring to breathe as they helplessly listened to Chiff's convulsing.

"Stop crying like a pup, boy," came a woman's voice and Chiff instantly stopped sobbing. "They won't hear you if you talk soft, but crying like that'll bring those nightriders for sure."

The boys knew instantly who the woman was. The shredded hem of her skirt touched Jean's face as she moved among them.

"Stand up now," she said. "They can't see us."

On the woman's command, the boys rose to their feet. Jean strained to see through the darkness, barely making out the tignon the woman wore on her head.

"Chiff," she said. "You got to be strong if you want to make it out."

Stonewall let out a sobbing laugh.

"Aunt Luzinda," he said, and the woman grabbed him and held him.

"Shhhhhhh now," she said. "This ain't the time for talk. Just follow your Aunt Luzinda and keep still."

Jean caught a quick glimpse of Aunt Luzinda's eyes glimmering through the darkness, clear and illuminated. She touched his shoulder, her eyes locking on his, holding his gaze for what must have been only seconds but seemed longer. Jean lowered his head, then followed among the boys, each rushing to keep up with the old woman as she maneuvered the darkened landscape. They followed single file into a field of corn, then along a dry stony creek bed. Aunt Luzinda moved in the darkness with sure quick steps as the boys stumbled after her, up a rise and down the other side into a field of tree stumps and finally up another rise covered with scrub. Aunt Luzinda stopped near the top and glanced back at the River Road at lights bobbing up and down in the pitch blackness.

"There they go," she said. The boys peered in different directions into the darkness. "Come along, children," she said.

Monday, August 16, 1965

Nieting opened his eyes in a hospital bed in a small bare windowless room. The place was stifling. He struggled to breath. So, it would be the DP camp and not home to the Habberstrasse. The only question was whether it would be the camp at Fohrenwald or Duppel. Conditions between them were quite different and it was the latter from which Uncle Max would rescue him. He knew Uncle Max would come at some point, because he'd had the privilege of having lived this before. Nietzsche was correct. Eternal Recurrence was real. Except that now his head and part of his face were covered in bandages. His chest was wrapped with white gauze dotted with blood that made him appear as some kind of red-spotted lady bug. His right arm was encased in a thick plaster cast. Below a white sheet his legs and lower torso were wrapped in thick bandages. These were new twists to the eternal revolving door. A nurse walked from the room. Would she be kind or cruel? He'd seen both in his time. She appeared to be American. The facility was American, then. He must be at Duppel, just as it had been the first time. But, how could there be a first time if everything recurs eternally? In a moment, the fog began to lift or was he simply playing a game? He knew he was Dr. V. Nieting, and that he had comeback from a nightmare, myriad nightmares. Eternal Recurrence was a child's game he'd played long ago. Nieting chuckled at the thought in spite of the pain that rose like flames over his torso. The nurse came back in smiling broadly.

"You're awake," she said. "My apologies for the room. It's actually a storage closet. We've been overwhelmed with all the rioting. This was the only space available when they brought you in."

Nieting groaned when he tried to move. He could feel the stiff flesh and congealed lacerations stretch and tear at the slightest movement.

"Stay still," said the nurse. "Don't try to move. You're arm is broken and you have a concussion. I've never seen so many cuts on one person. You've been through the mill, all right. You'll be fine, but for now I expect you'll be pretty uncomfortable."

Nieting attempted to speak and a burning shot from his mouth to his forehead.

"Keep still now," said the nurse. "You're cut pretty badly, from head to toe, actually. It's not quite time for your shot yet, but we'll give it to you a little early anyway."

She must have given him something because the stinging that covered him like a sheet of steel wool embedded beneath his flesh subsided into a vague uncomfortable glow.

"I'm afraid that's the best we can do," said the nurse. She was a kind woman after all, older than Nieting, in her forties perhaps, with striking blue eyes and auburn hair pulled back under a white nurse's cap.

"You were in pretty bad shape last night when they brought you in. . . stark naked, as I understand it. They stole your ID, everything. I can't tell you how sorry I am. I mean, you're a tourist, right? The officer said you were from Germany. I'm ashamed of what happened to you. I just want you to know that there are good Americans too. We're not all vicious animals. Sleep now. The best medicine for you is rest."

When he awoke, she was in the room.

"Good evening, Valentin," she said. "The police officer was here checking on you. He told me a bit about you. I have the feeling they're taking a special interest in your case. Maybe because you're a journalist. It's doubly bad if you get a wrong impression because people will read what you write. I thought that might make you feel better, knowing you do have friends here. Nobody likes it when a guest to this country is treated badly. We're all heartsick over that poor French girl. She's here in the hospital, but she's in a bad way. You did sleep for a few hours. Would you like some food? Do you feel like eating? Just wink your eyes if you're hungry, don't speak. Good. I think I can rustle up some nice chicken noodle soup. That sounds good, don't you think? By the way, my name is Estelle, see?"

The woman pointed to a name badge pinned to her white uniform.

"I'll be right back and we'll get some warm food into you."

Next to the bed on the nightstand, just within view if he turned his head as far as he could manage, was a copy of the Los Angeles Times.

NEGRO RIOTS RAGE ON; DEATH TOLL 25
21,000 Troops, Police Wage Guerrilla War; 8 PM Curfew Invoked.
The guerrilla war of south Los Angeles claimed its 25th victim Sunday night as bands of armed Negro looters took to the streets and snipers defied efforts of 21,000 National Guardsmen and law officers to bring peace to the area.

At the bottom of the page was a photo of policemen stretched in a line across the street, marching against a backdrop of burned out buildings beneath rows of palm trees.

"That's 43rd Street," said Estelle. She'd returned with a tray containing Nieting's supper. "That's where the National Guard found you. At least that's what the police report says. I don't suppose you need to see the paper just now. I have no idea who brought that in here. You'll feel much better once you get something hot in your stomach."

Nieting strained to read the caption of the picture. *Guardsmen and Los Angeles police officers march down Avalon at 43rd St. in an action designed to free the streets of rioters and looters.*

Estelle laid the tray down, picked up the newspaper and left the room. She returned in moments.

"You don't need that paper. You can't even hold it. Now, let's eat."

She raised the bed and gently positioned her patient, swinging a table top before him and painstakingly pouring several spoonfuls of soup into his partly opened mouth. The liquid ran out and down his chin.

"You've got to help, too," she said, dabbing him lightly with a cloth. "When you feel a little better, I'd like to hear about where you come from. I've visited Germany several times. I love it over there."

Estelle chattered as she deftly wielded the spoon, and finally, after managing to get an acceptable amount of soup into her patient, she left with the tray.

"Be back in no time, Valentin," she said. "Try to rest."

The woman means well.

It was Emil who spoke. He stood stood bedside, wearing that same suit, that same mischievous grin, self assured, terribly odd, yet confident and charming as always.

Father?

Yes, Valentin. I'm here, now. That was my paper your pretty nurse confiscated. No matter. I don't read the news anyway. I thought you'd be interested in seeing your photo. Don't worry. They didn't expose your cock and balls to the public of California. You were strapped on to a stretcher, covered with a sheet. Your eyes were huge. If you had been an actor, the critics would have called your performance brilliant.

I'm happy to see you, father, said Nieting. *I've been waiting for you, hoping you would come. I don't want to be alone any longer.*

I know, son.

I've been thinking about the things you've said, father.

You're a good boy.

We'll be together from now on, won't we?

Until the end, Valentin.

Estelle was in the room. She stepped between Nieting and his father and bent over, examining the bandages covering the patient's skull.

"It looks pretty good from here, Valentin," she said. "I think you may be out of this place sooner than we thought. I mean, tonight maybe. You'll have to take things real easy so you don't open these cuts. Personally, I think it's way too soon to let you go. They'll send you home with some-thing for the pain, though."

Valentin, said Emil, *Looks good from here. Estelle has quite a nice ass for a woman her age. You should see.*

"I'll have to get you some clothes," said Estelle. "But, that's not a problem. I'm sure I can find something around here, nothing great, but at least descent enough to go out in public. It's not having any ID that's a bigger problem. You should probably contact your embassy, I mean, you're practically destitute. I hope that doesn't sound harsh."

She's all right, this one. said Emil.

"I'm pretty sure you'll be let go tonight," said Estelle. "If that's right, I'll see if we can get you discharged by the end of my shift. I'll be glad to give you a lift to your motel. Otherwise, they'll just put you outside and you'll have to fend for yourself. I'll take you back to your room and you can get a good night's sleep and call the embassy in the morning. You'll be just fine."

A real regular bird, this one, said Emil. *I don't suppose you'd be up for a bit of love making when she gets you back to the hotel. No, not in your condition. Too bad.*

"You rest now, Valentin," said Estelle. "I'll be back in a while and fill you in on everything." She walked from the room.

Things have taken a better turn, haven't they, said Emil. *We're going home, son. Everything will become clearer once we get back to Berlin. We have time now to talk. I don't want any sadness, Valentin. This is a joyous occasion.*

Emil looked closely into his son's eyes.

You're very quiet, Valentin, he said. *Are you disappointed about how things have turned out? Of course, you are. Don't be, please. To those who would say you've failed, we say to hell with you. Perhaps your col-ored friend was correct and this Negro revolution is simply none of your business. You're not a Negro, you know. By god, you're not cut out for that sort of action. That doesn't mean you've failed, certainly not that your entire existence is a failure. Your life is your work, Valentin. No single effort can define a man. Do you realize that not one piece of my work survived the war? Everyone who knew me or knew of my work is dead. To the last man and woman. I did make Goebel's list of degenerate artists. Isn't that hilarious? Isn't it ironic? The list of degenerates is a who's who of the best Germany had to offer. Raoul, Heartfield, my dear Hannah Hoch, Beckmann, Dix, Grosz, Richter, Schwitters, Ernst, all my buddies and pals. And that's just for starters. Not bad company. What other nation has such a prestigious role of honor? Where else do they celebrate the artists in such a manner? It's the only proof that I ever existed as an artist or as a man for that matter. Every other trace of my existence has been exterminated. The Nazis wanted to destroy us, to obliterate not only our bodies and our works, but the memory of us as well, and the only remnant of evidence that I ever lived is that damned list. For all of that, who is to say that my life wasn't a success or that I wasn't an artist or that I didn't live the life of an artist?*

Emil's words washed over Nieting like an acrid breeze, sweet for a battlefield, an easy wind lifting the veil of madness, allowing him to glimpse the truth it obscured; a half truth, not yet the entire truth. He would follow Emil, but not because of the things he said. It was all a sophistry created by Nieting himself. His father appeared small sitting in the chair, his boney legs crossed. He was petit and pale, holding his elbow in his palm as he chatted. Nieting desired to embrace him, but knew he would cause his wounds to bleed if he moved. Emil did not exist and Nieting loved him all the more for it.

After several hours Estelle returned with clothing and the paperwork required for Nieting's discharge from the hospital, and the one possession he had remaining, the key to his motel room. She appeared perturbed by the unceremonious dismissal of her patient in the middle of the night, but did her best not to share her misgivings.

"We usually have the doctor speak to the patient before letting anyone go," she said. "I guess there's no one around just now. It is strange. The police officer took your chart. Very strange. Here's the medication. I'll need to explain how to take it. You'll be just fine, though. I promise."

She helped Nieting dress, then she and a fellow nurse carefully assisted him into a wheel chair and to her car, a yellow Volkswagen parked in the hospital parking lot.

"Here, take this," she said, handing Nieting an envelope after finally sitting him in the passenger seat of her car. "There's money in there, five dollars. I don't know where it's from, the detective, I think. I guess they figure you need something to buy food. That's pretty descent, if you ask me. I wrote the number of the German Embassy on the paper and my number too. If you have trouble, give me a call. Really, I wouldn't mind at all. I'd like to help."

Estelle drove through the night time streets of Los Angeles towards the Imperial Highway Motor Lodge. The route she chose was unfamiliar to Nieting. In the glow of streetlight, all appeared calm and inviting, lush with trees and green lawns, the air thick with the scent of vegetation. He didn't notice the absence of the unrelenting sirens or the stinging stench of smoke and gasoline. He accepted the absence of struggle with a wearied abandon and wondered where Emil might be, even though he knew full well he carried his father with him. At a stop sign on a residential back street, Estelle shifted into first gear and the car gently picked up speed.

"I understand why you're so quiet," she said. "I mean besides the pain. That sounds pretty dumb, doesn't it? I mean, I understand your suffering. I understand how you feel. My parents are German, well, me too of course, I mean, I'm American, but they came from Germany. They got out before the war, before it was too late."

She glanced at Nieting for a reaction. Her voice barely roused his attention. She was in the distance somehow, like a twinge, as if the pain medication were wearing off. He didn't wish to converse.

"We had family and friends over there," said Estelle, "so we knew later how bad it got. Most people don't care much about what happened to the Germans, the regular people, every day folks who never wanted the war. They think everyone was a Nazi, and well, I want you to know I don't feel that way. I know it was tough with the bombing and all, and you must have been just a boy. I'm sorry you had to go through this on top of everything else you've been through."

Nieting nodded at the woman, hoping his recognition would satisfy her curiosity.

"I was a teenager during the war," she said. "My parents hated the Nazis, but we had relatives over there who couldn't get out when my parents did. I had aunts and uncles and young cousins in Germany. I'd never met them, but heard so much when I was growing up and had seen pictures. I felt just as close to them as I did to my American family. I used to lay in bed at night thinking of them, wondering how they were surviving, wishing I could do something to help, wishing I could comfort them. They all died, every last cousin died in Dresden in the bombing. I wanted you to know that. I think we have some things in common. I want you to understand, you have a friend."

If Nieting could have moved, he would have slapped the woman's face. He had made a deal with the past that she could never fathom. He'd not completely understood it himself until this moment. Emil was his Mephistopheles and would demand payment. He would do so because he loved his son with a love of great honesty and integrity. Val would see him again shortly. He would be awaiting Val's return.

The neon sign for the Imperial Highway Motor Lodge blinked bright red in the sultry summer darkness. Estelle pulled into the lot and stopped next to the motel office.

"I can take care of myself from here," said Nieting.

"Well, well," said Estelle, grinning. "The sphinx has finally spoken."

Nieting cringed as Estelle moved towards him, as if to embrace, but stopped short.

"Are you sure?" she said, gently touching his shoulder. "I could go with you to your room. I'm a pretty good nurse, you know."

"No please," said Nieting. "I must be alone now. So much has happened. I must think. I will be fine, I assure you."

"You have my number," said Estelle. "I may just come by tomorrow morning to check your dressing, whether you like it or not. I wouldn't mind talking a bit either. I wish you'd consider me a friend. At least call me if you need help, will you?"

"Yes, of course," said Nieting. "I can't thank you adequately."

"There's no need for that," said Estelle. "Just tell your friends in Germany, some of us Americans are good people."

Estelle waved as she pulled onto Imperial Highway and puttered off into the night. Nieting did not look back. He limped stiffly across the parking lot, cradling his plaster encased arm like a baby, towards the staircase to his room, passing a group of white men congregating next to a car parked beneath a spot light. All the windows of the car were smashed and the body badly dented. A man stood in the center of the group with his left hand wrapped in a blood soaked rag and held aloft. Blood streamed down from between his fingers, covering his arm and shirt. He held his right hand on his forehead, and spoke excitedly to the others.

"I been over by Hoover and 41st," he said. "I work down there. It's all burned to hell now. I had two niggers come at my car, right in the lot of my job. They put bricks through my windows. I was nearly killed. I was going home to El Segundo and my god damned muffler come off so I stopped here to have a look."

The man trembled as he spoke and began weeping.

"It's a race war," said one of the whites, "a goddamned race war."

"Those niggers oughta be wiped out, if you ask me."

"I got my gun. I'll shoot the first one looks at me cross-eyed."

The whites stopped talking as Nieting moved by, staring silently at his bandaged head and the cast on his arm. Nieting returned the stare blankly as the conversation resumed.

"Look at that poor bastard, will you?"

"I bet those god damned jigs got him too."

"We all need to get some protection. Who else got a gun?"

"We call'm nigger getters where I come from."

"Protection hell, we need to take this war right to the niggers."

"I'll shoot any coon that tries anything on me."

"I'm with that."

The white men's words were empty sounds to Nieting, ugly music, shrill like sirens but superfluous, harmless like an unpleasant stench. *How can one feel so expectant,* he thought, *when there is no future?* This single question occurred to him as he climbed the stairs to his room. In truth, he had no intention of answering that question or any other. The struggle was over. There were no more questions to be asked. No more theories to be considered. No more anthropology, no students, no re- search, no great works, and no revolution. *The Robert Charles Song* would remain where it was, lost in the collective unconscious of the Negro forever. Nieting wanted no more now than to see his father, to follow him. He desired nothing more than to pay an overdue debt in full. Perhaps it was he who would be collecting.

When he reached the head of the stairs, he saw that the door to his room was wide open and a dim light shown inside. He was taken aback. Even being mad and knowing he was mad, watching himself being mad, observing and marveling at the madness, seeing the door ajar jolted him nonetheless. Could Emil really be inside? To ask the question was shameful. One must at least have faith in one's insanity. Nieting moved into the room, ready to curl up in his father's lap and go to sleep forever. When he edged inside, the door closed behind him. A man stepped in front of the door and another emerged from the shadows into the illumi- nated doorway of the bathroom.

"Professor Nieting," he said. "Good to see you. You're much im- proved over the last time we meet."

The man appeared to float across the room, coming face to face with Nieting, flashing a badge that caught the neon motel sign blinking through a crack in the drapes and lit up like an electric light.

"I'm Detective Savino," he said, "and this is Detective Gibson."

Nieting heard the man behind him breathing and the smack of chew- ing gun. He could smell his sweat.

"I brought you in the night before last," said Savino. "You were nude, you know, when you passed out on 43rd? Do you remember? They wanted to take you to the psych ward, but I told'm you weren't crazy. I told'm the niggers striped you bare. You know, there was nothing left of your pants except the top part with the belt loops and one pocket. It was amazing, really. The only thing they left in that pocket was your room key. I recognized it because that whore that was killed next door two nights ago is my case. I would have picked you up sooner, but, well, you understand."

As Nieting's eyes adjusted to the light, he looked about, scanning every corner of the room, even stepping toward the lighted bathroom to see if Emil were there, but the detective blocked his path.

"You must have gotten pretty sore at that junky to cut her up like that," said Savino. "You carved her up pretty good, didn't you?"

Nieting wanted to call to Emil, but didn't dare.

"Carved up?" he said. "I don't know what you mean."

"I figured you didn't really intend to come back here," said Savino, "but I knew you had no choice after the blacks did that number on you. Then again, you know what those wet backs did to the crime scene. I nearly shit when I saw that. We could have picked you up at the hospital, but things have been a bit hectic. I was keeping pretty close to Estelle. Real sweet girl, don't you think? She seemed kind of sympathetic to you for some reason, so I made sure she didn't know how serious your situation is. I don't mind being soft hearted once in a while. Since there was no place else you could go, I figured we'd just wait and let you come to us."

"I don't understand how I can help you," said Nieting. "Please, tell me what you want. I've been ill, as you can see."

"That material you left behind is mighty inflammatory," said Detective Gibson. His voice slipped over Nieting's shoulder like a greasy hand. "What's your real reason for being in Los Angeles?"

Nieting's ears perked up. He could almost hear the voice before it sounded.

Real hard cases, these two.

Finally, Emil had emerged, standing at Savino's shoulder and nodding his head knowingly.

There's nothing there, Valentin," he said. *These two are ghosts. Empty. I mean, nothing.*

He winked at his son and nodded, as if to say, 'answer the man's questions, Valentin. Don't be frightened. This is merely a formality. You've been questioned by their ilk before. You've injured no one. Tell the detective what you know. He doesn't really care about a prostitute.' Nieting heard himself telling the story, how Oscar had commissioned him for an article on Buddy Bolden and financed his trip to America and that Kid Auger was to be an important component of the work, but nothing had turned out as he thought it would and now there was nothing left to do but go back to Germany. Emil stood by his side throughout the interrogation, whispering, never once suggesting that Val lie, simply telling him to leave out details that would have confused the detectives and obscure the deeper truth. His son's political views were irrelevant and need not be mentioned. The few sheets of writing found by the detectives were inconsequential musings, so unimportant Val had discarded them, left them behind.

"Professor, I'm afraid we're going to have to take you in" said Savino. "I don't believe your story. I don't know whether you killed anyone personally, but I do know your kind is responsible for a lot more than one dead whore. I'd say you have close to thirty deaths on your hands at this point and half my city burned to the ground. God knows how many arsonists, how many snipers got stirred up by that bullshit you write. You're a dangerous man, an agitator, and sure as hell an undesirable. I wouldn't expect to be walking the streets of America again if I were you, not in this lifetime. No need to cuff him, John, the shape he's in, he couldn't cause any trouble if he wanted too."

Valentin, said Emil, *there is nothing to worry about. As they say in the American cinema, 'they ain't got nothing on you.*

Emil chuckled and led his son out the door into the hot night as the two detectives followed.

At least outside of that filthy room, we won't smell these two so intensely. Rather unsavory types, wouldn't you say, son?

The corners of Nieting's mouth curled as he followed his father to the unmarked police car parked in the motel parking lot. Little Val was at peace. He was no longer alone. His father was here and he would take care of him.

We're going home, Valentin, said Emil. *We are going home.*

Wednesday, August 18, 1965

In the early hours of the morning, as Suzette and Celine slept, Auger stood before the gallery of photographs on his living room wall addressing the pictures of his friends, his lifelong colleagues, as though they were animate and not merely reflections beneath glass. There were no others he could speak to who might understand what he'd been through and consequently, what he'd learned from it.

"I'll admit it now," he whispered. "I do remember Robert Charles and I remember the trouble he got in. I don't blame myself for wanting to forget that mess. You all understand what I'm saying. I didn't understand that sometimes what you don't remember can hurt you more than what you do remember. You all know what I'm talking about. It just don't do no good to dwell on certain things. I just wanted to have a good life with my family. Never wanted to hurt nobody. You all know that. You know how I am. Yes, I sure enough remember Robert Charles. I remember his face. I remember his voice. He had a very nice lady friend. I remember her face too. I seen her and I seen a man that was his and Bolden's friend. We heard later on that that man and his entire family was sent to prison for hiding Robert Charles. We heard that sweet little girl was caught up in it too. She disappeared after the police questioned her. Vanished. Who can blame her? The whites was like monsters. I won't deny that. They said in their newspapers they wanted all the niggers dead. They said it many a time and that's what they tried to do. There wasn't nothing in the newspapers but Robert Charles for days and days and all that rioting the whites was doing.

"When it was over they put them police on trial, a half dozen of them, the ones who couldn't capture Robert Charles that very first morning when they had him trapped. They was cowards. That's what they was charged with and I expect it was true, except who could have stood face to face with Robert Charles? He had a fire in him that no one could have stood up against. Hell, it took thousands to finally bring him down. That man with that big handle bar mustache, the one who gave me so much trouble, he tried to kill me, he was one of those police charged with being a coward. The trial was in all the papers and that man, oh he was a mean fella, he was thrown off the force. I don't believe it was the first time they got rid of him either.

"Pops, you was just a bitty baby so you don't know nothing about all this. Most of you all was too young to remember these things. Those were bad times for colored people. You know as well as I do, it's always been tough but we're talking about something else now. Seemed like every day or so some colored man was strung up somewhere. Sometimes women and even children was killed by the mob. All across the south. Hell, it happened up north too. I was there in Chicago in 1919 when the white mobs went after the colored people. You was there, Pops. We was both working with Joe Oliver at the time. They stoned a small boy just for drifting over onto the wrong beach when he went swimming in the lake. You all know this. They still killing children today, as much as it breaks my heart to think of it. They killed those four little girls in that church. Nothing has changed. They had to bring the National Guard into New Orleans way back, sixty five years ago to stop the rioting just like they done in Los Angeles today. It stopped after the Guard come in and after they killed Robert Charles. I forgot it for a long time, but I remember now. The papers said twenty thousand whites was crowded around Saratoga Street where Robert Charles was hid. It was between Clio and Erato, twenty thousand jammed in there firing into the house of that man I seen talking to Buddy that day. I remember it because Stonewall had a newspaper and was reading about it the day they buried Philo Baptiste out in Pine Grove Plantation. All those thousands firing at one man in the upstairs of a wood framed house. It took hours to bring him down. It took burning the house to get him out of there. Even when the flames was flying, Robert Charles would suddenly appear in a window and shoot his Winchester and every shot hit home. With every shot he took one of that mob went down. Finally, the fire drove him out and of course, there was so many people all over, on every roof top, every angle you can think of and when he came out they shot him. I don't know how many hundred shot they found in his body but it was a lot. Then, you know, they just destroyed his carcass, his corpse was torn up, played with by the crowd like dogs fighting over a dead rat till the police wrestled what was left of him away and tossed it in a wagon and sped off. My god, I do remember reading these things along with Wall Mathews. He was reading the papers to the boys, like I say, the day we buried old man Baptiste.

"Philo was from Pine Grove. His family was there as far back as anyone could remember, long before anyone even knew what the English language was in that part of the country. He was working in the French Market in New Orleans when he was killed, kind of like a night watchman, and the mob came through and he was shot down dead, an old man at work and he was gunned down and left to die. They brought his body home to be buried among his folks. Us boys, the Pine Grove boys, why, we played for his final journey to the grave yard. That song. That very song. The one Buddy and that man made up. It was *The Robert Charles Song* they played that night so long ago. I forgot it for so long, but now I can hear it real clear. Buddy played it after the man sang those words about Robert Charles. The words were true, but so deep terrible sad it was like they wasn't even words no more, like the truth was being shot, kind of injected-like, right into our bodies, and of course, it made you sorry, but also somehow . . . well, I think it was . . . I think it was beautiful . . . that a man could do that, tell something so hard like that, make it into something else.

"Well, Buddy played right on the heels of this man's words and the amazing thing was, his cornet sounded just like the man's voice. You would have thought it was the man singing but it was Buddy playing, so soft and so clear it broke your heart. I can hear it, yes I can still hear it, a very lovely melody, sweet, tender you could say, right there with that hard metal sound of the guitar that Buddy was duplicating somehow too. It was all in the music, all the things that happen that can make people into animals, make us less than human, make us hard or make some men into monsters, real true blood-thirsty monsters. That was the hard quality from the guitar and the people was all listening, the room was filled with folks, not saying a word. I don't think anyone could have spoke if they wanted to. The guitar man and Buddy was doing all the talking for all of us. There wasn't nothing else to say so we just listened and it was sad, deep sorrowful and that cold metal striking was cruel and we all knew what cruelty was, by god, we all knew what cruel was, and that melody, I can't tell you how pretty it was, a beautiful line Buddy played and played a few different ways before he quit. It made us understand that we was human beings, still human after all we'd seen, all we'd been through, and human beings was, could be a beautiful thing, it could be a beautiful thing to be human after all, and we was, we was human beings and no one could take that from us.

"I thought all the Pine Grove boys, cept Wall and me, had slept right through all of what I'm telling about. I thought they missed Buddy and that guitar man making up the song, but the day of Philo Baptiste's funeral, we was leading all his people down that dusty road on Pine Grove Plantation. It was hot and the dust would just about stir if you wiped your face with a rag and we was going on, leading old Philo's family to his final home and we start to playing that song. None of us knew what we would do and I thought sure none of the others besides Wall and me even heard the song but we picked up that melody, *The Robert Charles Song*. It was the song made up for Robert Charles, in his honor by Buddy and that guitar man. Of course, we wasn't singing the words, just playing. No one on Pine Grove ever heard it before, but we played it, just the melody as best we could, trying to catch it all, the hard sounds, the truth about suffering that gives music its heart and the sweetness everyone knows about, anyone who ever knew a mother's love or had a child. It's a kind of innocence, maybe, in the melody, swimming in a storm of hardness, anger, things you can't never understand better than when they're in music. We sent Philo Baptiste home this way. I know his folks appreciated it the way they carried on, the way they thanked us. And we never, not one of us boys ever mentioned a word to each other or anyone that I know of, about what we done, about that song or where it come from. We just never did speak of it. What could we have said? There wasn't one thing we could have said that wasn't said perfect in the music and in what we did for Philo . . . and what Buddy did for us. We just never spoke of it.

"Dear old Wall Mathews died about ten years ago and we never did get a chance to reminisce. I don't know if we would have brought all this up if we did. Some things are perfect as they are and there ain't no use saying anything more. I guess that song belongs to all the folks who was in that cabin the night Buddy and that man made the thing up. Most of'm got to be dead by now. I don't expect none of the Pine Grove boys is alive. Rabbit died driving a truck, some kind of accident when he was still a young man. I lost track of Raymond so long ago . . . they lived hard lives in Louisiana in them days, working in the fields. Life was tough for a colored boy in the city, too. Maybe more so. There ain't that many that live into old age back there. Me and my boys was the only youngsters in there with Buddy that night. I guess *The Robert Charles Song* belongs to me now. I'd lost it for so many years. It was hidden down there with all those bad memories. I thought I was going mad or was finally over the hill and it was just all those folks struggling back into my memory. They refused to die. Robert Charles refused to die. I expect they'll die anyway when I die. I don't intend to mention anything about the song to any living soul. Won't do it. Why should I? Even if I told someone, what would they do with it? Use the song to make themselves rich? Why would I want to make another white man rich? I'll be god damned before I wake up one morning and hear Buddy's melody on some top 40 station. Even if it was black kids that made it first, next thing you know some English boys'll make a million off of it. Not this time. Buddy's song belongs to me this time and I won't allow no funny business. Why would I give the story to some young black kid who'll just use it to make trouble? Some kid who been blinded by agitators and communists would just love to bring back *The Robert Charles Song* and all the trouble that came with it.

"Now, I could transcribe the tune and pass it along to Duke. They'll all be in town in a few days so I could do it in person. Duke's just the man to put it in some piece of music that could do justice to the people who created it. My only request would be that Buddy's name be listed as composer. I might want a bit of the royalties too, like a finder's fee. I got a family. The song wouldn't be around if it wasn't for me remembering. I'm the last man standing who knows about it. I think sharing the profit would be a just arrangement. Duke might not even be interested. I wouldn't give it to no one else. There ain't no one else could do it justice. I believe in fairness, but I ain't a greedy bastard either. I don't even know if I'll write the tune down. Could just let it drift back down where it was. Not everything should just be given away. Not in this world. That's clear enough. But then again, the song is a bit of all those folks. It's a bit of Wall and the boys and of course, Aunt Luzinda. They was all there when it was first born. It'd be kind of sweet to let it be free, be like they was alive again, another chance for their spirits to ramble in the world. No one would know but me. Of course, that song is a whole lot of Robert Charles himself. If that's true, then I sure as hell want to keep it under wraps. We don't need any more trouble. I don't know what I want for the song but I do know what I don't want. I just got to write the thing down before I forget it. If anyone is gonna make money off this tune, it's me. Money never was the important thing for me but fair is fair. I just don't know what I'll do with my song."

Auger laid awake most of the night, unable to stop talking in his head, yet the bright morning found him cheerful and energetic. There was an air of celebration in the Auger household on Wednesday morning. Suzette was on the verge of closing a deal for the sale of the house at an excellent price. She'd even had a lead on an apartment on Waikiki where the family would live until she found a new home. They'd be sitting pretty with the money they made on the Brentwood house when the deal closed. Celine had gone off, gaily, on a day trip to Santa Barbara with her girlfriends and Suzette was at home organizing for the move west which she was determined would take place by the middle of September. Since the decision to relocate to Hawaii, the Auger's had lived in a whirlwind of activity or a breeze, as Suzette described it. She amazed her husband with the ease with which she shouldered all the business, the sale of the house, packing, contracting movers and the realtors in Hawaii. She was tireless and overjoyed.

Auger hopped from bed on Wednesday morning and headed straight toward the sound of tape ripping and being slapped onto a cardboard box. He came up to his wife with his robe open and grabbed her from behind, rubbing his naked body against her. She squealed with laughter and wriggled away. Auger pranced about, exposed to her, strutting as she looked at him with wide eyes.

"Don't tempt me, Jean," she said. "You've got to get to work and I have so much to do as it is."

He ignored her admonition and approached her, taking her into his arms.

"Jean," she said giggling. "The car from Disneyland is supposed to be here soon. You better stop horsing around."

"It won't come for three hours," said Auger. *Old man, my ass*, he thought.

"Later sweetie," said Suzette, "I promise," and Auger relented, striding barefooted over the plush carpet to the bedroom. In no time, he was showered, shaved and dressed, sweet smelling and slick haired. He flipped on the TV in the living room and machine gun fire rattled from the box. Auger's heart jumped as a great explosion thudded and helicopters chopped and men shouted. He thought, *My God, when will it end?*

A newsman answered, "This action in the Mekong Delta is indicative of the American effort to clear the area of communists."

"God damn, Vietnam," said Auger. "There's trouble all over the world. Communists just won't let people live in peace. Well, that ain't my problem. I'm through with worry for a while."

At two o'clock when the limo driver rang the bell Auger was ready and waiting. He handed the trombone case to the driver and deep kissed his wife. He did a little dance for her sake as he walked down the path and before he entered the limo he turned to where Suzette stood and blew her a kiss. The radio was on in the limo as Auger stretched his legs on the plush leather seat.

"At 11 o'clock this morning the curfew was officially lifted from the riot area. At noon bus service was restored to most of the curfew zone. Crews from the gas and power companies are out assessing and repairing the massive damage incurred over the last week of chaos. Governor Brown announced that the National Guard may be able to begin withdrawal as early as tomorrow afternoon."

Auger slid open the little glass door to the front seat and said to the driver, "It's about god damned time, don't you think Murray? I couldn't stand another day hearing nothing but that bullshit."

"You bet, Kid," said the driver.

"How about switching on a little music?" said Auger.

"Sure thing," replied the driver and punched the radio button. "You mind the Beatles?"

"I don't mind," said Auger. He sang with the radio, snapping his fingers. "I've got a ticket to ra-hide. I've got a ticket to ra-ha-hide. I've got a ticket to ride and you don't care."

The driver laughed and when the song ended flipped the channel again.

I'm sure I could make that tune into a Jazz hit. I can hear Barbarin funking that rhythm, take it right into an uptown street beat like the kids do today. Man, they'll be dancing from New York to LA. Bout time I modernized my thing a bit. That's where the money is. Might send back to New Orleans for some youngsters. I don't know if Paul could get the right beat. Man, I sure do miss him and John. Hope ol'Paul ain't mad. He ain't the kind to hold a grudge, but I sure was hard on them. Paul didn't mean nothing. It's just his way to be outspoken like that.

"Well hello Dolly. This is Louis, Dolly."

"There you go," said the driver.

"Nah," said Auger. "I don't go for that stuff. That's old folks' music."

The two men laughed.

Armstrong's trumpet slid into one of his patented high notes, rising up until it slapped the beat with a big wet tongue kiss.

"Louis **is** always funky, though," said Auger.

"Louis got soul," said the driver and Auger responded, "Amen."

"You can hear it all in Louis," said the driver. "He goes all the way back past King Oliver, Buddy Petit, right back to Buddy Bolden. It's like all their spirits still live inside that sound."

"You're right," said Auger.

For a brief moment Auger felt uncomfortable, as though the driver was able to read his thoughts, as though he might know something about what he'd been going through. Yet, no one could possibly know. Then, the sound of Buddy Bolden's horn was there. It came in so low, so sly and sneaky, Auger didn't know how long he'd been playing. Perhaps he'd been playing since he'd gotten into the limo. Maybe he was there all morning. The cornet growled playfully, teasing out the first few notes of the little melody of *The Robert Charles Song*. It was indescribably tender and sweet, so pretty until the guitar hit like an anvil, vibrating like a red hot poker, striking viciously three times and Bolden's ditty dancing like the cornet and guitar were incongruous, agonized lovers. There was no anger in Louis' song on the radio, but there sure as hell was anger in Bolden and that guitar man. There sure as hell was anger in Robert Charles.

Auger slid the window to the driver closed.

I don't want to hear my song just now, he thought, but Bolden did not desist. He picked up the tempo as the guitar struck relentlessly. Auger's chest tightened. He needed air and lowered the window and came face to face with a small boy, six or seven years old, in a car in the next lane. The boy was chubby faced with a deep brown complexion and large almond shaped brown eyes. They watched each until the boy smiled and waved.

"That song belongs to you, don't it?" said Auger.

The boy cocked his head curiously and Auger looked away.

"It ain't my fault the world is like it is," he whispered, then thought, *I got my own family to look after. Other folks' kids are their own look out. What if I just up and give the song away? Give it to Paul or John or better, give it to some youngsters in the Lower Ninth. I ain't got to be involved at all. My name don't have to be attached to it. I can go about my business. It would be a shame to have that kind of property and not make nothing off of it. Nah, money never has been the important thing in my life. I do have a family though. Then again, there's plenty ways to make a living. I know who the god damned song belongs to. It belongs to that child yonder. His people paid for it with their lives. But it's me that's got it. I better write it down fast before it goes away, man, I shoulda done it already.*

The guitar man stroked the instrument furiously as Auger peered out the window.

God damn, that tune is lethal, he thought. *I don't want no god damned trouble. The riots is over now, the damned riots is over for Christ's sake. We don't need no trouble breeding song to stir things up. Some wise ass punk is sure to put lyrics to it, especially if they know what it was about. They might even dig up Robert Charles again, god forbid. Not too many folks alive even know who he was. Let sleeping dogs lie. I don't want to be the one that gets the fires started again. No way. It's a trouble breeding song. Always has been. It used to be dangerous to even mention Robert Charles. That's why that song never went nowhere to begin with. For Christ's sake, why would I bring it back. A man could get killed for playing that song in public. That's why they all forgot about it. I should just keep it to myself. Who knows, maybe I'll hum it to Celine on my deathbed, if she keeps with her music lessons, never know with that child she's so hot or cold on things. I could give it to her just as I die, just Buddy's sweet melody, keep that other stuff out, all those strange angry voicings, those days are gone, folks don't need that no more, look what it gets them, turns people into animals and they nearly burned the city down, caused my family to leave the mainland. No, we need sweetness. Melody belongs to everyone not just a few. I don't care who they are. Black or white. Melody belongs to all that hear it. That's only natural.*

I'll give my melody to my child before I go, let her benefit from it. That black boy in that car can keep his boogaloo and mine can have the pretty songs. Hell, sounds like a French ditty anyhow. Buddy took plenty from the Creoles. Who's to say who that song belongs to? I know who. Me. Cause I'm the only one has it.

The limo took a long swing around a curved driveway and pulled smoothly into the lot where the talent performing at Disneyland parked their cars. The driver stopped the limo and in an instant was at the door, deftly hoisting the trombone case off the seat and smiling broadly as Auger stepped onto the black top. A large bus with tinted windows and the words, THE DUKE ELLINGTON ORCHESTRA on the side idled nearby as men worked unloading equipment from the baggage compartment.

"Well, I'll be dog goned," said Auger, shielding his eyes from the sun. "That's Barney Bigard standing there. Hey Barney."

A portly man in a light colored silk suit standing beside the bus turned at Auger's words.

"Jean Auger," he said. "I was hoping I'd run into you."

Bolden and the guitar man beat out a fanfare in Auger's head as if they were mocking him then turned back into the song. He felt dizzy and he tapped the side of his head with the heel of his palm and tried to breathe deeply. Suddenly, the strength of the sun was too much.

"Don't look so sorry to see us," said another man, stepping around the bus, carrying a saxophone case. "You must owe me some money from a card game I forgot about."

"You ain't never beat me at cards," replied Auger. "Not on the best day of your life."

He approached the men with an outstretched hand.

"Johnny Hodges. How you been?"

"Dukes' running us ragged with one nighters," replied Hodges, taking Auger's hand in his.

"We ain't slept in a real bed for a week," said Bigard. "How you been, Jean?"

"Oh, I been just dandy," said Auger. "Me and the wife is fixing to go off to Hawaii. Gonna make our home there. This just may be my last official day working. You're looking at a retired man."

"Congratulations, Auger," said Hodges.

"That won't last long," said Bigard. "You know our kind can't retire."

"Right," said Hodges. "We just die."

The men laughed.

"I tried retiring," said Bigard, "but I couldn't keep to it. Every time Louis or Duke called, I'm back out on the road. My poor wife always threatens to leave me. I suppose they'll have to drag my dead body off the band stand."

"If I know Duke, he won't even stop the number," said Hodges. "Probably have somebody step over your body and pick your part up where you left off."

"That's right, you'll be calling him Barney for a week before you realize I'm gone," said Bigard.

"Where's the Duke at," said Auger. "I want to say hello."

"His majesty won't be here until tomorrow," said Hodges. "We gonna run through a quick rehearsal and take the day off."

The Robert Charles Song rang in Auger's head, blasting in full dissonance, the guitar man hammering the chords violently and Bolden growling, popping notes and making sucking sounds.

"What's going on with all that mess in South L.A.?" said Bigard.

"We heard things was pretty bad down there," said Hodges.

"Well, it was bad for a minute," said Auger. "But not no more. They had some trouble makers, hard cases, you know, some fire bugs, but they got to'm and things calmed back down right quick."

"That ain't what we heard," said Bigard.

Someone shouted.

"Hey you old men."

"Is that Johnny St Cyr and Paul Barbarin coming this way?"

"That looks like Barbarin," said Hodges.

"That's him," said Auger.

Auger conversed with his old friends just like everything truly was just dandy as *The Robert Charles Song* intensified in his brain. St Cyr and Barbarin approached, smiling, pointing at the three men next to the bus, elbowing each other and chuckling. The song was unrelenting even at the sight of Auger's two friends striding across the parking lot. They were wearing Hawaiian shirts.

"Look at them shirts," said Hodges.

"They sure won't get hit by no car wearing those," said Bigard.

"I need to find out where they found those shirts," said Hodges.

"Suzette must have told them we was moving," said Auger. "That's my boys' way of saying congrats."

Auger gazed at Hodges and Bigard, weary from a long bus trip, yet dressed elegantly, and his two friends coming towards him, all of them happy, healthy, all survivors, success stories, they'd all lived through it – if not the Robert Charles ordeal, some ordeal somewhere. They knew what he knew and like him they'd arrived at Disneyland intact. Auger jumped nervously at what sounded like Bolden stomping his foot, but was a leather bag dropped by one of the men unloading the bus hitting the black top. The guitar man picked up on the thud of the bag and spit metal terror on the beat and Bolden laughed through the horn, a knowing laugh that chilled Auger. *That song is lethal,* thought Auger. *It's a curse. We don't need it no more. Look how we've made it. Look how good we done. We're all right. What would these fellas want with such a song?*

Barbarin and St Cyr slapped hands with Hodges and Bigard, then they embraced.

"How you been?" "Still walking around." "Ain't getting any younger." "Auger is the old one." "Hell Hodges is still chasing the ladies." "No shit." "I ain't stopped that myself." "Bigard, your wife would cut your balls off is she heard you say that."

Let sleeping dogs lie, thought Auger and it struck him that the song had ceased sounding in his head. The silence was abrupt, echoing like wind inside of a seashell. The song was gone. Auger began to panic. *Where'd my song go? Where the hell is it?* He tried to bring it back, tried to hear Bolden's horn, to summon the melody and nothing came but a distant wind sweeping. He hummed to himself, reaching for the tune and the Beatles' *I Got a Ticket to Ride* popped into his head and would not go away. *The Robert Charles Song* was gone.

◆ ◆ ◆

At the Los Angeles County Jail, Professor Nieting was placed in a small room with mirrored walls where he remained for the next day and a half. He was deposited there by Detective Savino just after midnight on Tuesday morning. There was nothing in the room besides a table and two chairs. Occasionally, voices could be heard through the walls, screams, cries, curses, even laughter, coming in waves, sudden surges like a raucous party or brawl going on somewhere in the building. They were the voices of Negroes, the insurgents, prisoners of war, still defiant, their boundless rage reverberating, echoing through the building. If the hospital was filled beyond capacity as Estelle had said, then surely the jails must be. The metal table top where Nieting sat was smeared with bloody hand prints only some of which, as was pointed out by his father, appeared to belong to Nieting. Red spots showed through his trousers, as well, yet he did not seek assistance. He would have had to pound on the heavy door to call for help and that would have worsened the bleeding. He was content to sit with Emil and wait. They spoke calmly across the table, his father sitting with his leg crossed over his knee, an elbow resting in his palm, the hand pivoting on the wrist in passionate yet restrained gesticulations. A comment that he'd made on Kid Auger's door steps occurred to Nieting. Emil had uttered it as a taunt, a cruel retort, at least that's how Nieting took it at the time. Yet even then, in all the madness, there was the sweet breath of truth to the statement that caused Nieting to take note, to keep the words inside until they floated up out of the depths, bobbing onto the surface of the still lake of his consciousness. The stillness was the gift that came with the acceptance of his father as teacher. 'If you are going to take your life," Emil had said, "there is no longer a reason to deny the truth." It was something like that he'd said, his way of selling the idea of suicide to his son and Val had resisted. He'd resisted for the longest time, yet his father had persisted, even as Val refused to listen. *You can possess the truth, the truth you cannot live with, once you resolve yourself to die.*

Uncle Max had described his father, affectionately, as one who had always acted strangely, was a true odd ball, an eccentric, he was an artist after all, and funny, comical, yet a profound thinker. He truly was Val's sweet Mephistopheles, who hadn't come to claim Val's soul, but to return it to him. No father could have been more concerned with the welfare of a child. They spoke the truth to one another now. They discussed everything. Not like the old days, when Val was a child. There were few words uttered between them then. The bond between them was close, just as it was now, yet Kid Auger had done most of the talking with his trombone. He sang for them of the beauty of life and suffering, offering succor when death seemed the only escape. What could move a child to take his own life? When little Val was lifted to safety in the sound of Auger's music, he did not ask himself why he'd sought death in the first place. He was so young, after all. Now, he was a man. Now, he could ask the question. Truly, that was the nature of the deal. He always believed there was one goal to living and that was the attainment of truth. Uncle Max had taught him this. Hadn't the child's instinct been brilliant? The time to make the exchange was near.

Emil described his death in the gas chambers of Auschwitz with amazing detail and composure. *How can I know he died in Auschwitz unless he is real, unless he truly exists and is telling me these things and is not my creation but truly my father?* Nieting understood he was insane, yet the love he felt for his father and comfort he took in his presence did not abate simply because his father did not exist. Auschwitz was never mentioned by Uncle Max. The truth was uttered by a man of Nieting's invention. That he knew the truth in all its unimaginable sadness was the gift his father had promised, knowledge in exchange for life. Emil was a kind wizard, a healer, a physician of the sick soul. He explained to Val that he and his mother had been victims and that she'd tried desperately to protect him, to bring him through the war safely, to keep him from his father's fate. Her love was the essence of motherly love. Her suffering caused her to love her son ever more even as the agony of living consumed her spirit. Her death could not be his fault. He was merely a small boy.

"You know more about her final suffering than I," said Emil. "I was gone then."

Val described to his father how they'd lived during the war, of hiding that he was a Jew, of the bombing, of the hunger and fear, of the invasion of the Russians and the Americans. The two wept in each other's arms. Val's words were as strange to him as his madness, yet they came easily, were waiting for him, lined up behind a door he didn't have to go through, rather merely open and his suffering came to him like children crowding around, asking to be loved, begging his embrace. It was a homecoming, a reunion with himself just as Emil has promised. It was part of the pact, the deal, the agreement. The clarity after weeping was an endless blue sky. When little Val began talking, he could hardly stop. He even described his stint in the Hitler Youth, cut short by illness. His mother had sent him to dispel any suspicion that he was not of pure blood, that his Aryan soul was tainted in any way. Emil and Val laughed at the thought of the little Jewish boy who'd only recently discovered he was a Jew, who had no idea what it meant except that it was a matter of life and death that no one else know, maneuvering in a camp of National Socialist child patriots. Emil stopped in the middle of a laugh and sighed, taking Val's hand in his.

He told Val of happier times, how as a young man, he'd first met Val's mother.

"I was in love with Hannah Hoch, but she was older than I. She called me the kid. She was in love with Hausmann who was really in love with Johann Baader, I think. One day, I asked her why she felt so strongly about Raoul when he clearly would never love her. She shrugged her shoulders and pulled me along the path in the park where I'd stopped her to make my declaration of love. 'But Raoul is married and has children,' I said. 'You have no hope.' She smiled a rather sad smile and didn't answer. I felt sorry that I'd asked her, because I'd clearly hurt her. Then I remembered, it was I who should be sad. I told her she could have me, that I did love her. But, she shrugged again, a quick little rise and fall of the shoulders, lovely, very lovely, she was quite a charismatic woman, and she told me she loved me as a friend and as a colleague, but not as a lover. I cried, Valentin, right there in front of her. I stamped my feet on the gravel path and cried, and just as sweet as a flower, she poked me in the ribs, called me kid again and laughed. She was bursting with magic, the sight of her laughing made me laugh too. Then I said, 'If you won't have me, I want you to find me someone else. I want someone as great as you. Not just beautiful, but a brilliant artist like you are. Nothing less. Greater perhaps, but nothing less. I want a woman with a great mind, just like yours, someone who will give me a real run for my money.' She said she knew just the person I was describing and not long after she introduced me to your mother. Of course, your mother was beautiful, strawberry blonde, lovely full lips, broad hips, you know?" Emil winked. "A figure like a goddess and she was an artist just like I told Hannah I wanted. She turned out to be far more dynamic and, I must admit, more prolific than I. We hit it off on our first meeting and my love for Hannah transformed into the love for a sister. I was consumed by my love for your mother. You were conceived in love, Valentin, blind, blissful, idealistic love. Good times didn't last long in those days, but that can never change what came before, the joy your mother gave and received. I believe you were her most prized gift, her most wonderful possession. She succeeded in her most important goal, Valentin. She saved you, she kept you alive, which was what she'd wanted most of all, and her brother picked up where she left off."

Emil stroked Val's head, lifting the curls from his eyes, gently running his finger tips over little Val's rosy cheeks.

"I wish we could play Kid Auger's records, father."

"We will, Valentin. Not just yet. I promise you, we will."

It wasn't until sometime around mid morning on Tuesday before any-one else entered the room. A man was shown in by Detective Savino. Savino didn't bother to look at Nieting, rather he simply opened the door for the man to enter, then disappeared. The man identified himself as Mr. Koeppan, Secretary to the Deputy Consul General to the German Consulate General representing the Bundesrepublik in Los Angeles. He handed Nieting a bag containing stockings and underwear and a suit of clothing. He presented him with temporary identification papers and explained in a rather curt and summary fashion that the authorities in Los Angeles, including the FBI, had released him to the authority of his home government.

"You are going back to Berlin, Herr Professor," said Koeppan. "You have no choice. The City of Los Angeles and the government of the United States of America no longer wish to extend their hospitality. You are being thrown out, professor."

Nieting remained silent. Only Emil spoke, tossing quips about Koeppan's shiny bald pate, his pasty plastic face, his stuffy manner and disgusted disinterest.

"It's only a little after 11:00 in the morning" said Emil. "Baldy never gets up this early. That's why he's such a grump. He stinks of alcohol, doesn't he? He must have come straight from an orgy at the consulate. How in god's name did he become so stout? This one knows how to take advantage of his position, which is down on all fours, I'll wager. That's why he won't sit down. Too tender. Look at that grimace." Emil circled Koeppan. "What did I say? There's a grease spot on the back of his trousers. He's soiled his monkey suit. He has the stink of the SS if you ask me and a desk jockey to boot. I'll bet this putz will give us a lift to the airport though, and buy us a ticket to Berlin. We're in Valentin. We're going home."

Nieting stared silently at Koeppan, unable to resist grinning at Emil's routine and when a chuckle escaped, surprising Koeppan, who, clearly annoyed when he entered the room, became even more so at Nieting's blatant disrespect.

"Your case will be evaluated in Berlin, Herr Professor, your mental condition, that is. The report from the American authorities expressed the opinion that on top of your communist views and anti-government agitation, you have lost your mind."

"By all means, Koeppan," said Nieting, coldly. "An examination, if conducted swiftly and efficiently, may be acceptable without my taking legal action. I've broken no laws and have had no hearing. This expulsion, although quite in accord with my wishes, is not without questions regarding legality."

"That's my boy," said Emil, clapping his hands and cackling.

"You don't seem to understand the gravity of your circumstances," said Koeppan. "You are a suspect in a murder investigation. Even if you weren't involved in this disgusting underworld intrigue, and there is no doubt that you were close to it, Nieting, close enough to be culpable, compromised morally in the very least, you would not have a leg to stand on."

Koeppan ran his eyes over Nieting's bloody trousers and smirked.

"Legal leg, that is," he said.

"That may or may not be true," said Nieting. "As I said, your suggestion is in accord with my wishes."

"Very well, then," replied Koeppan. "There remains the question of the future, Herr Professor, when you return to Berlin. You were dismissed by the Free University for the same offenses that have caused the Americans to expel you. I am sure you realize there are elements among the students that continue to disrupt the operations of the university. We have far too many agitators stoking the flames as it is. You influence has already been far more pernicious than we intend to accept in the future. I believe your friend and former student, Herr Dutschke will soon discover that our government will not accept sedition, not from students and not from their professors."

"What is your question, Koeppan?" said Nieting.

"What are your intentions, Herr Professor?"

"You have no reason to answer the prick," said Emil. "Keep your trap shut. He's here to take us off the Americans' hands. He can fuck himself."

"Perhaps the comparison with Dutschke is not apt," said Koeppan. "After all, you are an intellectual and he is a man of action. However, you are equally dangerous. No, I believe a writer of your capacity is the more heinous type of subversive. We have no need of opportunists of any sort. One Meinhoff is enough. I insist upon knowing your intentions. What will you do when you are in Germany?"

"Don't say a fucking word, Val," said Emil. "Look at him squirm. Look at his eye twitch."

"I assure you professor, you can be detained on psychological grounds if you indicate a proclivity towards disruption."

"Quiet, Valentin," said Emil. "Don't respond. No one knows you're crazy but you and I."

"Your silence speaks loudly, professor," said Koeppan. "You are arrogant and smug, just as your last employers stated you would be. I would not be so foolish as to take your safety for granted if I were you. One can easily end up in the same condition as your colleague, the poet Snellman. We are aware that you've had meetings with Snellman this past week."

"I didn't tell him," said Emil.

"Are you a drug addict, professor?" asked Koeppan. "Perhaps you had some involvement in Snellman's death. You do seem to keep company with drug addicts. You could easily end as Snellman has. No one would question another dope fiend found dead. I won't be any more explicit. You have been warned."

"Don't be shocked, Valentin," said Emil, "Your friend, the poet is free now. There is nothing more they can do to him, or to us."

"We will discuss these issues again, professor," said Koeppan. "I assure you that we will. Your problems are far more acute than you seem to understand. However, you are a citizen of the Bundesrepublik and the Americans want you out of their country immediately. We have no choice but to take you back. Not as a matter of courtesy to the Americans, but of official protocol. I wouldn't consider that a victory, either. It may be the worst news you've ever received."

"By the way, Koeppan," said Nieting. "You have been to university, correct?"

"Of course," said Koeppan. "I graduated from Humboldt University with superb marks. I received my Baccalaureate in . . ."

"Catch that, Valentin?" said Emil. "He hesitates to say the year. Nazi pig."

"Baccalaureate?" replied Nieitng. "I trust that is the minimum level required by our consulate?"

Emil screamed with laughter, holding his belly and shaking all over with his mouth wide open.

"My god, Valentin, you educated prick, you're a chip off the old block. That bag of shit is about to explode. Don't go too far, we need the dirty bastard to get us home."

When Koeppan finally left the room, Nieting fell into the chair, exhausted. He'd put a show on for the benefit of his father, but had taxed himself greatly.

"Take it easy son, rest, rest, we have a long trip in front of us."

Nieting and his father waited several hours, uninterrupted in their explorations of Val's life, speaking in quiet tones, awash in the light of truthful remembrance where even the fire of past suffering cools, refreshes, until Estelle entered the room with Detective Savino sometime in midafternoon. Koeppan would be along shortly, Savino told Nieting, to take him into custody in the name of the German government and place him on an early evening flight to Berlin. When Savino left, Estelle changed Nieting's dressing and bid him farewell with misty eyes, unable to illicit any more than the most formal expression of gratitude.

A black Mercedes Benz transported Nieting to the airport where Koeppan transferred his charge to another German in a dark suit who he identified as a Mr. Ludendorff. Ludendorff was a business man, or so Nieting was told, who had agreed to assist him back to Berlin. He eyed Nieting suspiciously and announced he would be seated in the row behind him on the airplane and that Nieting had better cooperate or he would have more trouble than he could handle. Koeppan added that

Ludendorff was an ex-military man and would know exactly how to handle any funny business. They all continued to the boarding area where
Koeppan instructed Nieting to sit. He walked off with Ludendorff, stopping ten or so yards away and conversing in rather jovial tones, finally
shaking hands whereupon Koeppan departed. Ludendorff took a seat
a good distance from Nieting and began to examine papers he'd taken
from a leather case, perhaps Nieting's dossier, raising his head from time
to time to check on the condition of his charge.

"Couldn't ask for more, could we?" said Emil. "Businessman my ass.
If he is, the business is assassination. Fucking fascist prick. I wonder
where he was in 38. I don't suppose he'd like to answer that one. At least
he thinks he's too good to speak to us. Thank god for that."

Later, as the jetliner rose into the air, Nieting peered out the window at
the smoldering rubble of the city disappearing beneath the thick garment
of gray smoke of the fires of the Revolution. A woman in the row behind
Nieting, sitting next to Ludendorff, said," I think we're the first flight back
on the usual path. For the last week they've had to divert. We're directly
over the riot area. They were shooting at airplanes, if you can believe
that."

Ludendorff grunted and shuffled his papers. Emil peeked between
the seats, shook his head disapprovingly and winked at Val.

When Nieting reached Berlin there was a small but insistent group of
friends there to offer assistance. Hans Gartenbauer, having received
news of the mysterious death of Arnold Snellman in a Venice alleyway,
was anxious to attend to his friend Nieting. There was Oscar Worst and
the MerzKraft circle, a hand full of old men and women, survivors of
National Socialism who had known Val for most of his life. But Nieting
was silent, even among those who expressed concern for his welfare and
offered their support during his convalescence. He wasn't completely
mute, rather he was distant, not forthcoming. What had happened in
California among the Negros of Watts was unknown to his friends. The
only information they had regarding the American trip was sketchy and

based entirely on the testimony Koeppan had received from Detective Savino which amounted to no more evidence than Nieting's presence at a motel frequented by drug addicts and prostitutes on the same night a prostitute was murdered. They were told that he had been victimized by Negro hoodlums after wandering into the Negro section to proselytize his communistic views during the now world famous Watt's Riots. Knowing their friend's intellectual temperament and academic orientation, they dismissed this story, originating solely from sources within the Los Angeles Police Department, as a neofacist fabrication, suspecting instead that it was the authorities that had victimized Nieting, silenced him for purely political reasons. In their view, there was no doubt that this was the case. However, their friend was unwilling or unable to corroborate their theory or give any details whatsoever regarding his experiences in America.

Nieting was reinstated in the flat on the Zossener Strasse where he'd lived with Uncle Max and Heinrich, thrust back into a former life among the possessions of his two old guardians. Nieting had sealed the flat after Max's death, had left it as it was during the last decade of Max and Heinrich's life, planning to go through the contents upon his return from America. He'd insisted that the task be put off out of necessity, so that he might pursue the American adventure, yet Oscar suspected it was sadness and perhaps fear that made him reluctant to sift through the artifacts of their lives.

During the first month after Nieting's return to Berlin, there were many visits from old friends, colleagues from the Free University, ex-students and the old timers in the MerzKraft circle, until Nieting's silence drove them away. This was his intent. He no longer wished to converse with anyone besides Emil, who had taken to visiting his son only when there was no one else at the flat. It was rude, he said, to carry on a conversation between them and ignore guests who were loyal friends, who truly cared for Val. After all, Nieting was able to struggle through only the most basic pleasantries and beyond that would sit silently, his gaze drifting inevitably away to some corner of the room. His behavior did not offend or incur unkind judgments from his guests, clearly something terrible had happened in America, most likely some kind of poisoning, a chemical or biological agent introduced into his body by the American and German police agencies, no doubt working in concert. It was impossible to know if Professor V. Nieting would ever return to the man he had been before the American journey. Nevertheless, Hans and Oscar diligently cared for him, visiting even after everyone else had ceased visiting, arranging for a nurse to see he was bathed regularly and a housekeeper to maintain order in the flat and make his meals. For months, Nieting lived in an isolated world of his choosing, unaware of the efforts of his friends to organize his comfortable existence. He was a cooperative patient for the most part, eating when directed to eat, allowing the dressing on his wounds to be changed, passively accepting sponge baths from the nurse. The only area in which he was recalcitrant was the cutting of his hair and shaving of his beard, both of which he refused. By the end of the third month of convalesce, his hair and beard had grown long, giving him the appearance of a towering emaciated Zarathustra with glowing eyes and no words. That he communicated exclusively with nods and rarely spoke added a mysterious aura, as though he possessed some great truth. Hans and Oscar had always admired his thought, had believed in his brilliance. They'd always anticipated great things. Their program now was to bring him out, to reignite the fire of his intellect. Yet Nieting remained immune to the stimulation offered by his friends.

They could not know that Nieting had not fled them, rather he was ensconced in another world, far richer, more rare and rewarding than the world they wished to tempt him back too. To stand upon a mountain with his father at his side and examine the events of his life played out on the vast valley floor below, beneath the misty clouds of madness, with courage, with acceptance, brought a sense of peace he'd never before known. He wandered with Emil on Berlin streets as the bombs fell. They haunted the ruins in search of food and discovered corpses beneath the rubble. They became delirious with hunger and with the cold. They walked shoeless until their feet bled. Nieting observed himself living as a child, hiding that he was a Jew from Germans and being cursed for being German by the victorious invaders. The joy of loving his mother and mourning for her, of seeing himself crushed in the filth of war and grieving, weeping as he watched himself weep, stroking the head of the sad boy, or was it Emil who stroked the poor child? These visions brought a profound stillness.

One day in late January, five months after Nieting's return to Berlin, Hans arrived at the flat in a state of high excitement. He was breathless as he spoke.

"Valentin, have you heard? Someone detonated a bomb at the SDS teach-in at the university this afternoon. No one was injured, thank goodness. Only some windows and furniture were destroyed. Now, our dear Rektor has banned the next teach-in at the university this Friday. The students are furious. The Rektor is attempting to crush open debate. He is excluding free speech from the campus, Valentin, do you understand? The students will never accept this. I promise you. Those were our students. They remain our students. We've taught them a thing or two, haven't we?"

Nieting's eyes flashed and he said nothing. In the days to come, however, Hans did not relent. He kept trying to bring Nieting out of his private world, force his engagement in a revolution he'd helped precipitate. Hans would often read the columns of Ulrike Meinhoff, the radical Christian pacifist and anti-nuclear activist aloud to Nieting. Meinhoff's writing was succinct and daring, reminding Hans of the speeches of Malcolm X, so clear and direct one felt joy and surprise at hearing the truth couched so starkly. The readings however, elicited no response from Nieting. He appeared thoughtful enough, yet one had no idea what it was he was thinking. Oscar also tried to stimulate his young friend, leaving newspapers and back issues of MerzKraft at strategic points in the flat turned to provocative articles and sensational headlines. When he would return on his next visit, the papers would be neatly stacked on a shelf by the housekeeper and Nieting unwilling to discuss their contents or anything else. It was Hans and Oscar, more than anyone who grieved over their friend's retreat from the present, from real life, and most tragically from productive activity.

Nevertheless, Nieting's wounds healed well over the ensuing months. He gradually regained strength. He'd never possessed a robust constitution and had become more austere during his convalescence, yet he was clearly on the mend. His inner well being was discernable in his appearance, encouraging his friends, yet perplexing them as he became no more forthcoming, remained disinterested in all but what must be going on inside, in his mind. Yet, he had attained a stability of sorts. One day in June, when Emil failed to visit the flat, Nieting was able to maneuver his internal world with confidence nevertheless. In fact, his joy may have been greater, acting on his own on the precipitous heights of remembrance. Perhaps Emil was no longer required as a guide as Val lived his life over and over, savoring the incomprehensible truth. With each reliving the diamond center grew more brilliant. The day after his father failed to show, Nieting's sense of independence was verified. Emil appeared suddenly, seated at a writing table. He finished writing a note and turned toward little Val, smiling sweetly.

"I'll leave you now, son," he said. "You've no need of a father's protection any longer. You are a grown man. I'm proud of you and I'm grateful we could journey together after all, after all the adversity we've seen. We have shared our lives. It is because of you that we have. We will remain connected in time. I do love you, son."

When Emil left that day he was gone for good. He'd departed, never to return. It was a strange coincidence that Hans and Oscar arrived later that afternoon at the same time. The two always came when they could and rarely crossed paths. They greeted each other affectionately on the street with a long embrace. They'd come to be friends in their service to Nieting and were comrades in much else besides. Revolution was truly dawning like a great sunrise. That Nieting would soon join them was their deepest hope. That afternoon, they had reason to believe he might. They were shocked by the man they encountered. Nieting appeared glad to see them, shaking their hands as they entered. He offered tea and giggled with embarrassment when he realized he did not know where the tea pot or the cups or the tea were stored. All three men laughed shyly.

It was as if Nieting had not seen his friends for a long time, as if he'd just returned from a long journey. That Nieting could engage in such pleasantries was a great step forward. Hans and Oscar beamed, winking at one another each time Nieting turned away. They were no less enthralled when their friend slipped back into silent preoccupation. There was no need to go all the way at once. Their friend had started his way back. Hans and Oscar waved their arms about, explaining the news of the day. Nieting flashed his eyes as they spoke.

"The students have had enough, Valentin," said Oscar. "Tell him, Hans, tell him quickly."

"They're going to march on the university, regardless of the Rektor's threats. Tomorrow they will march en mass and take over the Henry Ford Building."

"Take over, Valentin," said Oscar. "They will occupy the place. Shut down the university's business."

Hans and Oscar laughed as the corners of Nieting's mouth seemed to curl slightly.

"The fucking Henry Ford Building," shouted Oscar. "That fucking Nazi fellow traveler is going to have his namesake occupied by anarchists and communists, by our dear students."

"Yes," said Hans, "Tomorrow afternoon they will march. Their route will travel past your flat on the way to the university. You will be able to see them pass by. The administration has no idea what they're up to. They're going to hold teach-ins like those in Berkeley. There will be thousands of students, Valentin. Your students will be among them. Go to the window when you hear them go by. Show your encouragement. They'll be looking for you. Your influence is part of what is animating their determination."

"You deserve to see your students, Valentin," said Oscar. "And, they deserve your acknowledgment."

The excitement of the day's events and the spark in their friend's eyes, still smoldering inside, caused Han's and Oscar's passions to overflow. After months of silence, the movement of eyes seemed akin to vocalization. They choked back tears as they discussed the irresistible force of the students. When time came for them to depart, Nieting became still more animated, embracing each, kissing their cheeks, thanking them for their attention. Hans and Oscar wept as they walked down the stairs to the street. Nieting would rejoin his comrades after all, they thought. He would begin to write again. Professor V. Nieting was not irrevocably lost. He would return and join the struggle. Neither man could have known that what appeared to be a great step towards robustness, health and normalcy was a manifestation of completeness, an ending rather than a beginning. His long beard and blue eyes set deep in the sockets and the white skin appearing translucent and stretched over his skull, gave him the look of a holy man, child-like and sage-like, earnest to the point of agony. Yet his gaze remained fixed on a world that existed within.

Nieting heard Han's and Oscar's voices shouting farewell on the street and imaged them hurrying in different directions, excited and determined, willingly caught up in the fight of the students, animated by their thirst for revolution. He smiled at the thought. Hans' voice echoed one last time, trailing off into the sound of traffic. Emil was gone. Nieting was truly alone. The thought frightened him, yet he did not hesitate to stroll through the Kurfurstendamm, watching himself walking on the opposite side of the street. The once expansive Kurfurstendamm had become an alley not ten yards wide at the foot of mountains of debris, crumbled brick, twisted pipe and splintered beams. He crept along, looking out for soldiers, stopping to climb the rubble at the sign of an object that might be traded for bread. He scaled the slope with amazing dexterity, bloody knees, *poor child, yes I see you, you are innocent, no more than a small animal driven by hunger, lost child, my dear lost child.*

Nieting returned to the flat at the sound of the key in the door. The housekeeper had arrived to prepare his supper. He surprised her with a smile and a cheerful greeting. He ate heartily of the food she prepared and thanked her warmly when she left for the night.

The next day around mid morning, after the housekeeper left, he began to hear the trombone again. It was Kid Auger serenading him as he always had, distilling the beautiful sadness inside Nieting into velvet rivers that flowed about the room endlessly, rich colors moving in zig zagging patterns along the floor, walls and ceiling, glowing, radiating warmth. Breathtaking vistas shown between the streams of colors, dark green forests, white tipped mountains, endless blue skies. Auger's trombone played the role of heartbeat. He had entered the room as a family member would, without greeting, simply going about his business of manifesting the pulse of existence, creating visual images of continuity, projecting the shapeliness of mind onto the walls of the flat.

There was the pistol, locked in Uncle Max's chest of drawers. It had been there all along, unbeknownst to anyone other than Nieting. Now, it sat on the writing desk. Nieting noticed the gun as he marched past the desk time and again to Auger's jaunty march beat. He eyed it across the room when Auger played a slow blues and Nieting rested in his uncle's chair. Perhaps Emil had placed it there. Perhaps he'd come in, not wishing to disturb his son, had done the service of retrieving the gun and had left unnoticed. The gesture was sweet. His father no longer had any desire to be pushy or presumptuous. His boy had indeed grown into a man. Nieting flushed with affection for his father. He loved the gun as well. How natural everything is when one can stand up to the truth.

Nieting, too went about his business, moving back and forth between the past and the flat on the Zossener Strasse – the flat was no longer of the present, it had moved elsewhere. Each time he returned to the flat from his wanderings Auger's trombone was sounding softly like a warm fire, a welcoming embrace, reassuring, sending him off again, back into the other realm. He spent the morning laughing with his mother. It was really more a vision of her laughing seen from the bed of an infant. She was young and healthy, humming gaily as she wrapped her arms around her son's tiny body. It was nearly too much for Nieting to bear, more difficult than seeing her ravaged by the filth of war. His weeping brought him back to the flat. He found himself standing in the center of the living room, his face wet with tears. For once, Auger could offer no solace, yet Nieting knew he was acting as he should, as he must, grieving for the irreconcilable, the undecipherable. This was where wisdom resided.

At midafternoon, Nieting was awakened from an unintended slumber by the booming whine of police sirens bouncing off the façades of the buildings lining the Habbetrasse. He'd fallen asleep in Uncle Max's chair, opposite the windows facing the street. The sirens jolted him awake, knocked him into the present. Someone on the street shouted into a loud speaker, short unintelligible barks. Nieting closed his eyes. Returning to the real was one of the pitfalls of being alive. These intrusions were common and for the time being must be endured.

He heard an electronic clicking sound, apparently from the loudspeaker, and the growling of a large motor turning over. Several moments of silence followed, a pause that caused Nieting to sit up and listen. Then, a roaring sound rose up in a wave, thousands of voices, singing and chanting, just as Hans said would happen. The students were on the march to the university to take over the Henry Ford building, to teach themselves how to build a new society, to tear down the old unchanging order by force if necessary, by any means. It was the joy and anger of the Revolution flooding the Zossener Strasse. Nieting hurried to throw open the windows and stare down at the street. The students were there, the force of their presence hit him like a blast of pure oxygen. A trumpet called from below and voices shouted, 'Long live the Revolution.' They filled the street like water rushing, filling every space from one side to the other. They strode arm in arm, beautiful young comrades, carrying banners, some moving solemnly, deliberately, as others pranced joyously. Nieting swooned in the fresh air. His work was done, but THE work was beginning afresh before his eyes. He held his hands aloft and clenched his fist as a passing contingent thirty strong shouted together, "Long live professor Nieting," greeting him with fists thrust into the air. They were his students. No doubt Hans had told them he would be watching for them, that he would be with them always. Nieting listed forward as if the voices had grabbed him, were pulling him towards them.

He nearly tumbled over the window box, landing on his elbows in the dirt of the planter and pushed himself up. He waved to the students and his name came miraculously back in dozens of voices before it melted into the single voice surging onward.

Nieting stepped from the window as the noise outside intensified. Even Auger joined in. He was there in the room in the flat on the Zossener Strasse. He'd come all the way from New Orleans. He didn't look at Nieting, he simply played, punctuating each step of each member of the multitude with driving tailgate trombone beats. He danced, as well, shouting with his body, *The Revolution will not die, cannot perish until every child, woman, man lives in peace and health and liberty.* That was it. There were no more words. Nieting held the pistol. The noise on the street rose higher, so loud it was inside and outside of his body. The air congealed with the voices as Auger stomped his feet and played, twisting his torso, thrusting the trombone slide to the sky and swinging it down inches from the ground. He danced around the room weaving the sound of the horn in and out of the noise on the street, drowned out for an instant, then emerging, pushing the rhythm, a rope tossed, a lifeline amidst the cacophony of voices and sirens and barking loudspeakers and in the center the trajectory of a single bullet leading like Bolden's cornet into the overflowing of the unending Revolution.

The Lost Song Found

"Look at those palms trees, man. See, that's why I always dug California. If you just raise your head up it looks like you're in paradise."

"No shit, but you'd better keep your eyes down or you're gonna cut yourself on all that glass."

The two men, one of whom carried a trumpet in a black case and the other, an alto saxophone in a cloth bag, stared at two LAPD officers staring at them from a patrol car on the corner of Avalon and 51st Street as they crossed the intersection and entered South Park.

"They didn't learn nothing, did they?" said the man with the trumpet.

"Whad ya expect?" said the other. "We learned plenty, though. Things are different now. Won't be too long before they know how different."

In the park it was a typical Saturday afternoon, except that the atmosphere was more festive than usual, as children, set free after eleven days of war played and laughed with abandon like they'd been turned loose in kid heaven. The streets of south Los Angeles still smoldered and the debris-filled main thoroughfares were hazardous, particularly to children. Yet, for all the destruction around them, the people in the park seemed happy. There was a sense of celebration. For days they'd suffered death, countless injuries and thousands of arrests yet the people appeared as if they'd won a victory. In the fields of the park friends met who hadn't seen each other since before Marquette Frye, his mother and his brother were arrested by Office Minikus setting off the great conflagration. People greeted one another with handshakes and embraces. The two men carrying the instruments gabbed as they walked past groups of folks, responding several times to their names called.

"Michael, I heard you got shot. God damned good to see you, baby."

"Good to see you, brother."

"Bobby, our band gonna play today?"

"I don't know. Seems like a good chance though."

"We got to hear our band."

Life set back on its daily course piqued the awareness of the two men, stimulated the appreciation of what they each possessed and quickened their steps. They smiled in anticipation. They knew where their friends would be. No one had called a meeting or a rehearsal, yet everyone knew where to go and that they would there today. Ahead, beneath a large Maple tree, twenty or so musicians and their friends milled and buzzed about, voices animated, instruments out and shining in the sun. It looked like a party, everyone happy to see everyone else, holding horns at the ready, drums poised, talking, talking, talking. A van had pulled up on the grass next to the Maple tree and a gas generator rumbled inside the open back doors as two cops watched from a patrol car in the parking lot, scowling, yet not making a move. A young man struck an electric guitar, chopped a rhythm and the group lit up like the juice from the generator in the van flowed through the guitar right through all of them. The drummers, scattered about, joined in from where they sat, casually, one after one, entering the pulse, a complex congregation yet a heartbeat none the less. No one else stopped what they were doing. The talking went on and shouts of welcome when someone joined the group as a few lay on their backs beneath the tree in the sultry heat heads propped on instrument cases and others joked and chatted with the growing number of children arriving, drawn by the drums, taken in by the pulse of the universal body. It was joyous. It was what they did. Was this what the rebellion was about? Was the rebellion an extension of this? No one spoke about it in those terms at this particular junction in time, although there is no doubt the philosophical implications of the prior week's events, implicit and explicit, were, had been and would continue to be explored. It was theirs. It was what they did. It was joyous.

The pulse was their substance, all their minds projecting out, a balm for the flesh. What the young man said was true. If you looked straight up, past the residue and stink of smoke, away from the rubble of war and cop cars watching, palm heads languished against the blue sky of heaven.

The guitar player stopped playing when he greeted a young woman with a kiss, smiled and spoke to her two girl friends, shaking their hands like it must be a first introduction. His laying out altered the rhythm, but did not cause it to abate, rather it morphed into another groove, a hand gently stroking a naked back on a luscious bed inside the heart, bright and warm in the sunlight.

A young man pushed a wheel chair carrying an old man along the paved path towards the group beneath the Maple tree.

"Hey, Rene."

"Good to see you, brother."

"You bring your drum?"

"Yeah, I got it on my back."

"He got his great grandpops."

"What's happening Floyd?"

The old man nodded as one of the group approached, assisting Rene as he pushed the chair onto the uneven lawn.

"Hello, Mr. Lawson."

The old man nodded again.

"Great to see ya, Morris," said Rene, beaming, and the two embraced and proceeded to push the chair into the shade of the Maple.

"Pop's got something to tell you," said Rene.

"Is that right, Mr. Lawson?"

"You can call call me Floyd, Morris," said the old man. "I ain't no undertaker."

"Why thank you, Floyd," said Triplett, chuckling. "You know when I was a kid I used to walk past your house every day going to school, carrying my trombone in that case and you'd call out, 'how's my fine young musicianer this morning,' and man, I'd feel it all over, just thrilled. I thought, I am that, wow, a musician. I'm a musician. I think

I walked past more than once just to hear you say it. That's why I call you Mr. Lawson to this day. You're still that grown-up man, Gerald's dad, up on that porch making me feel good, feel like I was something, a musician."

The old man closed his eyes and laughed a big laugh with very little movement.

"You was a good boy," he said. "I've seen all kind in my day and I knew you just had it. That's all."

"Pops been asking me everyday, 'take me to see Morris,'" said Rene. "'I got something to give to Morris. He wouldn't tell me what it was for days."

Rene looked at his great grandfather and the old man said, "Go on, son."

"Pops couldn't sleep all during this last week," said Rene. "It wasn't just all the noise going down, helicopters, cop cars, fire engines, guns, cars screeching, bullhorns, explosions, shit I couldn't sleep myself for all that racket. But just knowing what was happening – you know he don't go out much, he's eighty nine now, but he was watching on the television and he could hear it out there and he lives off Avalon and he could look off the front porch and catch some of the action so he understood full well what was going on. Well, he must have got pretty upset."

"Okay, okay, Rene," said Floyd. "Thank you, son."

Rene stood behind the wheel chair gripping the handles. Floyd reached back and squeezed his hand.

"I'll do my own talking now," he said. "See Morris, all that stuff got me to thinking. Wasn't the first or the second time I seen it happen. I been around a bit and I started to remembering. All kinds of memories come back. There was a song once made up about just such a thing. We had a song, but I done forgot the words, so help me, they're gone, but I do remember Robert Charles."

A few others in the group had turned towards the three men and were listening to several conversations at once, when a middle aged man with sparse gray hair on his head, sunglasses and a pointy goatee remarked.

"Robert Charles? I'm from New Orleans and my grand dad told us about Robert Charles when I was a kid. He was a newsboy or something and the pigs came by and told him to get up off his front steps where he was setting and when the pig came round again Robert Charles was still setting there. They tried to take him in and he hold up with a rifle and killed a whole bunch of white people."

"Is that right?" said Floyd, shaking his head. "We had a song about Robert Charles. I played it once or so myself. Wasn't the kind of song had to many venues you could sing it."

There were almost a dozen listeners now and they broke into laughter at Floyd's remark. Floyd smiled at the response.

"Yes, it was a real trouble breeder," he said. "The song started coming to me last week. Like I said, it wasn't the first time I lay in a bed listening to those kinds of things going on outside. I was in New Orleans when Robert Charles had his ordeal, then I lit out quick as I could cause they was killing all the black folks they could get their hands on."

"No shit." "For real." "God damn motherfuckers" "It ain't changed at all."

Nearly all the musicians, all the people beneath the Maple tree were facing Floyd now, listening to him speak.

Triplett said, "Why don't all you in front sit down. Give Mr. Lawson some air. Spread out. Good. Go on, Floyd."

The old man flashed his eyes. He was on and the air was electric.

"Well, there was this New Orleans boy, a cornet player, who put a melody down one time. We was all together and I commenced to singing some lyrics, just whatever come into my head about the situation we was all in, all hiding out, laying low cause the night riders was running the country roads looking for Robert Charles. We was all together in a kind of cabin, hid real good. It was built against a rise in the land just about underground and we spent the night in there."

The old man rubbed his stubbled face with the palm of his hand.

"Seems like more of its coming back to me now," he said. "I spose cause I'm telling you'all."

"Take your time, Mr. Lawson," said Triplett.

"I had my ol'geetah with me, naturally," said Floyd. "That's how I made my living in them days. Never did take kindly to no work."

A wave of laughter hit the group, then silence.

"We was sitting around in the dark. An old black woman brought us in, each and every one of us there that night was brought in by this woman. I can see her face now. She filled that cabin with stragglers she found out on the road and brought us to safety. How that woman did it – she was skinny as a reed and wiry, black like night – how she could move around in that country like she did in the pitch dark is something I never could figure out, but she did it and she brought us to this safe house and I commenced to playing after awhile and making up words about our situation which meant I was singing about Robert Charles cause he was the reason we was there, because he stood up to the white man and was gonna die for it if he wasn't dead already. I started to singing and this boy with a cornet, from New Orleans . . ."

"Was it Buddy Bolden, Mr. Floyd?" asked a young woman.

"I couldn't truly say who he was," replied Floyd. "I don't remember. I wasn't naturally from those parts and only met the fellah that one time. He was a strong looking young guy. Looked like a city boy. He sure could play some horn."

"I"ll bet it was Bolden," came a voice.

"Well, he just played this melody over my guitar. I think I was hitting the hardest, meanest notes I could find cause that's how I felt. Now, I don't mean to say I was hitting them hard and mean, there was women and children in that cabin, but the notes I was hitting had that meaning and everyone, down to the smallest child knew what I was saying. New Orleans, he commenced to playing a melody so sweet over the bitter notes I was striking. That was my style in them days. That's how I felt about the world. I wanted my songs to burn cause this is what life was like. I was young and full of it."

Sounds of amusement and recognition rippled through the group.

"Yes, sir."

"We understand."

"Tell it like it is, Mr. Lawson."

"Go on, Floyd."

"I knew things was different in that cabin," said Floyd. "I still had my style, but I was trying to hit it soft so the strings rung like bells. I wanted the sound to hang in the air real light and not so hard. I was trying to soften things, but the notes and the rhythm, they had my rage and I expect everyone else's rage in that room. Then the cornet played over top of me and it was so sweet, like that part in a person that'll always be like a child, if you're lucky and they don't kill it in you. I do know one thing, you'd have to be brand new like a baby to believe that any thing that pretty could still be made in the world. Remember, we was all huddled in the dark on the cold clay floor so the night riders wouldn't get us. How could anything beautiful come of that? That terrible situation we was in, not just in that room but everywhere I'd ever been in my life was in those notes. Robert Charles wasn't no different from so many others, only he was rare cause he fought back. He wasn't the only one fought back but he was rare how he did it. Robert Charles was a brave man. Real brave. He sure done them Mau Mau proud."

The group under the tree erupted into laughter and applause, startling the old man.

"We all know how that turns out," he said. "Robert Charles went down hard and that was in the guitar too, tough lessons to take, deep blues and New Orleans was laying a melody over the top of my guitar like a mother humming to her newborn. Those two things don't go together, they got to cancel themselves out but they didn't. The guitar and the cornet melted into one thing, more real life, more like a real man and woman feel than any music I ever heard before or since."

"Do you remember the song?"

Floyd snapped back, annoyed and sighs of relief floated from the group.

"Of course, I do," he said. "Why the hell you think I made Rene cart me out here?"

There was laughter beneath the Maple tree, hushed chatter, then silence.

"Guitar man, let me have that guitar," said Floyd.

"It's electric, Pops," said Rene.

"I know," replied Floyd. "I'm eighty nine, not one hundred and eighty nine. Turn it down is all. Turn it down low. Hey Morris, my fine young musicianer, pick up one of those trombones. Guitar man, first I lay out your part then I'll play the melody for Morris. All you others, listen. I'm passing this along to you all now. This is it. I can't do this more than one time. I don't have it in me. I'm fulling my responsibility to my brothers and sisters in that cabin so many years ago and to their children. That's who you are, so listen good."

The old man's fingers fumbled at first, yet in moments the twisted hands, nearly a century old, squeezed what he wanted from the instrument, slipping into a rhythmic pattern, simple in appearance yet intricate in its implications, a basic beat, a distillation of polyrhythms he circled again and again allowing it to sink into the breathless group. Then he handed the instrument back to its owner who tried to emulate what he'd heard. At first, the young man played some kind of funk rhythm, *chucka chucka chucka* and everyone laughed. He looked surprised at the group's reaction. He was doing his best. Floyd sang the part in a low raspy voice and the young man tried again and failed again and failed several times until with the old man's correcting and encouraging he arrived momentarily at a satisfactory rendition. As long as Floyd counted, the guitar player had it, but when he ceased, the beat altered like a piece of twisted rubber reverting to its original shape.

The musicians watched attentively with complete sympathy for their band mate as Floyd, who had become overtaxed, signaled Rene to take over. The entire group clapped along with Rene, the drummers joining in and even the large, ever growing contingent of children joined the clapping, the combination finally receiving the nod of approval from Floyd.

"Now, all you drummers and you children that was clapping, you all go over with Rene. Rene go out onto that field there and work on it a bit. All you other musicians stay here. Guitar man, can I borrow your axe one more time? Morris, what say we try the melody."

Floyd paused for a moment, listening for the song, then slowly sounded the notes, lining them up, looking them over, dismissing one here, welcoming another there, finally subjecting them to the breath, teasing out the phrasing as the musicians watched, rapt. To them, Floyd was revealing a great truth, a truth to be added to all the great truths, lost, found, lost again and found only to be submerged once more. Floyd was proving their most precious conviction, that the music was alive inside of them, that it might be obscured or hidden but would never be lost. Triplett played back the melody.

"Like this?"

"No, like this."

"This?"

"You hitting a wrong note and the phrasing ain't right."

"Stay with me, Floyd."

"I ain't going nowhere."

It took a short time for Triplett to get the melody, at which point the horns, two trumpets, four saxophones, baritone, tenor, alto, soprano, and another trombone, stood up and following Triplett's lead and a correction or two from Floyd, worked through the melody in unison. When the nod came from Floyd, Triplett said, "We need Rene and the others back here," and a dozen children shot off into the ball field shouting for the return of the great rhythm section. When the entire group assembled, Triplett asked Rene to lead the drummers one more time and once again the rhythm had fled, transformed into something the Magnificent Montague might have played on his radio show and not what Floyd have initially shown them.

"Damn it, boy," said Floyd. "You done lost it again. No, no, that ain't it. Now listen."

Floyd sang the part and a small boy standing at his elbow clapped along, nailing each beat and each agonizing hesitation on the dime.

"What's your name?" said Floyd.

"Soloman."

"Show us the beat, Soloman. Yes, good, that's it. This young man is a natural musicianer. Everybody, listen to what Soloman is laying down."

Soloman hit the beat and the group followed, first all the children, then Rene and the drummers grinning.

"Don't fall into that backbeat now," said Floyd. "This ain't gut bucket and it ain't Motor City."

Floyd winked at Triplett and Triplett motioned to the horns to get ready, raising his hand then dropping it on the down beat and they blew. The sound of the ensemble surprised everyone, including the players themselves. There was a sadness to the melody and a sweetness that coaxed a wide vibrato from the horns, a full throated lament like the last song one might ever hear, a melody that could sum up all of life's travails and cap them with a kiss, a final sweet embrace. Yet, they played the song with blistering verve and power so even the drummers stopped, hesitated until Floyd said in a near whisper, "c'mon drummers. You all is taking the part of my guitar. We need you too." Rene led the drummers in, slipping beneath the melody as the children clapped time, some landing perfectly on target and others hitting here and there like glittering rain. The horns eased down onto the rhythm gently like they were straddling a wild horse. The sudden creation, the instant existence, seeming to come out of nowhere, of such a mass of shapes and colors, astounded everyone and filled every corner of the park. A hundred children crowded around and grown-ups came over or watched from picnic tables and blankets spread across the grass.

As they played, the energy rose higher and higher. Floyd and Triplett could do nothing but watch. *The Robert Charles Song* was alive. It had a life and a mind of its own, as if Floyd's rhythm and the New Orleans cornet player's melody were components of some ancient alchemical formula interacting or was a living thing released from a box, which it was, the box being the old man's mind. Just like that with no signal from anyone, the brass players and the drummers and the children took off across the field, kicking up dust on the diamond, filling the outfield with scores of tiny second liners, dancing past picnickers, the sound vibrating everyone's flesh.

"Our band's doing their thing."

Floyd Lawson and Morris Triplett watched the celebration, the rebirth of *The Robert Charles Song* from the shade of the Maple tree. Floyd winced as the rhythm morphed and Rene struggled to hold it right. When he saw that Triplett noticed his reaction, he chuckled.

"I think that song was only played the right way once," he said. "I guess that's the way it's supposed to be."

"We'll work on it, Floyd," said Triplett. "I promise we'll make you proud."

"Hell, it don't matter," said Floyd. "Things change, everything changes. We ain't trying to keep things from changing, we're trying to keep hold of the thread, keep what has value so it can help us change like we need to and still be ourselves."

"That's the way our music is," said Triplett. "Always remaking itself. Just like anything that's living."

"Amen," said Floyd.

"It was real good of you, Floyd," said Triplett. "It was the right thing to do, bringing that song down here today."

"I had to do it," said Floyd. "I had to do it for those folks in that cabin, for New Orleans the cornet man. He might have been Buddy Bolden, I don't know. I had to do it for that old woman. She changed my life."

"She changed your life?" said Triplett.

"Yes sir, she did. They all did. Morris, I was a hard living man in them days. Riding the rails, drinking, chasing women, playing music for change. Seemed one way or the other, the white man always had me leaving town on the run. It wasn't no way to live but it was all I could see to do. Until that old woman brought us together. She saved a heap of us from the noose. I can tell you that. They was stopping every train going into town and taking any black man they could find. I woulda been doomed for sure if she didn't wave me off that train, if she hadn't took me to that safe house. I recollect, the night we made *The Robert Charles Song*, she was talking about black people being one thing, like a big family . . . no, that ain't it . . I'll be damned, you know she said we was a nation. She said black people is a nation. Hell, that's what the youngsters are saying today and this was back how many years ago? It was around the turn of the century and that old woman, she had to have been a slave when she was a girl and she said this. At the time, she got me to thinking about how I was living. Seemed like maybe the best thing I could do was to stay in one spot and try to help my people the way that old woman done, raise a family and teach the children who they was, who they really was. I might not have done the best job, but I tried. Wasn't too long after that night in that cabin that I came out west and gave up the road for good. See, I had to bring that song out here, once it come back to me. I had to do it for her . . . and I suppose for Robert Charles, too."

In the distance, the musicians, surrounded by the mass of children, appeared to be heading inexorably towards Avalon Blvd, like they might keep going and parade down the war torn streets.

"Oh good lord," said Floyd. "Rene don't let those children out onto that street with all that glass and such."

"No, he knows better than that," said Triplett. "I hope he does."

Triplett cupped his hands and shouted, "Hey don't go out, don't leave the park."

"They can't hear you," said Floyd.

"Hell, I think they're gonna go," said Triplett.

"No, no, they're turning."

The two men laughed and Triplett leaned over and gently patted Floyd's hand. The procession swung to the opposite corner of the park, dancing past a police car, flooding around it, enraptured children following the musicians as the clapping and even the drumming transformed into some kind of dance beat, African, Afro Cuban, Louisiana Funk, Kansas City Jump, Central Avenue shimmy, jumbled joyously as the horns improvised. Triplett danced as he watched and old Floyd, exhausted by the heat and the activity of sharing the song, danced deep inside.

Rene walked backwards leading the group, hands visible over his shoulder bouncing off the drum head as they turned sharply to the left and headed straight towards the Maple tree. The musicians danced and played, swinging their horns over the heads of the children who swarmed joyously over the grass fields. A siren from a police car ran on Avalon past the park and the alto sax picked up the shrill cry, pulling it into the collective sound and screaming high notes as it receded into the distance. All the musicians talked to each other with their instruments, everyone reacting to everything, every sound, every movement, maybe even every thought. They threw the sounds out as fast as they could finger the keys, comical baritone honks, great lamenting tenor sax shouts, profound moaning trombone beats, blistering trumpet runs, all the horns emitting gasps, sighs, laughs, cries, whispers, yells, every sound ever made by man or beast tossed like wedding rice upon the people in the park. And when the musicians hit the dirt of the baseball infield, it seemed as if the wild cornucopia of every sound ever uttered was channeled instantly into a funnel, the collective sound flowing with no instructions or direction, back into the melody that Floyd Lawson had first played for everyone. The drummers too, pulled the rhythm down, naturally, with no cue besides the concerted action of the others, into the beats that Floyd had so painstakingly showed them. They marched loosely and the children acted no differently in their joyous dancing yet *The Robert Charles Song* appeared in a perfect manifestation of the old man's memory.

He and Triplett looked at each other and then at the approaching musicians, unable to say a word, rather listening to what truly must have been an ancient alchemical formula after all. Something was happening between the musicians and the music, some force transmuting, distilling it all into a single element. Somehow the vessel that emerged must have contained human souls past and present, the soul of the old black woman who'd changed Floyd Lawson's life must have been there, and the soul of Robert Charles himself. It was then that Floyd Lawson and Morris Triplett heard it. Somewhere in the center of the sound, in the middle of the brass, a raspy vibrato pulling everyone forward, the lead cornet guiding the ensemble into a perfect distillation of Floyd's vision. Triplett knew the sound of every player on the field like he knew the voices of his own children. There was no cornet among the horns. He and Floyd did a double-take, their eyes holding together as the cornet paused on the beat and the others did as well then started again in perfect concert with the cornet. Everything was enveloped in the phrasing of the cornet now. Floyd and Triplett looked back to the field in unison at the musicians and the children walking in a mass spread across the grass, traversing the diamond, clapping crisply yet slowly, the ensemble quivering the melody as if it was only just being born. They were all riding the sound of the cornet, following the breath. The cornet was lodged right in the center of the living song. Everyone must have heard it, even if they didn't know exactly what it was. The cornet was there as sure as Floyd Lawson was there, in the hot park under the Maple tree in that wheel chair sixty-five years after he'd huddled on that cabin floor with the old black woman who'd changed his life and New Orleans, the cornet man, who'd made up the melody the band was playing and that the cornet man was leading himself at that very instant as sure as Floyd Lawson was there, and Floyd Lawson was there, sure enough.

FINIS

Made in the USA
Lexington, KY
10 April 2017